not my
MATCH

Lena —
Thank you!
xoxo

OTHER TITLES BY ILSA MADDEN-MILLS

Very Bad Things

Very Wicked Beginnings

Very Wicked Things

Very Twisted Things

Dirty English

Filthy English

Spider

Fake Fiancée

I Dare You

I Bet You

I Hate You

Boyfriend Bargain

Dear Ava

Not My Romeo

The Last Guy (w/Tia Louise)

The Right Stud (w/Tia Louise)

not my MATCH

ILSA MADDEN-MILLS

 Montlake

Published by Montlake, Seattle

www.apub.com

Amazon, the Amazon logo, and Montlake are trademarks of Amazon.com, Inc., or its affiliates.

ISBN-13: 9781542021890
ISBN-10: 1542021898

Cover design by Hang Le

Cover photography by Daniel Jaems

Printed in the United States of America

not my
MATCH

Chapter 1

GISELLE

Tuesday, August 4

This night is a death sentence. Pretty soon the executioner is going to pull me off this barstool and drag me straight to the guillotine. I'm so fed up and tired I won't even struggle. *Just make it fast and painless,* I'd tell him. *And might you spare me a sip from your flask to see me off?*

My esteemed date is Charlie, but he's insisted I call him Rodeo. A short guy, maybe five-four if you count the Stetson. He's a belt hitcher, tugging at his jeans from the back, making the rearing horse on his buckle jiggle. The spinning lights from the club grazed that gold buckle earlier, and the ricochet nearly blinded me. Nothing against height-challenged men or country attire, but the weasel is checking out every girl in the Razor.

Just another nail in the coffin for one of the crappiest days ever, from my car being broken into this morning to my advisor glee-fully telling me he would *not* be recommending me to study abroad. Disappointment, heavy and thick, slams into me all over again. Forget the busted car window and some thief's poor attempt at hot-wiring my car—I was living for the chance to study in Switzerland. Everything

I've been dreaming of, hanging on to with bated breath, has evolved around the fellowship at CERN, the European Organization for Nuclear Research.

A fresh start—dead.

Goodbye, particle accelerators. Hello, devastation.

My chest hurts, and I lift a hand and press it there.

I'm blaming these past few days on the birthday curse. Bad things happen around my birthday, and I'll be twenty-four in five days, so it stands to reason fate is taunting me as she loves to do.

"You like?" Rodeo drawls in a lazy southern accent, preening as he gives me a view of his textured olive-green cowboy boots. "Alligator. Flew to Miami to buy these. Custom made by a real designer. They go from casual to dressy in a snap."

"Uh, nice." He's a fairly handsome guy; I'll give him that. A face. Teeth. Hair. Arms. Legs. But it's the sneaky, mean look in his dark eyes that gives me pause.

Pretty soon I'm going to find my wits and the good sense Mama gave me and get out of this date, but right now, I yearn to finish my whiskey.

"The texture of the boot comes from the young alligators, since their bellies are softer. More malleable in the tanning process. They raise 'em on a farm, then kill them and make boots. Fascinating process. I'd like to see it in person, to tell the truth. Do you think they put them to sleep or just kill 'em outright with a knock to the head?"

A second passes. Or a minute. I inhale a breath. "I don't want to know."

"Ah, you've got a soft heart, honey." He waves away that idea and holds his foot up a few feet off the ground, and part of me thinks about giving him a teeny tiny little push. "Now don't be shy; give 'em a feel. Might be your only chance to feel quality."

Quality? Well, isn't that just rich. I've sunk low tonight. A guy who wants to see baby alligators killed is what I attract.

"I prefer not," I reply with ice in my voice—not that he notices.

"Feels like silk." His eyes linger on my legs suggestively as he inches in closer to me, giving his belt a little hitch.

A girl pops up next to him on the other side and orders a drink, and I visibly blow out a breath as he gives her the up and down.

The man is here to get laid. I get it.

I picked him off the app only because there was an emu next to him, and I felt nostalgic. They're regal, odd birds, their height reaching six-ten by maturity. Daddy used to keep an older mated pair on our farm after a local safari place closed and left them to wander aimlessly. I used to feed, pet, and gaze at them longingly, lovingly, amazed at how fast they ran (up to thirty miles an hour), how they seemed to look at me and see that I was just as strange as they were: a tall lanky girl with oversize glasses, braces, and no friends. Daddy, who recognized my affinity with unique things early on, built them a two-acre enclosure, pond included. To see them play in the water . . . grief swells up and washes over me—for the loss of them and Daddy.

In hindsight, I realize that Rodeo must have been standing on something—a box or a ladder—when he snapped his bio pic. Taking a sip of my drink, I squint, trying to picture us having sex. I'm five-nine, so how would that even work? I'm really into eye contact, and if we had sex missionary-style, then his head would land somewhere between my breasts and my stomach. He'd have to crane his neck to look up at me. Maybe I'll buy some Ken and Barbie dolls, cut Ken's legs off at the correct ratio, and test it out. A shame, but sometimes science requires sacrifice. When you don't have a clue, testing is important. I never want to be unprepared. My curiosity isn't because I plan on having sex with Rodeo—heck no, I just love random tidbits to squirrel away.

"You come to the Razor a lot, honey?" Rodeo asks, attempting more conversation as the other girl wanders off. His dark eyes hold mine over the rim of his frosted mug of draft beer. At least he isn't ogling my breasts any longer—no, he gave that up when I slipped on my navy blazer and buttoned it up to the collar. A bead of sweat drips down my back. It's August in the South, over a hundred degrees outside, and if I don't get out of this club soon, I'm going to pass out.

"No. I've never been here. I don't get out much. I'm a grad student and teach—"

He nods, interrupting me. "It's close to my apartment is why I picked it." A pause. "It's hard meeting girls online."

At that remark, at the hint that maybe he's not the jackass he appears to be, I relax a little. Maybe he was just babbling about watching baby alligators die.

I infuse my voice with interest and ask the number one question Mama always asks me about my dates. "Are you employed?"

He fingers his gold belt buckle and chuckles. "Not a desk job like most. I'm the reigning Ride 'Em Till You Die champion for the past three years. I made a million dollars last year in the circuit. You into rodeo guys?"

"I love horses," I push out, floundering to find a commonality between us. "I grew up outside Nashville, a small town called Daisy—"

"Whips, saddles, spurs, bridles—I've got it all at home if that's your kink," he interjects with a sly tone as he goes from nice to sleazy in a blink, the insinuation of it making me squirm as I shift around on my stool. A dark chuckle comes from him. "You look uptight, but I bet your waters run deep, honey."

Uptight. He gets a gold star for that. My ex-fiancé, Preston, would agree.

He continues, tugging me away from the dark path those thoughts want to lead me down. "And I know what you're thinking—I'm short. Most girls do at first, but just you wait, 'cause what's in my pants is a God-given gift. Ain't had one complaint since I started. Been riding fillies for a long time, and they always come back for more of what I got." His lids lower as he gives his crotch an endearing, loving look, as if his small head is sentient and listening.

There you go.

My first instinct was right. Death sentence. Must escape.

After turning away from him and looking at the mirror across the bar, I watch as red creeps up my face. My hair is chaos, the blonde strands once in a sleek chignon now dangling next to my temple, the finer hairs sticking to my damp forehead. My pink lipstick has faded, and there are smudges of mascara under my eyes from the heat.

I push my black glasses up on my nose and swipe at a bead of sweat on my forehead. Why am I even wearing a stupid blazer in the middle of the hottest summer on record? My fingers toy with the top button, loosening it a little.

Rodeo sees me unbuttoning my jacket, and his eyes light up. He takes a step closer, and now his checkered shirt is brushing against my breasts, and I see his nose hairs. His smell wafts around me: spicy, male, kind of leathery—horsey.

I lean farther away, arching until I bump into the person next to me. Without glancing back, I mumble an apology and straighten myself on the stool.

Rodeo indicates my empty tumbler, his tone low and husky. "You want another drink? That whiskey you sucked down is long gone."

Using my foot, I press on the lower part of the bar and scoot my stool away from him. I check my phone and put on a frown. "Actually, it's getting late, and I need to leave—"

"Hey, bartender! My little filly here needs a drink," he calls out and waves his hat around at the busy server behind the bar.

The petite bartender comes over to us. Her name tag says **SELENA**, and I'm envious of the confident sway of her hips in skinny jeans, the deep-red lipstick on her lips. Her dark hair is sheared close to her scalp in a pixie cut, her eyes defined with dark eyeliner. We're like night and day, me in my faded makeup, mud-brown pencil skirt, and low-heeled pumps.

Selena focuses her eyes on me, dismissing Rodeo. "You sure you want another drink?" The dry tone says, *Girl, why are you with him?*

A long exhalation comes from my chest. All I need to do is get rid of him and just enjoy the burn of a good bourbon.

I give her a quick nod, keeping my eye on Rodeo.

"Same as before? Woodford on the rocks?"

"Please," I say.

Selena turns around to reach up to the top shelf while Rodeo lets out a whistle under his breath, watching her voluptuous figure.

She turns back around, pours the drink, and slides it over to me, her face composed and blank. She has to have heard Rodeo, but you'd never know it. She's cool. I want to be cool. Maybe then I might find the right kind of guy.

"Thank you," I say and take a sip as Rodeo watches me with a smoldering look, then reaches out and toys with my necklace. "So this is obviously working between us. You're hot. I'm hot. The electricity is sparking. I'm already picturing you riding me. Ever hear of reverse cowgirl?"

I pry his hands off my pearls and push at him as anger rises like a tidal wave, overriding my earlier politeness. When he's at a safe-enough distance, I take a sip of my drink and slam it down on the bar. After digging around in my computer bag, I grab my wallet, pull out several twenties, and toss them down.

"You're leaving already, honey?" There's a plaintive whine to his voice.

I turn to face him, teeth gritting. "Yes, and I know what reverse cowgirl is." I have to answer his question; it's a thing. If you ask, I crave to respond with the truth. "And there is zero spark. My protons are not attracted to your electrons."

"Protons? What—"

"Plus, it's incredibly rude of you to suggest sexual acts when you've just met me—"

"Hot damn, you've got a temper. Gotta admit angry sex is my favorite. How's about me and you getting out of here—"

"Keep dreaming—"

"And I might even let you stay the night, make you some pancakes in the morning, sprinkle some chocolate chips on them or some organic blueberries. You look like the granola type."

I do like organic blueberries, but . . . "This was a drink-only meeting, and I told you that when I messaged you. And please, for the love of everything, stop calling me *honey* or *filly*, or I swear I'll dump what's left in this glass over your head."

My chest rises at my outburst. I just threatened physical violence on a person. This isn't like me. I never get angry. I let people run roughshod over me time and time again . . .

His gaze flares as I jerk to a standing position, stumbling a little in my heels as I ricochet off the person next to me. "Forgive me," I murmur to the fellow, steadying myself by latching on to the bar like a lifeline. I throw a wary glance at my glass. I actually had one before Rodeo showed up, and considering I haven't had dinner—yep, I'm buzzing.

"Giselle?" comes a deep voice, dark and sultry, the tone recognizable even over the loud music.

No, it can't be.

My heart flips over, and my entire body flushes as I look past Rodeo to the tall man who's standing a few feet away on the edge of the dance floor, a questioning look on his movie-star face.

My hands clench. I should have known I might see him. I just assumed he would still be working out or doing whatever professional athletes do early in the evening. My sister, Elena, mentioned he usually pops by on the weekends, but that's about it.

Devon Walsh, superstar football player, arches a dark brow at me, the one with a silver bar at the edge. I run through my mental checklist. Voted Nashville's Sexiest Man of the Year. All-Pro for three years straight. Best friends with my new brother-in-law, Jack. Owns the Razor. Wicked lips. Beautiful tattooed body. *Hot.*

"Is everything okay?" he asks as his gaze drifts over me, starting at the top of my half-down, half-up hair and moving all the way to my pumps. I squint, and even though it's not possible in the dark club, it feels as though he's put a spotlight on my form as he surveys every inch of me.

"Fine," I call, tossing up a hand. "Couldn't be better! Good to see you! Bye!"

Leave. I want no witnesses to this debacle.

"I see." His discerning eyes flip to Rodeo, and that maddening eyebrow goes up again. "Are you on a date?"

My entire body rebels at the questioning, teasing tone in his voice, and I stiffen all over.

He thinks I'm *with* Rodeo.

I did meet him here, but . . .

"Yes, we are," Rodeo calls and throws an arm around me as I wrestle unsteadily out of his grasp.

A small frown etches itself on Devon's forehead as he sticks his hands into the pockets of his low-slung designer jeans. Maybe he sees I'm close to passing out from heatstroke or that I'm about to murder one of his patrons.

My insides feel like jelly, and it has little to do with the whiskey and more to do with Devon, although I'm not interested in him like that—just curious. Yes, he's hotter than a Bunsen burner, but we're friends—well, not *real* friends. Okay, whatever, I'm overthinking this, and my brain is not firing on all cylinders. We're *acquaintances*, if you really want to split hairs, and when he looks at me, I'm firmly in the "you're Elena's sister, and she's married to my best friend; therefore, I am friendly" category.

That doesn't stop me from appreciating his chiseled, bladed jawline and the deep-green eyes that are framed by thick black lashes. At six-two or six-three (I itch to measure him), his body is toned to perfection by time in the gym, his shoulders muscled inside a tight black T-shirt, his chest tapering to a trim waist and long legs, with faded Converse on his feet. Rolex on one wrist, a black leather cuff on the other. One part civilized, the other side all bad boy and oh-so decadent.

His skin is a pretty tan color from the sun, a sharp contrast to my own milky paleness. His hair is mink brown and thick, mingled with royal-blue highlights, the top long and swept back off his face with lots of volume, the sides clipped close to his scalp. He uses more hair product than I do. When I first met him back in February, he wore a gelled faux hawk with purple tips, but he changes his hair more than any girl I know.

Diamond studs wink from his earlobes, just another way we're opposite. I let my holes close up when I was eighteen and never went back to have them repierced. Two full sleeves of roses mixed with fluttery gold-and-blue butterflies dance along his forearms. Those, I like. A lot. Nervous, I stroke the pearls around my neck.

"Giselle?" he asks.

My brain jerks to a halt as I realize I'm ogling him. Sputtering, I rack my brain for an intelligent response—*come on, Giselle, you're working on a PhD in physics; you have a plethora of words in your arsenal. Tell him Rodeo isn't your date!*

But all I can think about is the last time I saw him—Saturday at Elena and Jack's wedding, where he was the best man to my maid of honor. He wore a mouthwatering fitted gray suit, the fabric so devastatingly soft I bit my lip when he took my hand and looped it through the crook of his arm. Did his fingers linger on mine longer than necessary? Maybe. He probably didn't notice. He was just doing his job as Jack's best man. He did stare a hole through me. A level-five gaze, which involves intense eye contact lasting ten seconds, meaning I either had a giant zit on my nose, or he really liked what he saw. I asked him—well, whispered—as we walked down the aisle toward Jack and Elena if he was feeling unwell. He said he was fine—curtly—which was strange, because Devon is the opposite of grumpy.

Later, when I was alone in my apartment, I dissected the interaction and came to the conclusion that he stared at me only because I looked washed out and hideous in the strapless silver dress Elena had picked out for me. I'd told her I didn't have the breasts to hold it up, but she'd insisted.

Yet inside that church, standing next to my sister as she recited her vows, my thoughts about Devon wandered. Was he attracted to me? *Me?* It seemed impossible.

The truth was abundantly clear once his supermodel date showed up to the reception. He never glanced at me again.

"Oh my God, are you . . . are you . . . *Devon Walsh*? I'm a huge fan of yours since your Ohio State days! I have your jersey on my wall," is the screech that comes from Rodeo as he shoves past me to reach the football star.

The jostle to my shoulder causes me to lose my grip on the bar, and I stumble to the side, knocking into the guy next to me on his stool— again. He flips around with a scowl—*oh, I think I know him*—and then his beer bottle smacks me in the cheek.

"Jesus! Are you okay?" the stool guy calls out and tries to steady me, but it's too late.

"Wonderful," I mutter and rear back, causing my heels to teeter on the slick tile. Time seems to stand still as I grapple with balance. My body obeys the laws of gravity—thank you, Newton—and flails forward and down. My knees hit the floor with a slap—

Right in front of Nashville's sexiest man alive.

Damn you, birthday curse.

Chapter 2

GISELLE

"How does it feel?" Devon asks as he presses an ice pack to my right cheekbone. Wincing at the contact, I put my hand up to my face, and our fingers brush as he slides back and lets me hold the pack in place. Butterflies dance in my stomach as tendrils of awareness buzz along the nerve endings where we touched, and I swallow down the feeling. He's just a guy who happens to be drop-dead gorgeous. He isn't attracted to me. Whatsoever.

"Fine," I say, forcing brightness into my tone. My head does throb, but I'm not sure if it has to do with my face or just the lack of food in my stomach.

I'm at a table in the VIP room of the Razor, a roped-off area in the back. The place is mostly empty, except for a few guys watching a game in the corner. I imagine this place doesn't get crowded until much later. Thankfully, the music from the club seems to be turned off in here.

From his standing position, Devon bends his knees, crouching down to peer into my eyes, as if to make sure I'm lucid. The scent of him hits me, masculine and heady with a hint of sea and summer, some expensive cologne.

"You hit the floor pretty hard. How are your hands and knees?" This close, the glints of gold in his irises flicker like fireflies, mingling with the velvety forest green. His gaze is lush, mesmerizing, and deep—

Stop with the adjectives about his eyes, Giselle! Right.

"Good, just sore from the fall."

"You might have a bruise or two tomorrow. Want more ice for it?"

"No, but thanks." I want to forget it ever happened. More than anything, I'm wallowing in embarrassment.

His fingers graze over my knee, not lingering any longer than necessary, flicking at a piece of something. "When you flung yourself at me, I thought you might tackle me," he murmurs.

"Hey. I was ping-ponged between two guys and had nowhere else to go."

An image of me on my knees, palms on the floor to keep myself from face planting, dances in my head. Devon helped me up—careful, strong hands on my elbows—then barked at his teammate Aiden, the guy on the stool, and told him to grab an ice pack from the kitchen. Then he escorted me to the VIP room, shoving past dancing people. I half expected him to sweep me up in his arms like in one of those romance novels.

"According to your hype, it would take more than me to take you to the ground," I say with a small laugh. "If I was going to tackle you, I'd need stealth. I'd hide in your closet in the dark and pop out when you least expect it. You'd open your door, and I'd be hiding in your fancy shirts wearing a hideous mask." I smile, ignoring the pain from my face. "What makes you jump . . . creepy crawlers? Freddy Krueger? Michael Myers?"

A rueful laugh comes from him. "Sharks. Their teeth creep me out. Watched *Jaws* when I was a kid and wanted to throw up."

"Beware," I say. "I'm coming for you soon."

"First, you'd have to get in my penthouse. Hard to get there when there's a private elevator."

I laugh. "Never underestimate the grit and determination of a southern woman with a goal." I know where he lives. Never been there, but . . .

His warrior body unfolds as he straightens up to his full height. "There she is, right as rain. It's okay to fall to your knees. I tend to have that effect on women."

I roll my eyes so hard it hurts. Did I mention he's cocky?

"But not you, right?" he adds. "Nope, you're as cool as they come."

Wait . . . what?

My throat feels tight as I try to decipher how his comment settles. I see—*oh, I see*—exactly what he thinks. He's put me in the same box as everyone else. It shouldn't hurt, but it does.

I swallow thickly. "That's me. Cold as ice."

His forehead crinkles in a scowl. "Hey, hang on a minute; I didn't mean it like that—"

"No, I get it. I know what everyone thinks. Unemotional robot. Stuck in her head. Oblivious. Impervious to sexy men."

He cocks his head, lips puckering, as if he's deep in thought, then sticks his hands in the pockets of his jeans, his tell that he's uncomfortable. I would know. I watch him. "Those thoughts never entered my head. I just meant you're not like other girls—ah, never mind." He opens his mouth, shuts it, then says, "You think I'm sexy?"

"*Pfft.* No."

He grunts, his face unreadable. "Good."

"You're too old for me."

He sputters, and I can't stop my genuine smile at his incredulous face. Oh, goody, I got him. "I'm twenty-eight, for fuck's sake. There's what, four years between us?" He rakes a hand through the top of his hair, yet it still settles in a sexy mess, the blue highlights gleaming amid the dark brown. Dammit. He's effortlessly beautiful.

I force a nonchalant shrug. "Age doesn't matter as long as you're my type—you know, the three *T*s: textbooks, tweed, and timid. You have that whole rock star vibe."

And those lips. I could write a book about his mouth, the soft-pink color and how the lushness contrasts with the hard lines of his jaw, the overly full bottom lip, the deep V on his upper one.

"Smart. You should stay away from men like me, pretty girl." He gives me one of his signature teasing smiles, and yep, we're totally in the friend zone. He calls everyone *pretty girl*, even Mama and Aunt Clara.

"Mmm." I nod.

"Is Cowboy your man? He got left behind when I brought you back here, but I can send someone after him."

He takes a step away from me, as if to do just that, and I groan. "No, please. I can't take another minute with him."

He stalks back and dips down, bending his knees as he kneels, closer this time than before. His body radiates tension. "Did he do something?"

I chew on my lips and stare down at my lap, letting the earnestness of his husky voice wash over me. Oh, Devon. He may be an arrogant superstar wideout for the Nashville Tigers, but underneath that surface beats the heart of a good man, so when he says nice things to me, my gut knows it's not because I'm special. He'd help any girl out.

"He was . . ." A dick. "Someone I met on this app. I figured if he liked emus, we'd have something to talk about." I raise my gaze to his, trying to get him to understand my logic, but he's frowning. "Then he tried to mess with my necklace, and nobody touches Nana's pearls." I twist the strand in question, pulling them up to press my lips to them for a second.

"What else did he do?" he asks gruffly. His eyes land on my necklace as I settle it around my throat, then move to my mouth. I wish I had lipstick on.

I steady the ice pack on my face and try to will my heart to slow down. Can he hear how fast it's beating? "He mentioned reverse cowgirl, which sounds fun with the right person, but ugh, not him . . ."

Oops. Something about Devon makes my tongue loose—or maybe it's the whiskey. Regardless, that position sounds hot. I imagine it takes strong leg muscles for the female. I run almost every day, so I could hang. Where would my hands go? Behind me on his hips or in front of me for balance? Either way, I'd be faced away from my partner, alleviating inhibitions. If I can get my hands free, there's access to my own pleasure. It's settled. Reverse cowgirl is going to the top of my How Giselle Gets Her Groove Back list.

"Your face is red, Giselle. You feeling okay?"

I clear my throat, shaking those images away. "It's hot in here."

"Take your jacket off," he says. "You're making me sweat just looking at it."

After setting down the ice pack, I unbutton the blazer, slide it off my arms, and toss it on the table, then notice how damp my white silk shell is. My lace demi bra is clearly defined, but the cool air is a religious experience. I undo the first three buttons of the shirt and wave the delicate lapels.

"So, so much better." I groan as my hands tug at the bobby pins in my hair and place them in a neat line on the table. Massaging my scalp, I straighten out the long tangles, moaning at the sensation. "I need Chris Hemsworth to rub my feet, and it just might make this day bearable." I kick my sensible shoes off and wiggle my toes.

"Isn't he married?" Devon mutters. I raise my head from where I was leaning it back over the chair and take him in. He's moved a foot away and rubs the back of his neck. His eyes linger on my blouse, then slide away.

"Not in another universe," I say in a light tone. "Someday I'll tell you my ideas on the multiverse. In one of those, there's a world where it's entirely possible he's married to me, and we have ten kids."

"Damn." He laughs. I melt.

"In the Giselle-and-Chris universe, he can't keep his hands off me, and we procreate like bunnies on Viagra. He's not a movie star but an architect, and we live in a villa he built for me in the French Alps. I spend my days researching dark matter, baking cookies, and crocheting baby booties. My nights, well, those are devoted to him."

His lips twitch. "Where am I in this universe?"

I cup my chin. "You're a teenage girl who works at Cinnabon with a penchant for charm bracelets, bubble gum, and pink berets. On the weekends, your dark side emerges, and you sneak out your bedroom window to spray-paint meaningful graffiti on billboards."

He gives me a full-blown smile, lush lips curving. The effect is devastating, and I suck in a breath. "Quite the imagination there, Bunny. You amaze me."

I blush. "My randomness drives my family insane." I pause. "I can't decide if your nickname should be Cinnamon or Pinky. Thoughts?"

"Neither. I only answer to Badass."

"Spoilsport."

Devon searches my face. "Back to the online-dating thing. My cousin Selena did that and barely got out of the car with some guy she met. Dangerous to use."

I sigh, regretting the loss of our banter. If he only knew that in one of my other universes, he ravishes me on a bathroom countertop. He's *him*, sexy with rippling naked muscles, and I'm some girl he picked up on the side of the road as I was running away from an evil bridegroom. I'm wearing a ruined white dress, and I have long pink hair—but glasses, because yes, I must appear intelligent in every universe. He's in deep lust from the moment I get in his Maserati, and he takes me home—where he makes me his. I chide myself internally. No wonder I can't keep up in my classes. I live in my own head too much to focus on the facts. There's no universe where Devon and I are together.

I blame these vivid thoughts on the virgin issue. It's taunted me horribly for five months, since Preston's parting words when he admitted to cheating. *If you won't give it to me, what did you expect, Giselle? You're frigid.*

I was his fiancée (for almost a month), and I still couldn't . . . well, want him. I just kind of fell into dating him, then accepted his proposal.

And now, here I am, trying to prove I'm normal, looking for love in all the wrong places. That's a country song, I think.

"Just because you have women all over you doesn't mean that the average person has it so easy," I say rather hotly. "I made sure to not come alone, and I wasn't planning on leaving with him. I had a plan. I have a plan each time."

He takes a step toward me, indignation on his face. "You've done this more than once?"

My brow comes down, annoyance sparking at his incredulous tone. "The first guy, Albert, was a handsome accountant. I met him at Starbucks. Things were going fine until he showed me a pic of his ex on his phone and started crying. Apparently she wanted him to put a ring on it, and he has commitment issues. I advised him to talk to her."

"How many others, Giselle?"

I shift around on the chair. "You make me feel like I'm in the principal's office."

"How many?"

My hand clenches. Oh, he's so aggravating!

"I don't understand why you need to know, but there was only one other one, Barry, a bit on the slick side. His bio said he was a chemistry major, so I thought, 'He likes science, and so do I,' so I swiped right. Turned out he just wanted me to sign up for some pyramid scheme to sell kitchen things like Pampered Chef but not. I passed on being a rep but ended up buying a spatula from him." I sigh. "I even paid for his latte. Then came Rodeo, and he had that adorable emu . . ."

"Giselle." There's a heavy dose of frustration in his voice, and it makes me lift my chin defiantly.

"Sometimes you have to go through a bunch of duds, Devon. Don't pretend like you know a thing about it. You have a new girlfriend every month. Who was the girl at the reception? Pity I never got introduced."

A long exasperated breath leaves his broad chest. "Who'd you come with tonight?"

"Is this twenty questions?"

A small knowing smile tugs at his lips. "I know you have to answer me. Elena told me about your little question problem."

"That little minx," I breathe. She's on her honeymoon in Hawaii with the man of her dreams, yet I feel as if she's right next to me. My beautiful, sweet older sister, whose shadow I've never truly been able to escape. I sigh. At least she's happy, and no one deserves it more than her. Before she met Jack, I ruined our relationship last year when Preston, *her* then boyfriend, kissed me that awful day in his office—right before she walked in. Is it any wonder that he and I never felt right? We started off wrong.

A ball of emotion clogs my throat, and I gather myself, trying to push those memories away. It takes effort.

"Topher drove me," I say grudgingly. "When I took my car to the shop in Daisy, I walked to the library, and he was closing up. He drove me back to Nashville and insisted on coming with me here since I'd never met anyone at a bar before."

Devon wants to know about my car, and I tell him how I came down this morning to a failed attempt to steal my older-model Camry.

"Are these dates about getting over Preston?" he asks in a careful tone as he gingerly sits down across from me.

"Best way to get over someone is to find someone new."

A few ticks of silence go by, and the air around us resonates with tension, and as soon as I catch on, I sit up straighter and focus. I don't understand why the space between us feels charged, but it's crackling.

"Right," Devon grinds out as his eyes drape over me, lingering on my blouse before coming up to my face. Our eyes cling until he looks away and scrubs his jaw. "You should get a friend to introduce you to someone—"

"Uh-huh. You're my friend. Right?"

He frowns. "Of course. Why would you even ask?"

Oh, I don't know, because I can't figure you out. Why did you give me a level-five gaze at the wedding? Was it the ugly dress? Was it me?

"Fine. Who do you suggest I date? He needs to be kind and good in bed—no, scratch that, spectacular. I'm talking fireworks, Devon—mind blowing."

His gets up and paces away from me.

"Did someone say *spectacular*? If so, I have arrived," says Aiden as he swaggers in the door and over to the table. About six-two with short brown hair and glittering ice-blue eyes, he's a farm boy from Alabama with a megawatt smile that makes female hearts patter. Currently, he's the Tigers' backup quarterback, but he has his sights set on Jack's starting position.

After settling down in the seat vacated by Devon, he hands me a glass of water, the one he dashed off to get after Devon ordered him to. "Word to the wise, I have excellent hearing. Part of my superhuman quarterback skills. Can you define how many orgasms you need? I'm good for five a day and have references."

I burst out laughing, and he joins me. He's about my age, and I've never seen him without a grin or a girl. He showed up at my sister's wedding with two. Twins, no less, and he danced with both of them at the same time at the reception, slow, one in front with her arms around his neck, and one behind him, her hands around his waist. It worked better than I thought it would.

"You are ridiculous," I say. He reminds me of a puppy, sweet and rambunctious, begging for you to throw the ball during the day, then curling up next to you at night.

Devon, on the other hand, is a panther; one minute you think he's lazing in the sun, twitching his tail, and the next he's vibrating with barely suppressed power. Like he is now as he scowls at Aiden.

What's his deal?

The football guys joke around me all the time.

Aiden watches me drain the glass. "I didn't mean to hit you in the face. Sorry, Giselle. I didn't even realize it was you until you landed on the floor."

I glance at Devon, who's taken a couple of steps back to lean against the wall. He has his phone out, seeming to have forgotten about me. Good.

"I didn't know it was you either," I murmur.

He leans in closer. "Dude. Your date left with some brunette. Hope it wasn't a love connection."

I laugh. "Guess he found a little filly to take home."

He guffaws.

"He said he'd let me play with his bridles and spurs. I half expected him to whip out a . . . whip."

Aiden roars with laughter as I recount the date, reciting Rodeo's words about his God-given talent and his angry-sex suggestion, all the way to his offer of putting organic blueberries on pancakes. When I finish, he wipes a tear from his eye. "What a douche."

"She met him on some app," Devon growls, stuffing his phone in his jeans.

"Perfectly acceptable," I reply coolly.

"You can do better."

"I'm not Nashville's sexiest woman!"

"You're not unattractive!" He glares at me.

Well. I blow out a breath.

There's several ticks of silence as Aiden looks at him, then back at me, a thoughtful expression on his face. He taps his fingers on the table, seeming to come to a decision. "So about these fireworks. How do you feel about—"

Devon straightens up from the wall, moving faster than I anticipated, and slaps a heavy hand on Aiden's broad shoulders. "Give it up, Alabama. She's off limits."

My spine straightens. *Off limits?*

Back in February when I was engaged, yes, but now that I'm single?

Aiden brushes Devon's hand off and flashes me a grin so big it looks like his cheeks might crack. When he speaks, his words are directed to Devon, but he's looking at me like I'm a slice of pie. "If you think I give one rat's ass what Jack Hawke thinks about who I talk to, then you need to check yourself. I was the Tigers' first-round pick in the draft—"

"You aren't special, pup," Devon growls.

"And no one, even the team captain, tells me who I can chat up," Aiden adds. "He isn't even here. We're in the middle of training camp, and he's at the beach."

"He'll be back, asshole, and he'll punch you, injured arm or not," Devon snaps. "Or I can do it now."

Competitive athletes. So. Much. Testosterone.

They bicker, then toss back beers in the next heartbeat.

"Tell me more about this off-limits decree from Jack?" I say in my calmest voice to Aiden, attempting to hide my building anger.

He gives me a disarming smile. Underneath the country-boy charm, he's smooth as silk. "Now, don't be upset. Jack gave the team 'the talk' a while back. 'Keep your meaty paws off Elena's sister, or I will demolish you' is pretty much how it went down."

I put two and two together fast. No doubt Elena told Jack I'm a virgin; then toss in the broken engagement, and Jack's trying to protect me, and I appreciate the concern . . . but *come on*, am I that fragile?

Jesus. What if he told the whole team I'm a virgin? No, no, he wouldn't, right? If he did, I'm going to . . . my chest tightens with tension. Shaking my head, I shove the idea away. I'm jumping to conclusions.

"I'm a big girl, Aiden. Trust your instincts. Isn't that what big football players do?" I bat my lashes.

Aiden gives me a surprised glance, one that turns heated, and I smile because yes, the geek knows how to flirt.

"Aiden," Devon warns.

"What?" he replies, gazing at me.

"Stop eye-fucking her."

"Shut it, Dev. This is my regular look. We're having a moment here."

"Are we?" I ask, my tone dry.

Aiden holds my gaze. "Oh, hell yeah."

Devon lets out a grunt just as his cell buzzes.

I refuse to look at him. Part of me is enjoying pushing his buttons. I get that he's Jack's mouthpiece, but the mere idea of a group of men discussing my love life makes me want to throw a table—or a football player.

Aiden grabs my phone, asks for my passcode, and, once he gets it, types in his number. "Those are my digits. Call me. We can recreate the Fourth of July"—he winks—"or we can watch some good horror movies. Lady's choice."

"I love horror but prefer sci-fi."

His blue eyes gleam. "Hmm. Sci-fi and fireworks in a movie. You thinking what I'm thinking?"

It takes me two seconds. "*Independence Day* with Will Smith?"

"I like you." He gives me a fist bump. "Love that movie. Let's do it."

I let the hammer fall but soften it with a smile. "I see what you're doing. You think messing with me would screw with Jack and his season as quarterback. You really would do anything for that first-string spot, wouldn't you?"

A slow blush crawls up his neck to his face as he grimaces. "I want that position, yes, and it will be mine someday—"

"No time soon," Devon growls. "Jack's at the top of his game. His shoulder will be fine in a few weeks."

Aiden flips him off without even glancing at him. "I also think you're fucking hot."

I arch my brow. I'm a tall skinny girl with no breasts, and my nose is a hair too long. Maybe I have good cheekbones and nice blue eyes, but I tend to dress like my mother. The sexiest clothing items I own are a pair of frayed denim shorts and a pink thong I bought on impulse. Neither are appropriate for a serious grad student.

"Yeah, me and you," Aiden says huskily and spears me with what I'm sure is his most intense, mesmerizing, come-to-me-baby-doll eyes.

Devon throws up his hands. "The bullshit in here is deep."

"Go check on your waitstaff, Dev. You're down a few servers tonight," Aiden quips back.

"What about those twins from the wedding? Won't they get mad?" I ask Aiden. We're both ignoring Devon.

Aiden grabs my hand. "I barely remember their names."

I shake my head, laughing as I disentangle our clasp. "I adore you, but tell someone who believes that lie."

Aiden clutches his chest. "Come on; you're not taking me seriously. You were engaged when we first met, and this is my chance. Consider this our meet-cute, and go from there." He pauses, his tone serious. "I have this event at the mall next week. Something my agent set up. I really hate going alone. You wouldn't believe the women who throw themselves at me."

"Sounds awful," I deadpan.

"You wanna go?"

"Fight off your pantie-throwing fans in the middle of some smelly sports store in the mall?" I pause. "I could be persuaded with food and a good cabernet."

"Enough," Devon calls and storms over, his eyes flitting between us, seeming to measure the distance between our faces.

Aiden chuckles and leans back in his chair. "You're a piece of work, man."

"What does that mean?" Devon grouses.

Aiden narrows his eyes at him, pushing out his lips, and I can tell there's something on the tip of his tongue.

"Spit it out, Alabama," Devon mutters.

They seem to share a long look, one with meaning I have no clue about, but I imagine it has to do with the fact that even though the three of them are friends, Devon and Jack go way back, and Aiden is the new guy on the team and ambitious as heck. He wants to be the star quarterback, and Jack's in his way.

"Nothing, man, nothing," is what Aiden settles on.

Devon crosses his arms. "You said the party at your place starts at nine. You're supposed to supply beer. I'm guessing you haven't gotten it yet. Maybe you should."

Aiden huffs. "Plenty of time." He glances at me. "You had dinner yet?"

"No."

"Want to grab something?"

I am starving, but . . . "Ah, um . . . well, let me—"

"She's having dinner with me," Devon says, and I can barely keep my mouth from dropping open.

"Well, well," Aiden murmurs as he takes in Devon. With a subtle shift of his shoulders, Aiden turns to me and shakes his head in disappointment. "Maybe next time, Giselle."

Devon pulls him up by his arm. "I want Guinness. You drink Bud Light. Hollis likes Fat Tire. Sounds like a lot of beer. Best go find it."

"Party?" I ask.

Aiden rolls his shoulders. "We're watching an MMA fight. Dudes only, I'm afraid, or you'd definitely be invited."

Then, he directs a long look at Devon, one that screams *try and stop me* and leans down to kiss my cheek. He brushes past Devon with a smirk and sends me a wave as he mouths *call me* before he exits.

With a silly grin, I watch him go. Of course I won't call him. He's fun and sweet and a huge flirt, but there's no tug toward Aiden, no push-and-pull connection—not like with *someone* I know. Who's really pissing me off.

A text from Topher pops up on my phone asking if I need anything and saying that he's sorry he bailed on me at the bar, explaining he's outside on a call with a coworker who's having an emergency. I type out a reply, briefly explaining that the date was a bust.

The entire time, silence rings loudly in the room, reverberating and growing. I feel Devon's eyes on me even before I move.

After tucking my phone back in my computer bag, I stand and face him, our gazes locking.

One, two, three, four, five—and he breaks, dropping his focus to somewhere over my shoulder.

"Dinner, huh? Don't manipulate me like that again. I can handle Aiden. Topher's outside waiting for me, and I'm leaving."

"Fine."

He wasn't even serious about dinner! My fists curl.

He sighs. "Giselle. If you need someone to talk to about dating . . ." The words are dragged out of him, and he grimaces, his muscular body striding to me, then halting, as if he doesn't want to get too close. "Look, I don't mean to butt in, but Aiden isn't someone you should . . ." He scrubs the shadow on his jawline.

If I weren't annoyed, I'd feel sorry for him. It's plain as day the man doesn't know what to do with me.

"He enjoys yanking Jack's chain; I get it—but a girl has needs, Devon."

His lips part. "Giselle—"

I cut him off. "Thank you for the ice pack and getting me away from Rodeo, but no more of this telling me who I can see or how I meet them. I'm a grown woman."

"Wait a minute, now," he says as I make a move to sweep past him. He grabs my elbow, and I shiver at the licks of fire that trace up my limb. Stupid arm. I should chop it off. Why does it like him?

"Giselle." His eyes drop to my mouth.

The way he says my name, raspy and low, gives me pause, and my breath snags in my throat.

"I know you're a woman . . ." He stops, seeming to search for words until he notices his hand on my arm and releases me. Then takes a full step back. A long exhalation comes from his chest. "Sorry."

He is acting so . . . strange. First the wedding, and now this.

Nerves hit as I contemplate my next words. "When Jack said I was off limits, did he give a *reason*?"

"Jack is your new brother-in-law, and he's a protective guy. He doesn't trust us." He pauses. "Don't be angry at him."

"That's for me to decide. So he didn't say *anything* else—about me personally?"

Devon's face shutters, his demeanor stiffening. He tucks his hands in his pockets.

"Devon?"

His green eyes lower, shielding his gaze. "Look, can we talk later? I've had a hell of a day and need to get going."

He's brushing me off.

My heart hammers, unease curling as thoughts tumble through my head. I shouldn't be embarrassed to be a virgin. Plenty of people are. I *am* a sexual person. I can pen a scene between a tall sexy alien warrior and his earth girl that curls my toes, but still, the thought lingers that maybe I'm—

"I'm not frigid," I mutter.

He freezes mid hair rake. "What does that have to do with anything? I didn't mean what I said earlier. You misinterpreted—"

"I'm a virgin!"

Every second that goes by without him saying anything, just him staring at me as if I slapped him with a two-by-four, is drenched in tension. He inhales a sharp breath. Curses. Several times.

"Everyone out!" Devon yells, pointing to the people at the back of the room. They take one look at his face, grab their drinks, and shuffle out of the room.

I watch it all with bated breath. "He told you, didn't he?" I whisper.

"Giselle—"

"I asked you a question. Courtesy demands you answer me." My hands clench, waiting, waiting . . .

He wipes at his mouth, then slides his hand down to rub the shadow on his chin. "Yes."

Chapter 3

Devon

Giselle Riley has gone off the deep end.

Ninety-nine percent of the time, the girl is straight-up prim and proper, all the way from her little topknot to her heels. Nothing ruffles her. After that asshole Preston cheated on her, she never uttered one unkind word about him. I've never heard her curse or seen her with her hair down.

And there it is now, tawny-gold-and-white strands shining and cascading down her back like a blonde waterfall, the ends drifting below her slim shoulders. It's the kind of hair a man wants to wrap around his hand.

Is it any wonder I can't stop staring?

Who is *this* girl?

Her cheeks are twin spots of color, her silvery-blue eyes snapping as she paces around on her bare feet. She shoves her glasses up to her head and pivots and comes back and stops in front of me. She's breathing rapidly, and her damp shirt draws my eyes, the points of her nipples pushing through her lacy bra as her chest heaves. She's got small tits, but enough for me to look at. I bite back a suggestion on the tip of my tongue that she put her jacket back on. At this rate, she'll slap me.

I almost want her to. It might make me stop staring at her like an idiot.

Jack is going to flip when he knows I blabbed, but he can fuck right off. He's on his honeymoon, and here I am doing damage control with his slightly insane family. Perfect.

"I knew it!" she calls. "You've been acting off, and now you think I'm even more boring and weird than you did before. I'm going to strangle him when he gets back from Hawaii!" She mimics throttling someone. "I hope a shark takes his throwing arm right off."

Jesus.

"I never thought you were weird!" Why am *I* yelling? "And you're the least boring person I know!" I toss in.

Her eyes sparkle like lightning in a storm. "Oh, I can picture it now, him in the locker room, giving you guys the lowdown, talking about poor innocent Giselle and how she's never . . ." Her full bottom lip trembles for half a second before she sucks it in and straightens her spine. "It's wrong. And personal."

I hold my hands out. "It wasn't everyone, okay? It's just me who knows that part."

She stops in her tracks. "Just you?"

"Only me—"

"Ah! He leaves it with you to make sure everyone falls in line. Do you always take orders from Jack?"

I groan. "He trusts me, Giselle! I'm his best friend! Aiden doesn't know, which is why you should beware around him. If he knew the truth"—I cringe, not really quite sure *what* the unpredictable ass might do—"I'm sure he would stay far away." He better. "I may need to sit him down for a serious talk." And box his ears.

Red flames on her face. "You'd tell him? Just take out a banner in the paper, Devon; post it on Insta!" Lifting up on her toes, she gets up in my face, which doesn't take much. She's tall and willowy. Little puffs of angry air come from her chest. Steely eyes glare at me, and her pouty mouth purses as she pushes a finger into my chest. She smells good—not that heavy flowery stuff, but light and sweet and fresh, like after a soft rain in the spring, and how could I have missed how creamy her skin is, that peaches-and-cream color, translucent—

I shake myself as her words dawn in my thick skull.

"I'd never tell him! Good God! It's not my place. I just meant . . ." Why can't I say the right thing around her? She's always made me uneasy. Too smart. Too something.

My phone goes off again, but I can't move a muscle. It's the crazy girl in front of me who has my attention. She pokes me in the chest again, and I grab her finger and tug her in closer.

"You trying to tickle me?" I arch a brow, trying to defuse her anger.

She blinks, as if just realizing how close she is, and licks her lips. "No."

Her chest presses me, those pert little boobs soft and—wait, what was I saying . . . ? "I'm not going to tell anyone, and it's nothing to be ashamed of. It's admirable that you're saving yourself—"

She cuts me off, but at least her voice has lowered, rather hiss-like. "Stop patronizing me. You know nothing about my reasons, Devon."

"I didn't *want* to know," I mutter as she finally pulls out of my grasp and flips around to start pacing again.

"I wish he'd never told me," I tell her rigid back.

But boy, did the info cool my jets. When we first met, she was engaged, but since then, the thought of her spread out on my bed has crossed my dirty mind. I'm male. She has a way that gets under your skin, and before you know it, you're in the shower, thinking about her in those big glasses, pearls, heels, and nothing else—

I shake my head at the unreasonable image. Blasphemy. She's like a pal. One I can't touch. There's a clear thick line drawn between us.

She scoffs as she drifts back over to me, her lips still pursed, and the image is seared in my brain, her heaving chest, the heart-shaped face, the swish of her legs under the skirt. She's graceful and smooth, as if she took one of those deportment classes on how to carry yourself. Etiquette, probably.

She's, well, a lady. Nice.

And I'm bad. Very, very bad.

She wasn't far off with her new-girlfriend-every-month snark. Women flock to me, drawn to the persona and fame, and I pick and choose the ones I want. When it's over, I send them off happy and smiling.

"You won't have to worry about keeping my secret much longer. I'm getting rid of *it*. Pronto."

An image of some shady guy fucking Giselle pops into my head. Inexplicable anger rushes like a tidal wave, and my hands tighten. I'm ready to rip his imagined head off right now. "Explain."

She levels me with a stare, and I swear she's counting the seconds. "I could draw you a picture, but I'm not an artist," she says. "Imagine a slot, then you take a tab, and you stick it in. No more hymen. It's over, and everyone can stop discussing me *behind my back*!"

And with that line, she's flouncing toward the door. Her ass sways inside her little skirt, which has a long slit up the back. Normally, she's a dressy-slacks kind of chick, and I guess she wore the skirt for her date—which makes me mad all over again. Nothing has made sense in this room since she let down her hair, unbuttoned that damn shirt, and got angry. Why couldn't she just be the old Giselle?

She turns around, her lips set, anger directed at me. "I will never use you on my Pinterest board as Vureck again."

"I don't even know what that means!" I call after her.

She ignores me as she exits, and dammit, with her in a strange temper, she's liable to pick up some rando cowboy and bang him before the night is over.

I curse. "Giselle, wait a minute! Let's discuss this. You forgot your shoes and . . . fuck." I grab the shoes and bobby pins off the table and take off after her. By the time I get out of the door of the room, she's already ten yards ahead, gliding between patrons, ducking and swerving. She dashes past the bouncer at the podium, the door flings open, and she's gone.

At least she's out of the club. She'll go home and calm down, and I'll call her tomorrow. We'll talk, and everything will be fine, but on the other hand, I don't want her fuming all night, angry. And I *had* wanted to take her to dinner once the opportunity arose earlier. Sure, I was circumventing Aiden, but we could have gone to Milano's and had a decent time. She would have sat across from me, maybe explained exactly why she decided to take up serial dating, and I would have been on my best behavior. I could have offered advice, tips—dammit, I don't know. I do know all those guys she mentioned are wrong, wrong, wrong. She's been a little lost lately, a wounded look on her face, and shit . . . I jog to the exit, determined to catch up and talk to her.

"Devon! Yo! Wait up." I feel a hand on my shoulder.

Cursing, I come to a halt as I hear the edge in Selena's voice.

"I'm in a hurry. What's wrong?" I study her frazzled expression, the way she's chewed off her red lipstick. The closest thing I have to a sibling—we look alike. Dark hair, green eyes, chips on our shoulders. Our moms were sisters, and we grew up next door to each other. I got her settled here when she moved here from California last year.

"More like whose shoes are those?" She indicates the heels in my clutch. "If you want to explore female footwear, I know some great consignment boutiques downtown."

"They belong to Giselle, the girl who fell earlier. She ran off," I add, feeling torn all over again, part of me pointed toward Selena, the other to the exit.

"Like her already. You have my approval."

"She's a friend, Elena's sister. Someone you haven't met."

"Huh. Her date was a jerk, but I kind of liked her."

"Not for me." I like my women only mildly interesting, someone I can forget. Giselle is not in that category.

Selena sighs. "One lousy girl broke your heart once, and now you're a cynic. Someday I'd like a niece or nephew to cuddle. Wherever Hannah is, I hope she's miserable without you."

Not this again.

"All right, let that go. What's going on?" I ask and tap my hands against my legs, antsy.

She twists her lips. "Besides the fact that another server didn't show up tonight and the air is on the fritz, everything is peachy. I'm working on getting new bartenders, and the air guy says he'll be here first thing in the morning."

"Sounds like it's under control." I tend to not dabble with the internal workings of the club. I bought this place as an investment. Football is my one and only. "What else?" I want to focus on what she's saying, but my head jumps between hoping Giselle's feet aren't being fried by the hot concrete on the street and wondering if she's found Topher yet—and why my dad keeps calling me. I should have just answered his call earlier, but I didn't want to take my eyes off Aiden. Jack said to keep him away from her. That was the only reason I butted in like I did.

"After Randy quit, you said I could hire someone for the new GM position. No one I've interviewed works. We need someone before this place becomes a shit show." She's holding a tray and cocks it on her hip as she stares at me expectantly.

It takes me three seconds to decide. "You're the new GM. Should have made that call when he resigned. Hire a new bar manager to take your place. Solved."

Her eyes flare, tinged with excitement. "No way. I can't manage the whole club. I don't even have a business degree!"

"You're smart, hardworking, and everyone respects you. You're it. Now get back to work."

I'm about to turn back and see if I can catch Giselle in the parking lot, but Selena jumps at me for a tight hug. Her tray goes flying, hitting the floor, and the shoes poke me in the chest. I chuckle and pat her back. "Aw, you love me."

"Fucking A, man, I don't know what I would have done if you hadn't given me a job, and now you're promoting me? Feels like I won the lottery." She gives me a kiss on the cheek. "What's my salary, boss man?"

Giselle has to be gone by now. I sigh. "What do you think you deserve?"

"What Randy was getting plus ten percent."

"Two. Randy had experience. He managed three other places before this one."

She bites her lip. "Five, and I'll hire some new servers by the end of the night and find the best bar manager in Nashville by the end of the week. You know I can do it."

I grin. She does work her ass off. "Three percent raise. Now go."

She laughs, does a little pirouette, and takes off for the bar.

My cell buzzes again, and I hold the shoes under my arm as I pull the phone out of my jeans.

I press the green button, expecting to hear my father's voice, only it isn't him.

◆ ◆ ◆

"Once you go in there, phones are gonna be out. People love drama, especially celebrities. Everything you do, man, under a microscope," Lawrence says as we get out of my car.

"I know," I say dryly. I've been in the limelight since college, but Lawrence likes to jabber.

He grumbles. "You didn't need to drive Sex to this part of town. People notice. People like to steal shit."

I flick my eyes down at the red Maserati. She's my pride and joy, and driving her reminds me of how far I've come from a poor kid in California. "Her name is Red."

34

"Sex is better."

I smirk. "Your Tom Ford five-thousand-dollar suit sticks out like a sore thumb. 'Over here; come take my wallet.'"

He strokes his tie. "Can't believe me and you and Jack used to party in places like this in college. All that energy and zero hangovers? Dude. I'm old now with an ex-wife and alimony. Damn, I miss those party days; don't you?"

"Nah." I don't miss college. Sure, we won a national championship our senior year, and that's what I try to remember, but there's heartache from Hannah in some of those memories.

He blows out a breath as we both come to a stop in front of Ricky's Bar on Wilbur Street, several blocks from where I live near the stadium.

I slip a roomy sweatshirt over my head, flip up the hood, and slide on a pair of shades.

He squints at me. "Last chance. I can get him, and you can stay in the car. Nobody has to know he's your family."

I exhale. "He won't go with you. Trust me. It will only make it worse."

We roll into the bar. The usual place. Sticky floors, tattered beer signs on the wall, a long bar with red stools, antiquated light fixtures hanging from a yellow-spotted ceiling. Shotgun-style layout, four exits, I bet. The one we came in; one down a dark hallway past the pool tables, where I guarantee there's a dingy restroom; another in the kitchen; and, if the owner is smart, one that leaves from his office. A long sigh comes from my chest. I spent most of my teenage years in places like this, washing mugs, sweeping the floor, taking out trash. My dad owned a bar, then lost it, then spent the rest of his life crawling in and out of every one he passed.

The place reeks of body odor, greasy fries, and cheap perfume.

Three guys are shooting pool, two older women nurse beers by a jukebox crooning Tammy Wynette, and several stools are occupied, but mostly it's a sparse crowd. No one looks up as we make our way to the front, except for the old guy behind the bar. With a white beard and glasses, he's wearing a shirt stretched out over his belly and a Nashville Tigers hat. He's a fan. Not sure if that's good or bad.

I lean in, keeping my voice low. "You called about Garrett Walsh?"

He sets down the glass he was drying, nods, and points to the dark hallway. "He went in the restroom half an hour ago and hasn't come out. You his son?"

I grimace, studying the grooves in the wood of the bar. "Yeah."

He puts his hand out and shakes it. "Ricky Burns. Love how you run with the ball. I got your number off his phone." He reaches behind him and tosses me a cracked cell. "He left it unlocked, so I just rang up the last person he called. Didn't realize it was you till I saw the name." He frowns. "Much respect to you, Mr. Walsh, but he ain't welcome back here. Runs off good customers and gets belligerent. He tried to start a fight with the guys playing pool. Next time I see his face, I'm calling the cops."

My stomach turns over, and for half a second, anger at Ricky bubbles, until I squash it down. His words are nothing I haven't heard before. It just hurts. "I appreciate you not calling the police tonight."

"No problem." He picks up another glass and takes the towel to it.

Lawrence pulls out a wad of cash from his wallet, but Ricky pushes it back. "No need for that. Just get him gone." He pauses, keeping his voice hushed as he gives me a beady-eyed look. "Two men came in looking for him before you got here. Rough types. Bruisers with tattoos." He flits his eyes over the bar in my eyebrow, down to the peek of butterflies on my wrists. "Told 'em he wasn't here but thought you should know."

"Any clue what they wanted?"

He raises an eyebrow, as if I'm crazy, then huffs out a laugh. "I don't ask questions, but judging by the hard look on their faces, my guess is money. I'm just an old man, and this bar is my life. I don't want any trouble in my place; you feel me?"

Loud and clear. "Thanks, man."

36

Lawrence takes a gander at the patrons again. "Ricky, you mind if we take him out the exit in the back?"

"Be my guest. An alarm will go off, but I'll turn it off up here."

I tap the bar, and we flip around and head to the hallway, where a single light bulb hangs from a dangling cord. Rapping out a sharp knock on the men's room door, I call out, "Dad? Open up. It's me."

Checking the door, I find it locked, and frustration builds. Images from my childhood flit through my head: me coming home from a football game to find him passed out on the front steps of our trailer. I'd drag him inside and put him to bed.

"Let me try." Lawrence eases me to the side and beats hard. "Get the fuck out of the fucking restroom, or we're calling the fucking cops."

"Subtle," I say.

He shrugs. "I know what works. I brought the hoodie. I tried to bribe the old dude. You're missing out. Just think, me at your service twenty-four seven. I love this shit."

"Nashville adores me." It's what I tell him every time he inquires about doing my PR for me. I don't need PR. Jack, on the other hand, has a rocky past, and Lawrence has come in handy. It's a small world that the three of us ended up in the same city. Jack was drafted to Nashville straight out of college, Lawrence is from here and has opened his own firm for athletes, and I went to play in Jacksonville, then luckily got traded to Nashville a few years ago. Three amigos back together.

"Here, move. I got this." I pull out one of Giselle's pins and pick the lock. It takes three tries before the cylinder clicks, and the door opens.

"Should I ask why you have bobby pins in your pocket?"

"No."

"You're better at that than you should be," he muses.

"He used to drink and lock me out. I got inventive."

"Fuck me; it smells like piss." Lawrence covers his mouth with a hankie as we slip inside.

My dad lies faceup on the floor in front of the sink, splayed out in the shape of an X. His chest is moving, so he's alive, and some of that knot in my chest loosens. The last time I saw him was a month ago, when I took him to dinner. He seemed fine—a bit antsy, but sober.

I push Lawrence aside and bend down and shake his shoulder. "Wake up, old man. We need to get you home."

Eventually he comes to, his eyes blinking as he grimaces and lets out a groan. The smell of beer hits me. "Where am I?" he rasps.

"Filthy bathroom. Not yours." My lips compress. Seeing him like this reminds me of why I've been trashed only one time in my life.

"Ricky's?"

I nod. His words slur, but I peg him as not bad off. There are degrees to his drunkenness, and I've cataloged them all. At least he seems to recall where he was at some point.

"I had a fight with Dotty," he mumbles. "Tried to call you, Dev. You didn't pick up. You mad at me?"

Guilt ratchets up my spine that I missed his earlier calls.

Dotty is his on-again, off-again girlfriend he met at AA.

"Come on." I lift him up by his armpits and grunt at the weight as I place him on the toilet. He sways back and forth and scrubs at the stubble on his face. His once-white Grateful Dead shirt has brown stains on it. I wince, my shoulders tightening, as I take in the oily hair, the black shadows under his eyes, the nasty cut on his hand. Not wanting to look back at Lawrence and see judgment on his face, I busy myself with dampening some paper towels and dabbing at his hand.

"How'd this happen?"

He stares down at the dried blood, squinting. "Can't remember." He tries to pull his hand back, but I hold tight.

"You don't need stitches, but it needs antiseptic." There's a slight tremble in my voice, and I grit my teeth. My sophomore year of high school, he stepped off a curb, got hit by a car, and was hospitalized with two broken legs. The night before I was supposed to leave my past behind in California and play college ball, he got into a shouting match with our neighbor across the street and ended up with a broken nose, two busted ribs, and a concussion. His injuries set me back three days for summer camp while I took care of him.

"Had worse," he grumbles, as if he's read my mind.

Our eyes meet, his bleary road maps. His face is sallow and gaunt, the lines of a much-older man of fifty. "Your liver can't take much more of this," I grind out. "When did you fall off the wagon?"

He staggers to a stand, using the wall for leverage as he presses his fingers into his eyes and rubs. "Shit—I—don't worry about it." He ends with an attempt to take a step but trips over his own feet.

I catch him and prop him up. He's as tall as me, so Lawrence jumps in, and we put him between us, his arms around our shoulders as we head out the door and down the hall to the exit. Sweat drips down my back inside the sweatshirt. Pushing through, we step outside to a quiet parking lot, where I gulp in fresh air.

We move slowly to the front and reach Red. Lawrence holds him as I pop the lock and open the door; then we get him inside, buckling up the seat belt for him.

"Call Dotty. Tell her I'm sorry . . ." He trails off as he leans his head back on the seat. His eyes flutter shut.

Nah, not calling her. His love life works like mine. Once they've seen his true colors, his cesspool of insecurities, they are done. I haven't let a girl see who I really am in seven years. I slam the door and face Lawrence.

His face is, thankfully, blank. I don't think I could handle pity right now.

"You've done this a few times." His words are quiet. "Fuck, Devon. Why haven't you ever told me he was . . ."

A long exhalation comes from my chest. Jack knows the most, but even he's never *seen* my dad like this.

He shifts his feet and pulls out his phone, tapping away. "It's all right. I'm here if you need me, okay? I'll get an Uber. Call me tomorrow, and we'll chat."

"About what?" If he thinks I need to rehash this episode, he's deluded.

His eyes rise and pierce mine. "Men were looking for him. We need to find out why."

"He's just a drunk." He's an alcoholic. But I hate to say those words out loud.

"How much money are you giving him a month, Dev? Besides paying all his bills?"

"None of your business." Dad has a job, but I do give him money. He's my dad, and I have plenty of it. It's the same with Selena. They are all I have.

"Just as I thought. Too much," he murmurs, along with a look that seems to peer into my soul. He steps away toward the corner where a black car has pulled up. "Hate to miss the party at Aiden's, but I've got a girl to see tonight. Call me. If you need me, superstar, I'm all yours." He blows me a kiss.

I smirk, letting some of that tension ease. "Be safe, asshole. Thanks for the unpaid help," I call as he opens the door and gets in.

He drives off, and I swing around to get inside my car.

Of course, just as I crank it, Dad opens his eyes and hurls.

After scrambling around in my glove box for napkins to get him as cleaned up as I can, I drive the twenty minutes to the east side of Nashville to a small subdivision with cookie-cutter ranch-style houses and modest-sized front yards. I picked it out for him before he moved here a few years ago, when I did. I got him the job at the car dealership a block away.

I help him inside, wrangling him into the dark house and fumbling for the light switch in the entry, one that doesn't come on. Cursing, I half carry him to his bedroom, sending up a *fuck yeah* when the light comes on in there. At least the electricity is still on. I help him get his clothes off down to his boxers, lay him down on his side, and set a trash can nearby in case he gets sick again, and before I pull up the covers, he's back asleep, snoring.

After washing my hands and face in his bathroom, I check on him. My eyes catch on the photo on his nightstand—a pic of me and Mom and him when I was ten. Even with her smile, her face is distant, as if she's thinking of anything but the husband and kid pressed against her.

Couldn't make her happy. Dad's voice grates in my head. *Got her pregnant.*

The day she stormed out of our trailer, kicking beer cans out of her way, a shabby duffel bag clutched in her arms, pops into my mind. She drove away with another man, and I chased her down the driveway, begging. *I'll be back,* she promised, a pinched expression on her face. She wasn't there when I got sick with mono the following month. She wasn't there for my thirteenth birthday. Or Christmas. She erased me from her memory, as if I'd never existed, then left us to pick up the pieces.

Dad shoved women in my life, a revolving door of girlfriends, and I looked to them for love, craved it. They won my kid heart, only to follow in Mom's footsteps. *Bye, Devon. Be a good boy, and take care of your father.* Bonnie, Marilyn, Jessie—they never stuck around. In retrospect, most of them were barfly floozies, but hell, I just wanted someone to stay.

Still, he keeps that damn pic. I snatch it up, hands clenching around the frame. Part of me wants to rip it apart and remove her from our lives forever.

Where are you? I bought your beer, asshole, pops up on my phone.

Sorry. Unexpected errand, I reply to Aiden.

And you told ME not to be late. What's your ETA?

Leaving the frame and my dad in the bedroom, I head back to the kitchen, halting at the mess. Empty beer bottles, takeout containers, and dirty dishes litter the table and countertops. I close my eyes, wishing it would magically disappear. Of course it doesn't. Shit. I plop down at the table and fire off a text: Something came up. See you tomorrow.

He sends a flurry of pissed-off messages. I ignore them. Dad comes first.

Chapter 4

GISELLE

With a kiss to my cheek, Topher lets me out at the curb, and I pad over to the stoop of the brownstone, an old three-story building with a spacious apartment on each level. With lots of charm and close to Vanderbilt, it comes with the perfect landlady.

Dressed in her orange-and-purple muumuu, Myrtle stands on the sidewalk, her Yorkie, Pookie, sniffing at the one tree we have. Sixty and the closest thing I have to a bestie, she plucks a joint out from behind her ear and lights it. Mostly it's for her horrid migraines, but she gets it illegally, and it worries me. Pink lipstick outlines her lips as she takes a deep drag. A former model forty years ago in New York, she married a middling movie producer, eventually divorced him, and moved to Nashville to pursue a country music career that never panned out. Now she owns the building and writes poetry, some of it published.

With a grimace at my bare feet, she says, "Prince Charming?"

I plop down on the third step. "Charlie was an alligator-wearing weasel."

"Ah. The emu?"

"We didn't get that far, and I was afraid to ask. I need some wine with a side of Ragnar Lothbrok. You up for a *Vikings* binge session?"

She takes a toke. "Maybe tomorrow."

"How's your head?"

"Better now. How did the advisor meeting go?"

Dread inches up my spine as I tell her about my meeting at Vandy. "He isn't going to recommend me for CERN, he isn't happy with my teaching methods, and my work last semester was not impressive." I sigh as the words fall out. He's not wrong about last semester.

She lets out a wave of smoke, and I inhale the smell. "I'm still waiting on the next Vureck and Kate chapter. Is she going to escape the ship?"

I've been writing a sci-fi novel for the past five months. A romance, of all things, although the writing didn't quite start out like that—it just sort of happened. Science has been the center of my world since I discovered Einstein in elementary school, but writing is a way to vent my frustrations. "He's finally given her clothing after scanning her for disease, but now he's locked her in an antigravity chamber, and she can't cross the threshold. She needs to disable the control pad to escape. Haven't figured out how."

"Loss of power on the ship?" she offers. "His pet snake slithers into the chamber with the tools to get her out?"

"Because a snake can carry tools." I smile.

"It's an alien snake. Give him little fingers."

I jerk out my phone and take notes. "Maybe. Or the big guy is tormented in his sleep, since he has a murky past, and he sleepwalks up to her prison, opens it himself—"

"Because he secretly wants to bang her—only he hasn't acknowledged it. Just give the purple alien a big dick. Size does matter; I don't care what *Cosmo* says."

I grin. "She pops out and makes a run for it, and he grabs her, and they fall to the ground. His seven-foot muscled frame lands on her, and she's soft and silky, and he's never seen a female form the color of hers . . ." My voice trails off as ideas flash in my head, and when I glance up, she's smiling wryly at me.

"Your eyes light up when you talk about them. There's an artist inside you."

Ha. I sigh, stuffing my phone back in my bag. "My classmates would think my writing is ridiculous."

"Ah, you care what people think. My old age gives a fresh perspective, I guess, but if you want to be happy, do what makes your heart fly. Every breath you inhale must be meaningful. What do you *really* want, Giselle?"

I don't know. Not anymore.

Her words settle inside me, twisting around. Now that CERN is gone, my career goals feel uncertain. What *will* I do now? Graduate. Teach. Research. Sure, but is that all? What about love and my dreams of a family? When it comes down to it, physics is all I have left, the only thing I trust, and that life stretches in front of me, empty. That tight feeling in my throat rushes back.

Pookie pees, then runs over and jumps in my lap.

I stroke the dog's hair, plucking at the pink barrette on her head. "I've made so many bad choices lately—Preston, ugh, what a disaster. At least physics won't disappoint me." My voice cracks, surprising me, a testament to my very bad day. "I had an argument with Devon."

"Oh dear. You hate confrontations. Tell me everything, and leave nothing out," she says, sitting down next to me, and I recount the date with Rodeo, then reenact both sides of the minifight between me and Devon. Sometimes it's torturous, especially for those bad things you'd rather forget, but I have an eidetic memory, where I remember almost perfect mental images as well as auditory occurrences and other sensory recall. I'll never be able to forget how Devon smelled and how he felt when I was pressed against his chest. Hard chiseled muscles, the scent of summer and delicious male. I sum it up with, "I had a good old-fashioned hissy fit and stormed out. It's Jack's fault, but now Devon sees me as someone he needs to protect." I scratch Pookie under the chin. "Every time he looks at me, he's thinking about my virginity. He's wondering what's wrong with me. Explains the gaze at the wedding."

She pats my hand, her mascara heavy on her lashes as she juts the joint at me. "You look like you need a toke."

I grin.

"You're already getting a contact high. Might as well. Opens the brain waves for free thinking." She waggles her eyebrows.

"I need my brain cells to stay focused at the moment."

She laughs just as my phone buzzes. I groan at the caller, Mama, and press straight to voice mail as I stand up. "Maybe next time. A daughter's duty calls."

Setting the dog down at her feet, I study her face. "I didn't ask about your day. How was it?"

She twirls her bejeweled hands. "Fuse box in the basement is on the fritz. Something electrical. Garbage truck never showed. Pookie crapped in my kitten heels. The usual." She wets her blunt by pinching it, then sticks it back behind her ear as she ambles behind me to the wide front door.

"Nothing exciting, huh?"

She grimaces. "If you're asking if I talked to Mr. Brooks, I did not. His bald head and wrinkled lips can kiss my petunia."

I throw my arm around her. Mr. Brooks was her long-term boyfriend until they broke it off around the same time Preston and I ended. We've commiserated together ever since.

"Sorry."

"Fun to ride but not worth the trouble," she adds, giving me a squeeze.

"We're quite the pair, you and me," I say as she walks inside with me, and I help her up the last few steps.

"Didn't bring my cane," she mutters as we approach the elevator—a small one, rather dinky and dark, but it gets the job done. It's on the basement level, so I push the button for it to come up. The doors slide open.

"You should just get the knee replacement," I tell her, taking her elbow. "You know I'll help you with the recovery."

She waves me off as she puts her foot at the door to keep it from shutting. "Sushi tomorrow night?"

I bob my head. "It's on. Spider roll and fried wontons. Your place."

She points a finger at the door off the foyer on the first floor. "Let's invite the new resident. His name is"—she leans in to whisper—"John Wilcox. Moved in today. Handsome fellow in his fifties."

I see that glint in her eyes. She's already tried setting me up with the grocer, the baker, and the boy who throws the Sunday paper. None worked out.

"He's all yours. Please."

She mulls it over. "He has a cat. I'm allergic."

"Take a Benadryl."

She taps her chin. "Sushi night is historically girls' night."

"Rules are made to be broken!" I toss in.

She sends me a droll smirk. "Live what you preach, Giselle."

"Ask him. Tomorrow night is going to be lit," I chirp, waving good night as she pushes the button for the second floor, letting the door slide shut. I take the stairwell up to my place on the third level.

◆ ◆ ◆

I don't have any whiskey, but I'm midsip on a glass of wine when Mama calls back around nine.

"Mama!" I say brightly. "Missed you earlier, but I had to get situated."

"Was he employed?" No *hello, how are you.*

"He was a rodeo star, belt buckle and all." Then: "I thought I'd at least have until tomorrow before Topher told you about my date."

47

Topher and Mama had some unsure moments when he lived with my sister—*not right to cohabitate with a man*, she insisted—but now that Elena's married to Jack, Mama is satisfied and treats Topher like one of her own. Not sure that's a good thing.

"Topher can't keep a secret. If he wasn't gay, I'd tell you to marry him. He came by for some Sun Drops at the Cut 'N' Curl while I was doing some late-night cleaning."

"He's in trouble for running straight to you." I shall plot my revenge.

We chitchat for the next few minutes, until she drops her bomb. "Your birthday is Sunday. I get home from church at noon, so be here by one, dear."

I set down my glass and lean in, gripping the phone. Something about her voice . . . "I don't want anything fancy, Mama. Just you and me and Aunt Clara and Topher." I pick at the threads on my blue couch. "Elena and Jack won't be back. Maybe we should wait—"

"We will celebrate on the actual day."

I groan at the determination in her voice. She's a bulldog. "Mama, let's wait."

There's a beat of silence, and I picture her in her stately brick house in Daisy. She's probably already wearing her blue nightgown, the one that goes all the way to her feet with lace at the hem. She's curled up in her recliner watching *Dateline*, hair perfectly coiffed, nails tapping a copy of *People* magazine in her lap. A warm cup of peppermint tea sits next to her.

"Mama?"

"I don't like the ghosts in your eyes, dear. Preston . . ."

Sick of his name and annoyed, I hold the phone at arm's length for the next ten seconds. Sometimes I think she was more devastated than I was when we broke up. She'd been hesitant at first since he'd previously dated Elena, but he's a lawyer, lives in Daisy, and has money. He checked all her boxes, and she couldn't resist him. She planned our wedding, made an album with her favorite color scheme (pink and more pink), and selected flowers, venue, musicians . . .

I bring the phone back.

"Didn't you used to have a crush on him?"

"Who?"

"Aren't you listening? Mike Millington, the new principal at Daisy High. Recently divorced. He married some girl he met at Tulane. She ran around on him, and there's a child, but she's adorable. Only three years old—plenty of time for you to ease your way in and be a good role model—"

"I did not have a crush." Four years older than me, he lived next door to us until he left for college. I totally wrote our names in my notebook and drew little hearts around them. When I was thirteen.

"He handcuffed me to a tree once," I throw out.

"They were plastic handcuffs. Don't embellish."

I leave the memories behind as realization dawns. "Mama! You invited him to my birthday lunch? Why?"

"Dear, be nice. His dad passed, and his mom just a few months later. He's moved back to Daisy and is living in their house. He's starting over, dear, and I'm just being neighborly. Don't worry about details. Let me take care of it all."

I get that she thinks I'm unhappy, but no, I pick my own bad dates.

"I haven't seen him in ten years," I sputter, standing so I can pace around the living room. "I don't want to stuff food in my face while he sits across from me. It's my birthday—"

"I'll put him next to you."

I groan. "Why?"

There's a long silence, just the sound of her breathing, and when her voice comes, it's subdued, a tinge of hurt echoing in the tones. "It's a bittersweet day, dear, but you deserve a party. I want some happiness for you."

My eyes shut. While I was under the bleachers at the high school, mostly naked and getting videoed, my dad wrecked his car, went into a coma, and never came back. It was my sixteenth birthday. I've refused a party ever since, and the curse was born.

And the coldness.

My chest exhales. "We should just do it like we always do. Low key."

I hear the tinkle of a teacup as she sets it back on the saucer. "I can't take back the invitation. It's rude. Any good hostess knows this. Once everyone gets here, you'll be glad. I know you better than you think."

I pinch my nose. "Once everyone . . ." What is she planning? "Did you invite my preschool boyfriend too?"

"What's his name?"

"Jude—whatever, Mama, you can't fill the house with prospective husbands! I don't need a man. I have my work." This is the direct opposite of my thoughts lately, but I can hardly tell her about my quest, which has nothing to do with love. Feelings don't have to be involved at all. Just the act itself.

I glare at the wall, fingering my necklace. "If we're doing this, I want alcohol."

"It's the Lord's day."

"Champagne. Jesus would understand."

She pauses. "Okay."

I stare at the phone, as if expecting to see her come through the phone with two heads. She's . . . compromising?

I let out a sigh and grit my teeth. "I'm not dressing up."

"Of course, dear," she purrs, victory in her voice. "Wear your usual. You always look so nice."

Because my style is modeled after hers.

"Uh-huh. Just you wait."

"Don't be bratty like your sister."

I smirk. Elena was the one who went off to New York to college (the nerve of her leaving the South), traveled Europe, then gave up her chance to be a physician to be a librarian turned sexy-lingerie maker. She's the rebel, and I'm the spare, the one Mama believes will never step out of line, but these days I'm teetering on a tightrope, and I don't know which way I'll fall. With a sigh, I end up telling her about CERN, and she can't keep the relief out of her voice. She never wanted me to even apply. At least someone is happy about it.

Later, after the wine has chilled me, I circle back to the party. "Did you invite Devon?"

Dialogue in the background vanishes; she's clicked off the TV. "Do you want me to?"

My hands grip the phone. "Just trying to get a feel for how many people will be there."

"Have you seen him since the wedding?"

I don't like her tone—it's as if she's taking notes.

"Briefly." It's not an outright lie, but I don't want to get into a convo about Devon and all that entails.

"He's not really your type, dear. He's from *California*."

She says it like he's been in prison. I roll my eyes.

"And he has not one, but two earrings."

"I can count."

"And those tattoos? Bless."

Which is why she's never seen my pitiful attempt at ink.

"He's a playboy," she continues. "Who was that girl at the wedding? She had on enough makeup for a glamour shot."

"All women are different, Mama. Don't judge us."

"Well, y'all don't go together. You need a hometown boy and babies."

I exhale. "Never mind him. See you soon . . ." Before she can say anything else, I rush out "I love you" and hang up.

I plop down on the couch and pour another glass. After pulling out my notebook, I find my goals and pencil in a new one, right under Go to Switzerland, V-Card Must Go, and Write a Sci-Fi.

Buy a Dress Up To My Ass.

By midnight, I'm at my desk typing away, wearing my favorite cutoff frayed shorts and a tank top, listening to the sky rumble with a summer storm. At least the front will bring cooler air. I'm headed to the kitchen for water when the power goes out, shrouding my apartment in splotchy darkness. Glow from my laptop sends shafts of light to parts of the apartment, slicing through the black. Maybe it's the storm or a car hitting a transformer nearby. Power outages aren't the usual, and I can't recall a single one in the year and a half I've lived here.

I peek out the window and see that the rest of the city is still lit. After fumbling around, I grab a flashlight out of the kitchen drawer and head to the front door, stiffening as the light catches a curl of gray mist slithering in from the hall and dancing under the crack at the bottom of my door. For a moment, I'm frozen.

The fuse box. Myrtle mentioned an electrical issue in the basement.

Fear inches up, and I snap out of my daze and jerk open my door. No flames or crackling sounds, but the smell of smoke drifts to my nose. There's a layer of the fog around my feet, near the stairwell, and my heart flies, even as I recognize it's not dense or thick.

Instinct takes over, and I shut my door to block as much smoke as I can and dash to the stairwell and take the steps three at a time. I fall down the last two in my haste and fall splat on my ass on the landing, not noticing any pain, and jump up. I reach the second-floor door to Myrtle's hall and fling open the door, already running. The smoke is thicker here, two inches off the ground and rising with every second. Jerking my tank up over my lower face, I'm already screaming her name before I reach her brass knocker, beating on the wood.

My chest rises rapidly, and I count the number of times I slam my fist on her door. Fifteen. Calling her name.

She opens her entrance just as the annoying sound of smoke alarms pings around us, ratcheting up my anxiety level. Took them long enough!

"Thank God! Must be a fire! Smoke is coming from the vents and up the stairwell!" I take her arm, not mincing words. "Where's Pookie?"

"What?" She looks disheveled, apparently asleep for hours, her robe askew, feet bare.

A rumbling, cranking sound reaches my ears just as water spouts from the sprinkler system in the ceiling. She had it installed years ago for the hallways. "Myrtle! It's a fire! Get the dog!" I tell her, and she pales and weaves on her feet.

"Can't be. Electrician said it was fine—"

I put my hands on her shoulders and lower my voice, infusing calm under the urgency. "Come on, Myrtle, sweetie. Where's your dog?"

"In my bed." She points back into the apartment as she steps out in the hall, looking around with wide eyes. She gasps as I leave her and fly inside, grabbing the lump of trembling brown fur off her comforter and stuffing him in my arms. On the way out, I snatch her purse and cane. She has the alarm system wired to 911. Fire trucks will come. I strain to hear them, but it's only just gone off . . .

She scoops Pookie up and follows me at a slow pace that makes me want to scream. I hurry her along to the stairwell, giving orders as I help her the few paces down the stairs to the first level. "Walk slowly down the steps—yes, that's good. One at a time. You're doing great." Horror hits. "The new guy!" If the fire's in the basement, he's getting the worst of it. "Don't open any doors to the basement," I tell her, thinking out loud. "Back draft."

"What?" she yells, her face draining of more color.

For half a second, I think about explaining that a back draft can be caused by introducing oxygen to an oxygen-deprived fire zone; then the combustion would reignite, and the carbons and black smoke would explode and take down anything in their path. But there's no time.

I take a deep breath, and it's mostly clean. Must be calm for her. Reaching out with my palms, I don't feel any heat on the last door and open it to a roll of smoke on the first floor. "Just go slow, okay, Myrtle— awesome, you got this. Shut the stairwell door—yes, good—now, let's get you out the front door. I'll get the new tenant, okay?"

She nods, clutching Pookie, her eyes wide as she coughs. Fear rising, I dash past her as she walks outside to safety. Just as I reach his door, the tenant opens it, cat in his hand. Thank God. "Fire," I breathe, and he gives me a jerky nod and heads to the exit at the front of the building. Smoke tumbles thick and dark, and my eyes water as they dart to the basement door, hearing crackling sounds but no visible flames.

"Where are you going?" the man yells as I turn back to the stairwell.

I bite my lip, eyeing the smoke level in the stairwell. It's not bad there, not thick yet, just tangling around my knees. There's an escape ladder outside my kitchen if things get hairy—but they won't.

"My nana's pearls." His mouth drops, and before he can yell at me, I take off in a sprint, legs pumping.

Once inside my place, I slam the door shut and tear the place apart, counting the seconds in my head. I reasoned on the way up and gave myself forty seconds to search. Less than a minute but doable and safe.

Ten seconds . . . no pearls on the coffee table or under the cushions.

Twenty . . . not in the kitchen, where I opened the wine.

I skid around the corner to the bedroom, eyes bouncing over text-books on my desk, clothes on the bed. Nothing. Frustration washes over me, mixed heavily with fear.

Thirty . . . smoke dances around me as I hit the bathroom, kicking open the door, fumbling through lotions, perfumes, and makeup. After jerking out a washcloth, I use it to cover my mouth. It's fine, it's fine. I have good lungs. I'm a runner. Just . . . Nana. She died after Dad, and nothing was ever the same. And she wore them every day. She loved them; she touched them. I wasn't her favorite—Elena was—but she did love me.

Forty . . . I jerk back from the room and run to the door and stare at the smoke rushing in like a tidal wave from underneath. My eyes water as I cough. Can't go that way now. Don't know what's waiting for me. Could be flames. Could be smoke gets me before I get down the stairs. Nausea sits in my stomach like a thick wad of concrete.

Backpack in hand, I stride to the bedroom; snatch my laptop, phone, and purse; and shove them inside and run back to the kitchen, my frantic hand already working the window latch next to the small table. Off in the distance, I hear the blare of fire trucks, see the flash of red and white lights.

Rain drenches me, a bolt of lightning crossing the sky as I swing my legs over the ledge to the barely there balcony and stare down at the concrete below. Perfect, let's add electricity to the mix while I get on a metal ladder. I look over the edge. Forty-five feet, I estimate in my head quickly. "Not afraid," I mutter.

Water pelts me from the sky as I sling the backpack on my shoulders, then unhook and push the metal ladder, listening to it clatter down, screeching and groaning. It's rusty, but I know it works. A girl like me has a plan. The day I moved in, I was checking the exits.

Fear zips down my spine as I take the first wobbly steps, my grip tight as I concentrate on staring at each brick I pass.

Forty-five feet. I can do it.

Grip of death on the ladder. Move foot down. Repeat.

Wind buffets me, tugging at me, and the grasp of my right hand slips. My left pulls me back just as fast, but I take a minute to take deep gulps of air and get my heart under control. At least the air is fresh. I adjust the backpack and start again. Dimly, about halfway down, I'm aware of my name drifting up from the chaos, a roar of a sound layered in under the rain and sirens, but I don't look, just keep going. I'm on the side of the building next to the street, so I can't see who's at the front, where firemen shout orders. Out of the corner of my eye, an ambulance flashes past. *That's normal,* I tell myself. They always come when the fire truck is called.

I reach the top of the first floor and freeze at the huge floor-to-ceiling window that Myrtle loves, the antique glass old and wavy. Flames flicker and lick from the basement door just a few feet away, crackling and dancing. Smoke hovers thick and black, billowing like a monster down the hall. At the end is the stairwell, although I can't see the door.

I drop down off the last rung and sprint down the alley and circle to the front.

"Myrtle!" I call as a paramedic puts her on a stretcher. What happened to her? She got out! How long was I . . .

Guilt slams into me, and I bend over to catch my breath at the street, gasping for air, some of the adrenaline dropping. I made it, I made it. But if she's hurt—

My gaze scans the scene, past the red trucks, and every thought stops at the man I see.

What's he doing here?

"Devon!" I scream over the melee, at the men who are holding him back from the entrance.

It feels like a million seconds before he flips around, his wild eyes zeroing in on mine. Then he's turning and walking—no, running, running so fast, like I've seen him on TV, only . . .

Strong hands land on my shoulders, fingers digging into my skin. His normally tan face is white, his mouth pulled back in a snarl.

I lick my lips, gasping for air. "We . . . really . . . need to . . . stop . . . meeting like this—"

He jerks me to him, growls, and kisses me.

Chapter 5

GISELLE

"I'm fine," I tell the paramedic who made me sit on a bench across the street from the building a few minutes ago.

She shines another light in my eyes. "You didn't hit your head? Fall? No dizziness, nausea, coughing?" Her businesslike tone is calming, but nothing stills the jackhammer in my chest.

"One cough." I take in the pacing man behind her, the one who's currently sending me looks that say, *I plan to kill you as soon as I know you're okay*. Not able to hold his eyes, I inhale more air and check out the firemen scurrying around the building. The fire is out, but smoke spills from the windows. God, it happened so fast.

"Her ankle is swollen," Devon barks, and I flick my eyes down at the ugly yellow bruise on the outside of my right foot.

The paramedic looks at my ankle.

I wince. "Oh. I fell down the stairs to get to Myrtle. It doesn't hurt, just a little sprain . . ."

"You should have come out with her!" Devon rakes a hand through his hair. Another tell that he's upset. He's said this only a hundred times since the moment he grabbed me.

The paramedic turns around and asks him to take a few steps back. He heaves in a great breath and paces off.

I tear my eyes off him and press my hand to my chest. My heart still hasn't slowed, teetering on exploding.

After checking out my ankle, the paramedic rises and tells me what I already know, that it's fine and just needs some ice and for me to go easy on it. She's been sweet, especially since I refused to let her look me over until I talked to my best friend. *Myrtle's okay,* I keep telling myself. Before she left in the ambulance, she patted me on the cheek and assured me she only twisted her knee on the last step of the stoop. Worry knots my stomach. She's frail. Ugh. And John's cat jumped out of his arms and ran away as soon as he came out. We'll find his cat. I'll find him if it's the last thing I do.

John left in the same ambulance with Myrtle, his complexion gray as he held an oxygen mask to his face. *Welcome to the neighborhood, new guy. Normally, it's not on fire.*

A whine comes from my lap, and I smooth a hand over the Yorkie left with me. "Shh," I croon. "It's over now, sweet Pookie. Your mama is fine."

"I can hold the dog at least," Devon says, walking over from where he was pacing. He seems to have calmed down, and the paramedic nods, giving him permission as he takes the shivering animal. I frown, half expecting her to nip at him, but she takes one look at him and stuffs her nose right in the bend of his elbow. I give up. He's irresistible to all females.

With a final searching look at me, as if looking for other injuries, he marches over to a group of firemen huddled near the building, ignoring the yellow tape someone has already put up. Just shoulders his way in and starts asking questions. They don't seem to mind. Must be nice to be famous.

I catch snatches of conversation. The fire was localized in the base-ment. Structural damage is widespread. Fire marshal is en route to assess. Yes, a crew will be out to board up the busted windows and door so looters don't get in. We need approval to get inside once the tape is up. My eyes go up to the third floor. Did my stuff get wet? No doubt it reeks of smoke. At least the rain has stopped, the cool air rolling in.

Shit.

I . . .

What was I thinking?

Forget that for a sec.

He kissed me.

My hands touch my lips. My first kiss in months. Hard and swift, not a drop of sweetness. No tongue. No saliva. I'm a little disappointed.

"He's your boyfriend?" the paramedic says as she nudges her head back at Devon, a smile on her face. "Hot as hell, and boy, what a temper. Devon Walsh, right?"

"He's a friend."

Her eyebrows pop. "Nearly got himself arrested trying to burst into the building and get you. Lots of colorful words he used." She laughs.

My eyes shut as more remorse beats at me. "No one was hurt?"

She pats my hand, seeming to read me. "Our guys are well trained. We've seen much worse. You were on the third floor, right?"

I nod.

"You showed up before anyone went inside to search, and even if they had, these firemen know how to handle it."

I don't feel any better. Devon. My lashes flutter. If he'd managed to get past the firemen and gone in after me . . . I recall the image of the first floor, and my stomach lurches. My hands tremble as I press them to my face.

She walks away to put her things up, and Devon stalks back to where I am. He stops in front of me and hitches Pookie into the crook of his arm. A gladiator of a man with a tiny dog should look ridiculous, but not him.

"I can take her now." I stand up and force myself not to weave.

His face twists as a muscle pops in his jaw.

I limp the two feet over to him; my ankle isn't bad except for a twinge, and he blisters out a curse and meets me before I reach him. He takes my hand, then laces it with his, his clasp reassuring and firm—me in one hand, Pookie in the other. He leads me slowly over to where his Hummer is parked.

"Shouldn't we stay and see what's next? At the least, I should look for the cat." Frustration builds as I realize I don't even know the feline's name. "Can you take me to the hospital? Myrtle is by herself. She'll want me to call her daughter in New York and the insurance people—"

"It's two in the morning, the cat will show up, your friend is fine, you don't have shoes, you're swaying on your feet, and I need to get you home."

I don't have a home.

He unlocks the black Hummer, opens the passenger side, and motions for me to get in.

My chest rises. "Myrtle—"

"Get in the goddamn car, Giselle, or you don't want to know what I'll do next."

Kiss me?

Ravage my body?

Nope. Just be angry.

"What were you doing at my place this late?"

"Get. In. The. Car."

"Fine!" With a huff, I slide into the car, sinking into the opulent black seat, inhaling expensive leather and sexy male.

After settling Pookie in the back on the floorboard with surprisingly careful hands, he dashes to the hatch and throws stuff around. After jogging back, he wraps a sweatshirt around the dog, tucking her in gently so she won't roll around in the car.

He gets in and cranks the car, and I wait for him to pull out, but he doesn't, his hands on the wheel, twisting around the black leather, his knuckles white.

Nerves hit, and I deflate, all brave face gone. "Devon, please, I shouldn't have gone back inside, but I know how a fire works—the smoke wasn't bad on my floor, and I had the ladder. I monitored my dizziness, gave myself less than a minute—"

"You can't predict fire, Giselle," he says, his face etched with a deep scowl as he glares out the windshield. I wish he'd look at me. "Just to get a necklace."

"Nana's. They remind me of her." I kick at my backpack on the floor, which he must have put there before I got in. "At least I grabbed my work—"

"A laptop is replaccable. *You* could have died." He throws his head back on the headrest and turns to look at me. His eyes are a vibrant green, gleaming with suppressed emotion.

"I'm sorry," I say after several moments, searching his gaze. "You're right. I reacted on instinct. It happened so fast, and there wasn't time to think straight—" I suck in a breath as pent-up fear claws at my insides and inches its way up to my throat, stinging and harsh, reminding me of my dangerous choice. My eyes blink rapidly, my hands clenching in my lap.

He looks horrified. "Giselle, fuck, don't . . . cry . . . I . . ." He stops. "They wouldn't let me go inside, and I wanted to kill them." He abuses the steering wheel with his grip.

More regret rises as I see how he must have felt. I terrified him. He was here and couldn't do anything to save me, and he would have been the one to tell Mama and Elena if something horrible had happened to me. Wetness tracks down my cheeks, and I hurriedly brush the tears away.

"Come here, baby." He reaches over the console for me and pulls me in for a hug, his hands stroking up and down my back. Electricity arcs between us, a hyperawareness that races over my skin. Sadly, I'm the only one who notices it. Devon is just being kind.

Pressing my forehead to his chest, I breathe in his mesmerizing scent, sea and sunshine. "I thought I had it. I did have it. But you tried to run inside, and if something had happened to you, I'd want to die." I place my cheek over his heart, listening to the rapid beats. Highly trained athletes have a resting heart rate of below sixty beats per minute, but his is out of control. I sigh. He's still upset, and I tighten my hold around his waist.

I don't know how long he holds me—a minute, maybe five. Time feels distorted as his hands move up to my scalp, palming my head under my hair. His lips brush the top of my head.

"You can let me go." *Don't.* "I'm soaked," I whisper, noticing for the first time that he's changed clothes since the club. His black shirt and jeans have been replaced with slim-fitting gray joggers and a white damp T-shirt that clings to his chest, outlining his pecs. In the dark car, he feels bigger, more muscular.

"You're shivering."

He lets me go to crank up the heat, and I sigh, missing his comfort. He stares down at me, tilting my chin up as he inspects me.

"I'm really okay."

His eyes land on my tank top.

"Not wearing a bra," I say, stating the obvious. "It's the first thing to come off when I get home. Then, the pearls."

His eyes drift up from my erect nipples and cling to mine. Whoa. My brain is too scattered to count the seconds, but I think it goes past ten.

The angry kiss is on my mind, but I don't dare bring it up. Logically, I connect the dots: his inner caveman reacting out of fear and anger or adrenaline, a heady cocktail of epinephrine erupting straight from the medulla to the bloodstream—that is, alpha Devon at his peak, ready to tear the world apart. Probably the same way he feels when a pass intended for him gets intercepted. Nothing sexual.

"I would have gone in there for you a hundred times."

I swallow thickly. "You'd do that for anyone."

He pulls away and settles back in his seat. "Right. Where do you want to go?"

"There's a Hilton a few blocks from here."

"No."

I eye him. That was fast. "Why not?"

"You need someone tonight."

"Mama's, I guess."

He studies me. "Is that really what you want?"

I groan. "No, she'll ask me a million questions and be upset. I'll call her tomorrow. Same for Aunt Clara." I stare down at my bare legs. "I have a key to Jack and Elena's house while they're gone, but the hardwood is being redone this week, so the fumes will be awful . . ." I wince at that.

"Topher?"

"He just got a small rental in Daisy, but the new roommate situation is tricky. I'm assuming I'll need a few days to get situated, and I don't want to bother him."

"Any other friends?"

I bite my lip, not wanting to explain my small social circle. Most of my friends are still in Memphis, where I did my undergrad and master's, or have moved on to graduate work across the country.

"Stay with me until this gets sorted."

Surprise makes me blink. "The fuck palace?" I say, reaching for levity because, hello, *stay* with him?

"I see Elena shared her nickname for it with you."

I shrug. Devon purchased the penthouse from Jack, who had bought it only to bring his girlfriends there while he kept a separate apartment for himself and Devon. The penthouse was where Jack and

Elena had their drunken one-night stand, when she didn't know he was a famous football player. Elena hated the penthouse with a passion and had it sold to Devon a week after they were engaged.

He pulls out on the street, driving to the intersection. "Beggars can't be choosers. I imagine you'll need several days to find a new place. I'll hardly be at the penthouse anyway, since I have training camp."

"Sounds good." Sounds terrifying—in an exhilarating way.

He darts a look at me. "You think staying with me is a good idea." He says it as a statement, not a question.

I smooth down the frayed edges of my shorts. "With the giant *V* on my forehead, I'm in the safest hands in Nashville." I snort. "Funny. You're a wide receiver."

He mutters something under his breath, and I study the hard lines of his profile, the blade of his nose, the glints of blue in his dark hair, the slope of his broad shoulders. I can't mistake the tension rolling off him. Did he expect me to turn down his offer?

"You never said why you were at my place in the middle of the night," I say, searching for a way to break this strange tautness between us.

He makes a left onto the street. "Wanted to tell you I was sorry for yelling."

"At midnight?"

"Didn't say it was a good idea. I drove past and was gonna check if your light was on. I was going to call you if it was, but then I saw the fire trucks." He gives me side-eye.

"I didn't know you knew where I lived."

He shrugs, his expression casual. "Elena mentioned your building once. I heard you tell someone what floor you had."

Ah, I see. Just a coincidence that he knew where I lived. Not a real interest.

My fists clench at the next topic I want to address. "Back to the club, I don't think I can go another minute without explaining. First,

I'm sorry I lashed out. Jack is the one who needs to be yelled at. Second, you must know I haven't been saving myself for someone special. If that were true, then I would have slept with Preston as soon as he put the ring on my finger—which, in hindsight, is what he really wanted anyway." A long pause comes as I let out a breath. "I just couldn't do it."

He frowns. "What did you mean by your comment about being frigid? Did that jerk tell you that?"

Unwelcome memories wrap around me, and as much as I try to shove them off, they linger. "He did."

"Asshole." His eyes flick over to me. "He didn't deserve a nice girl like you. Don't let him get in your head."

I stare out my window.

"Hey," he says. "Talk to me."

"You like long stories?"

"Hit me."

I chew on my bottom lip, and before I think too hard, the horrible truth spills out. "When I was fifteen, almost sixteen, this lacrosse player in high school caught my eye. Handsome with dreamy eyes, he reminded me of Lord Byron, you know, with dark hair and a pout on his lips, like a girl's. I was a year younger but had skipped a grade, so we were in the same class." I sigh. "Needless to say, I adored him, and anytime he looked at me—and boy, he had a way of just looking—I did his bidding. Wrote his term paper, let him copy my chemistry notes, saved his seat at lunch—but he never asked me out. He really laid it on thick the summer before our senior year, asking me to come to his practices and watch. After one of those, he led me under the bleachers, and I went, knowing that's where all the cool kids go to get high or laid. Did you know they voted me the most boring girl of my class? It's one of those secret lists they make, not the real ones that make the yearbook." My voice cracks, just a little, and I jerk it back. "Anyway, he kissed me, my first real one, and had me down to my underwear in no time. Then I heard his friends laughing. They were hidden, videoing me on his phone. It was my birthday." Heat rises in my cheeks, and I'm glad Devon's looking at the road, his face hard.

"By the time I got home, my daddy was in a coma. Looking back, now that I have distance, I know all guys aren't like him, but it's made me hesitant about sex."

"What's this dickhead's name? Where does he live?"

My fists curl. "I took care of him."

He flashes his eyes over to me. "Good."

We've reached the Breton Hotel, where his penthouse sits at the top. Close to the stadium, the building's exterior is a dark-gray stucco color. The night valet, a young guy dressed in a black uniform, dashes for the Hummer like it's the best day of his life, his wide face spreading in a grin.

I take Pookie from the back, and Devon waits for me, his eyes low and heavy, as if he doesn't want me to read his thoughts. He takes my hand in his, his thumb brushing over mine—*killing me with the sparks*—as we head inside. The interior is all marble and glass with a chic sitting area encircling a four-tiered stone fountain made of black monolith-style granite. Lush plants and bright flowers in textured gray urns decorate the corners around a twenty-foot fireplace. An older woman at the front desk waves at him, her eyes appreciative as she rakes her gaze over his broad shoulders. I swear she puts her hand over her heart as we pass by. Yeah. Everyone adores him.

My heart flutters, not from the fire but from his proximity. He stalks across the lobby like he owns the whole place, and I keep up with him. He leads me around a hidden alcove and shows me the penthouse elevator and the code to use it. It slides opens, and he tugs me inside.

The air feels thick as we rise to the top.

He lets go of my hand.

"So did you confess to doing the lacrosse player's homework and get him in trouble?" he asks.

"Worse."

His arm brushes mine as he takes Pookie from me and arches a brow, the one with the piercing. I have the insane urge to lick it. "Spill your devious ways, Giselle. What did you do to him?"

"My stories can get long, Dev."

"I want to hear them."

Butterflies dance in my chest, and I push them down. This is Devon. *Friend.*

"That night, I sat at the hospital and forgot about Carlton for the moment—that was the lacrosse player's name."

"Last name?"

I smirk. "Anyway, Daddy passed that night. When I checked to see if Carlton had posted the video, he hadn't. Maybe he heard about my dad—it is a small town, and Daddy was the mayor, and news travels fast, so perhaps he felt bad. I don't know—maybe he never intended to make the video public but planned to use it to hold over me in some way. School was set to start the next day, so I was terrified he planned to do something with it on the first day back. What he didn't know was that I may be the quiet sort, but I will make a plan."

"Revenge?"

I nod.

He grins. "You're fierce."

My lashes lower. *Oh, if you only knew the thoughts I've had about you.* "I worked at the school office, organizing and cleaning. I had access to info you'd never believe. Records, test papers left on the copier, teacher's computer passwords—I never used those, by the way."

"Of course. But you wrote his paper."

"A mistake. Anyway, I came to school the next day—Mama had no idea. I was exhausted and heartbroken, and my head wasn't right, but I was angry—God, so angry. At everything." My breath hitches. "I wasn't myself."

He puts an arm around me and tugs me to his side. "I'm sorry about your dad."

I nod. "I didn't get my name on the attendance roll, because I wasn't planning on staying, just slipped into the office, hugged the secretary—she was the sweetest old lady and had heard about Dad—then grabbed Carlton's locker combination. Keep in mind all students had to leave their phones in their lockers. Then, while everyone was in class, I opened his locker and swiped his phone. I left the textbooks. A man needs an education. With the state I was in, I wanted to blow up everything he had."

"Ballbuster."

"Are you bored yet?"

"You never bore me."

"People put crazy things on their phones. I went home—because remember, I was never at school—and found two videos of him drinking and snorting coke at various keggers over the past years."

He gives me a surprised look. "How did you get the passcode?"

I tap my head. "I'd watched him unlock it several times, and I mostly never forget what I see. I sent the videos to his parents from his own phone. Pretty easy since I had all their contact info. If you think about it, I was helping him. He was on the road to drug addiction. His parents got him in rehab the next week, and he missed half of our senior year." I pause, feeling the weight of his stare, green and intense. "Too hard core?"

"Hell no. I'm kind of . . . turned on."

A blush steals up my face. I see it in the reflection of the elevator. "Interesting."

A long second stretches out—until the ping of our arrival makes me jump.

He pulls me along as the elevator opens, and we walk down the hall. "No one ever saw your video?"

"Just his buddies, I assume, but then they saw it firsthand anyway. There was some talk amongst their crowd, sly jokes directed at me, and it hurt—it really did—but I just put my head down and kept going. Losing my dad had me in a haze anyway." I think about those blurry days of dealing with my father's death. "If Mama had seen that video . . . she couldn't take any more. She would have been arrested for killing him."

"Huh. Did you get your revenge on Preston?"

I shake my head.

"Why?"

I shrug, feeling the weight of his question, wondering the same thing myself. "I don't know."

We reach his door, and he opens it for us, a grin twitching his lips. "Welcome to the fuck palace, baby."

Laughing, we walk in. He sets down a squirming Pookie, who promptly finds a pair of sneakers by the door, squats, and pees.

Devon blinks. "Shit."

"Just pee. She only does that when she's nervous—which is ninety percent of the time."

"Great."

"Hate to break it to you, but you're now living with two females." I hit him with a blinding smile. "Let's hope our cycles don't sync up. We'll clean out your ice cream and cry over nothing."

He blanches.

"Kidding. Small dogs typically go into heat only three to four times a year—a larger dog, every six months. She's spayed, so you're safe." I pat his arm and pick up the shoe, and he stops me.

"Leave it. Come on; let's get you settled."

I follow him past the foyer and into the massive den, taking in the open floor plan, noting the expensive gray leather couches, two huge black loungers sitting on chrome legs, the giant big screen, the trophies stuffed in the white built-in bookcase along the back wall. The floors are a wide-planked bamboo. Framed art of Devon dots the walls, one a blown-up image of him at a game in his blue-and-yellow jersey as he snatches the football from the air, his face a study in concentration. I take in a candid of him with his helmet gone, sweat misting his face as he smiles and accepts an MVP award. I watched that game. It was last year's AFC Championship.

To the right is a huge window overlooking the gleaming lights of downtown. Farther out, I see the east bank of the Cumberland River and Nissan Stadium.

He hasn't finished unpacking yet, judging by a few boxes lining the wall. My eyes snag on my heels, sitting like they don't belong on a rectangular, heavy concrete coffee table. His style is modern and bare. How's he going to feel when I start leaving my laptop and glasses everywhere? It's just for a few days . . .

He gives me a quick tour, and I estimate it's about four thousand square feet or more on one level. I follow him to the ultramodern kitchen with a spacious granite island in the middle. The cooking area is decorated with shiny black subway tiles all the way to the ceiling, the appliances a stark white. The formal dining room sports a Scandinavian pale-oak table with lush velvet high-back chairs. A brushed-nickel chandelier hangs from the textured ceiling. He leads me down the wide hall with thick molding around the baseboards and along the ceiling, all in white. He tells me I can have the best guest room, then shows me the en suite bathroom it opens to and the closet that's as big as the bathroom in my apartment. The bed itself is a king, the headboard padded in tufted cream linen, the frame draped in a white duvet with pops of furry blue and gray pillows. There's a whitewashed eight-foot armoire, an elegant mirror that leans against the wall, and two matching end tables. Everything looks like it came straight out of a magazine.

"You're gaping," he murmurs.

I close my mouth. "You'll have to kick me out of here when it's time to go."

He shrugs. "I hired someone to decorate. Never had a home that was all mine."

Once out of my room, he opens the door to another bedroom across the hall, but it has zero furniture; it's just sparkling clean. Two more rooms are the same. All have private bathrooms.

He points out his room at the end of the hall but doesn't offer to let me peek in, and I'm disappointed but tuck it away. I follow him into a laundry room with its own kitchen, and he grabs a handful of clothes and stuffs them in my hands. He tells me there's some of his cousin's underclothes in the chest in the bedroom and maybe other things—he really isn't sure what's there—and I nod, barely noticing. This place is like a resort! He frowns, worried I don't have enough clothes; dashes to his room; and comes back with more and takes them to the guest room as I pad along. A huge weight feels lifted, and I'm not sure if it's the fact that he's given me a place to sleep and is taking such gentle care of me or that I told him what happened all those years ago, and we laughed about it.

We head back to the kitchen, and he tells me to sit at the black-and-white island in the center while he grabs me a water bottle from the built-in stainless steel fridge, then checks out my ankle. He props it up on a stool rung and bends down to run light hands over my skin. Warm tingles dance over me, and I bite my lip. I've known him for months, but he's never touched me this much. Finally, he sets my foot gently down and moves away.

"Keep the ice pack on it tonight while you sleep." He sets one down on the counter.

I huff out a laugh. "We're like characters in a book—me the damsel in distress, you the dashing hero. Twice in one day."

"Hmm."

I suck down a drink of water while he leans against the fridge, his lashes lowering every so often as he does that thing where he looks at me—but doesn't.

The city outside is quiet, the kitchen is silent, and time feels frozen: just us—in this beautiful penthouse.

Is it odd that neither of us seems to notice we're wet from the rain?

We stare at each other, and heat builds and rises inside me, a yearning to touch him that makes me feel light headed. I'm losing my mind. He doesn't want me like that.

His green eyes flicker over me, lingering on my body.

I'm afraid to move, almost paralyzed, as if he's a predator and I'm delicious prey. I'm aware of every excruciating detail of *him*, the span of his broad shoulders, the long tan column of his throat as he drinks his water, the roped muscles in his forearms.

"You were right, you know," I murmur. "I'm glad I'm not alone tonight."

"Ah." He bites his lower lip, his teeth digging into the plump skin.

"Thank you." I push my glasses up. "I shouldn't be here long—just until I get things figured out with my insurance."

"All right."

More quiet. More staring at each other.

What is he thinking?

"I should shower," I blurt.

His gaze drifts lazily over me. Again. "Me too."

Oh Lord. I cling to the edge of the granite, imagining him under a spray of water, the droplets slicking over his skin—

Nope. Must stop.

"Why did you kiss me?"

He frowns and straightens, seeming to shake himself. "Why not? See you in the morning." And then he's striding down the hall to the last room and shutting the door behind him.

Chapter 6

Devon

Sleep refuses to come, even after a hot shower and fifteen minutes of watching *The Office*. All the usual tricks. I check my phone aimlessly, wincing at the late hour, then toss it aside. Training camp will be here in a few hours, and I should be exhausted—but my blood pumps overtime, my heart rate still erratic. That moment of thinking she was still in her apartment in the fire rushes back, and I let out a heavy exhale and scrub the bristles on my jaw. I was out of control, ready to barrel through the firemen holding me back, just to get to her. I wanted to rail at her. I wanted to throw her over my shoulder, spank her ass, then . . . *fuck her* hard and fast until she got some sense.

Jack's face appears in my head. *Keep your eyes on her. She's a virgin,* he told me at his engagement party a few months ago. At the time, he was scowling as he watched her talk to a group of rambunctious players. The guys like talking to her . . . I mean, why wouldn't they? She's smart and sexy in an understated, unassuming way, a sharp contrast to the blowsy jersey chasers who dance attendance on them. She's a bit aloof and reserved, too, as if she's holding part of herself back. Little does she know that to an alpha male, that means *challenge.*

But shit, why, why did he have to tell me *that*?

I mull it over, trying to get to the bottom of it as I kick my covers. *Maybe he thought* you *needed to know,* a sly voice says.

And here I am, with her just a bedroom away.

A scream pierces the quiet, and I jerk out of bed and dash to her room, flinging open the door as I reach it. I was worried she'd have bad dreams. Risking her life for a string of pearls—shit. What a crazy girl.

Pookie stands on the bed and shivers, all six pounds on alert as Giselle tosses and turns.

"Giselle?" I murmur, not wanting to startle her as I sit on the bed. "Babe, you're dreaming."

She cries out again, unaware, and flails at the duvet, twisting around as a tear falls down her face.

Forget this.

After untangling her from the comforter, I cup her shoulders and ease her up to my chest. She makes all my protective instincts flare to the surface.

"Dev," she whimpers. "What's happening?"

"Bad dream. You're sleeping with me." Makes perfect sense.

I sweep her up, and she clings to me, her arms tightening around my shoulders as her face presses against my chest. "I'm sorry. God, you must be sick of me."

"Not yet." I walk with her down the hall. Nothing wrong with this. Nothing.

"I keep seeing Myrtle in my head. She's . . . she's falling down the stairs, and it's my fault. Her knees are bad." Her breath hitches. "I should have walked her all the way out the door."

"Shh, I got you." She's worried about Myrtle when she should be thinking about herself.

I ease her down on my bed, keeping my gaze averted from her toned long legs, the shapely curve of her hips peeking out from one of my old shirts, the fall of her damp hair curling around her shoulders. Nope. This is so she can sleep. This isn't weird.

After grabbing a pair of light flannel pajama pants, I slip them over my underwear and crawl in next to her, settling her under the covers and myself on top.

"Come here," I say.

She pauses for half a second, then scoots over while I rest on my back. Even with a layer of sheets and a duvet and a few inches between us, I feel the warmth of her body. She smells like my shampoo and bodywash—mango and citrus. In my head, visions dance around of me sliding under the covers with her, parting her thighs—

"You're unexpectedly . . . sweet," she murmurs.

I shove away my erotic thoughts. "Sure."

I turn my head to see her blinking up at the skylight over the bed. It lets in more light than I thought it would when I had it installed, but something about the stars speaks to me. My hand reaches up and traces a line from one star to another. "You think there's life up there?"

"Yes. Do you?"

"It pays to keep an open mind, but not so open your brains fall out," I quote.

She lifts up on her elbow and stares at me. "Carl Sagan?"

I smirk at the surprise in her tone. "Not just a jock, Giselle. I read, mostly on the road."

She blows at a piece of hair in her face and plops back down. "Devon Walsh, squashing stereotypes one quote at a time."

"I don't think we're alone in the universe. We're just a speck, simple humans walking a life unaware."

She laughs, a hint of bemusement there.

"What?" I ask. "You don't agree?"

"Oh, I agree. Not everyone believes in aliens." She sighs. "'For small creatures such as we, the vastness is only bearable with love.' Sagan again."

Love? I arch a brow. Not touching that quote with a ten-foot pole.

"Tell me . . . these alternate universes you mentioned—where are we right now?"

"I love that you're curious about my theories." Then . . . she presses a light kiss to my shoulder—nothing sexy, for fuck's sake—but heat licks me from head to toe. *Ah hell, keep your face blank, asshole, and your dick better chill out.*

I clear my throat and ease an inch away. "Come on. What are we doing in this universe? Don't make me a teenage girl."

"You might not like it . . ." Her voice trails off.

"If I'm some ugly insect or demon, yeah, I may not, but help a guy out. I need a story to put me to bed."

She laughs under her breath. "Are you sure?" Then: "Ohhhh, a demon universe—"

"Focus, woman. Hit me with your best one."

"Fine. You're a seven-foot purple-colored alien from Sector 4, the Triangulum Galaxy, 2.7 million light-years from Earth—"

"Is that a real place? Why am I purple?"

"Yes, it's real, and purple is your favorite color."

"How do you know?"

"I just imagined it's your favorite color. Is it?"

"Let's say it's purple or blue." I grin. We're not looking at each other, both of us staring up at the stars. "So as an alien, do I look like a man?"

"You have a humanoid form, yes, much like now—broad shoulders and long sleek black hair. Your prehensile tail is four feet long with a pointed end, and you use it as a whip when you fight. Your skin is made up of scales—"

"What the fuck?"

"Your scales are very small and shimmer when you're excited. They're very soft and warm."

"Sounds prissy." I'm enraptured, hanging on every word.

"Nothing girlie about you. Muscles abound. You're a virile, alpha alien—"

"But I have a tail." My voice is dry. "So this alien *is* a demon."

She huffs. "Fine. I'll take away the tail, but you could have used it for . . . pleasurable . . . activities . . ."

My dick twitches. "Like what?"

"Nope. You don't want it, so it's gone."

"Please continue."

"I'm trying!" She pokes me in the side. "You stalk around in a loincloth—rather strange since your world is so advanced—with metal gauntlets on your wrists. You keep an amethyst stone on a necklace around your neck. It belonged to someone important who passed away. You're a mercenary sent to Earth to procure a woman for your king. You find me, er, her in Los Angeles. She's a twentysomething scientist with a D cup. Her name is Kate, and she has blue hair." She pauses. "Are you sure you want to hear this?"

"You said D cup. I'm riveted."

She sighs. "Twenty days into the yearlong journey to your home planet, your cloaking goes on the fritz, and the ship is attacked by your enemies. You release her to protect her from being taken, and you and Kate fight them. A tentative friendship is born after you defeat them. She also knows how to fix your cloaking issue. You teach her your language but force her into the antigravity chamber every sleep cycle. Big alien jerk. You've taken an oath to hand her over untouched, yet one night, you sleepwalk to my, um, *Kate's* cage, let her out, and forget your oath about keeping her pure—"

"Giselle," I say, my voice low and husky, images flitting through my head. "Is this about to get dirty?"

"It's my story, actually. I'm writing it."

Oh.

"That's amazing. You're . . ." So fucking hot . . . "Obviously not only smart but, um, creative." I pause, inhaling a breath. "Maybe we shouldn't talk about the sex part."

"You asked. I responded." Her voice lowers. "I want to lose my virginity before I turn twenty-four, Dev."

I start. "When's your birthday?" I ask a few beats later, battling to keep myself from pouncing on her. *Hands off the innocent girl. Hands off the innocent girl. Jack will kill you.*

"Sunday. Mike Millington's going to be there."

"And he is . . . ?"

"My tween crush who's recently divorced. He's probably bald with a beer belly." A long sigh comes from her. "If he's kind and there's something there, I don't know, maybe . . ."

My chest rises, and I'm racking my brain to come up with a reply, but my head is going haywire and wants to say, *Well, if you want to get rid of it that bad, then what the hell is wrong with the man you're in bed with—*

A whine comes from the open door.

Pookie runs to Giselle's side of the bed, and Giselle gets up to scoop her up, climbs back in the bed, and flips over to her side, away from me, as she settles the dog under the covers.

"Good night, Dev," she murmurs. "Thank you for letting me sleep with you. Just this once. You're the best."

Yeah, the best. Right.

I mutter out a reply, heave out a breath, and turn over to face the wall.

Chapter 7

Devon

When I come out of my room at seven, Giselle is sitting on a stool at the island with her back to me, laptop open, earphones on her head as she types like a maniac.

It's weird coming out to someone in my domain. Usually girls are gone before the sun comes up—not because I'm a shitty host, but because they don't feel the need to linger. The light of day isn't pretty after casual sex.

She balances precariously on the seat as she reaches up to grab a pen, another one of my old shirts riding up. She must have tied it in a knot at the front. Her frayed shorts are on her ass, snug and dipping down far enough that I can see the waistband of a pink thong. I take in a familiar image at the base of her spine.

"Why do you have half a butterfly on your back?" I ask, sliding up next to her so I don't freak her out.

She turns and smiles and takes the earphones off. "Morning, sunshine! Let's kick today's ass. You with me?"

I wince. "God, you're one of those."

She throws her arms around me for a quick hug, gets off the stool, and dances away to the stove. "I've never needed much sleep. Up at six, and I made you breakfast. Banana-nut muffins. I found the mix in the pantry, so I figured you liked them." She takes in my track pants and workout shirt.

Quinn, Jack's younger foster brother, buys most of my groceries. I didn't even know I had muffin mixes. Normally, I eat oatmeal and a protein bar, then get out of here as fast as I can.

"I was going to make some eggs once you got up." She smiles, and I feel the tension from last night falling away.

"All right. Bacon?"

She grins, and I grab the food from the fridge. She takes them and starts cracking eggs and whisking them in a bowl she pulled down from the cabinet. "I made coffee."

"You're fucking beautiful," I exclaim as I pour myself a cup and take a long sip, watching her with bemusement as she blushes. I shove down thoughts of alien Devon ravishing her on a spaceship.

After my first few sips, I help by putting the bacon in a skillet and watching it sizzle. "Don't think I didn't notice that you evaded my question about your half-assed tattoo. How did it happen?" I'm anxious to hear her talk, and shit, I don't know, she kind of fascinates me.

She throws in some sour cream and salt and pepper with the eggs. "Got it when I was in college, right after my freshman year. I stayed in Memphis for summer classes, and, well, it was my birthday."

"Bad shit happens on your birthday."

"You have no idea." She sighs. "Anyway, I'd had a beer and was tipsy, and we walked into a tattoo shop. My girlfriend was getting E = mc^2, but I picked out a butterfly, had it in my head that it represented change, a metamorphosis." She attacks the bowl with the whisk. "So, the tattoo . . ." She pauses to take a sip of coffee, then sets the cup down. Her nose scrunches up. "I can't tell you."

I turn to her and point the tongs at her. "You have to answer. It's your thing."

"I can't." She crosses herself.

My eyes narrow. "Giselle Riley, you aren't even Catholic. What happened? Did it hurt?" Somehow I don't think pain makes her squeal. She fell to her knees at the club and barely complained; she climbed down a flimsy ladder in the middle of a thunderstorm and never thought twice.

I turn the bacon while she pours the eggs into a hot pan, her face blank. "Hard or soft? I like them soft, but I can cook yours a little longer."

Oh no, she won't get out of this that easily.

"I like them any way you want. Now . . . why did you get half a butterfly at the base of your spine?"

She shoots me an evil eye. "You're horrible, you know?"

"Tell me, or no bacon for you."

"Fine! Earlier that year, in January, I was kind of seeing this guy, nothing serious. Big football fanatic. One night I went to his place to watch the national championship game between Ohio State and Georgia—"

I freeze and face her, realization dawning. "Holy shit. That was my game, my senior year. I caught three passes and *won* that game." I preen a little, flexing my arms for her. "Did you like my tight body, little college girl?"

She rolls her eyes. "My date did. Quoted your stats from memory—whatever, he had a hard-on for OSU. I didn't know who you were, just some player in a red-and-white jersey."

"Number eighty-nine. Write that down. You're coming to a game this year."

"I know your jersey number." Her face flushes a delicious pink color.

"So what you're saying is you took one look at me, saw my ink, fell in love, and went out to get a matching tattoo." I chuckle when she throws a piece of bacon at me, and I catch it in my mouth.

"I was inspired by your ink, okay, just a little, and it stuck with me when my birthday rolled around in August."

I make her a plate, then make mine, and we sit at the island across from each other. "Why didn't you finish it?"

"I had to push my pants down more than was comfortable so the artist could get the right spot. Then my friend left the room for a few minutes." She shovels a forkful of eggs in and chews while I frown.

"What happened?"

Her silvery-blue eyes hold mine as she pushes up her glasses. "He set his tattoo machine down, put his hands on my ass, and squeezed so hard I saw stars. He held my arms down and tried to bite me there. I fought, elbowed him, fell out of the chair, and ran out." Her lips twist. "You've got your mad face on. Told you I didn't want to talk about it."

"How far is Memphis? Three hours?" I calmly eat a slice of bacon, chewing hard. First the lacrosse dude from high school, and now this prick? I, Devon Walsh, swear to never hurt Giselle Riley.

"I hope you got your revenge," I mutter.

"Went to the cops and filed a report. I didn't want him assaulting any-one else, especially since most of the clientele were college kids." She gets up and puts her plate in the sink, rinses it, then arranges it in the dishwasher. Pookie whines at her feet, and Giselle gives her a piece of bacon. "He got six months' probation but lost his license in Tennessee. His defense was it was consensual." She chews on her lips. "Anyway, it was a long time ago."

She moves to walk past me, and I grab her hand. "Hey. We're not all jerks."

"I know," she says, her face softening as we stare at each other. "Just some bad early experiences."

"Did it mess with your head?"

"Maybe. I'm sure it added to the list of reasons not to date much, but we don't have to worry about that much longer. Mike." She gives me a thumbs-up. "Looked him up on Insta this morning. All his hair. Nice physique. It's on."

And just like that, I'm ready to rip heads off. "Yeah, well, what about caring for someone? Huh? Getting to know them before you bang them?"

She blinks. "This is your advice? *You.*"

I stiffen. "I just want the best for you. You deserve . . . love or whatever."

"Do I?"

"Yes."

"So do you."

I frown, shoving that sentiment away. I don't let anyone close enough for love. Not anymore. "You just need a good guy."

"He can be a bad boy—in bed." She eases out of my grasp and walks to the den to grab her heels, leaving me uneasy. This Mike topic needs a serious conversation.

She stops at the mirror in the hall to let her hair down, only to finagle it into two plaited braids, tying them off with string she must have found in my kitchen junk drawer. She looks at herself for several seconds, frowning.

"Where are you going?" I ask as she walks to the den and grabs her backpack, stuffing her laptop and phone inside. Part of me isn't ready for her to run off. I liked breakfast. I like talking. "You look cute in shorts and heels."

"Need to check on Myrtle, and these clothes will have to do until I get more." She makes her way to the door while I tag along. She pauses and glances at a shivering Pookie at her feet, then down at a pair of expensive Italian leather loafers. I already tossed the three-hundred-dollar sneakers into the laundry room. I have no clue if I can even wash them, but I can't seem to bring myself to care.

She winces. "I took her out earlier, but she's a nervous wreck, and she might pee again. I guess I can run down real quick—"

I open the door for her. "I'll take her down. Go see your friend."

Her phone pings with a text, and she looks at me warily. "It's Elena asking how my classes are. She must be up early in Hawaii or hasn't even gone to sleep yet. I'll call her later and tell her about the fire."

I see the problem right away. "Don't mention you're staying here."

She nods quickly. "Mum's the word. Jack will never know. I'll be gone before they get back."

"Right." I stick my hands in my pockets and follow her to the elevator and push the button for her, eyeing her legs. "Is your ankle all right?"

"Fine."

"Knees?"

"Good."

"Any more bad dreams?"

"No."

I heave out a breath. "Giselle. About this Mike guy . . ."—who I don't like on principle—"instead of rushing out for a fling with him, why don't you let me find you a nice guy? Not Aiden, not any football player, and not any guy on the app."

The elevator opens as we stare at each other.

She frowns. "Not Lawrence."

Fuck no. Lawrence is a woman-eater of the first order. "Let me work on it, okay? I have someone in mind." I think.

She stares at the floor, then back up at me. A strange expression flits over her face, and I think it's disappointment.

"Whatever. You find him, and I'll meet him."

Relief wafts around me. I dangle Red's key, the extra one I grabbed from the foyer. "Well, if you're gonna do the walk of shame to my lobby, at least drive a badass car."

"We slept together because of my dream!"

"Uh-huh. The valet's name is Richard. Password to drive my ride is 'Pour Some Sugar on Me.'" No one drives her but me, but because Aiden begs to drive it when he's over, I made up a silly password to taunt him with, and he keeps trying to guess it and approach the valet.

I laugh and toss her the keys. She catches them, her eyes wide. "Devon! Are you sure?"

I usher her into the elevator and push the button for the lobby. "Can you drive a stick?"

"Was driving a tractor when I was ten."

I wince. "Not quite the same, baby, but I trust you. Bring her back in one piece, and I'll tell you why I kissed you."

She sputters just as the door shuts in her face.

◆ ◆ ◆

After letting Pookie have another pee, I leave the penthouse, stopping at the valet's desk and asking for the Hummer to be brought around. I add Giselle's name to the list of people allowed up the elevator in case she comes back when I'm not here and can't recall the code. Security is tight around here, one of the many reasons I bought it from Jack.

I'm sliding into the car when a man across the street calls my name. I'm used to people seeing me around town and asking for autographs if they bump into me, but he's not the usual fan. Shaved head, tattoos, work boots, and a determined grimace plastered on his face as he holds up traffic to reach me. I eye the car he was leaning against. Blacked-out sedan.

"Mr. Walsh!" he yells as he runs across the parking lot to the overhang of the hotel.

I've been mauled by women and bombarded after games by overzealous fans who've managed to get on the field, but I don't hang around for strange dudes who drive dark cars. Living with my father has taught me to be on the defensive, and coupled with the stardom, I'm a paranoid fuck. How does he know where I live? Because he wasn't just walking past. No, he was waiting.

I lock the door and pull out in the opposite direction, glancing in my rearview mirror. He's standing with his feet apart, hands on his hips. He kicks at a piece of the asphalt with his boots. It's not hard for my head to wonder if this guy is related to the men looking for my dad. Annoyed, I pull over a few blocks later and send a text to check on my dad, but he doesn't reply.

After parking behind the locked gates of the stadium, I jog to the gym, where we spend the first few hours of camp. After working out, we'll do a team meeting and watch tape, then separate for offensive and defensive strategy sessions that last an hour or so depending on the day before. Next is our first practice of the day, more mental preparation than physical, where we'll jog through plays and discuss pros and cons. By late afternoon, playtime is over, and we'll put pads on for the grueling, challenging second practice.

"Where the fuck have you been?" says Aiden as he runs on one of the treadmills. "I've gotten a massage and a leg workout in."

I get on the treadmill next to him and turn it on. "I may be late, but I can still kick your ass."

He snorts—as much as he can going at full speed.

I match his pace, increasing my incline so it's steeper than his.

He cocks an eyebrow, and it's on.

"How was the fight?" I rasp out a few minutes later.

"Slick. McGregor took him down in the second round."

I nod.

"What was your big errand?"

Flashes of me taking care of Dad and cleaning up his house come to mind.

"The model? You go see her?" He ups his incline.

I shake my head.

"Huh. Okay, so you flaked on one of your friends because you're a dick."

I grin at him in the mirror, and he flips me off. I like Aiden, and we've become friends over the past year—when he isn't aggravating Jack—but nobody gets the lowdown on my dad.

"You gonna see her again?" He pants, upping his speed on the machine. Damn twenty-three-year-old rookie.

"Don't kiss and tell," I drawl as I finish my run. Besides, nothing happened between me and the girl from the wedding.

I wipe my face with a towel, then suck down water before I head to the weights.

"I can spot you," Aiden calls, getting off the treadmill.

"You just wanna see if I can press more than you." I get settled on the bench and wait for him to prep. He's a competitive bastard, but it's good for both of us.

"Two hundred?"

I roll my neck, cracking my fingers. "Two twenty-five."

He chuckles, moving the weights for me. "Now we're cooking with oil!"

I roll my eyes at his southern slang. Straining, I get the first ten reps up; then my arms tremble.

"Come on, pussy; you gonna quit now?"

Sweat drips down my forehead, and my fingers curl tighter in the gloves. "Been playing longer than you. I got this."

Five more pushes, and my arms burn.

Aiden leans in. "Who are you? Who the hell are *you*?"

"Devon Walsh," I mutter, shoving the bar up.

"That's right, motherfucker. You're a constant threat. Running or getting the ball. Your body is a well-oiled machine, the best wideout in the NFL. You make defensive guys cry. You catch a jump ball as easy as a post. Shallow, deep, or on a slant. Nobody can catch your ass."

I grunt. "Tell me how pretty I am."

"So damn pretty. Not as much as me, but nobody is."

"Not working," I heave as I struggle to get the bar up for another rep.

"Twenty, man, that's all you got? Hollis beat your ass yesterday with five more. Push it up, or I swear I'm gonna escort Giselle Riley all over Nashville. She'll be in love with me, 'cause come on—who isn't?" He pops my leg with his towel. "I might just love her back. I'm sick of the women, dude, annoyed with the attention, and she's not like the rest. Did you see her in that skirt? I went to bed thinking about her—"

"Shut up," I call, the bar wobbling.

"Why? You got a hard-on for her?"

"No!" I shout.

He gets in my face, his voice low. "Why are you so angry? Huh? You think I'm blind? I might be a farm kid from Alabama, but I ain't stupid."

"I'm going to kill you," I say, letting loose a long string of curses.

"You can try. Just don't hurt the throwing arm."

I glare up at him, seething.

"Come on, old man. Three more, and you're done."

The bar rests on my chest, and I swallow. Digging deep, I press my lips tight, clench the bar, and push it up for three more reps. Once it's secure, I jump up off the bench, adrenaline pumping. I point my finger in his face. "Don't use her as motivation, man—not cool."

He holds his hands up between us. "Whoa, man. So you aren't into her? 'Cause last night in the VIP room, you had this look on your face. And you took her to dinner. Was that your errand? Did you hook up—"

"She is my friend!"

He scratches his hair, studying me. "For real? You swear?"

"Yes!"

"Huh." He paces around me. Something about the look on his face, almost hopeful, causes my shoulders to coil and tighten.

"What's eating you?"

He stops, rubbing his face. "All right, all right, I won't talk smack about Giselle. She's your friend, and it bothers you. I'm glad you clarified, because I was wondering—I mean, I know I joke around a lot, but she's got something about her, you know?"

My hands ball up, dread pooling.

He paces around. "It's been years since I had a real date with a girl who wasn't after my money and fame. I'm tired of coming home to an empty apartment and not having someone I can vent to. Hard to trust people, especially after what Jack went through."

Jack's ex wrote a tell-all book about him full of lies. It was a bestseller and nearly killed his career. Aiden took her out once and claimed she was a devil.

"Giselle gets the lifestyle—she knows we're real people, and she doesn't care who I am." He rubs at his neck, a slow blush crawling up his face. "She's interesting. I like how she thinks. Plus . . . she's looking for someone."

"Jack will flip." It's all I can come up with, battling the impulse to put my hands around his throat.

He holds his hand up. "But . . . but if I do this right, maybe talk to him and explain that she's different, that I'm not doing it to piss him off and rattle him . . . I'll be on my best behavior. I'll wine and dine her—like, really woo, no pressure—be sweet and give her time before I throw the whole charm at her. If we clicked—and obviously we will—I could have what Jack has. A chance for a real relationship . . ." His voice trails off as he frowns. "Dev? You okay?"

I've been trying to keep the anger under wraps, but his whole wooing shit sent me over the edge, and I erupt and shove him. He stumbles back into the wall. Shocked blue eyes glare at me. "What the hell, man?" he shouts as several of the guys run over, their gazes darting between us.

"Everything all right?" Hollis asks, panting since he dashed over from a treadmill. He's the toughest and stands between us, a brawny defensive lineman with dreads, medium-dark skin, and fists the size of bowling balls.

Everything with my dad, Giselle and the fire, her horrid encounters with men—and now him saying he might really *like* her and want to be serious—even talking to Jack? What the hell . . . I can't . . . no.

"Stay away from her!"

"What's your problem?" Aiden's chest heaves, his fists curled.

"Your attitude!"

His jaw pops. "Dude. I won't hurt her!"

"You're a kid! You don't know how to treat her!"

He shakes his head at me, his face reddening. "You're an asshole—you know that? I'm not gonna hit you, even though you deserve it. But I can guaran-damn-tee you that I'm gonna see her again, so you better get used to the idea." He snatches his towel off the weights and storms out of the gym.

Chapter 8

GISELLE

Driving a red Maserati to Walmart makes me cackle. On the inside, though, I'm freaking out. I googled how much the car was worth as the valet drove her around for me, and I started sweating. Over $140,000, but knowing Devon, it has more bells and whistles than the one I looked up. Sweat slides down my back.

With my hands gripping the black leather steering wheel, I inch along at two miles an hour for a place to put Red so she won't get a door ding. I picture Devon's face if I were to wreck. Dark and stormy. Maybe how Vureck looks when Kate crash-lands his ship on that rocky planet.

A horn blares behind me, and I check the rearview. An old lady in a Cadillac flips me the bird.

I whip to the back of the lot, away from all cars, park, and head into the store, already pulling out the quick list of essentials I made. Some cheap shirts and shorts, underwear, a pair of flip-flops, apples to snack on, makeup and toiletries, and some food for Pookie. Definitely pee pads. Deep in thought, I don't notice the man at the entrance of the store until I bump into him.

"Sorry, excuse me," I say with a smile and move to step to the right—only he puts his hand on my elbow.

"You know Devon Walsh?"

First instinct is to always tell the truth, but self-preservation knows when to kick in. "No." I pull my arm away, and he holds his hands up in a placating manner.

He's older, around forty, with clipped brown hair. I catalog other details: height, weight, a scar on his right cheek, tattoos on his neck. I frown at his shirt, an old black one with a lion crest and faded writing.

"Sorry, Miss, but I know you do. It's my job. Tell Devon we're looking for his dad. He owes us money."

My gaze narrows. "You look familiar." I point down to his shirt. "Daisy High School. Small world."

He takes a big step backward, eyes wary. "Look, just tell Devon—"

"No, you look, buddy," I say, my southern accent thickening as I inch closer to him. I put my hands on my hips, feeling brave, maybe because this has to do with Devon, and I'd slay a dragon for him. "I'm assuming you followed me from the penthouse, which is just horrible. Don't you have better things to do? Not to mention it's downright *rude* to approach a young woman with your demeanor and an ominous attitude—"

He blinks. "I can't help the tattoos or the scar!"

"Regardless, I never forget a face, and yours is tugging at me. I may not know your name—yet—but my mama is Cynthia Riley, and she knows everyone." His eyes bulge. "That's right. You must know her, and when I tell her you put your hands on me—"

"Please don't tell your mama! I just had to get your attention!" He's already walking away, darting looks over his shoulder as he mutters something that sounds suspiciously like *Get the hell away from her.*

My lips compress as I call out, "Creepy message received. Now scurry on back and hide. Cynthia is coming for you."

I watch until he gets in an old black truck near the back and squeals away, relief swamping me as he disappears down the road. Worry inches up my spine as I walk inside the store. What's going on with Devon's dad? Frowning, I text Devon what happened and hit send. My phone dies right after, and I groan and add *phone charger* to my list.

◆ ◆ ◆

"She needs another day or so for us to monitor the arrhythmia in her heart." The doctor looks at me. "Besides the atrial fibrillation, her glucose and iron levels are low. Her knee is sore and swollen, and the cortisone shots we administered will alleviate some of that in the next few days. However"—he gives the woman in the bed a firm look—"a knee replacement is recommended. I have a list of orthopedic doctors who are excellent."

Myrtle pushes up in bed. "Like I already told that nosy nurse, all I need is my cannabis. Some studies show it helps arrhythmia."

The doctor arches a brow. "I'm going to pretend I don't know about your cannabis. I'm not aware of this study."

"Well, get busy earning my money, and read it and write me a prescription," she huffs. "As it stands, I have to sneak around and buy my special cigarettes on the sly." She looks wary and a little scared. My protective instincts flare; they've been doing that a lot today.

The doctor is a tall man with white hair and wire glasses and *seems* acceptable to treat my bestie, but he's in a hurry, already eyeing the door to get to his next patient in line. That bugs me. "Where did you go to medical school?"

"Vanderbilt."

Well, of course, it's top notch, but I stand firm. "Nice. Now, perhaps we should revisit the issue of cannabis. It's the elderly who benefit the most from medicinal marijuana," I tell him, not even caring that I don't have a medical degree. This is Myrtle, and she's been enjoying her Mary Jane since the eighties. "She smokes because of migraines and her knee pain." Mostly. "What are the guidelines for getting a recommendation for a prescription?"

"It calms me *and* improves my appetite," she adds, a hopeful gleam in her eyes.

"Unfortunately, medical marijuana in Tennessee is all but nonexistent." His words are flat. No budging there. I can tell by the hard look in his eyes. I exhale.

She huffs. "I should move to Colorado."

"I'd miss you terribly," I say sadly.

After he's gone, I reach over and pat her hand, wishing I could convince him to help us, but my gut tells me it might be impossible. "You're back to being feisty. Guess I should have known you'd bounce back, but I'm mad you didn't tell me about having A-fib."

"Give me a mirror. My hair is everywhere." She fingers her scalp, trying to arrange the wayward brown curls.

I pluck one from her bag and give it over.

She cries, "I look like death! Lipstick, stat. Mr. Wilcox said he might drop by with lunch. Can you believe they released him last night? Apparently he's very healthy."

I tug out her usual pink, and she swipes it on.

"Patricia? Did you call her?" I ask.

She grimaces, that worried look back on her face. "I did. My daughter has five-year-old twins and is too busy to fly from New York to see me."

I grit my teeth but dip my face so she can't see. If my mama was in the hospital for a few days, I'd be on the next plane to see her.

"How long have you dealt with A-fib?" I keep my voice light. Apparently after they brought her in, her heart went into arrhythmia, and they sent an electric shock to restore the regular beat.

She throws her head back on the pillows. "Years. As long as I take my meds, I'm fine, but sometimes . . ."

A fire can throw everything haywire.

"When we get you home, we're going to start eating healthier. No more red meat, more exercising, and less alcohol—"

She pouts, cutting me off. "I have maybe twenty years left, and that's being optimistic, and I refuse to spend them being an old fuddy-duddy. I want fun, Giselle, crazy laughs, roller coasters, and men with big schlongs—"

"Hey, ladies!"

I look over at John Wilcox. He's about five-eleven and lean with thinning hair and a big smile. He looks so much better than last night that I jump up and give him a hug, squishing the takeout bag from a sushi place. He chuckles and pats my back. "Ah, it's good to see you well. Guess we didn't get a proper introduction last night. I'm thankful you saw the smoke so soon. This is my son, Robert." He indicates the younger guy behind him.

"And you delivered sushi."

John grins and holds up the bag from Myrtle's favorite restaurant. "It's just what she asked for. I brought it. That's how I roll." He looks at his son. "Get it?"

His son shakes his head, smiling. "Dad, we all got it."

My grin feels like it might split it's so big. *I like him,* my eyes tell the lady in the bed.

Yeah? her expression says.

I lean over and whisper in her ear. "Big hands."

"One minute in the room, and they're whispering," John muses, setting the food on the small table in the corner.

"If we don't make you wonder what we'll do next, it's not worth the effort," Myrtle chirps.

He smiles at her.

I feel the zing between them.

Robert looks a little older than me, in slacks and a summer blazer. Rather handsome in a studious way. We chat for a few moments, catching them up on Myrtle's situation, sans the marijuana request. John tells me they ran by the apartment and found his cat, and I mentally cross that off my list of things to do. They settle in some straight-backed chairs his son finds in the hall and divide up the food. They offer me some, but I tell them I had a big breakfast.

John says he's staying with his son until a new place comes up, and it dawns on me that Myrtle doesn't have anywhere to go when she's discharged. Once the apartment building is open, it may take weeks for the restoration. I pick up my phone that's still charging and type a few notes.

1. Research A-fib.
2. Find M a place to stay.
3. Find myself a place! Can't stay long at Devon's.
4. Call All-State Insurance.
5. Call Patricia. Come on . . . she's your mom.

I glance at the clock and jump up.

"Sorry, guys, I have to go," I say, grabbing my things and stuffing them in my bag. After my Walmart visit, I came straight here, and the time flew while we waited for the doctor to show up so I could talk to him. "I'm on rotation to teach a summer class today." I dash over and kiss Myrtle on the temple and give her one last squeeze. "I'll call you later and let Pookie hear your voice. Maybe I can get a night visit in, yes?"

"Only if you have time," she warns me. "You need to study and write more chapters and email them to me. I can read on my phone. Thank goodness it was in my purse."

"I can sit with her tonight," John calls as I make it to the door. I look back, and he and Myrtle are gazing at each other—level five all the way.

A long sigh comes from me. Maybe something good came from the fire after all. If my bestie found zing, well, that's pretty awesome.

On my way to Vandy, driving in a car I could never afford, my mind tumbles around to this morning.

Devon saw my tattoo, and now he has an inkling that I knew of him before we ever met. He's not going to let me live it down, I bet. After getting out of the car, I'm smiling as I fast walk across the quad to the physics building, where I alternate with other cohorts to teach a summer-session class to underclassmen.

I pause before I go in the door, thinking about my curse. *This birthday, this month, is going to be fine,* I tell myself. The worst was the fire, and it already happened.

Fate laughs.

◆ ◆ ◆

"So *Stranger Things*—could it be closer to the truth than we realize?" This comes from Corey, a lanky baseball player who's retaking Intro to Physics.

Like me, he's a little fascinated by the multiverse. We've mostly wrapped up our lesson, and we're running through notes—but we tend to get lost on topics that aren't part of their curriculum. "Well, no."

"Dang," he mutters.

"Am I saying it's completely impossible? Of course not. It's an unsolved mystery, which we don't have the capability to test for. The Large Hadron Collider at CERN may be able to point us in the right direction someday." I cross my legs as I sit on the grass in the shade under a huge oak tree. We left the musty classroom because these kids need a break; plus, it's not as hot as it was yesterday.

Addison, who was doodling, stops. I've been working hard on her this summer, trying to get her enthused. "Why do physicists study the possibility of a multiverse if it's so far out of reach?"

"You can't dismiss an idea until you study it for years. For example, long ago, people saw the sun rising and setting, seeming to go around the earth. What did they believe?"

"That the sun orbited the earth?" She scrunches up her nose.

"Exactly!" I toss her a yellow sucker, her favorite. "We have to be ready to see possibilities."

"I think the multiverse is cool," Corey says. "I dig that theory you brought up last week. Made my head hurt, but hey, I learned something. You're not like that other dude who teaches us. I sleep through his lectures."

"Tell me more about superstring theory from last week." I wave a sucker.

He sits on the grass, legs crossed as he cups his chin, thinking. "I don't know; it's about quantum mechanics and the theory of relativity, right? Like, a theory to make a single mathematically consistent framework to explain the universe."

Pride swells so big I want to pop. I give him a fist bump. "Corey! You rock!" It's more complicated than that, but this isn't a theoretical physics class.

"You explain it better, Ms. Riley. You're the best teacher here." He grins, and I chuckle. He'll do anything to get in my good graces.

Addison grumbles, throwing up her hands. "I have no clue what he just said. Why is this class so important?" A long sigh comes from her. "Obviously, I shouldn't be in engineering."

Corey elbows her. "Chill. We have to pass this class, and she's our best shot."

I don't want to crush her dreams, but engineering requires two to three physics classes, so I lie back in the grass and raise my arms over my head. "Stretch it out, guys. Let me think a second before I answer Addison."

Why is physics important to a girl who would rather sleep until the afternoon than come to class? Yes, she admitted to skipping several classes last semester, this one included, to recuperate from hangovers. Now her parents are making her do summer school to make up for it.

Everyone moves around, adjusting and getting the kinks out. After a few ticks, I sit up and look at Addison, wanting to inspire her and not turn her away from what I love.

"Do you have a car?" I ask her.

"A new Prius."

"Ah. What kind of engineer do you want to be?"

"Mechanical."

Perfect. I point at her with my pen. "Without physics you wouldn't have that sweet car. Physics determines style, speed, drag force, engine efficiency—knowledge you'll need for that degree. All manufacturing depends on physics-based technology. Tested formulas explain how things work: cars, cell phones, this pen, even quarks. Physics is here to explain the universe, how it started, the why of it, and where we'll be years from now. It's limitless. All the secrets of the universe are just waiting for us to discover them!" I wave my hands at the blue sky.

"You lost me at *quark*. Kidding. I remember. It's a subatomic particle." She laughs. "You get really excited about weird stuff, Ms. Riley."

"Just grasp the basics and build. I'll help you. You can always call me if you get stuck in your notes," I assure her. We need more girls in STEM.

Corey grins. "Also, still waiting on more superstring explanation."

I settle my textbook on my lap, trying to think of a way to break it down without being overly scientific. I like to think I'm a good teacher, but sometimes I do get lost in my head and spout terms they've never heard of—nor care about. "The theory is an attempt to describe the universe under one theory of everything by adding extra dimensions of space-time and thinking of particles as miniscule vibrating strings." I grab the thick stick I picked up on the way to our spot and show them. "We only *see* three dimensions on this: width, breadth, and height. But what about the particles deep inside, the ones we can't see with our eyes? Theorists think that tiny curled-up dimensions—"

"What's the fourth dimension?" asks Corey, getting me off track. "It's time, isn't it? Can we travel through time? I'd really like to go back and tell myself the winning lottery numbers."

I grin. He's incorrigible. "Einstein indeed called it *time*, but it's a spatial dimension and can be only described by mathematics." I smile to soften the blow. "It's a fascinating concept, but there's no proof of time travel or a multiverse." But someday . . .

A dry tone cuts across from the building. "Ms. Riley, your class is dismissed. I'd like to speak with you, please."

Glancing over, I see him standing on the steps, eyes squarely on me. Dread inches up my spine as I pick a piece of grass out of my hair.

"Ohhhh, he looks pissy," Corey says under his breath as we gather up our things.

Several of the students tell me bye as they leave, and I wave, reminding them to study their notes.

"Go on now," I tell Corey, who's hanging behind, still darting looks at Dr. Blanton.

"You sure? I'll walk you over to him if you want."

Oh, Dr. Blanton would just love that.

"No, that's okay."

He winces. "I don't think he likes our class—or you. He's always poking his head in and glaring."

I smile and pat his arm. "Don't worry about me. Study this week instead of hanging out at the ATO house."

"I'll chug a beer for ya, Ms. Riley."

"Be safe at least."

He nods, gives Dr. Blanton a wide berth, and leaves.

I reach Dr. Blanton on the steps of the building, acutely aware of the shorts, T-shirt, and flip-flops I bought. I should have changed into jeans at the hospital but didn't.

He presses his lips together, looking warm in his tweed jacket. I have the female version of that blazer. "Taking a class outside? Is that conducive to learning?"

"Not all kids learn in a classroom, especially these. There are actually seven different types of learning: verbal, visual, auditory, physical—"

He cuts me off with a slice of his hand. "Ms. Riley, spare me the rhetoric. I overhead your lecture."

"It wasn't a lecture; I prefer learning experiences."

He exhales, having heard this argument before. "Regardless of where you teach, the lesson plan was relativity this week."

I bob my head. "I did that. Just adding to the objective, Dr. Blanton. Isn't that what I'm supposed to be doing? Expanding minds? Creating questions? Getting them interested?"

He studies me through his wire spectacles, as if I'm a bug. His eyes land on my bare legs, and I inhale. We're supposed to wear slacks or a skirt. "I prefer traditional methods. Just the facts—in a classroom with an overhead. You can't be friends with students."

I'm not! I just don't want to see them struggle.

He's used to teaching upper-level classes, students with high IQs and a drive to absorb anything put in front of them.

"Most are terrified of physics. They flunked—"

"Enough."

I bite my tongue but take two steps until we're on the same level, not comfortable with him being higher than me. "Was there anything else?"

"Yes. The multiverse is not a legitimate topic of scientific inquiry. Don't encourage them."

It is, dammit, and many physicists would stand next to me and argue the case.

"The topic came up because the students find it interesting, and it's a way to introduce string theory. I see nothing wrong with exciting students."

He glowers at me. "The mere idea erodes public confidence in science. It's a philosophic notion."

"Are you saying that some of the major theorists of our generation are wasting their time? Theoretical physics questions everything. It's why I'm here."

He takes his glasses off and cleans them with a hankie. Stuffy man. He needs a Myrtle in his life. "Ten percent of our female doctorate candidates don't make it to the end of the program, Ms. Riley. You're about to start your second year, and I'm not impressed."

My heart drops, my failures creeping in. First Preston, now my career?

"Your level of work dropped dramatically last semester. Don't bother to apply for CERN again unless I see marked improvement."

The knife of that disappointment cuts deep. "I'm aware. I had a few personal issues earlier in the year—"

"No excuses, please." His jaw grinds as his eyes sweep over me. "Women," he mutters under his breath.

My anger coils up, and my face heats. Before I can tell the misogynistic jerk to go fuck right off—

"Wear decent clothes, Ms. Riley. You look like one of your students." And then he's stalking back inside the building.

He isn't wrong, but my fists curl, and I let out a string of muttered curses once he's out of earshot. Sure, I can stand up for Devon and Myrtle in a heartbeat, but when it comes to myself . . .

Chapter 9

DEVON

"No frat-boy innuendoes, and I'm sitting at the table with you for the first fifteen minutes until she's comfortable. We clear?" I tell Brandt Jacobs the next day as I walk over to his silver Porsche.

"Let me get this straight," he replies as he shuts his car door and faces me, huffing out a laugh. "You called me about this girl you want me to meet, and you're going to monitor my behavior? Am I being punked?"

"You're here to meet her. That's it. Drinks only. If she asks you to stay for dinner, you do whatever you want, but she has to invite you. You've got half an hour with her." Those are the guidelines Giselle and I worked out over breakfast this morning. She liked knowing I'd be close, and it was her idea to wait until they met and chatted before she asked him to eat dinner with us afterward.

Last night, she was in her room when I came home tired and exhausted after training camp. She had a light on, and I thought long and hard about knocking on her door, just to see her face, but I didn't. The less I see her, the better. Plus, the fire must have finally caught up with her, and she needed to rest. Then, this morning, there she was in the kitchen all perky and working, and I offered up Brandt.

He laughs and slaps me on the back, pulling me back to the present. "Good to see you, man. Love how you always get to the point. Let's talk contract soon. That fourteen million a year can be negotiated to eighteen. I feel it. Look at Carter with the Panthers; he just got a bump, and your stats slay his."

"Soon. How's the new house in Brentwood?"

He talks about his home and the pool he's putting in as we head toward Milano's, a classy Italian restaurant Jack has in his portfolio. I tell him about training camp, and we discuss the upcoming preseason game we have in Miami.

"I was surprised you weren't seeing someone," I say.

"Recent breakup." He shrugs broad shoulders in a gray suit, a rueful look on his face. "Turns out she liked my bank account more than me."

"Sorry, man."

"Right." He grimaces.

"Giselle doesn't care about money. She's got her own future ahead of her." Someday, she's going to get out of this funk and find her way.

"I didn't know you were such a matchmaker."

"Is that what I am?"

He laughs. "Yeah, and thanks for thinking of me. I'm ready to meet someone nice."

"Good," I say as I study him. He's a blond all-American type with a keen mind and the tenacity of a bulldog. Early thirties, handsome, and successful—I can see Giselle with him. Still, I feel uneasy, and for the hundredth time, I second-guess the setup—but it's happening. It needs to happen. She deserves a good guy, and I'll pull out the best I've got.

"What's her story?"

"Recent broken engagement. He's a dickhead."

We step into the foyer, and he looks around, taking in the fancy farmhouse decor, rustic metal chandeliers, and wood beams across the ceiling. The place bustles with waitstaff and clientele. He lets out a whistle. "Damn, Jack is raking it in."

"You're a good agent."

The maître d' sees me and smiles, nudging his head toward the back of the restaurant. Craning my neck, I find her sitting at a booth near the bar, hair down in a sleek fall of blonde, glasses perched on her nose, her laptop open as she types. My lips twitch. The girl likes to write stories about aliens. Or she could be studying. She's a dichotomy of contradictions, and since the night in the VIP room, I never know which Giselle I'll get.

We walk to the back, maneuvering past tables, and the closer we get, the antsier I feel, hands tapping against my leg.

"So, friend of yours? Related? How's your cousin, by the way?"

"Giselle's a good friend. Smart as a whip and has a big heart. Selena is great. Just moved her up to GM at the club."

"Is she hot?"

"Selena?"

He laughs. "What's wrong with you? *Giselle?*"

Want me to make a list of what's wrong? *My dad is a train wreck, and he isn't answering my calls; strange men are approaching me at my place and Giselle at Walmart; my teammate isn't speaking to me at camp; my best friend's sister-in-law is staying with me; and I want to put my hands all over her so bad I can't fucking stand myself, so I'm setting her up with you.* Yeah, best to not say that.

I push my hands into the pockets of my navy slacks, seeing visions of Giselle cooking breakfast this morning, her lips curved up as I ate most of the bacon she made. Her hair was up in a messy bun, and she kept pushing her glasses up her nose. "Yeah, she's hot."

He follows my eyes and shoulder bumps me. "Is that her?"

"Hmm."

"Niiiiiiice."

I inhale, unease crawling in my gut. "She's a serious kind of girl; you feel me? She isn't a one-nighter."

"If I didn't know you better, I'd say you like this girl for yourself."

"No." I brush past him and arrive at the booth and slide in next to her while Brandt sits across from us. Her eyes take him in, glancing over his tailored suit, the hundred-dollar haircut, the boyish grin. Her lashes flutter, a blush rising on her cheeks as he shakes her hand.

Well? my eyes ask her.

She nods in my direction, smiles, and adjusts one of my tailored blue dress shirts she's fashioned into some kind of top, the ends tied together, the top buttons undone, her creamy skin glistening. I hide my grin. She bought clothes from Walmart, but here she is, in mine. I told her to check out my closet and take whatever she wanted.

I keep sneaking glances at her as they chat. Her profile is a soft curve, her lashes long and thick against her cheekbones. She's wearing makeup, and her pouty lips are a deep-pink color. My traitorous eyes can't seem to *stop* looking at her. And since I'm being honest with myself, it's been going on for a while, maybe since that first night I met her months ago at the community center for *Romeo and Juliet*.

Maybe it was the overwhelming sense of desperation on her face when she looked at her sister. I knew that gaze, familial love mixed with loss, a yearning to right a perceived wrong. She hurt her sister with Preston and didn't see a way out. I saw a girl who took a chance on a guy, sacrificed her relationship with her sister, gave up pieces of herself, and was vibrating with the repercussions, wondering how the hell she'd gotten there. Every pleading look she gave Elena was a testament to how badly she wanted to set things right. By the end of opening night of *Romeo and Juliet*, the shortest engagement in history was over, and she withdrew further into herself, hiding her heartbreak behind closed doors, I imagine, while Jack and Elena fell deeper in love and planned a quick wedding. In our interactions since then, I've checked her out but armed myself with restraint, not willing to chip away at the edges of a fragile woman. Instead I wasted my time with brief physical connections that fulfilled a need.

Pushing that aside, I sit back and watch them. He sips on a whiskey and tells her about his days at Princeton, then his family in Boston. His dad's a heart surgeon, his mom a nurse, his sister a lawyer. He moved to Nashville several years ago, heading up the sports department of a company that also deals with country music stars.

"Giselle is getting her doctorate in physics," I mention.

"Theoretical," she tells him when he asks which field.

"Like Sheldon on *The Big Bang Theory*?" he teases. "You don't seem to lack social skills like he does." He gives her an appreciative glance, a low look in his eyes as he lingers on the V of her shirt. I shift around in my seat.

She smiles. "I love that show, and yeah, same field. I want to study dark matter with particle accelerators."

My ears perk up. "Like the Large Hadron Collider? Supposed to be the biggest accelerator in the world. It's in Switzerland, right?" I lean in toward her. She smells like vanilla today . . . is that a new bodywash or perfume? Heat builds in my spine, tendrils of desire—shit, nope, not going there. I clench my hands under the table.

Her eyes light up. "Yes, in Geneva. It's called the LHC and sits in an underground tunnel below CERN. It's twenty-seven kilometers in circumference and built to push ions to near the speed of light. I just want to put my hands on it." A wistful expression crosses her face. "Maybe kiss it."

Brandt smiles. "I took a few physics classes." He tells her about a recent trip to Switzerland, where his family toured CERN. "Have you ever been?"

Her hands twist. "No, I applied for a fellowship to study there this year, but it didn't work out. Maybe next year."

What?

She wants to move to Europe? Since when? How long are these fellowships?

I'm still tumbling around the idea of her leaving Nashville when Brandt reaches over the table, showing her pics on his phone of his house.

Brandt nudges me under the table with his shoe, meets my eyes, and looks at his Rolex. Right. My fifteen minutes are up. I ease up out of the seat and tell Giselle I'm going to grab a drink at the bar.

She nods and turns back to Brandt, and I hear him ask about where she lives. She tells him she's staying with a friend after the fire at her apartment while she looks for an apartment close to Vandy. An exhale comes from me as I walk away. *Friend.* That's all she can ever be.

I'm sitting at the bar with my back to them, watching the thirty minutes tick down on my phone. On the dot, Brandt appears next to me, leaning in. "Dude. Definitely want to see her again. Alone. She's perfect, and those long legs—"

"Did she ask you to dinner with us?"

He slaps me on the back. "I didn't give her a chance. I've got a phone call tonight anyway, new quarterback out of USC."

Good. No, wait, not good. He *should* stay.

"She didn't give me her number. You'll get it for me?"

My skin prickles. "If she wants."

"She will," he says confidently. "We had a nice convo. I'm already picturing her in a bikini at my pool."

My jaw pops. "Uh-huh."

With a wave back at Giselle, he leaves, and I head back to the booth, sliding into the seat he vacated.

"Well?" I ask, tapping my fingers on the table until I stop and tuck them in my lap. I don't know why *I'm* nervous. She's the one who had the meetup.

She's got the menu up and is studying it, a little pucker on her forehead. "Pasta or salmon? You got a favorite? Oh, dang, they've got emu burgers on here. Gross."

"He wants your number," I say, cataloging her reaction.

She cocks her head. "Crab mac and cheese or creamed spinach as a side? Maybe I'll get both—"

"Giselle. Are you going to see him again?" My shoulders feel tight, and I roll my neck.

She sighs and sets down the menu. "He played lacrosse in college."

I'd forgotten. "He did. Big star in the Ivy League."

She takes a sip of her soda, and when she speaks, her words are careful. "He's not my type."

"He's perfect! He's mentioned a few times he wants to settle down and have kids!"

Her finger traces the condensation on her glass. "Meh."

I gape at her. "Seriously? He's handsome and has a j-o-b. Your mama would love him. What's wrong with him?"

Pale-blue eyes rise and drift over my forearms, where I rolled up my tailored shirt, her gaze lingering on my tattoos.

"Too slick, too much lacrosse."

"He likes physics."

"So? You do too. You know what the LHC is. You quote Carl Sagan." She pauses, that frown on her forehead growing. "There was no . . . zing. Like with Myrtle and John."

"Zing?"

"Physical chemistry was zero." She cups her chin. "I'd be bored. I like . . ." Her eyes brush over my hair, the diamond studs in my ears . . . "Someone who'll keep me on my toes."

"Poor Brandt. I don't think anyone has ever said he's boring." It's been a long shitty day, but I grin, feeling light, and I can't bring myself to feel bad for him. "Pasta is good. The bolognese sauce here is divine."

She smiles. "Sounds good. And I'm telling Jack to take the emu off the menu."

We're eating dessert, sharing a chocolate soufflé, when she brings up the man at Walmart. "Is your dad in some kind of trouble?"

Just the idea of telling her my theories about who they are makes my skin crawl. I settle for "Maybe."

"Tell me about where you grew up," she asks quietly.

I wince. "Glitter City in NorCal. Funny name for a dump of a town. Best thing I ever did was leave."

"Never went back? No friends or relatives?"

"Nah." I set my spoon down and wipe my mouth. "My mom ran off and never came back." I pause, fiddling with my water glass. Giselle's family is apple-pie American, with a mom and aunt who dote on her. We're like oil and water, soft and hard, bitter and sweet. "My dad owned a bar, but the bottle eventually ruined him. Spent most of my free time playing football or mowing lawns and working at the concession stand at the drive-in." A long breath comes from me. "Every time I see an old drive-in movie, I think about me as a kid."

I don't tell her about the two weeks our electricity was turned off, leaving me scrambling and borrowing money. Later, I discovered receipts from an ATM in Vegas, and Dad and I had a big blowup. He threatened to toss me out, and I wanted to slug him. *I* was all he had. Woman after woman walked out on him, yet I remained, picking up pieces and gluing them together.

The space between us swells with silence, and when I look up, she's chewing on her lips.

Rubbing my neck, I say, "I didn't grow up like you did. Family, people that stick, you know?"

"You turned into a wonderful human," she says, and her face is earnest—and sweet, so damn sweet.

My chest shifts ever so slightly, tugging at me, making me *feel*. I take a breath. It feels hot in here. Like maybe I can't breathe. "Better than Hemsworth?"

"Well, he did buy me a villa in Switzerland, but he can suck it. You're the man."

She frowns, then reaches across the table and rubs her fingers across the side of my neck. Her lashes flutter as she looks at her hand, then wipes it with her napkin. "Lipstick. Red. Not sure how I missed it earlier."

I roll my eyes. "Some random ran over to me when I met Lawrence before I came here. He always wants to meet at a bar to talk business." I decided to hire him after all. At this rate, I might need him. He does more than just PR; he looks into people, and right now he's running checks on my dad.

She sighs. "You don't even have to encourage them, do you? I bet she slipped you her cell—"

"Hotel key."

Her chest rises. "Ballsy. I should write this down."

"You don't need ploys. Stay you, Giselle. Smart and funny and—"

"Virginal."

I sigh. "That's not what I meant. You don't need to be flirty. Just wait for the right guy—"

"Seduction 101 with Devon Walsh. You give blow job lessons?"

I bite down my groan, my body tightening at the image her words paint in my head. Her on her knees, starry-blue eyes looking up at me, her lips wet and wrapped around—

"Do you want lessons?" Keep your face blank, dude, totally blank.

She rakes her gaze over me, expression closed. Girl is cool. Her face cracks in a grin. "Ah, I'm just messing with you. I don't need lessons. I have books for that."

"Books?"

"Mmm, ordered a few on Amazon. Hope you don't mind I used your address. *The Ten Best Sexual Positions for a Female's Enjoyment* and *How to Give Head without Biting His Cock Off* should be here tomorrow."

"You're joking."

"Of course," she deadpans, a half smile tugging at her lips, verging on full blown.

"Wait. You're serious? I can't tell."

"Forget that. Let's go somewhere. I have what we need for our bad weeks. I'm gonna show you how us southern girls deal," she says and slides out of the booth while I lay out the cash plus tip on the check.

She purses her lips. "We'll need the Hummer for sure. Glad I took an Uber here."

I check my watch. It's nine. "Where are we going? I have to be at the gym—"

"Old man."

"Four years between us," I remind her as we walk to the exit.

She grins. "Let's grab beer on the way—can we? Just a couple. You drive; I drink."

"Anything else, Princess?" I murmur as we walk out to the Hummer.

"Yes, do you have any old golf clubs you don't use? One will do. If so, we can run and grab it—if not, I'll make do with what I have."

"I'm intrigued." I open the door for her and help her inside the vehicle. Before I realize it, I'm reaching over and strapping her in while she watches me. Can't help it. My stupid . . . body . . . wants to be near hers.

She smiles so big I lose my breath. "This is going to be the best night of your life," she murmurs.

"Really?" I stare into her eyes. I've never noticed the glints of white, a burst of lightning inside the blue.

A moment goes by. Maybe longer.

"Ten seconds," she breathes.

"What?"

"Nothing."

I should just get in the car, but here I am, standing like an idiot. "Am I going to regret this adventure?"

"'Little filly,' as Rodeo might say, 'When I'm done with you, you'll be begging for more.'"

I laugh.

An hour later, after grabbing beer from my fridge and an old club, we're bumping over a gravel road in Daisy with Sam Hunt blaring. Our windows are down, and warm air rushes through the interior, each of us lost in our thoughts. She's braided her hair on each side and changed into a tight green T-shirt that she got on clearance, a Saint Patrick's Day leftover. **READY TO GET LUCKED**, it says, which made me laugh when she pranced out in it.

I park next to an old two-story red barn. It's pitch black, my headlights illuminating the rolling hills and meadows in the distance.

Leaving my lights on, I grab a couple of flashlights, toss her one, and follow her in the barn. Cicadas trill, frogs sing, and leaves rustle in the quiet. A man could get used to the peacefulness of it.

"You gonna murder me out here in the middle of nowhere?"

"And bury you in the cow pasture. They'll never find you." She laughs and turns around, watching me as she walks backward inside the depths of the barn. She flicks on a switch, and the buzz of fluorescent lighting reverberates, the glow dim but adequate. The place is big, airy, and mostly clean, hay stacked in the corner, a tractor parked to the side. Various tools hang on the walls.

"This place belong to your family?"

"Mine." She smiles. "Elena got the big fancy house in town, and I got the farm."

"How much is the land worth?" Real estate is pricey in Nashville, and Daisy is close.

"I'll never sell. I grew up here, rode horses, and followed my dad around. He used to farm, mostly as a hobby. We kept these two emus until they died of old age. The true farmer was his dad. Someday, I'll build a house out here and have ten kids."

"Hemsworth. I'm starting to hate him and his damn villa."

"You keep bringing him up."

I do? Whatever.

My gaze snags on a faded circle of flowers hanging on a hay bale. "Is that a black wreath? What did you do there? Satanic rituals?"

When I look back at her, she's on her knees beside some boxes, her flashlight at her neck, eyes crossed, teeth bared. "Death is here," she growls in a deep voice. "Prepare to be sacrificed!"

I flinch. "Jesus!"

She bursts out laughing, dabbing at her eyes as she gets up and walks over to the wreath, patting me on the shoulder as she sashays past. "If I'd known you were that easy to scare, I would have been jumping out at you when you walk out of your bedroom."

"I might jump back."

She bites her lip, amusement in her eyes as she fingers the obviously spray-painted dried flowers. "No satanic demons. This sad wreath is in memory of my twentieth-birthday debacle." She crosses herself. "May the curse be broken soon."

I laugh, spellbound by her theatrics. I'm discovering her, layer by layer, every little piece, and I crave more, every tiny detail of who she is. "I sense a good Giselle story. Ugly black wreath, a barn . . ."

She leans against the wall nonchalantly. "It's a horror story. You might get scared."

"Giselle Riley, please, what happened here?"

She flashes a cheeky grin, clearly wanting to tell me. "Rascal. You really want to know?"

I want to know every fucking thing. "Yes."

"Bobby Ray Williams met me here three days before my birthday for a tryst. He drove his four-wheeler."

"There's a country song there."

"I'd made up my mind. He was the one. I liked him; he was sweet, a good guy who wouldn't gossip about me to his buddies. His daddy owns some of the land adjacent to ours, and we spent summers together."

Real jealousy rides me, and I kick it down. "Uh-huh."

"So that night, he comes in the barn, and things get hot and heavy. Lights are off, Coldplay is singing 'Magic,' and I can feel it in the air—this is it; it's gonna happen. He'd brought a blanket, and we put it over some hay bales. We're mostly naked, and things are going good; I'm all in, and he's fumbling around—he was a virgin too. And he thinks he sticks it in, but he didn't; he's screwing the blanket and the curve of my ass—"

I rear back. "Say it isn't so."

She grimaces. "Yeah. Before I could say, *Hey, you missed your target,* an owl flew in—how, I don't know. It headed straight for Bobby Ray, clawed him good—I mean sunk into his back like it was never going to let go. He rolled off me, fell off the bale, and hit his head on a rake. Thank God the tines were down, but he blacked out for a few seconds, maybe from the blood. He comes to and is puking and yelling, and I'm running from the owl. Finally, I get the doors open, and it flies off. I tell him he has a concussion, and we spend ten minutes just trying to get his pants on—that was fun—then hop on his four-wheeler. On the way to his house, I could barely see and steered us off into a pond."

My mouth gapes. "You're making this up."

"Sadly, no. Dragged a hundred-and-eighty-pound grown man from the pond, nearly carried him back to my car—why didn't we take it in the first place? I don't know. I wasn't thinking clearly, and neither was he. Just thought we'd get to his house faster cutting across the field. Anyway, I'm almost to his house when a cop pulls me over for speeding. Well, Bobby Ray gave me a bloody nose when I was pulling his flailing body out of the water, so the cop took one look at the mess in the car—and us—and called an ambulance. Spent the night in the ER."

She gives the wreath a sad look.

"He's married now with a baby, so I guess he figured out where the vagina is. What's really funny, and now I can find the comedy, is I never told him he did it wrong. He still thinks to this day that he took my V-card." She giggles. "Your face is killing me. Let it out, Dev."

My face splits in a grin, laughter spilling out as I try to talk in between breaths. "That's the worst . . . almost-sex story . . . I've ever heard," I gasp, clutching my sides. "Cursed is right. You need to see someone."

She executes a curtsy. "I'm here every birthday for your entertainment. When was your first time?"

"At the drive-in, in the bed of my old truck, with a girl three years older than me. The place was closed, but I had keys to the gate."

"Good experience?" Her tone is wistful.

Honestly, I can barely remember, except that I came too soon but went in again. "Yours will be, Giselle. With a guy who cares about you. Don't get in a hurry."

She stares at the wreath for several beats, her jaw working. "So you've said." She swings her flashlight as she walks over to several container boxes, tearing them open and pulling out dishes.

"Here, carry this." She points to a box she's set some in, and I pick it up and follow her back out, then set the box down in front of a stump by the door.

She pulls a pair of goggles out from the box while "Body Like a Back Road" blares, and she hums along. "Get that club from the Hummer. Shit is about to get real."

I do as she says, swinging the club as I walk back to her, wondering what the hell she's going to do.

"Here, hold my beer."

"Said every redneck before they wake up in the hospital." I chuckle as I take it, and she slides on her goggles, sets a white mug on the stump, and picks up the club.

"Stand clear," she says. After backing up a few paces, she arches her back, her stance confident and sure as she grips the club.

"This one is for my asshole advisor. The one who thinks women aren't as good as men." Swift and sure, she swings the club. *Crack!* The cup shatters, the pieces flying through the air.

I whistle, watching the glass fall. "Damn."

A satisfied grunt comes from her as she snatches an old blue vase and slams it on the stump. "This is for Preston. Cheating sonofabitch," she yells as she connects. The ceramic bursts as it sails across the field.

"Yeehaw!" I yell.

She pauses to take a drink of her beer, and my eyes eat her up.

"What?" she asks, threading the club through her fingers.

"You're like every guy's wet dream for a farm girl—you know that, right? It's dark, we've got a barn, country music is playing, and your shorts are killing me."

She moves her hips, making the frayed fringe swish. "I've washed them. I bought others, but these are my favorite."

"You played sports, didn't you?" I ask, taking her bottle, watching her line up with what looks like a candy dish on the stump. Confident. Efficient. Graceful. *Hot.*

"Volleyball. Considered a scholarship once, but I knew it would screw with my grades in college."

"I went the other direction, chose getting drafted over a diploma. Never was a good student. The game took most of my time."

She cocks her head. "Does it bother you that you didn't finish?"

"Football, it's always been enough . . ." I toe at a piece of gravel.

"But?" She leans on the club.

I shake my head. "I don't know. I'm set for life, but I wish I'd tried harder. Regrets, maybe?" I shrug. "It does feel like everyone around me is more educated—even Jack graduated with honors."

"What does this insecurity stem from?" She's lowered the club, giving me her full attention.

I grin, deflecting. "I don't see a couch around here, Dr. Riley. Stop trying to analyze me, and hit something."

She studies me. "You quote Carl Sagan, and you own a business. You have the best stats for a wide receiver in the league. Has someone said you aren't intelligent? Has someone made you feel *less* than? Give me their name. I'm going to smack them around."

"Savage, aren't you?" I grin.

"When someone hurts you, yes."

I smirk.

"It was a woman. I just feel it. Who was she?" She's got her mouth pursed, a hand on her hip, and I don't doubt for a second she'd hunt down my ex. "Come on; tell me. I told you about Bobby Ray, and you skirted over your first time. You owe me a story. I've told you so much!"

I open my mouth, then shut it, pacing around. I should tell her; it's Giselle, and she's brought me to a special place, and I *like* her . . . shit, no, I don't like her like that—I can't, I just can't. I chew on my bottom lip.

"Dev?"

I throw my hands up. "Her name was Hannah. I met her first semester of my freshman year at a frat party. She played hard to get, and I chased her, waited for her after her classes, texted her, all that stuff. I thought I could just get her out of my system, but she was different." A long exhalation comes from my chest. "Smart, working on a premed degree, and money, lots of family money. She was not my usual, though, not a fan of the party scene or into football. Finally, I convinced her to go out with me, and we fell in love. She didn't care that I lived and breathed football, and I didn't care that she spent a lot of time studying in the library. We just clicked when we were together. Our plan was for me to get drafted, her to start med school, then get married as soon as we could."

A harsh laugh comes from me. "She dumped me at the beginning of senior year for a guy in her premed classes. Some nerd guy with arms like sticks who couldn't run if a snail was chasing him, but he was really what she wanted; it just took her meeting someone smarter than me to know I wasn't her future. They got married on spring break, and I flew to Cabo and got the drunkest I've ever been in my life. Spent the entire week covered in tequila and bikinis. Haven't looked back since. She left me—just like everyone else."

I stop, my chest rising. Shit, I just . . . spilled all that out. My throat bobs, and I try to shake off the past. I roll my neck as the silence builds. I raise my eyes to hers.

No pity there, just acceptance and a nod. "She was not your destiny, Dev. You're meant for more. She did you a favor. Somewhere out there, a girl is waiting for you. She's going to rock your world and give you so many little football-playing babies—no stick-armed kids for you. I promise you wherever she is, she still thinks about you." Her gaze drifts over me, lingering. "Yeah, she messed up."

"You gonna let me hit some shit or what? I'm ready."

"One more for me." Leaning over, she wiggles her ass and taps another mug shaped like a pair of boobs. "This is for Myrtle. She needs to get out of the hospital, and her daughter better check on her soon!" The club crashes into the glass and sends it off into the night.

Laughing, we bump into each other as we maneuver around, and I take her spot at the stump. She hands off the club and presses against me as she helps me adjust the goggles. With a satisfied smirk, she moves away to place another ugly vase on the stump.

"Where do you find this stuff?"

"Aunt Clara is addicted to yard sales. She picks them up and brings them here. Her secret boyfriend, Scotty, comes out and gets the pieces and uses them for mosaics." She pokes me in the arm. "You can't repeat that. He likes his manly persona too much to admit he does art in secret."

I nod my agreement and whack the vase, and it disintegrates and scatters, the sound more satisfying than I imagined. "That felt good."

"But you didn't say what it was for."

I cup my hands and call out, "Preston, you suck!"

"Go again, and do it for you," she says sternly as she puts a teacup on the surface.

I swing the club and call out, "Hannah, hope you're happy! I'm fucking famous! And rich!"

A bowl appears on the stump. She backs away, and I swing. "Get your life together, Dad!"

She puts an owl cookie jar up, and we burst out laughing. "Had to," she murmurs. "It's fate."

"This one's for you, baby," I say and whack it. "Curses aren't real!" I yell.

We keep up a steady pace, her putting up random glassware, me hitting. By the eighth one, I'm bouncing on my toes like I'm about to take the field, catch the ball, and run it in for a touchdown. "Addictive," I murmur.

I shout whatever I feel like, from getting that Super Bowl ring on my finger to the Walmart dude who put his hands on Giselle, even though from the sound of it, she scared him with threats about her mama.

Another comes, then another.

I roll my shoulders, loosening the muscles. "What's next?"

She places something on the stump.

Wrapped in purple tissue paper, the item is half the size of the palm of my hand.

"A gift for you," she says, her face flushing, her eyes bright.

"Oh?" I prop the club against the barn, pick up the package, and stare down at it, pleasure mixing with adrenaline, heady and thick. "No one's bought me a gift for no reason in . . . well, never." My hands clench around it.

She moves from foot to foot. "Ah, it's not much. I grabbed it when I picked up some clothes for Myrtle at this boutique downtown after class . . ." She stops as I quickly undo the paper.

"Giselle, baby," I breathe, holding the carved stone butterfly in the palm of my hand. "It's beautiful."

She takes a step toward me and peers down at it. Delicate, with spread wings, the stone is soft and smooth, about an inch thick. "I saw the purple and blue colors mixed together, and it made me think of you. It's *a charm for strength*, the lady said—you keep it close and rub when you need to feel centered." She clears her throat. "You can put it on a desk or wherever, and when I'm out of your hair, you'll remember tonight and not think I was too much of a pain in the ass."

I close my fingers around it, rubbing my fingers over the surface. "I'll keep it in my pocket every day."

Her breath hitches. "You don't have to—"

"You aren't a pain in the ass."

"Give me time."

I stick my hand in my pocket, curling around the stone. "My guess is your apartment isn't going to be livable for weeks. The basement has structural damage. You're about to start fall semester, and you don't need the extra hassle of searching for an apartment. Stay as long as you want. Be my real roommate."

What the hell am I saying?

She licks her lips. "My family and our friends might think we're, you know, a thing . . ."

"We'll tell them we're not."

"Because we aren't," she says on a sigh.

"Just . . . stay."

Stay, stay, stay . . . the word bangs around in my head, ping-ponging around the blurry childhood memories of my mother driving away, lingering visions of every woman after that slamming a door and telling me goodbye.

I'm not deluded. Part of me knows I'm teetering close to a heady infatuation with Giselle, throwing my inhibitions aside and devouring her piece by piece. Then she'll wake up and see I'm not good enough, just like Hannah did. Unease pricks, making me itch, and I want to peel the sensation right off my skin.

"We need rules, though."

She swallows. "Yeah?"

My hands tighten at my sides. *Just say it, just say it* . . .

"I'm going to be up front. I find you . . . attractive," I say gruffly.

"What a nightmare," she replies dryly, eyes gleaming. "Devon thinks the nerd girl is cute."

"Shush. You're gorgeous, okay? Your ass is fine; your tits are small . . . ," I tease, "but perfect, and when you walk in a room, men look. They look real hard, Giselle—even me—and you're not even paying attention."

"Oh, I'm catching a clue."

I don't touch that remark. "All I'm saying is we keep our hands to ourselves. We're friends, and we don't want to ruin that. Plus, Jack . . ."

"Meh, we'd probably never mesh in bed anyway."

Unbidden, my hands clench. She went *there*? I take a breath. Steady now . . . "Really? I can assure you, fucking me would be the highlight of your damn year—"

"Promises you don't plan on proving." She pats me on the arm, then stops. "Oh wait, can I touch you there?" Her lips curl.

I shake my head, reaching for exasperation but finding nothing but bolts of heat at the sight of her. This is an asinine idea, asking her to stay, but . . .

"Don't split hairs with me, smarty-pants."

"Uh-huh. So what's off the table?" She steps in closer, her arms curling around my neck. Fire licks up my skin, and I suck in a gasp of air. What is she doing?

"Giselle—"

"I mean, sex is a no-no," she murmurs. "You've laid down the law, Sheriff, but what about first base? You already did that. You kissed me the night of the fire—and gotta say, it wasn't the best. We can't let it stand. Plus, you told me if I brought Red back safe, you'd tell me why you kissed me."

She smells fucking good, and I swallow down the thickness in my throat, my hands of their own volition reaching up and cupping her face. "Because I was angry, and it felt . . . right," I admit. "Was it that bad?"

"Just the first time I've been kissed in five months, only I didn't get any tongue." She plays with a piece of my hair, twisting it around her finger. "I propose we get a real kiss in and call it quits—after all, you let some chick kiss your neck tonight, so they don't mean much to you. I'm sure there wouldn't be a spark anyway, but once it's out of the way, we'll know for certain there's no zing. Truly, I need it for testing purposes. I plan on kissing Mike Millington at my party, and it would be prudent to have yours as a control to compare—"

Anger zips over me. "I want to meet this motherfucker. No one's getting near you if he doesn't pass my test."

"I do love it when you get all growly. What kind of test?" She presses her lips against my cheek, right at the corner of my mouth. It's not sexy or a come-on but gentle and teasing.

Regardless. My brain stops. Literally stops functioning.

Fuck, fuck, she feels so good . . .

"Dev?" She pulls back, gaze locked with mine as the moments tick down. "Level five," she murmurs, and I shake my head at her.

"What kind of test?" I grumble, trying to focus. "The douchebag-slash-asshole-slash-how-bad-do-I-want-to-kill-him test. It's evolving as we speak."

"Clearly." She rests her head in the crook of my neck, and my arms curl around her waist. I tug her closer, tipping her face up. She looks ethereal in the lights of the car, her blonde hair shining. I sigh. "All right. Come on; let's get this kiss out of the way and get on with our lives." My words are light, but my pulse beats like a jackhammer, already imagining how she'll taste, the slide of her mouth against mine, the satiny feel of her skin under my hands, because I'm going to run my hands all over her, touch her face, her hair, her arms, her tits. I can handle one kiss, for Christ's sake.

Can you? a voice cackles in my head.

"You were right the first time. No touching. I get it. I'll wait for Mike." And then she's twirling out of my arms, with her face averted.

I'm right behind her, and she whips around, and we bump into each other.

"Giselle, you're teasing me."

"No, I'm not," she replies, eyes flashing. "Don't you get it? I have thought about kissing you more than you may realize, and it's . . . not returned! We are just friends, not even really that, because you only know me because of Jack and Elena, but in my head—" Her voice stops. "What are you doing?" she gasps as I fiddle with her hair.

"When I kiss you, I want my hands in your hair. These braids have to go."

I work on one, and she does the other. "If you think I'm going to let you kiss me now, you missed your chance."

"You're right; I'm an ass. I don't deserve to kiss you at all," I murmur as she throws her rubber band on the ground, and I toss mine alongside it. "But we should get this . . ." Hot as fuck moment . . . "Experiment out of the way." My hands wrap around her waist.

She shakes out the braids with her fingers and glares at me. "You might discover, football player, that one kiss isn't enough—"

I kiss her, getting my first taste (and trying to go slow) by pressing soft brushes against the corners of her mouth before tugging on her bottom lip with my teeth, parting her lips, and swallowing her gasp, then swooping in to slant my lips against hers. We fit together as if we were made for each other, her head tilting in my palms as I slide my hands deep into her hair and clutch her skull. I give her everything she deserves, long and slow and languid, lazily sucking at her lips until she moans, her fingers scraping down my jaw, sliding across my shoulders, her nails digging into my shirt as she grips me.

I'm in control, in control; this is not affecting me. I am cool . . . until her tongue meets mine and tangles. A rush of desire rolls in, obliterating any good sense, and we go from gentle to feral in a millisecond. Our lips merge and battle, one of those long searing kisses meant for people who can't get enough with one taste and don't want to stop.

"Giselle . . ." Groaning, I pick her up, and her legs wrap around my waist like a vise. Somehow I've got her pressed against the barn, our mouths glued together in every possible position I can think of, my tongue dancing with hers, dueling and winning everything I want, taking and taking, then giving and giving. This is the longest kiss in history; it's like we're making out in high school, the best goddamn kiss, and everything I've wanted since the moment she walked into my penthouse. I can't think, and what am I doing? Just shut up, brain. She cups my ass and grinds, the feel of her nipples against my chest maddening. *Don't touch, or you'll be lost.* Fuck, she smells like vanilla and flowers—vibrant, heady blooms on a summer day, the ones that make you dizzy and weak for another inhale.

"Giselle," I gasp out her name as I rotate my hard dick against her core. Her legs tighten as she whimpers, urging me on as she sucks my bottom lip, dragging it out. My hand is up her shirt, and I graze over her breast, tugging on the erect nipple through her lace bra . . .

Something falls from above me, grazing my arm, and I flinch back, looking up and then down at the ground.

"What the—"

"Curse." She sucks in a deep breath and looks up. "Piece of wood came off the window. Rotted and needs to be replaced."

I gaze back at her lowered lids, swollen mouth, and heaving chest.

I'm in no better shape, and like a rubber band snapping against my wrist, I come to my senses and let her down, putting space between us.

The silence of the night is deafening, and I'm scrambling around in my head, looking for a way to explain that I didn't mean to take it that far, that we need to just take a second and breathe and pretend like this never happened. She searches my gaze, and maybe she sees it, maybe she does, because she straightens her spine and gives me a tight-lipped nod.

"Giselle . . ." I still don't know what's going to come out of my stupid mouth, but she beats me to it.

"No need to say what is on your face, Devon. That kiss was terrible, and we can never do it again."

My eyes shut. What a lie.

But . . .

We can't. There's Jack, but shit, mostly there's *me*. I can't hang on to girls like Giselle. I don't want to.

"Yeah."

She picks up a cup, slams it down on the stump, and smashes it to smithereens.

Chapter 10

GISELLE

"Ever since you were little, you kept a secret journal. Always knew you'd pick up writing again, just didn't think it would be about sexy aliens," Aunt Clara says as she ushers me in the door of the Cut 'N' Curl. Wearing a bright-red maxi dress and strappy sandals, she's a ball of energy.

I inhale the slight scent of ammonia mixed with fruity shampoo inside the salon. A block from the center of town in Daisy, everyone comes here to gossip and get their hair done. Even me.

I kiss her cheek, waving the bag of lunch I grabbed for her. I can't drive past a Chick-fil-A without getting her something. "Got their new mac and cheese. Figured you'd be too busy to get your own, with Mama running errands today."

"Bless your little heart," she squeals and snatches up the bag, pulls out the mac and cheese, then holds it up like it's the holy grail.

I grin, then recall her comment and give her a steely look. "First Topher told Mama about Rodeo, and now he's talking about my book. The man will suffer."

"Shush. Let me shove this in my mouth before you get huffy." She's already sitting in the chair, her feet up on her station as she takes a big bite and swoons.

I blow out a breath, wound up, feeling tense and ready to do *something*—especially after my morning with Devon. He marched out of his bedroom, not meeting my eyes as he grumbled about a bad night. He ate his oatmeal and drank his protein shake, careful to step around me in the kitchen (as usual), but oh, you can bet he loved all over Pookie, who'd peed in his loafers. He told her, *It's okay, little doggie, you've been through a trauma,* then grunted out a *Later* at me over his shoulder and left for the stadium.

It was a bitter pill to swallow, sitting next to him on the ride back from the barn. He never said one word, unless you count *May I turn the music up?* He blasted it, and I clasped my hands and stared out the window. His face after we kissed had been just . . . granite hard and crawling with regret.

Alone at the penthouse after he left, I forced myself to study until the words blurred on the page, so I pulled up Vureck and Kate and pounded out a chapter. It was a glorious fight scene, where Kate got to say everything I couldn't last night—how frustrated she is because Vureck refuses to see what is right in front of him, and how dare he stay resolute in delivering her to his king. She's not meant to be a harem girl; she is his.

Ugh . . . Devon . . . he doesn't *want* to get entangled, and it cuts deep, so sharp and visceral, that I don't understand the heaviness in my body, the pain radiating in the center of my chest.

Yes, he kissed me like a man drowning, but that was just a natural response to someone he admitted to being attracted to, his brain releasing dopamine, his serotonin levels increasing, thus producing oxytocin, the "love hormone." He probably hasn't gotten laid in a while. A man like him, well, he gets it on the regular, all those women kissing him on the neck. My hands curl.

Besides all that, last night I saw the anguish on his face when he talked about his college sweetheart. He trusted me with deeply personal things, and if he wants to call me *just a friend*, then I will be just that.

I don't want to *lose* him as a person in my life. I don't get close to a lot of people, and with him, there's a beautiful connection I'm afraid of destroying. On the drive here, I made a pact with myself to be his ear if he needs one, but no more kissing. It's not his fault that I'm the one with weird feelings. I will take all my frustrations out in my story.

"You rascal," I call out to Topher when I spot him leaning against the Sun Drop machine, thumbing through a magazine, pretending like he didn't see me come in. I bet he walked over on his lunch break. He meets my eyes in the mirror and walks over and swings me around.

"I'm supposed to be mad at you for gossiping about me," I mutter, but it's hard to stay annoyed when he plants a big kiss on my head.

He's in his midtwenties; his long blond hair is in a ponytail, and he's wearing a shirt with little kittens on it. "Don't be mad," he teases. "You know I can't resist the Daisy Lady Gang when they ask me questions. It's like the Spanish Inquisition with them, and I didn't spill about the book to your mama, just Clara. She was reading *Mated to the Alien* when I came in, and your book just fell out of my mouth."

"Shameless," I reply, shaking my head. "I'm never going to let you read it. That's your punishment."

He laughs. "Forget that; I love to write myself, so I can be one of those early beta readers." A serious look grows on his face. "I've been so worried about you since the fire. Have you seen this?" He pops open his phone and brings up a grainy video of a girl on a fire escape. "It was on Channel 5 News the morning after the fire. Some bystander took it. 'Unnamed woman escapes apartment fire.'"

I close my eyes. "Mama's not here, right?"

Aunt Clara puts down a nearly demolished bowl of mac and cheese and eases in, always ready for a conspiracy. "She's at the Piggly Wiggly; then she's getting her tires rotated and oil changed." Her eyes flare as she watches the video. "What on earth were you thinking, Giselle!"

Mama knows about the fire. I called her the next day, but she doesn't know I went back for the pearls, and she doesn't know I'm staying with Devon. I haven't mentioned the guy from Walmart to her, because Devon is private and asked me not to.

"You're staying with Devon," Topher announces, and I gape.

"What? How did you—"

He nudges his head toward the huge window in front of the salon. "For someone so smart, you forget I see all. Might start working at a psychic hotline." He holds up a finger. "First, you drove Red here." A second finger appears. "Second, and most telling, last night a black Hummer whizzed through town. There's only one vehicle like that I know of and only one hot-as-heck wide receiver who drives it." A third finger springs up. "Next, I saw you in the passenger seat. Windows down, music blaring as you swigged a beer."

I shake my head. We did have to drive past his new rental because there's only one road into Daisy. "Geez, I really hate small towns. Why were you even awake?"

"Out walking Romeo. He'd had too many cucumbers and had to go."

Romeo is Elena's small pet pig, and Topher and Mama are alternating babysitting while she's in Hawaii.

I sigh. "My car is still in the shop from the busted window, and Devon was sweet enough to let me borrow his."

His eyes dance. "His superexpensive baby. Where did you say you were staying since the fire?"

I forgave him too easily. "I didn't."

"Giselle?" Aunt Clara asks, lips curled. "Are you shacking up with Devon?"

Shifting my feet, I adjust my glasses.

"Giselle?" Topher waggles his eyebrows. "Where are you sleeping at night?"

I throw my hands up. "At the penthouse! But there's nothing going on." I cover my face. "Just let me be the one to tell Mama."

"Oh Lordy, Cynthia can take it. Jack is going to flip," she says.

I stiffen, recalling Jack's warning to the players. "It's my life. Jack just worries because of Preston."

Topher grimaces.

"What?" I ask, sensing a shift in the air.

He bites his lip. "Preston is dating Shelia Wheeler. I've seen them at the pizza place a few times."

"Oh." Shelia was in *Romeo and Juliet* with me. Gorgeous girl.

He flicks his gaze to Aunt Clara, and they share a look.

"And?" I ask.

She shrugs. "Her aunt Birdie says it's serious between them. She comes in every week with the lowdown."

A sting hits me, yet there's something flat around the edges. "Well, we all know he moves fast. He jumped from Elena to me in a heartbeat." I plop down in the seat Aunt Clara vacated and stare at myself in the mirror.

"The usual today?" she says, and I grimace. I come in every third Friday for a trim, predictable and boring as usual.

My mind churns as I glare at myself. "Not cutting an inch today, Aunt Clara. We're gonna do something crazy."

Her eyebrows arch. "Spiral perm with loose curls? Lots of volume . . . yes, yes, yes . . ."

I roll my eyes. "I don't want to revisit the nineties."

Topher jumps in. "I'm thinking red. Dark and mysterious, à la *Devil's Angels*."

"That's Elena's color."

"We can add some depth with some lowlights?" Aunt Clara says, lifting a blonde lock and twirling it around. She's disappointed about the perm.

If I'm going to be cliché and change my hair after a breakup, I'm going to make it worth it. A curl of excitement makes me smile.

"Giselle. I don't know if I can!" Aunt Clara says after I describe the vision I have, bringing up a few pics from my Pinterest board to show her Kate.

"You are amazing, the best stylist in town—"

"I'm the *only* one in town besides your mama," she replies. "You have your birthday coming up and—"

Emotion clogs my throat, feelings I think I'm in control of, yet apparently not. "I want to be different." A badass who knows how to drive a spaceship. "Just do it. Before Mama gets back."

A long sigh comes from her. "Never change for anyone except yourself."

"It's not for anyone. It's for me." I've decided it really is.

"You're sure?"

A while later, she's rinsing the color from my hair as we discuss my book, when Topher brings my cell over. "It's been going off straight for the past five minutes. Someone named 'Corey From Class.' Thought you might need to get it."

After sitting up, I wrap my hair in a towel and call him back.

"What's going on?" I ask.

Corey breathes heavily, his voice low. "Ms. Riley, I really hate to bug you. I know you study all the time."

I look around at the Cut 'N' Curl. "Um, yeah. It's cool. Just wrapped up some research." On my romance book.

"Class was bad. Me and . . . say hi, Addison!"

I hear her voice in the background. "Hey, Ms. Riley!"

"We had a terrible fu—freaking teacher today, one of those TAs, only we didn't understand a word he said. Talked in fu—freaking circles about relativity and black holes for an hour, and now he wants a summary of what we learned emailed to him by tonight. I can copy straight out of Wikipedia, but you know I really want to understand." He huffs. "The jerk ruined one of the coolest things in space."

"Black holes are still awesome," I assure him.

Aunt Clara pops an eyebrow. "Are they?"

I shoo her.

Another huff from Corey. "To me, black holes are the vacuum cleaners of the universe, and when I said that, he nearly flipped a table. He also said they're invisible and don't even suck everything!" He exhales. "In *Zanthia*, it's a swirling black spiral that you can clearly see, and it destroys a whole fleet! All the good space movies are ruined. It's okay when you do it, but not him."

Annoyance at my cohort makes me frown. Why stifle a kid's imagination and dismiss a somewhat fair analogy? It's not really a vacuum, but it's a common misconception. "What he meant is that black holes don't really suck; they have a gravitational pull, just like everything does, plus an event horizon, and once matter passes that point, it will be pulled in. Also, event horizons appear to emit a light when accelerating matter passes the boundary, so *invisible* is not quite accurate. What was his name?" I usually pay attention only to my teaching schedule and not everyone else's.

"See!" he calls to Addison. "Dude was a dick. I don't know his name. He never told us."

I close my eyes. Why couldn't he try to be personable with these kids? "Back to the vacuum and the idea that it sucks everything—you ever watch *Sesame Street* and see Cookie Monster devour cookies?"

"I have a Cookie Monster shirt. It says 'Eat Me,'" he chirps. "Girls love it."

"Of course they do. Think of black holes as Cookie Monster eating anything that gets close, munching and spitting, some of the bigger crumbs falling out. Some of the matter that's pulled in *is* large, but once it hits the event horizon, particles fly everywhere—some in, some out."

"I like my vision better. Giant Dyson. Black spiral. Maybe a wormhole to another dimension."

"No. An invisible Cookie Monster with a flash of light when matter approaches."

He sighs. "He was just up there spouting off facts and pissing me off when he didn't explain them—like I'm supposed to just get those words he used." He groans. "I shouldn't have called you. You're busy—"

"Where are you now?"

"The library. I've got a stack of books in front of me, and frankly, I'm ready to rip them apart with my teeth. Dude. I usually only rip off beer tops with my teeth."

I bite back a smile at the image of him and Addison disgruntled in the library. "Books are expensive, and it's not their fault. Take a breath. Wait for me." Auditorily is not the way Corey learns. He needs to see my face, and I can draw some diagrams . . .

"Would you really come?"

"I can't have your black holes dream dashed, so yes."

He yells, "I told you she would, Addison!"

She squeals in the background, and I hear him rustling back to me. "I . . . shit, Ms. Riley . . . thank you, thank you. I swear I won't drink this weekend just for you, just in case you ever need a kidney," he says.

After getting off the call with him, I grab my purse, then pull out several twenties and leave them on Aunt Clara's counter.

Her mouth twitches. "Hate to miss whatever color your hair turns out, but go and save little Corey."

I run a quick brush through my hair.

"Can I come?" Topher calls out as I head to the exit. "I want to watch you in action, and I really want to ride in Red."

"Don't you have to work?"

He grins. "The Daisy Library is closed today after lunch. Let me be your ride-or-die bitch. I don't know much about black holes, but I can google on the way there. We can stop and grab some cookies and use my sock as a puppet."

Elation swells. Topher is Elena's BFF, and him wanting to hang out with *me* makes me giddy. I smile so big it hurts and nudge my head to the car. "Nobody drives her but me," I say as we walk out.

He smirks, delight on his face as he runs his hands over the sleek hood. "Uh-huh. I bet you go fifty on the interstate in this fine piece of horsepower."

"Sixty-five. I'm more of a rebel than you know."

"Give me the keys. Devon never has to know."

"You don't know the password."

He chortles. "Damn, it takes a password to start this machine?"

I pop the locks, liking the clicking sound it makes. He's insisted I drive it every day. "Nope, just a song you have to know before you get the keys from the valet—who knows me now."

"What is it? Come on; tell me." He slides into the passenger seat. "Devon's password . . . hmmm . . . is it 'Closer' by Nine Inch Nails—no, how about 'Get Ur Freak On' by Missy Elliot?"

"You can keep guessing all the way to Vandy, but I hold that man's secrets to my heart."

He smiles as I pull out of the parking lot, dodging the potholes. "Do you now? How interesting."

"We are friends," I say grimly, repeating the mantra in my head. If I keep telling myself over and over, it might just become the truth—on my side. It's already truth for him.

He throws his head back and laughs. "Oh, Giselle, that man has been checking you out since the night he met you at the community center for *Romeo and Juliet*. He didn't take his eyes off you at the wedding. Looked to me like a man conflicted."

I pause, then tell him how Devon showed up at my apartment during the fire, about how I ended up sleeping in his bed after my nightmare, and then about last night at the barn. I break down my gaze levels and describe the best kiss of all time.

He fiddles with the music, looking for a station.

"He had a date at the reception," I say.

"Want to know a secret?"

"If you truly have one, I can't believe you haven't told me already," I muse, sending him a wry grin.

He taps his fingers on his white skinny jeans, his Converse shifting around as he turns to me. "I didn't really put it together until you said how adamant he is about staying friends, but . . ." He stops, tapping his chin.

"What?" I groan after he's let ten seconds pass.

"When we were getting in our cars to head to the reception, I heard him talking to Lawrence about when this girl Lawrence knew would be showing up, because she was late."

"Lawrence knew her? Like he set them up?"

He shrugs. "Maybe. He arranges dates all the time for some of the guys. Public appearances, galas, that sort of thing."

"Who told you that?"

"Quinn."

"Oh." Quinn is Jack's foster brother and a reliable source. He manages some of the players' apartments and cars.

"Anyway, from my perspective, he wasn't into her," Topher adds, nodding his head, as if an idea is taking root. "When you weren't looking, he was checking you out like you were a shiny gold championship ring. I bet he called in a date to put some distance between you and him."

I frown, easing onto the interstate, being careful as an eighteen-wheeler roars past us. I haven't analyzed why he showed up with a girl no one knew, who didn't have a relationship with Jack and Elena, but then, it's not unusual to bring a plus-one to a wedding—although technically it was a very small affair. And he hasn't mentioned a girl he's been seeing, but then maybe he wouldn't . . .

Ugh. I don't like this train of thought and tell Topher as much.

He gets quiet for a few moments, then: "Giselle, how are you? No sugarcoating."

My hands clench the wheel, and I swallow down the tightness in my throat. "Preston may have broken my heart, but I fucked over my sister. I can barely stand myself." There it is. The reason why this whole year has sucked.

Guilt hammers at me as I recall the day it happened. I'd been in town only a few weeks when Preston asked me to meet him at his law office to talk about Elena. He was handsome and oh-so sad with his "I love her, but your sister is ignoring me" routine.

One minute he was behind his desk dabbing at his tears; the next he was kissing me right as she walked in. In retrospect, I think he heard her in the office and wanted to shock her or screw with her or who knows— only Elena never reacts like a normal person. Instead of blowing up, she told us to enjoy each other, then pretended like it never happened. And like a chump, I let Preston weasel into my life.

Topher sighs. "I know what it's like to disappoint those who love you—heck, I'm a gay man in a small town, and my parents won't even speak to me. She forgave you, yet you're punishing yourself. You made a mistake. You owned it. You deserve to be happy."

"You do too, Topher."

When I glance over, he's squinting at me. "Your hair is drying." A pair of sunglasses appears on his face. "Yeah, it's so bright I gotta wear shades."

Chapter 11

DEVON

The scent of herbs mixed with . . . is that *skunk*? It hits me in the face when I walk into the penthouse around seven. I toss my keys on the foyer table and step into the den. An older lady sits in my favorite recliner with her face averted, her feet propped up as she snores. A bright-pink walking cane rests next to her. I almost pivot and walk out to make sure I hit the right floor, but my key fit, and Giselle's laptop is on the coffee table, her books scattered, her bag on the couch. This *is* my place.

The lady snorts, pushes at her brown hair, and mumbles under her breath, then appears to drift back to sleep as the door quietly opens behind me. I hear Pookie's nails clicking on the hardwood. Without looking back at who I hope like hell is Giselle, I murmur, "Why does the apartment smell like a frat house?" I don't even bring up the stranger. It has to be Myrtle.

I hear her behind me, kicking off her shoes. A long sigh comes from her. "I picked her up this afternoon from the hospital, and her migraine hit before we even got out of the parking lot. She smokes to alleviate the symptoms. Her dealer is an elderly man from Brentwood, a retired executive from a bank. Nicest man ever. He usually delivers."

"Did he deliver here?" I wait for the outrage to hit, but . . .

"He came to the hospital. No one ever suspects old people, and Myrtle makes her own rules. She acts like a teenager," she mutters.

My shoulders relax, and a smile twitches at my lips. It hasn't passed my notice that Giselle is drawn to interesting characters, from a pot-smoking old lady to emus.

Another snore comes from my recliner.

"I'm surprised you didn't recognize her," she murmurs, still behind me. My skin is electric, waiting for her to walk past me. Part of me wants to turn around and face her, while the other wants to pretend like last night never happened.

"Because I was too upset about the girl I thought was still in the damn building," I say tersely. Still not over that.

"I'm sorry about the pot," she says. "I was writing, and she snuck to the windows, cracked one open, and lit up. I'll grab some air fresheners."

I hear her snatch her keys back up, her shoes sliding back on. "Giselle, wait, don't leave—" Not when I just got here.

I pivot to her, my words stalling in my throat. "What . . . your hair—it's blue!"

Her back straightens, her eyes glinting with steel. "Electric Neon, to be precise. Not all of it, though. Aunt Clara missed a few spots in the back. She said it took a lot of dye, and we might need to put another application on."

I shake my head, trying to mesh the image of her this morning with the girl in front of me. I loved her hair, long and thick and down to her midback, silver and gold strands intermingled. "Why did you do it?" My words come out wrong; I see that right away by the quick flash of hurt on her face before she shrugs.

"You color yours all the time!"

"But yours . . ." I take a breath. I might be obsessed with her hair. My hands threading through the strands last night, my fingers cupping her scalp. "How long does the color last?"

"Forty washes." She exhales. "Thirty-five now. I stuck my head in the sink and scrubbed for an hour. My fingers are wrinkled up, and my hands need moisturizer. Maybe it will be gone by Sunday." Her shoulders slump. "It's still glowing."

Yes, yes it is.

"The doorman didn't know who I was when I took Pookie out. I had to show him my driver's license." She pinches the bridge of her nose. "It gets worse. When I went to the library to help some of my students, I sat down, and they asked if they could help me. Didn't even know I was there to save them from a black hole catastrophe."

I grin. "Come here, baby."

She crosses her arms. "You don't call me *pretty girl* anymore. You haven't since the night at the Razor."

"'Cause that's for women I don't know well."

"And *baby*?" She rolls her eyes.

"Fits you."

"It feels as if I should be offended."

"Are you?" My eyes drift over her snug lime-green T-shirt proclaiming her as the **WORLD'S TALLEST ELF**. Another Walmart clearance item.

She raises an eyebrow. "You call all your friends *baby*?"

Only you.

"Of course." I pull her forward and search her eyes, battling the instinct to taste her lips. Keeping our chests from touching—*Look at me; I'm doing good*—I lace my fingers with hers, but it's fine; I got this.

"I look ridiculous," she mutters. "Just another girl who thinks changing her hair color will make everything better."

"Shh. It's not that bad. It complements your eyes."

"You hate it."

"No, it just took me by surprise," I murmur, tracing my gaze over the bright locks of hair that brush against her T-shirt. "Reminds of Katy Perry in the 'California Gurls' video."

"Hers was a wig."

"I like it any color when it's down," I say, my voice husky. "And it matches my butterfly tattoos."

A strange expression flits over her face, and we stare at each other. I can't tell what she's thinking, probably about her hair, but my head is back at the barn the night before. "I have to tell you something."

"Blue jokes?"

"Thank you for last night, for showing me your special place. It felt good to break things."

She gives me a half smile.

"But I owe you an apology. I shouldn't have kissed you. Then I acted off this morning—"

"I goaded you into that, and you don't have to be perky just for me. I certainly don't want to make you feel uncomfortable in your own home." She disentangles our hands.

I frown. "I'm not." Hell, coming home and finding her here has been in my head all day, a beacon of warmth right in my chest. "I'm sorry for being a grouch."

She narrows her eyes at me. "So it *was* a terrible kiss?"

"On a scale from one to ten, I'd give it . . ." A billion. "Well, let's just say, it was—"

"Scale? Oh, how ironic." She huffs out a laugh.

"How so?"

She opens her mouth, then shuts it and shakes her head, muttering something about gaze levels.

I stuff my hands in my pockets, and she watches me. "Well. Now that we've established the rules, and kissing is over, things will be smooth sailing," she says.

"Right."

She nods, seeming to come to some sort of decision. "Want me to bake some cookies to get rid of the smell?"

"Can't say no to cookies." I turn with her as she brushes past me and heads to the kitchen. Of course, I follow her; I always do. It's her gravitational pull, and I'm as pathetic as Pookie, who trots after me. "Can I help?"

She hip checks me as she pulls a pan from the cabinet. "You could preheat the oven to three-fifty and get the cookie dough out of the freezer. I'll cut them up and make sure they're two inches apart. That's how I roll. Didn't you see the pizza boxes from dinner?" Her gaze darts to me. "Have you had dinner? I can make you something. Spaghetti? It won't be a homemade sauce, but Myrtle likes it when I make it."

"Nah, I ate with Lawrence." I'd thought about texting her to see if she wanted to go out for dinner, but worry for my dad kept rearing its head. I drove to his house and did a walk-through. It was obvious he'd been there—his sink was full of dishes—but he was gone. He's avoiding me.

I push those things away and focus on her. Lazily, I watch her flit around the kitchen, bustling like she belongs, stuffing pizza boxes in the trash, cursing as they tumble back out.

I move her to the side. "Here, let me do that." I pick up the boxes, folding and crushing them with my hands—*See how strong I am?*—only a pepperoni flies off and lands on my shirt. She erupts in giggles, and when I turn to mock glare at her, my foot tangles in the box on the floor, and I do a little slip and slide before I catch myself on the counter.

"Oh my God, pizza boxes are trying to kill you!" She crosses herself. "My curse is rubbing off."

"I swear this never happens," I muse with a grin. "Have you watched me play football? I'm a badass."

"Mmm, lots of times."

I arch a brow, satisfaction and pleasure rushing through me. "So it wasn't just my national championship game. Whatever happened to the guy you watched it with?"

"Jealous?"

"No." I'd like to meet him and check him out.

"Meh, he and I never worked out, but I can still see your bio piece they showed during halftime that night. Your hair was clipped short, and you sported a smirk as you flexed your muscles."

Most of the cockiness was for show. I was still reeling over Hannah.

"Impressed by my stats, I see. Why haven't you ever mentioned that you were a big Devon Walsh fan? I could have signed some footballs, maybe a shirt."

She throws a balled-up napkin at me, and I catch it. "Why do I need those when I'm *sleeping* in your old practice clothes?"

My body tightens at the image of her in a bed, my shirt bunched around her hips, a peek of her thong showing. Heat rises, my pulse kicking up. "What about when we first met? You never brought up recognizing me."

Her head dips as she avoids me, pretending to inspect the granite on the countertop. She pushes up her glasses on her nose.

"Giselle?"

"Haven't you put it together by now, Dev?" A pink flush starts at her throat and eases up her face.

I inch closer. "No, I haven't." *Seems I'm in uncharted waters with you, baby.*

We do that staring thing again where I can't take my eyes off hers, cataloging the microexpressions on her face, and then I get tangled up on a small heart-shaped freckle above her lips, that full sweet mouth that's perfect for—

Myrtle lets out a big snore.

"Are you going to make me use your name again?"

She scrunches up her face and throws another napkin at me. "My OCD for questions isn't foolproof. I can *not* tell you."

"Still waiting."

"Fine! I saw you play in college, had an instant crush, went and tried to get a similar tattoo, then met you years later and couldn't get the nerve up to tell you that I not only held my breath the night you got drafted and watched most of your games in the NFL—even when you played for Jacksonville—who I can't stand! Then you got traded to Nashville, Elena started seeing Jack, and there you were at the community center, in the flesh, and I couldn't even think of what to say, so I pretended like I wasn't a fan. Happy?"

"Fucking delirious," I murmur.

She laughs. "Really?"

"It's a layer to you I had no clue about. Smart girl who digs football, and I'm your favorite player. What else could a guy ask for?"

"Cookies?"

I laugh.

We're close, our shoulders touching as we hover over the island and look out into the den. I'm watching Giselle, drinking in her delicate face, the way her shirt clings to her chest—and she's looking at Myrtle. She leans into me and whispers, "Besides all that, you are very handsome. Eyes like a rain forest. Hot bod. Athletic grace. A black panther. Also, you might be the inspiration for a hero in my book—"

"Vureck?"

"You remember?"

I smirk, following her eyes to the lady on the recliner. "I see what's going on. You're buttering me up. Myrtle has no place to go, does she?"

She plops onto the stool and cups her chin. "Her place won't be ready until tomorrow morning." She gives me a look. "You mad now?"

I pick up a bright-green apple she bought and throw it in the air. No one's ever set fresh fruit in my kitchen before. "We only have two beds."

She nods. "She can take my room, and I'll sleep on the couch. You'll never know she's here."

"No, I'll take the couch."

She gapes. "You've done too much already! I will not take your bed. I insist on the couch."

Visions of her in my bed *with me* dance around me—until I push them away. "All right."

A small frown puckers her forehead. "I've moved in with a nervous dog who pees in your expensive shoes, invited a guest, let her smoke pot, and inadvertently nearly caused you to break a leg. You're living with a curse-ridden maniac."

I grin, and before I can stop myself, I kiss her temple (friends do that) and slide away. "Anything to keep you from being *blue*."

She gives me side-eye.

I laugh and head to my bedroom to change. "You really *blew* my mind when I saw you, Smurfette."

"Hey, you said you'd help me make cookies," she calls, and I dash back in the kitchen, grab the package of cookie dough from the freezer, turn the oven on with a flourish, then smirk at her. All without slipping. "We have any ice cream for the cookies? Blue Bell brand is my favorite."

A soft sigh comes from her, and before I can stop, again, I'm back and right in front of her.

She picks up a strand of blue and glares. "The new hair was supposed to be part of how Giselle gets her groove back, but—"

Nope, can't have that, and I do what I've wanted to since she walked in and I saw her anxious face. I wrap her up in a hug and swing her around until she squeals and yells at me to put her down, flailing her arms.

Laughing, I leave her there and head to my room, humming "California Gurls" as another napkin sails over my shoulder.

I'm grinning like a loon. I've got this friend thing down.

I'm lying to myself, but for some reason, I can't bring myself to care.

Chapter 12

Giselle

"You missed a cohort check-in this morning, Ms. Riley," drawls Dr. Blanton as he sits behind his desk in his office the next day. He frowns at my hair, a curl of distaste on his lips. "We discussed the upcoming fall schedule and bounced ideas for thesis papers."

I take a seat, even though he hasn't offered one. "It's Saturday. I must have missed the email. Thank you for letting me stop by instead."

"You could have joined us online. Most of your cohorts did just that."

"I'm sorry." I'm really not. Frankly, it's inconsiderate of him to expect us to be available for an online meeting in the summer—on the weekend.

He glowers at me.

I frown. "Dr. Blanton, look, my apartment burned down this week, and I've been helping a friend, and things are a bit scattered." I cross my legs, regretting that I still haven't had time to pick up real clothes and wore skinny jeans and one of Devon's shirts tied in a knot. There hasn't been time to upgrade my wardrobe to nice slacks and silk blouses.

Earlier this morning, while Devon went to the stadium, John and I moved Myrtle into a somewhat furnished lower-level apartment near our old place. After that, we got the call that we were cleared to go inside the burned building, as long as we avoided the basement. I raced upstairs and found my pearls under the coffee table, then left my apartment to help clean out hers, planning on going back later this week to retrieve other items of mine. All my clothes reek of smoke, but I'm praying a dry cleaner can remedy that.

Myrtle's place was less fortunate than mine—nothing burned, but she was upset at the wreckage on the first floor. She found her journals, books, and special mementos, and we left for her new place. She cried some and cursed a lot, muttering about insurance and renovations.

But for now, things are shaping up. I have a place to stay, Myrtle is situated, and John's new place is in the same building as Myrtle's, and he's offered to check on her every day. *It won't be a hardship,* he told me with a glint in his eyes. Now, it's time to deal with my professional life. Hence, the visit with Dr. Blanton.

The room swells with silence, and I shift around in my seat, touching my hair, then dropping my hands. I clench my fist.

"I'd like to have a new advisor," I announce, straightening my spine and meeting his gaze.

He grinds his jaw. I'm sure it's a cut to his ego. He is the head of the physics department; that's why I chose him. "I agree. You're not the caliber of student I usually mentor, your grades are mediocre, your attitude is shockingly lax with underclassmen, and your appearance is less than desired. I will put in a request immediately and see who's available to take you on. I'm not sure anyone will."

And . . . I stand up. Dick. "No, you will not put in a request. I will find my own advisor so I can make sure we have the same goals and outlook for my future."

I snatch my computer bag up and head to the door, but his voice stops me.

"Ms. Riley, the only assignment you had this summer besides teaching was to write a paper. It was due yesterday. You never sent it."

I turn and face him.

"I sent it Thursday." Right as Devon was going out the door, I pushed send, giddy by the topic of researching dark matter with the Large Hadron Collider.

He slaps down a thick set of papers. "No, you sent me *Sexy Alien Warrior and His Captive Earth Girl.*"

The world spins and my mouth dries as I dart my eyes from my manuscript, then back to his tight face. My hands clutch the back of the chair, and I inhale a deep breath. "Now that I hear it out loud, the title is a bit too on the nose."

He flushes. "Ms. Riley! You are not a serious student! You've spent your summer writing science fiction, not science fact. This"—he picks up the papers and tosses them in the trash—"is utter nonsense."

"Obviously you didn't read the chapter about Vureck repairing his laser beam using *my* fundamental knowledge of quantum theory, Dr. Blanton, so I beg to differ. My book isn't just fiction. It's written for people who appreciate science facts with their romance."

"Ah!" He points down at the trash. "Romance? That's what you call this drivel? It's the most ridiculous application of a student's bright mind that I've encountered. You're blowing your chance at a doctorate with this hogwash. Do you think your work will ever see the light of day in a serious publishing house?" he huffs.

"How do you know?"

He crosses his arms. "I can read, Ms. Riley. I thought your story was your paper. I read the first page and thumbed through the rest. Well, after that, it all made sense—your lack of motivation, your increasing distractedness, your horrible attitude. You don't have the focus it takes to be part of this esteemed program."

My heart drops at his criticism, part of me agreeing with him about my lack of motivation, the other part thinking back to all the diaries and journals of my childhood, dreams I wrote and drew squiggly hearts around, then to the more developed notebooks of my teens, where I first combined my love for Einstein with my thirst for books. My writing kept me sane through high school and my undergrad, little scenarios and science-type meet-cutes that made me giggle, and now, *now*, he wants to throw it all back in my face and say it's pointless? My story kept me from being lonely. My story encouraged me to get up every day and try again to be a better person, to take another stab at this degree I'm starting to think I'll never get.

I take another step and put my hands on his desk as I face him.

"You may be a physicist, but you are not my reader. My story is empowering for women—or men! It's a journey of one woman who starts out scared and afraid but learns to pilot her own ship and earns the love of a tough man. She realizes she deserves love and respect and happiness. And she's more intelligent than you are, but I digress. It's inspiring. It gives hope and healing with a side of entertainment, something you know nothing about." I rack my brain, looking for something to get through the holier-than-thou smirk he's wearing. "You can't put me in a box and give me a label and say what I write isn't important. Writers *and* readers come from all ethnicities, religions, genders, sexualities, languages, backgrounds, and, most of all, different fields of study. If I want to write a book, you can guarantee the science side of me is leading the way, because that's the part of me that needs fiction; it craves to mix the two and produce something wonderful. You don't get it, and it's your opinion. You lead with your head. I don't. But I refuse to let you belittle me for what I write." I dip down, jerk out the papers, and clutch them to me.

My chest rises as I grapple for control. I suck in air. "I wrote your paper. I accidentally sent you the wrong document. I will send the correct one immediately, sir."

He gapes at me, and I dash for the door.

Better to leave before he can tell me he's calling me before the committee and throwing me out on my ear.

I'd fight the chauvinistic jerk all the way.

I run down the hall and take the stairwell, my brain racing, hands shaking with adrenaline. I've never stood up for myself like that, and Jesus, it felt good. I fling open the door and jog out of the building and into the sunshine.

Half an hour later, I realize I've walked past the parking lot where Red is and ended up in a shopping center. I walk into one of the boutiques.

Shoving thoughts of Dr. Blanton and everything else to the side, I browse the aisles, and when the salesgirl asks me what I'm looking for, I almost say a tweed blazer and slacks but shut my mouth and ask her what she thinks might go with my hair. She grins, grabs clothes "to contrast," and tosses them at me as I hang out in the dressing room. She's young, hip, and full of commentary about my hair. "It's not that bad," she assures me and points me in the direction of a salon across the street.

With my savings account missing several hundred dollars, I walk out and head to the salon. Walking in, I realize it's no Cut 'N' Curl but is hard-core ritzy. I don't know if I'm staying or going when a young stylist walks up and asks if I need anything, and when she says she's just had a cancellation, it feels like fate.

She plops me down before a mirror, and I take in my streaky-blue hair. I laugh for a good minute while she gives me a bemused look. My hair really is horrid.

A person can't change the core of who they are. There's no sparkling personality underneath my quiet nature or sexy bombshell lurking inside my lanky frame. My identity isn't most boring, smart girl, or virgin. I'm just me, and I like me, dammit, even if I did lose myself there for a while after the Preston fiasco.

Myrtle's words haunt me . . .

Do what makes your heart fly. Every breath you inhale must be meaningful.

I'm done wondering what Dr. Blanton and my cohorts think, done trying to fit myself into other people's molds of what I should look like or be. I want my doctorate—that fact will never change—but writing is ingrained in my soul.

The stylist gives me a look. "Well, what do you want to do?"

I have a brief twinge of regret that Aunt Clara isn't here to do it herself, but she'll understand. Things are moving fast. It feels like something might just slip away from me before I can grasp it and hang on. Urgency rides me, making me tense, as I run through what I want, what I've really wanted for five long months. Devon's carnal mouth, his way of looking at me when he's pretending he isn't.

I want him, but in that direction lies peril and friendship ruined, and I sigh, refocusing. One thing at a time. First, let's fix this hair.

Chapter 13

Devon

I walk into the Razor and study the series of texts Giselle sent me an hour ago. I didn't see them until I came out of my last meeting; then I took off for the penthouse and showered. After rushing around to get dressed, I got here as fast as I could.

I am in need of your services was the first one, then a series of others when I hadn't replied.

I hate to even ask.

I really do.

Are you ignoring me after making you watch that movie?

I laughed out loud at that one (until I read the rest) because we did have a good time last night. After we ate cookies, Giselle put on an angsty, absolutely horrible French film with subtitles, where the main character cried every five minutes. In between cringes, I threw popcorn at Giselle. She threw back. Movie forgotten, we had a popcorn war in my den, and Myrtle was on my side—until our bowl ran out, and

Myrtle declared us crazy and went to bed. Afterward, I put on *Shark Week* to up my street cred (see, they don't scare me), and Giselle was instantly fascinated. She likes scary stuff. We sat on the couch for an hour and talked about the anatomy of a shark (mostly cartilage). She described how their skin is actually covered in millions of tiny teeth called dermal denticles that point backward and reduce surface drag, increasing a shark's speed. As the shark grows, it sheds the denticles and grows larger ones. Disgusting—but I like listening to her. She's the smartest person I know. Later, I helped her put sheets on the couch and got her a pillow. Then I went to bed. Like I should. I've got this!

I bet you're practicing and you aren't seeing these.

Topher has jumped the gun (he thinks I need cheering up for some reason?) and set me up with someone and he's meeting me at the Razor. NOT AN ONLINE GUY, so relax, but a real boy. Like Pinocchio! Anyway, could use your insight on scoring a homerun on this date. If want to text me some pointers, I'm ready.

I need to see this guy.

Random factoid: there's a meteor shower tonight, big rocks entering our atmosphere at 110, 000 miles an hour.

"Genie in a Bottle" reverberates through the dark club as I stalk in, say a quick word to the guy at the front, and weave through the Saturday-night crowd. It's not late, around eight, but the place is filling up. I fire off a text to Giselle: I'm here. Where are you?

When I don't get a response right away, I head to the bar, seeing Selena.

She catches my eye, grins, wraps up her conversation, heads my way, and runs down the recent issues with the air-conditioning and her new hires. My eyes scan the place for Giselle—at the bar, at the tables. For the first time, I wish the place was brighter.

She gets me a beer, and I take a swig, then check my phone.

"You heard from Garrett yet?" she asks, leaning in over the bar.

I grimace. "No. Hey, have any strange guys been in here looking for me?"

She purses her lips and shakes her head.

"If anyone comes in, call me."

"Your friend looks different," Selena muses, and my head snaps up from checking my phone again, like it might have changed in the past minute, following her finger as she points to the dance floor.

I see her seemingly lost in the peppy beat, head thrown back, glasses gone. I guess she grabbed her contacts at her apartment today. Her hair is different, the blue a lighter hue and evenly colored, the silky strands swaying as she holds her arms up over her head and shakes her ass.

Giselle stumbles into a couple, bounces off, and keeps going, her feet not in sync with whatever her hands are doing.

"She really can't dance," Selena deadpans.

"Don't think she cares," I say on a grin.

"Is she chasing dolphins?"

I take a swig of beer. "Nah, she's doing Uma Thurman from *Pulp Fiction*." Which pleases me more than it should. I love that movie. I make a mental note to see if she wants to do a rewatch with me.

Where is her date?

I run my eyes over everyone on the floor close to her, but it's either groups or couples, and she's by herself.

She wiggles her ass, and a guy appears behind her. He's moving with the music, getting closer to her, and she looks up, takes him in, then moves to the other side of the dance floor.

I laugh, sobering as she moves closer, and I take in what she's wearing: a tight cream pencil skirt with a sleeveless baby-blue blouse, the top buttons undone enough to show the flush and sweat on her skin. Her pearls rest in the hollow of her throat—and my dick gets hard.

"New clothes," I murmur under my breath, and for half a second it makes me sad, knowing she won't be in mine.

It happens again—another guy, this one more determined when he puts his hand on her hip. She removes it, gives him a glare, and stalks off to another spot.

"It's always the quiet ones. They'll surprise you," comes a deep voice as Aiden slides in next to me. He stares at Giselle.

"Aiden," I say, nodding and lifting my beer. "Good to see you." I mean it. We've been avoiding each other these past few days, but we need to get past it.

He grunts and orders a drink from Selena and swings his gaze back on me, his usual happy face flat.

"She dances like she's high," he muses.

"Don't ruin her fun."

His shoulders slump. "Dude, she never called me, I don't have her digits, and you're pissed at me."

I scrub my face. "I overreacted."

He exhales. "You blew up, man, over something I don't really get . . . unless you've got something going on for Giselle and you aren't telling me." He narrows his gaze. "Is that it?"

I stiffen. "Do I care about her? Yes. Do I want you talking smack about her in my face? No. Nor do I want you dating her. She is not one of your flings." My voice is firm and even, and I'm not going to lose my temper, not this time. I don't even touch on the Jack issue, because he knows how well that would go over. Those two are friends and enemies.

Aiden sets his beer on the bar and stands up from the stool. "There's another guy zeroing in on her. I'm going to help—"

Before he can finish, I'm up and gone, brushing past him, bumping his shoulder as I make my way to Giselle.

I hear him laughing behind me.

Her eyes open when my hands settle on her hips, a retort obviously on her lips until she sees it's me; then she throws her arms around my shoulders for a hug.

"Thank God! You didn't have to come, but I'm glad you did. Topher sprung this on me at the last minute," she says. I guess she hasn't checked her phone since she started dancing.

"Where's your date?" I say, huskier than I intended, staring down at her. I pull her closer as the music ebbs into a slower song. We fit together, her height perfect against my body. Her arms slide around my neck, and the air in the club feels thick, my lungs tight as her pelvis brushes against mine.

She nudges her head to the rear upper left of the club, an area lined with cozy leather booths. "Back there. He didn't want to dance, and I'm in a dancing mood. I told my advisor off." She smiles. "My date is kind of perfect. He said my hair is the color of a summer sky."

My hands tighten around her hips. "Let's meet him, then."

She gets a determined look on her face. "Right. You be the wing-man, talk me up, catalog everything, kick me if I say anything atrocious."

"Let's go take a look at him," I grind out, anger pulsing at this guy she thinks is *perfect*. I'm not being rational, and I'm aware, but I'm edging toward a steep cliff, step by step, as if pulled by an invisible force. *Just don't fall.*

She whips around, her ass swaying, stilettos on her feet, legs damn near making me groan as I follow her to the back.

We arrive at the steps to the mezzanine level, the wall lined with red banquettes and cozy sitting arrangements. "Greg, this is my roommate, Devon Walsh." She runs through the introductions as she slides in right next to him, and I take the seat across from him. She's telling him how we know each other, but I'm barely listening, sizing him up. She didn't have to tell me he's her type; it's obvious with the boyish good looks, the clean-cut haircut, studious glasses, and suit. Smart, business type, upper middle class—and his eyes are glued to her, following a trail of sweat that's slowly sliding down her throat to her blouse.

"Slide over," Aiden says to me, and I wrench my eyes off them.

"Aiden!" Giselle calls, her lips curving. "Meet my date, Greg Zimmerman." She quickly introduces them, and normally a guy would be into meeting two players for the Tigers, but he barely cares—because his hand has moved to the back of the booth, and his fingers are toying with her hair.

I bet he graduated from a fancy school, drives a luxury sedan, and has a regular nine-to-five job. Probably doesn't have an alcoholic parent with a penchant for gambling.

"What the hell," Aiden murmurs quietly to me as we watch them chat, and Giselle laughs at something he's said. "Who's the asshole moving in on my girl?"

My knee knocks against his. "She likes him, so be nice."

Feeling Aiden's glare on me, I flick my eyes at him. "What?"

"All you had to do was tell me the truth," he says under his breath. "There's a bro code for this, and even an asshole like me knows when to back off."

"He's the kind of guy she wants to be with," I hiss.

"Is Aiden your roommate too?" Greg asks Giselle, an eyebrow raised as he takes me and Aiden in.

Aiden starts in surprise, then smirks as he gives me a look that says, *When were you going to tell me that?*

Taking his eyes off me, he says to Greg, "No. Just friends."

"What do you do, Greg?" I ask abruptly, interrupting their conversation, studying him. His hand has slid around lower to cup her shoulder.

"Weatherman for Channel 5 News," he says, then proceeds to give us the forecast for the next two days. "With the cumulous clouds in the sky, we're in for more clear weather. Those are the puffy clouds, the ones that look like cotton candy."

"Fascinating," I say, infusing my words with enthusiasm. "Tell me more."

He leans in, his arm moving away from Giselle's shoulder. "Well, their name derives from the Latin *cumulo*, meaning heap or pile. They appear in lines, clusters, or on their own, the type you see in the summer."

"Indeed," I say, propping my elbows on the table, feigning a new love for weather.

Greg keeps going, his eyes lighting up. "However, cumulus clouds are influenced by weather instability, air pressure, and temperature. Cumulus clouds form via atmospheric convection as air warmed by the surface begins to rise. As the air rises, the temperature drops . . ." He goes into an honest-to-God five-minute TED Talk, and I keep interest plastered on my face. I can't stop the glee when Giselle's eyes glaze over.

"Of course, most people don't study clouds. I realize it can be quite boring." He darts his eyes at Aiden, who's checking out a girl that's swaying past our table.

"Never," I say as Giselle takes a sip of her water, her gaze on me, thinning.

Giselle says, "Maybe we should talk about something—"

Greg cuts her off. "Weather is important. As a scientist, I'm sure you appreciate that."

A frown wrinkles her forehead. "Science is wonderful." Her shoulders rise and fall in a soft sigh, one so tiny I don't think Greg sees it. He can't read her like I can. He can't see behind the cool facade to the girl with all the layers. "Sometimes I just want to have fun."

Greg thinks for a moment, a silent debate going on in his head, then smiles at her, his gaze softening. "My fun is painting clouds in watercolor. I have a few pieces in my loft." He takes a sip of whiskey.

"Maybe we can drop by there later, and I can show you?" His *later* is husky, and my hands are under the table, clenching.

"Mom would love to meet you" comes from him.

"You live with your mother?" I ask. My comment comes out a bit derisive, and he reacts by frowning.

"She's elderly and needs care. It's a very large apartment," he says to Giselle. "You'd love her."

Shit, she loves older people.

"Did she tell you she's writing a romance?" I blurt.

Greg's eyebrows go sky high. "Ah, no."

"Aliens," I say as I take a sip of my water. "Purple with sparkly scales and prehensile tails."

"I took the tail off!" she calls.

"Oh?" He blinks down at Giselle, who's currently giving me a flat look.

Focusing on him, I try to decipher if he's into it or thinks it's not worthy of a scientist, but dammit, he's not giving me any tells.

"Do you think that's silly?" she asks him.

I don't, babe, is on the tip of my tongue. *Tell me more about them. Tell me everything. Put me back on your Pinterest board.* (Yeah, I had to look up what that was.) *You be the woman who can rock whatever she wants because she's fascinating and intelligent and sexy as fuck.*

Greg leans in closer to her, his eyes heavy lidded. "I'm guessing you used real science to explain the details?"

"Of course," she says.

He bites his lip. "Damn. That's hot—"

"All right!" I announce and shove at Aiden to get up. Standing, I roll my shoulders and try to shake off the antsy feeling crawling all over me. "Let's hit the VIP room," I tell them, waving my hands in that direction. "More privacy and free food and drinks," I tell Giselle when she gives me a weird look. "Hard to talk over the music out here." It's actually not loud in the mezzanine. But who cares.

"I could eat," Greg says as he drains his glass.

Giselle nods, and they take off ahead of us down the stairs.

Aiden's shoulder bumps me. "What's the plan? How are we going to get this dude away from Giselle?" He bristles. "He paints clouds, for fuck's sake."

Is he boring? To me, yes, but . . .

Is he to her?

Regardless of the tangents on weather and living with his mom, she digs him, my head tells me as my chest tightens.

I motion to the bouncer to let Giselle and Greg in the area roped off by velvet to the right of the bar that leads to the VIP rooms as I hang back with Aiden.

"No plan," I growl.

Aiden gets a mulish look on his face. "All right, I see; you're leaving it up to me. Fine. I'll handle this."

"I hope your plan doesn't involve hitting on Giselle. Those days are done."

He shakes his head, a disappointed expression on his face as he takes me in. "We've established you've got it bad for her—whatever. I will let you have her, because you had dibs or bro code, whatever, but I'm going to cock up that date, and you can't stop me."

Before I say anything, he grins, backs up, and dances across the dance floor right in the middle of a group of women, who squeal and put their hands on his chest. He looks at me and calls out, "You want Giselle, and I can make it happen. She's yours." He's wearing his "I got this" expression, the one he gets when he's surveyed the defensive line and has a plan to score.

She's not mine, my eyes tell him, but my heart isn't in it.

That cliff looms, and with a few more tugs, I'll be falling over . . .

Chapter 14

DEVON

Aiden's version of *I got this* is clear an hour later. I came in with them earlier, got them a table with a view of the floor, and made sure they had a server for drinks. I told the waitstaff to cater to whatever they wanted, and they ordered several appetizers from the kitchen. I sat with them for as long as I could (about half an hour), but when Greg put his hand on Giselle's knee, I jerked up and went to check in with Selena.

Now, Greg is leaning against the wall with three jersey chasers around him: a blonde, a redhead, and the petite brunette from the dance floor.

Greg drains yet another whiskey as he shows the girls a video of him doing the morning weather, a bemused smile on his flushed face. The blonde has taken off his jacket, the redhead is currently loosening his tie, and the brunette is batting her eyes.

Giselle is dancing on the small raised dance floor in the middle of the room. Alone. I scan for Aiden and find him in the back, utter delight on his face. Several other players sit at a table close to the dais, and I watch as Hollis sets down his drink, eyeing Giselle, then gets up and dances over to her. Dammit. Jack's warning means nothing when a beautiful girl is in VIP.

Aiden gives me a grin, and I want to punch him. How can I be gone for thirty minutes and another of my teammates has zeroed in on her?

I can't leave her alone, ever.

I've moved before I'm aware of it, jostling him out of the way. "My dance," I tell him under my breath, and he steps back, hands up in the air.

After grabbing Giselle's hand, I twirl her around and pull her into my chest. She feels fragile when I gaze down at her, smoothing hair out of her face, trying to get a read on her.

"I went to dance, and the girls swarmed in on him," she tells me, her eyes shiny. "One minute he was telling me about precipitation in the Sahara—not much—and the next . . ." Her eyes dart over to Greg.

She has no clue she's the most beautiful woman in the room, and it's on the tip of my tongue to tell her, when another giggle sounds from their side of the room as one of the girls leans into Greg and gives him a kiss on the cheek.

I'm going to kill Aiden.

"Are you upset?"

Her nose presses into my neck as she inhales, and I lose my train of thought.

"Giselle? Talk to me."

She says nothing, resting her head on my chest, and I exhale, tightening my arms.

"Look, I'm angry for you. I'll beat the shit out of him," I say.

"Cumulous clouds are the mother of all other clouds . . . ," comes Greg's excited voice.

Her shoulders shudder, and my anger notches up, but I hold it in, tracing my fingers down her spine to rest on the waistband of her skirt, idly brushing at the place where her blouse is tucked in. "Baby, talk to me. How can I make it better?" My hands rub down her back, lingering at the top of her ass before starting at her shoulders again. Her hair brushes against my jaw, and she smells like vanilla, sweet and thick and heady. God. So fucking good.

Her body shivers, and I think she sniffs.

"Baby, don't cry, please . . ." I try to ease away and tip her face up, and she grudgingly lets me. "You aren't crying," I accuse as we stop moving, and I see the glint in her eyes.

She laughs, stuffing her face in my shirt again. "Oh God, no. He's so awful. I tried, I did, but if he talked about clouds one more time, I was going to stick a fork in his face."

A grin tugs at my lips. "You don't want to go meet his mom?"

She guffaws. "My own is enough."

"Ego bruised?"

"It's worth you dancing with me," she says with a smile and tangles her hands in my hair as we start dancing again, and I have no clue if it's a fast song or slow, but I don't want her out of my arms.

"Did you eat at least?" I ask a few beats later.

She smiles. "Should have just stayed home and ordered from Milano's."

"Nah, it's your birthday eve."

"I'd rather sit on your couch and watch *Shark Week*."

"Bloodthirsty beast."

"You like it."

"I love it."

She laughs, and I laugh with her. Watching her, the curl on her red lips, the way her eyes linger on me, holding my gaze . . . a sense of urgency flies at me, digging deep and taking up space in my chest. I want to be alone with her—just her, just me . . .

"Come on; let's get out of here." Clasping our hands together, I head to the exit, and she follows me.

Before we get there, I look over my shoulder to see if Greg is going to protest, but he's got his lips on the blonde. My fists curl, which is ridiculous, since she wasn't really into him, but he's a giant douche.

She seems to know where my head is, because she tugs me out. "Let it go, caveman."

◆ ◆ ◆

A while later we're deep into *Shark Week* as we sit on the couch in the dark, eating more cookies Giselle insisted she make.

She hands me another one, fresh from the oven, then wipes at my mouth as I chew.

"What?" I say, swallowing my bite.

"Chocolate," she murmurs. Her hair is up in a messy bun, glasses back on, her clothes changed out for her shorts and one of my old shirts. I whipped off my jeans and settled on gym shorts and a workout shirt.

She scoots closer and wipes at my lips again. "Stubborn spot."

"It's fine," I breathe, freezing.

"No, let me get it." She leans in and licks the corner of my mouth. A satisfied purr comes from her. "Yummy."

I snatch the nape of her neck before she can pull away. "Did you seriously just lick me?"

She pauses, giving me a sheepish look. "I was . . . hungry?"

My chest rises. What am I doing? I should just go to bed. Now.

She stands up. "I'm going to bed."

I grab her waist and pull her back down on the couch. "Oh, no you don't. We're watching TV." Obviously I have two personalities.

Her head leans on my shoulder as she settles back onto the couch. "I warn you, I may fall asleep. It's been a tough week."

"I'm sorry about your professor." She'd told me the details of her meeting with Dr. Blanton.

"He just made me more determined. I want my PhD, I want to write, and someday I will go to CERN."

"How far away is Geneva?"

"Eleven hours and twenty-two minutes on a plane, roughly four thousand five hundred and ninety-eight miles."

Too damn far.

"Stop! Go back!" she calls, her hands taking the remote out of my hands.

"What was it?" I say, expecting something horror related, but my face freezes when I see what show she's landed on, her gaze intense as she leans forward.

"French film. It's called *My Night in Paris*. Basically, the movie takes place during one night when the hero meets the heroine in a coffee shop, lures her back to his hotel, and fulfills her sexual fantasies. Here comes the part where he goes down on her. Best ever," she says—with a serious face.

I inhale sharply at the images of a dark bedroom and the couple on the bed. "So it's porn."

She smacks me on the knee. "It's art. The cinematography is beautiful and gripping—the shots of their faces and eyes, ah, so perfect. Notice how everything is in deep blues and gray, from the hotel room to the bedding. There's no corny music and no random pizza-delivery guy showing up to join in. Just her and him."

"How many times have you watched this?"

"Enough to almost speak French, *bébé*."

Realization dawns. "You want to see this—with me?"

"Why not? It's an excellent depiction of using sexuality to explore ourselves."

"Porn."

"No, I'm serious. There's nothing wrong with the sex here."

"Never said there was," I huff out. "Sex is great."

She nods. "It's who we are, no matter your gender or preference. Birds do it. Bees. Even eukaryotes. It's part of the universe. Essential. Everything is a push and pull—gravity, if you will—how we are drawn to certain people and not others. And when you get that zing with it . . . it must be amazing. They have zing."

She takes a breath, watching as the dark-haired man takes off the woman's blindfold and eases on top of her, sliding between the V of her legs. "There's beauty in this film, especially in how he gazes at her, the angle of that shot, like he's going to die if he can't have her—look at how he clenches his fists next to her head because it feels so good, and making her *his* is everything to him, and . . . and I . . . want that . . ." She reddens, her voice stopping abruptly. "Do you get it?"

Oh, I get it. And it's killing me. I adjust myself in my shorts as slyly as I can, which isn't hard since she's glued to the screen. "It's about the emotion, you mean, the depth of their connection, the yearning, the 'I have to have you right now, or I'm going to die.'" It's what I don't have when it comes to my own physical encounters.

"Yes."

The woman on the movie orgasms—I guess; I don't know, because I'm not looking at the screen, just staring at Giselle. My heart is hammering in my chest, and I feel light headed. "All right, I want to watch it with you."

Mistake.

Two minutes later—yeah, I have no control—I can't breathe, and I'm barely watching, my eyes flipping between the movie and Giselle's flushed face. The room is oppressive, the den a fucking furnace.

Her hand lands on my leg and curls around my thigh. "Watch this part. He's going to flip her over on her stomach . . ." Her voice trails off, her grip tightening as the woman moans as the guy slides all the way inside her.

Giselle's lashes flutter, her mouth parting, gasps coming as she watches them. My hands fist. I could put that expression on her face, make her come so many times she'd *pfft* at a French film. I could fuck her—and then what? Would I just be a way to get her V-card out of the way, like this Mike guy who's going to her birthday lunch? Annoyance flares. I don't want to be the one she uses, then leaves—for another country.

My chest twinges. Shit, honestly, she has some kind of weird power over me. Every time she moves, I'm following. When she smiles, I smile back. Every time she looks at me, I'm gazing right back. It's terrifying, and I don't like it. Makes me want to breathe into a paper bag. The last time I cared about a girl, my heart was decimated.

I jerk up off the couch, causing Giselle to fall back.

"Early morning for me! Good night!" I call as I stumble through the den, cursing when in my haste I slam my knee into the recliner footrest.

"You okay?"

I throw a hand up over my back. "Right as rain. Need to sleep." And a cold shower.

I'm breathing hard, leaning back against the door, when the knock comes.

"What?" I say through the wood.

"Did I . . . did I . . . we shouldn't have watched that. It's my fault."

"No," I say as I turn to face the door, feeling like an idiot as I talk to it. "It was really good . . . cinematography. Their faces . . . the sheets and pillows and stuff."

She pauses. "Thank you for rescuing me from the weatherman."

I open the door and stare at her. Her blue eyes are wide and starry. "Yeah, whatever."

She's so . . .

Dangerous.

"Good night," she says with a soft smile and walks back into the den, where I hear another orgasm.

"Night," I mutter and shut the door.

Chapter 15

GISELLE

Later, I head to my bedroom and pile up in my bed, headphones on, laptop open on my bare legs. I showered and changed into a blue lace camisole and a pair of booty shorts, fluffed up my pillows, and got to work. My story burns to be written. You'd think after finishing my movie, I'd be inspired for some off-the-charts sex scenes, but I'm deep into Kate sneaking like a ninja into the prison where Vureck is being held to rescue him after their ship was attacked. My story isn't just a love story between total opposites; it's the story of Kate figuring out her true self, a girl who's powerful in her own right, who is now the one to save him. Her dream of going back to Earth has faded; all that matters is getting back her man—er, alien.

My fingers tap away at about ninety words per minute, *Guardians of the Galaxy* soundtrack reverberating in my ears.

My ankle itches, and I give it an absent flick with my foot, tossing the covers off, still typing.

Kate uses her thin blade that Vureck gave her as a present to pick the lock to his cage. One of the lizard men wakes up from the sedative she put in his food and pounces on her—just as a tickle brushes against my leg, and I shake it off. The sensation prickles again, against my thigh, and I huff, look down, and . . . scream. Headphones are ripped off, and my laptop crashes to the floor as my hands fling around at what surely must be a million spiders in my bed. A brown eight-legged body jumps off the sheet and dives deep inside the covers.

Devon jerks the door open, hair soaked, body wet, a white towel knotted around his waist. My mouth opens, the scary arachnid of death forgotten. His chest—oh Lord, I've never seen his naked chest—is a work of art, the skin a light-tan color, sleek and muscled, his pectorals sharply defined, the oblique abdominals creating a distinct roll of muscles that tapers to the V at his hip bone. My eyes bulge. I've never seen a real six-pack on a guy, except online and in movies. A bead of water tracks down his throat, skating down the center of his chest, past the sparse hair, and right into more hair, at the top of his towel. Elena calls that a goody trail, and I agree. There's goodness in every part of him. He isn't beefy like some football players. He's a runner, all hard muscle and power, honed to outlast, outdistance, outperform—

"Giselle! What's wrong?"

I sputter. "You look . . ." Like a dream. "Wet." I swallow.

He marches in—one hand on the terrible, terrible towel—and paces around the room. I check out his ass and back—oh wow, back muscles for days, and if I was thinking clearly, I could name every single one. Think clearly! His lats under his arm are toned and tight, the rhomboids of his upper back tense and ready to fight.

A furry thing jumps on my foot, and I scream again, hands waving in front of my face. The bed bounces as I hop down to the floor—what took me so long?—landing with a thud, wincing at the ankle that still isn't right. My voice is breathless, and I'm not sure it has to do with the spider tormenting me or the fact that seeing Devon naked is a very bad thing for my vow to keep us just friends.

Devon shakes his head at me, his lips twitching.

"What?" I grouse.

"It's a tiny spider," he replies, eyebrow arched.

I cross my arms. "The giant spider has been crawling on me for several minutes! It jumped at me! You saw how fast it moved. Zero to sixty in a heartbeat. And now it's in my bed, and you have to find it and kill it. Meanwhile, I will be sleeping on the couch, because there's no way I'm getting back in that bed with a monster loose . . ." I stop, glaring at him as he chuckles. He shakes his head, his chest rumbling with laughter.

"Didn't know you'd go berserk . . . over a tiny, *tiny* . . ." He wipes at his eyes. "Giselle, baby, you're killing me."

After snatching a pillow off the bed, I double-check it for spiders (clear) and clutch it to my chest. "I saw hair on its legs!"

He throws his head back for more laughing, and I smack him with the pillow.

He isn't fazed, cackling more, so I whack him again. He holds his hand out to tell me to stop but moves fast, grabbing the other pillow. He hits me on my torso.

"Did you even check it for spiders?"

"No, and I bet the little guy is right on top." His eyes flare as he looks at my chest. "Giselle, don't move."

There's been a spider crawling on me, and he tells me *not to move.* The man needs to rethink who I am. I scream and brush at my chest frantically, heart pounding. Not seeing anything, I look back up, and he's grinning. "Psych."

My hands fist. "Oh, you . . . you . . ." I jump at him, shoving him with my pillow, and he falls down on my bed. I expect him to get up, but he just lies there, the rumble of his laughter making my lips curve. I like seeing him like this, relaxed and easy and so beautiful. His dark hair is slicked back, his eyebrow piercing glinting under the lights, the butterflies and roses on his arms—then a brown monster appears and sits on one of the blooms, right below his right shoulder.

Keeping my voice calm and even—*oh my God, you have a creature of death on you!*—I lean over and stare him straight in the eyes. "Devon. Listen to me. The *tiny* spider is on your right arm."

On your biceps I'd like to lick when the monster is gone.

"It's as big as a quarter, with multiple eyeballs—eight to be precise, arranged in three rows—and sharp fangs. I think it's a wolf spider. Agile hunters with poisonous bites when provoked, which we have done. Those bites hurt and sometimes require hospitalization. I know of a case where a healthy grown man nearly lost his foot from a bite."

He freezes, searching my face. "No joke?"

"Dead serious."

His face loses its mirth. "You're messing with me."

I shake my head slowly as I lean over him. "You know I don't lie."

His chest twitches, as if he's going to move, and I hold my hand up for him to stop.

"Not so funny when it's on you, is it?" I smirk.

He glares at me. "Kill it."

I rear back. "I like you at my mercy. In your towel. What if the little fellow hops on your towel or under it? Now that would be interesting." I let out a dark chuckle.

His throat moves. "Giselle, come on, baby doll, beautiful girl, *kill the motherfucking spider.*"

"I can't! I wanted you to do the dirty work. I don't want near it." I pause. "Plus, it didn't bite me, and she's just trying to live, and she probably has babies—"

He groans, his eyes darting to his side, but from the angle he's at, he can't see. "Oh, so now it's 'save the spiders' in here. Five minutes ago, you wanted me to crush her—how do you know it's a female?"

I take a step closer to him, sliding closer as I bend over him. "Because she's carrying her babies."

"Are you telling me there's, um, like *lots* of spiders on me?"

"Hmm." I grab my phone from the nightstand.

"This isn't the time to check your Insta," he growls, glaring at me.

169

I snap a pic of him sprawled out on my bed. That's for later. I peek at him from behind my cell. "Since you can't move, do you mind if I move the towel a little, just to see—"

"Lethal spider. With babies. Lots of venom. Football season. Must be healthy. Towel is not important right now, Giselle!"

I sigh. "Spiders have an acute sense of touch, by the way—it's what the hairy legs are for—so don't move, m'kay?"

"Giselle, are you screwing with me? I can't feel anything. Is she really there?"

"Shh, let me read up on this," I murmur as I quickly check Google. "Yep, I was right. 'Wolf spiders carry their young on the dorsal side of their abdomen for weeks, even after hatching. No other spider is known to do this.' Which means we can't kill her, Devon. Regardless of how she tormented me, she was probably just hunting food for her babies and got tangled in the sheets. We have to get her out of here uninjured. No telling how many fanged spiderlings she has. *Hundreds.*"

His nose flares.

"Okay, I have an idea." I dart out of the room, and he begs me to come back.

"Not laughing now, are ya?" I call back and hear an answering growl.

After grabbing a large bowl from the cabinet, I dig through the kitchen drawer for the longest kitchen utensil I can find, snatching a two-foot wooden spatula that I bet he uses on a grill. Perfect.

"How you holding up?" I say as I come back in the room.

"I felt something. Did she move?" he says in a wary tone.

"Nope. Still there. You're just paranoid." I creep closer.

He bites his lower lip as he eyes the spatula. "Are you going to hit me with that?"

"Of course not. I'm going to swoop her into the bowl."

He takes a breath, slow and steady. "Sweep her away from me, not toward me. If it gets on my face . . ."

"Trust me."

"Trust the girl who screamed so loud I'm shocked the police aren't here? Okay, okay, sounds good."

"I think Cindy likes you. She might be sleeping."

He rolls his eyes. "Fucking Cindy? Stop trying to figure out the damn spider, and get it off me. Please."

"I like it when you say *please*."

"Please, please, get Cindy off me," he groans.

I inch in closer on the foot of the bed, perpendicular to Devon. "I want something in return."

"Just ask," he bites out.

"I want to see you naked—not now, because you shouldn't move, but later, after the rescue."

His eyes find mine and lock, the pupils dilating in a rush, pushing out the forest green to nearly black. And his voice is thick when it comes. "Deal."

Steeling myself, and it's easy because I get a treat at the end, I hold out the spatula a few feet from Cindy and swing, knocking her as gently as I can. She sails off his shoulder and straight to the floor. I grab the glass bowl and place it on top of her. "I just scored," I say and look back at Devon and grin.

He gets down on the floor with me, and we stare at the bowl. "She's not *that* big."

"I disagree."

He huffs. "Do you really know of a man who almost lost his foot?"

"Um . . . ," I murmur, standing up.

He stands with me, a steely glint in his gaze. "You lied."

I hold my index and thumb close together. "Just a little. I can, you know, in times of danger or a prank. In my defense, the man did go to the hospital."

"This whole time, I could have just knocked her off and been done with it."

"Maybe, but I wasn't lying about the babies. Those are real, and I don't know how they haven't all scattered, considering the beating poor Cindy has taken."

"And now you feel sorry for the scary spider."

"But, but . . ." I laugh, clutching my sides. "You were scared! You were frozen!"

He gives me a glare as he bends down, and how in the world has his towel stayed on this entire time? I guess it's a very large towel. He nudges the lip of the bowl until it touches one of her legs, and she crawls along the side. He scoops up the container, and she slides to the bottom. He walks out of the room, and I follow him, soaking in the back muscles, the pert rise of the towel where his ass is—

"Are you ogling my backside?"

"Yes," I chirp as he grins and opens the door to the penthouse and stalks to the elevator.

"Are you going to take her out nearly naked?" I hiss, getting in the elevator with him.

"Yep." He pauses, sweeping his eyes over me before looking down and hitting the button for the garage. "You aren't dressed either."

I cross my arms, hoping to hide my nipples poking through my cami. "We're on a mission. Clothing can wait." And I really do want Cindy and family gone. I have to see it for myself.

The elevator stops, and we get off and walk near one of the concrete columns. I watch Devon as he sets the bowl down on its side, and Cindy eases out, slow and steady, then darts under Red.

"No!" I call out. "Not my car!"

Devon grins. "Your car?"

I feel a blush rising on my cheeks. "I love you, you know. Red is incredible, and I can't thank you enough. Everyone stares at me on the highway. I don't drive her fast and always clean out my mess—"

The rest of my words halt as Devon moves like a blur in front of me, his hands on my shoulders. "What did you say?"

I lick my lips, replaying my words telling him how much I appreciate him loaning me his car, which reminds me that my car is probably ready for me to pick up and has been for a while, only I haven't had time to get it—or maybe I haven't wanted to. Devon is still staring at me, and I know what I said—I do, totally—but it makes my heart dip and my legs shake, and I don't know *why* I said *those words*. I shouldn't have, because it wasn't like it was meant to be taken seriously—just words that slipped out, that are currently causing him to frown. I need to take a step back, mentally, and tiptoe my way through this, because if one little comment said in jest makes him wear that horrible hesitant "What am I doing?" look on his face, then I never, never want him to know how I feel.

"I just meant, thank you for letting me drive your car," I say quietly.

His throat bobs, his Adam's apple jumping up and down as he swallows thickly, his grip on me loosening before his hands finally fall to his sides. He stares at me—one, two, three, four—then drops his eyes to the floor. No level-five gaze here, just a man who is looking for a place to run.

"You sure that's all you meant?"

"Yes." Succinct and clear, my voice holds as I resist the urge to not gasp out in . . . pain? Yes, pain.

He gives me a final look and heads to the elevator. We don't say anything the entire way up, me on one side, him on the other, his countenance set in hard lines, a baffled, unhappy—yes, definitely unhappy—expression on his face. And I put it there, after the fun of Cindy. My words dug under his skin, confusing him and putting another barrier between us, because let's be honest: the man wants me. I know he does because of those long gazes, the soft touches, the way he kissed me, the way he held me tonight at the club. It's more than just hormones, but he doesn't want to want me, and that knowledge sits in my stomach like a boulder.

I wish I had more experience with men, that I knew the right thing to say to make my words not bother him. The scary part is that part of me meant those big words, and as that realization steals over me, I realize that I can't, I just *can't* fall in love with a man who wants to only be friends with me; I can't add it to my list of failures that keep piling up. Devon doesn't have the emotional capacity to return how I feel. No, he keeps that hidden piece of him locked away in his castle, with the drawbridge up, guards around the perimeter. People leave him. Because he served up his heart to Hannah on a silver platter, and she rejected him, hurt him when he was young and had a little bit of faith in love—

"Are you going to sleep on the elevator?" Devon's voice breaks into my thoughts. I shake my head and step off, following him back to the penthouse.

He comes to a halt in the kitchen, his back still to me, the lines of his stance tense and drawn, as if he's battling some internal struggle. Well, that's me, I guess. My fault.

"You don't have to carry through with our agreement to get naked," I say curtly as I cross my arms. I'm annoyed and hurt.

He turns around, hands clenched.

Well? my eyes say.

He stalks over to me, getting into my space, and I walk backward, my hands touching the wall for balance. His head dips, and his green eyes rake over me, lingering on my cami, taking me in all the way to my "Really a Waitress" red toes that Myrtle painted for me when she stayed over. "The problem is, Giselle, I want to be naked. I want to be all over you, inside you. I want to make you helpless underneath me, own every inch of your skin, until you smell like me, until you don't know where you start and I begin. I'm itching, my hands, *my fucking hands . . .*" The palms of his hands slam the wall on either side of me, caging me in. "Want to be in your hair; they want to strip you down and make you scream my name when you come. Then, I want to do it all over again."

My lashes flutter.

"Tell me how you really feel," I gasp out.

One of his hands slaps at the wall, jarring and loud, but I don't flinch, because it's Devon, and he'd never hurt me. Low and harsh, his voice is broken, as if dragged over rocks. "This is how I feel. I'm laying it out for you so you know the truth. Fucking is just sex to me, Giselle. No feelings. None of that emotional yearning stuff from your movie. That's who I am. Is that what you want? One night with someone who won't care about you the next day? Someone like a guy from your app?"

"It's not like that," I say sharply.

"Isn't it? That's what it will be with me. I'd fuck you and walk away."

My heart squeezes. "From me?"

"Yes," he growls, running his nose up my throat, his teeth nipping at my ear. His scent wraps around me, thick and heady. "Decide. Now. Do you want to fuck?"

That dirty word, from his mouth, directed at me, sets me alight like a match to fuel. Tremors start at my feet and work their way up until I can't form a coherent thought.

His chest brushes against mine as he presses a hot kiss to my neck, sucking at the skin. I pull his head to me, wrenching his mouth off my neck, truth staring at me, his eyes brimming with lust and promise.

I've made comments to him, flippant ones, about having sex just to get my virginity out of the way, but realization and clarity, *and him right now*, paint the truer picture. Having sex just for the sake of sex—no, that isn't who I am, and it never was; otherwise I wouldn't be a virgin. At any point, I could have given in to Preston's demands, but I never went there, because it wasn't right, a small kernel of wisdom that just *knew*. For months, I floated along with him, trying to extricate myself from him, not sure why and pretending like nothing was wrong. Part of that was guilt over Elena, but the rest was me, all me. He wasn't right for me. Neither was the lacrosse player from high school or the kind of boyfriend in college.

Is it Devon? Yes, this moment, his heavy-lidded gaze on me, the visceral need that's pouring off him, it feels damn perfect—if I want my heart broken.

My body wars with my mind, wanting him, the heat between us so hot it feels tangible. If I say yes, if I wrap my arms around his neck and pull his lips to mine, we'd be rolling around on the floor in a heartbeat. He's ready to pounce, hanging back by a tiny thread. Desire, dark and beautiful and intoxicating, swirls low in my body, aching and pulling. He's right here, waiting for me to answer, his chest twitching as he holds himself incredibly still. One little nod, and he'd do all those wonderful things to me, and then I'd be a nonvirgin—and very unhappy the next day. Still, still, I want him, and my body screams that it's worth it to hold him and kiss him and feel he's mine, if just for one night. My fingers twitch to delve into his dark hair, kiss him, and get lost. My chest inches closer to him, feeling that warm connection that drags me to him like a magnet.

I'd fuck you and walk away.

Yes, my body demands. *He's the only man you've ever truly felt this way about, who you dream about, who you've made the hero of your book.*

"No," I push past my lips, the hardest word I've ever said.

His breath hitches, and he shuts his eyes, breathing rapidly as he hovers over me.

Gathering strength and fortitude, I shove at him and dart under his arms. Space. I need space. My control is nonexistent when it comes to him. I have to get out of here. Out of this penthouse. I need to go for a walk around the block or get into Red—no, Cindy and family are there—or just get back on the elevator, ride up and down, and pretend I'm at a fair. I could sleep there, put down a pillow and a blanket, bring my laptop, and jump back into my story—

"Stop overthinking. Get dressed," he tells me, breaking into my thoughts.

"What?" I call out to him as he stalks to his bedroom door. "I'm going to ride the elevator! Why would I get dressed?"

He pivots around, his jaw popping, hands fisted. "We're getting out of this penthouse," he snaps. "Meet me out here in five minutes."

"It's late!"

"I don't care!"

I look down at the peek of his . . . member . . . from his towel. My throat dries. The top is all I see, mushroom shaped and thick and hard—holy shit, will my hand even wrap around that?

His lids open and follow my gaze. He places his hand over . . . it. "Ten minutes!"

He slams his door.

Chapter 16

GISELLE

Just pretend like that little showdown never happened. That's the ticket, I tell myself as we walk down a mostly quiet street to a diner across from the penthouse. A few people are out, darting in and out of upscale bars and moving on. Happy, probably tipsy groups that I gaze at longingly, wishing I had those kinds of connections. Myrtle isn't the kind who participates in bars, and shoot, I miss my sister most of all.

Devon opens the door to the diner for me, and I ease past him and take the place in. It's cute yet classy, decorated to resemble a fifties café, with red booths, black-and-white tile, and pictures of old movie stars on the white walls. People dressed in all manner of clothing, ready to eat after partying downtown, pack the inside, and I wonder how long we'll have to wait to be seated—how much longer I have to endure the silence between us.

In my peripheral I eyeball him while he talks to the server at the door. He came out of his room in jeans and a long-sleeved green shirt that might have exactly matched his eyes. *Pfft.* He took one look at me, because I hadn't moved since he'd left, and stopped in his tracks.

"Why aren't you dressed?" He argued with me when I told him I wasn't going.

He told me he was hungry—after all those cookies—and tossed a hoodie at me. I came because I liked the way he wanted me with him, that little thrill, so I stuck my feet into flip-flops and went.

I think he wants out of the heat of what's between us, but I can't figure out why he needs me to come with him. Isn't that just the opposite of what he *should* want? Men. And they say women are mercurial? Please. I tuck my hands in the front pockets of the hoodie, sniffing the smell of him in the dark fabric, swooning—nope. No swooning. Focus. The smell of waffles and butter and syrup teases me, and I sigh and look around the place.

Maybe food is the right thing. Can't have sex? Try eating. And now, I'm back to man logic. Is this how all men shore up their sexual urges? I picture Devon with a mound of pancakes in front of him, stuffing them in his mouth.

"Why are you smiling?" he asks as the server leads us through a myriad of tables to one in the back.

"Random thoughts." I slide into the red booth, and he takes the seat across from me. After grabbing the menu from behind the napkin dispenser, I place it in front of my face. He leans over and thumps it, and I lower it. "What?" I ask rather crossly.

He studies me, eyes ghosting over my hoodie. A small smile tugs at his lips. "Cindy."

I huff out a laugh. We had a tiff, but the effects of it seem distant now. He was honest with me, gave me a choice, and now it's done. Okay, moving on.

"She's somewhere celebrating by eating other insects. Familial bliss."

After pulling out my phone, I show him the image of him sprawled out on my bed, the spider resting on his bicep.

"Happy birthday, Giselle."

My breath whooshes out of me. "Oh, I didn't even realize . . . wow . . . I guess it is." It was my birthday when he and I cornered Cindy and took her to the basement. When I said those words.

I straighten my messy bun, which is all over the place after our antics, so I tug out the rubber band, slip it on my wrist, and rub my scalp. He's still watching me, and I'm twitchy and push my glasses up my nose.

He takes my hand on the table, his thumb brushing over mine, almost idly, as if he doesn't realize it. "Giselle, I freaked out—"

"What can I get you to drink?" the waitress says, and we both blink and look at her.

Relief washes over me. I don't want him apologizing for how he feels! I don't want him worried about me. I am fine. Totally. We are friends. Who must not, under any circumstance, fuck.

I order a Coke and Devon water.

Even with the baseball hat and long sleeves covering his arms, she catches on quick. "Wait. Devon Walsh?" Her eyes dart over the long hair sticking out of his hat, and her voice goes girlie, her body vibrating. She's about my age, dressed in a short red skirt, a black top, and a ponytail. Pretty.

Without an ounce of shame, she melts into the seat next to him. Devon sends me an annoyed glance and shrugs, then signs an autograph on a napkin. He pushes it back to her. She insists on a photo, and I wince for him as she ignores his attempts to get away and puts her head next to his and takes a pic with her phone. Unlike Jack, who hates attention, Devon isn't rude. No, he has a smooth finesse that he's gotten down to an art over his years in the spotlight. He takes her elbow and motions for her to get up, all with a fake smile on his face, telling her to please not tell anyone else and promising her a huge tip to make it worthwhile.

She dances away, a dopey grin on her face.

"At least she didn't kiss your neck," I say.

"Some are easier to handle."

"Hmm." I stare down at the menu. I'm going to eat everything on here if it helps me not want to chase after that sweet waitress and pluck out her eyeballs.

"Jealous?"

"You're a superstar," I deflect with a shrug, glad I squashed my urge to say *hell yes*.

"And you're a scientist who's writing a book. Yeah, you're just a little nobody." He grins and throws a napkin at me, and everything feels back to normal.

A few minutes later, we're both devouring chicken and waffles, until he pushes his plate away. We talked nonstop for most of the meal, him about his dad and how he took care of him growing up. He told me how he and Jack became best friends during summer camp freshman year.

"What's the best birthday present you've ever gotten?" he asks me.

"You'll think it's silly."

"No, I won't."

After wiping my mouth, I push the plate to the side and lean in closer, resting my chin on my hands. I push my glasses up. "What?" I ask, noting his weird expression.

He laughs under his breath. "You. When you get lost in thought, you get a wrinkle, right there . . ." He reaches over and rubs his finger over my forehead.

I smile. The man does watch me.

"The best present I got was on my fifteenth birthday—before all that curse business—"

"Which isn't real."

I wave him off. "Stop interrupting me."

He grins.

"Anyway, I'd been on this reading binge, had read almost every book in the school library. I was hounding Mama for something to read, and Aunt Clara had slipped me some racy books from the public library. She preread them to check for sex, but some weren't appropriate." I laugh at the memory of Aunt Clara bringing me Harlequins that just had *some light kissing*. "So on my fifteenth birthday, Mama gave me a bundle of letters from my dad, copies actually, written to her." A soft sigh comes from me, and I can only imagine the hearts in my eyes. "He got his medical degree through the army and was stationed overseas and didn't see her for nine months. Every day, he wrote her a beautiful letter, and it was in *his* handwriting and just breathtaking to think he wrote for her—he poured out his heart." Emotion clogs up my throat, and I push it down. "I got to witness how they met—at a bonfire on Halloween—and how he fell in love with her immediately; I read the little spats they had when she was dating other guys while he was gone, his heartbreak, and then I saw how she finally told him she couldn't live without him." A laugh comes from me. "Some were missing, of course, and those were the sexy ones. She denies it, but whenever I tease her, she blushes. I saw a glimpse of love, real love, and it . . . it . . . it was so sweet and perfect, but it also set the standard so high for me. And then, he died the next year, so I treasure those letters. I grabbed my copies when I went back for the pearls." I pause, watching his face. "What about you?"

"Your butterfly is in my pocket now."

Pleasure courses over me. "Really?"

He grabs my hand. "Really. And I've got a gift for you."

My eyes dart all over him, and he laughs. "Not on me. Soon."

"Giselle?" comes from the table behind Devon, from a couple just taking their seats.

I lean my head and take in . . .

Devon lets my hand go as the guy gets up from his seat and takes the few steps over to us.

"Robert!" I call when it clicks and hop out of the seat. "How are you? How's your dad? Everything okay?"

He smiles at me, a dimple in his right cheek winking at me. He looks different since the last time I saw him at the hospital with Myrtle and John. Or maybe it's just because I was harried there, barely knowing what I was doing. That day, he'd been in slacks and a jacket, but tonight he's wearing dark jeans and a blue dress shirt, the sleeves folded up. His sandy-brown hair is messy but stylish, and he's got his glasses on. He's taller than me, his build lean.

"Dad is fine. Talked to him tonight. I'm glad they found a place so soon."

"I need to call Myrtle and check on her."

He smiles. "We all had dinner together," he says. "She met my sister." He nudges his head back to his table, and I send her a wave. She looks like Robert, only the female version—tall with lighter hair and a sweet smile.

There's a pause, and I start, realizing I need to introduce. "Robert, this is my friend Devon Walsh." Devon stands and takes his hand in a grasp that looks a little hard to me, if the wince on Robert's face is indicative. Robert doesn't seem to know Devon is a football star, and I don't offer.

We chitchat for another minute about his dad; then, after flicking his eyes at Devon, he says in a quiet tone, "Let's have lunch soon. I'd love to talk to you more."

Is he asking me out, or is this about something else . . . ?

I dart my gaze at Devon, who's watching me, a taut expression on his face. He searches my face, then looks out the window.

Right, right. He doesn't care who I date. He wants me to find someone.

I give Robert my cell, and he gives me his card, which I quickly stuff in my pocket. He tugs on one of the strings from my hoodie, grins, and says, "Looking forward to it."

I'm still standing there watching him walk away, trying to decipher if there is any attraction there.

Robert flips around, a cocky smile on his face—okay, back up; when did he get cocky? "Oh, happy birthday!"

I smile.

He laughs. "Myrtle told us. Love the hair, by the way. Kate's, right?"

Heat rises in my cheeks. Oh. *Oh.* Myrtle let him read my chapters? Going to murder her. "Um, thanks."

I sit back down and stare at the table. It floors me that I managed to meet a guy I barely noticed, but he noticed me, and he just asked me out . . . maybe.

I look up at Devon, who's leaving a heap of cash on the table.

"Let's go." His expression is unreadable.

I nod, and we move through the diner—only I get shuffled back by a crew of drunken guys, and Devon turns and moves back to me, edging himself through them with his shoulders. He stares down at me in the midst of them—one, two, three, four, five, six, seven, eight, nine, ten, eleven—oh shit, we're gonna hit a record. Then he clasps my hand, threading our fingers together.

"You're with me," he says softly. Or was it, "You with me?"

Either way . . . "Yeah." *I'm with you.*

We hold hands and walk out the door.

Chapter 17

DEVON

"Do you have football camp tomorrow?" she asks as we walk back to the penthouse.

"Not on Sundays. Only day off."

"Good. I'm not sleepy," she announces.

"Me neither," I say, and the truth is I'm not ready to go back to the penthouse, where we'll be alone.

"Let's go for a drive. Not Red, though; let's give Cindy a chance to leave."

"Where do you want to go?"

"You're worried about your dad, and you haven't been able to catch him during the day, so let's do a drive-by. Check up on him. Maybe look for clues."

"It's your birthday, and you want to go see my dad?"

She tilts her chin up. "Yeah."

"All right. Let's go." That was not what I meant to say. What if she sees where I came from and thinks differently about me? What if he's there and trashed?

I kick those thoughts down as we hop in the Hummer and drive out of downtown and head to my dad's neighborhood. She's got the windows down, her hair blowing, belting out "Hollaback Girl" with the radio, and shit, I laugh. I don't know how she does it, but everything about her is funny. Bemused, I realize she's one of the best friends I have. In the space of just a few days, I've told her more than anyone else knows about me, besides Jack.

We sing the chorus together, my fingers tapping out the beat on the steering wheel as I whip into Dad's driveway and kill the lights. We get out and meet at the front door.

"You have a key?"

Feeling nervous, I nod and fish it out of my pants. Before I open the door, I take a deep breath and look down at her. "His place . . . it's messy."

She nods, face composed in a careful expression.

We walk in, and I flick on the light—the one I changed the last time—and take in the open space. The den is empty, but I can tell he's been here since the last time. More takeout containers litter the coffee table; an empty vodka bottle sits on the end table. Giselle heads to the kitchen, and I take the bedroom. It's empty, the bed unmade, clothes on the floor. His closet looks bare, though, as if he's packed a few things. Weird.

"Devon," she calls from the kitchen, and I jog to her, fear inching up my spine.

She's holding a piece of paper in her hand and thrusts it out to me. "It's a letter for you. It was on the counter."

"Oh." I swallow thickly and take it, sitting down at the table, my eyes eating up the words.

> Devon,
> My son. Remember that time you scored your first touchdown in JV for the hometown team? Remember the first girl you brought home—the one you really liked? Or that moment when you walked across the

stage to get your high school diploma? You do. You have those memories. I don't. Not one. I don't even know if I was there for that first touchdown. Maybe there's a game I recall, but I can't see your uniform in my head or that moment when you should have looked up in the stands to see if I was there.

I close my eyes and clench my fists, memories I don't want jabbing at me like thorns. *No, Dad, I looked, and you weren't there. And I never brought one girl back. Never.*

You've done so much for me—money, house, car, a job—things I tried to hang on to with everything I have, but I messed it up. I gave it a shot, tried AA, but I'm weak. So damn weak. Dotty is done with me, and I don't blame her. She deserves better. I can't hold a woman. You've watched them come and go, that look on your face, hope. God, hope is cruel.

I've done something bad. It hurts to even write the words down, but I can't do it to your face. I can't talk to you when you know that I owe people a lot of money, bookies, and not the legal ones.

Emotion rips at me, anger rising. My shoulders bunch as Giselle comes behind me, her hands moving over my neck and down to my arms. I shift and lean into her, my chest rising.

I have friends who are putting me up. You're a good kid with a big heart, but leave me be. Please, don't set this letter down and try to find me. I don't want to be found, so please listen to me when I say stay put.

My breath hitches, a desolate emotion replacing the anger. He's left me. He's fucking left. I'd pay his bookies, I could get him in rehab if he'd just go, I'll spend more time with him, I'll make it right . . .

"I know," Giselle whispers, and I realize I spoke aloud. She leans over me, running her hands through my hair—soft, easy strokes. "You love him."

> I'm sober as I write this. Woke up and promised myself I'd get the words down before the first drink kicks in. I want to say the right things to you, to make sure you know that these years in Nashville, the times we talked—I remember those moments, but when the end of the day is here, all I have is a thirst for the bottle. You've done more for me than a son should have. Just . . . don't give me anything else. I'll only hock it or drink it. I want to be better, but another side of me doesn't. It's a battle every single day.
>
> You're the best part of me.
> Forgive me for not being the father you deserve.
> I'll call you when I get settled.
> I love you,
> Garrett

Giselle eases in front of me, takes the letter out of my hands, then gets on her knees in front of me.

"Did you read it?" I whisper, my eyes stinging.

She shakes her head. "I just watched your face."

Shit, there's no telling what she thinks. "Read it." I want her to know. Out of the hurricane of my life, out of everyone I know, she's become a true constant, a calm breeze that eases me.

She picks it up and stands as she reads it quickly, then folds it carefully. "I'm sorry he's left you hanging. He's at rock bottom, I imagine, and feels guilty over the gambling debts. This letter was probably very hard for him." Her words are gentle. "I wish . . . I wish I had some kind of experience to draw on to help more, but I don't." She pauses. "There are groups for families of addicts. You're a star, so that's out of the question, but talking to someone might help."

My chest feels tight as I shove a hand in my hair. "Just you being here with me helps. No one's ever with me when things happen. I tried to give him everything." I stand up and walk to the sink and gaze out the window. A long minute passes as I grip the edge. After grabbing a clean glass, I fill it up with water from the fridge and drink it down. "I don't know what to do."

"That's okay," she murmurs, walking over to me. "Maybe he needs this time to decide who he is and where he's going."

I suck in air. "Part of me wants to find him, see if he's okay." I swallow down dread. What if he gets hurt, and there's no one to take care of him? I've spent most of my life being the adult for my dad, and here I am, still doing it. I can't make him change; I can't just snap my fingers and his addictions are gone—but I want to, so fucking bad.

"Yes, you can do that, of course, and if you want, I'd go with you and be your support. We can fly all over the country and look for him."

My eyes find hers. "You'd do that?"

"Of course." She pauses, thinking. "Just, I want you to know you aren't responsible for his actions. You can't make him change. It has to be him. Those are his decisions, and they don't make you any less of the wonderful, kind, beautiful person you are. You're such a good person, Devon, a true light, and every time I look at you, I see it glow with all the parts inside you. Seeing you hurt like this, it feels so unfair, and I'm trying hard, really damn hard, to be impartial and understanding on his behalf, but I . . . I'm angry for you, livid, that he's hurt you all your life, even though it wasn't intentional—he *hurt* you . . ." She blinks rapidly and takes a deep breath, her lower lip trembling. "You . . . you raised your own father, and it wasn't fair, and it wasn't pretty how you were abandoned by those who are supposed to take care of you—but you, God, look at you, the most . . . amazing man I've ever met." Her voice catches.

My heart tightens, the emotion so fierce I have to catch my breath. I meet her eyes, and there's a shimmer of tears there. Longing for her stretches inside me, clawing to get out and claim her, to listen to her heartbeat with my hand pressed to her chest, to have her in my arms for as long as she'd let me. "You really think that about me?"

"Oh, Devon. You are the best person in all my universes." She wraps her arms around me, holding me tight, so tight, and I cling to her.

Chapter 18

GISELLE

The alarm on my phone wakes me. Despite lids that don't want to open, I force myself to slap at my cell on the coffee table. Eleven. The sun coming in from the windows makes me squint, another niggling reminder that I have to be at Mama's by one for my birthday lunch.

Devon and I got back to the penthouse around three in the morning and sat down on the couch to talk, the TV droning in the background. I think he turned it on because he didn't want to look in my eyes when he told me more about his childhood. My head spins, picturing Devon chasing his mother as she left for another life. What does it do to a child when a mother never comes back? He escaped his dad with a football scholarship, but as soon as he made it big, he went back to his dad and moved him to Jacksonville, then Nashville.

No family is perfect. Mine is a roller coaster, but we get on the ride and cling to each other.

But Devon's . . .

Listening to his husky, quiet voice ripped me apart, but I wanted to be strong, an ear for him to let go of his burden. He locks down his emotions when he senses he's getting too close and retreats inside his castle walls, cannons pointed at the enemy. Because of his dad, because of that *one time* he gave his heart, he doesn't want to care, and I understand it. Love hurts when people leave, no matter the reason why. Even now, my heart pangs, knowing it's the anniversary of the day my father died.

I felt helpless as Devon talked, not knowing what to offer except to be the best friend I could and *listen*. Garrett is his father. The only one he'll ever have. And Devon, behind that cocksure smile and hard exterior, is a man who can care with a deep devotion that means forever.

Around four we were still awake playing video games, me sitting in the V of his legs, as we pushed aside talk of his dad and went into a serious game of *Madden NFL*; then I must have fallen asleep, my head back on his shoulders.

He's behind me now, his chest against my back, his arm curled around my waist as we lie on the couch. A muscled leg is on top of mine, curled, and his breaths are low and deep, his face in my hair.

I debate for a millisecond on begging off on the birthday lunch, but I promised I'd go, and Mama promised champagne.

Reaching out, I attempt to leverage myself up off the couch without waking him, but his arm tightens as he murmurs something.

He moves, his fingers slipping higher, inside the hoodie and underneath my camisole. He cups my breast, his leg drawing me in closer as he massages, brushing my nipple. The tip of my breast must have a million nerve endings, and every one shoots a blast of heat to my pelvis. He fondles me, caressing me against his thumb, and I feel drunk on sensation. A low groan comes from him as he breathes into my hair, the bristles of his unshaven jaw brushing against my nape.

His hand moves underneath my shorts and inside my panties.

He's asleep. And I'm letting this happen.

"Baby . . . ," he mumbles, and a finger slicks over my clit, lazy and slow. "So good . . . so fucking good."

I bite back my gasp as delicious sensations roll over me. I try to hold it in—I try—but I shudder from the tips of my toes to my hair, the combination of the scruff on my neck to his fingers erecting a rolling desire that's thick and sweet.

He flinches behind me, his breathing changing as he seems to come awake. I slam my eyes closed. Nope. I am not awake. I am in deep, deep sleep.

He slides his hand away, and I feel him shifting, rising up behind me, probably looking at my face and studying me. I picture his face, the chiseled jawline, the blade of his nose, those sensuous lips. I bet he's got that stricken look. The one he wears when he wants me but doesn't want to. Yep. He's going to rake his hand through his hair . . .

A soft whisper comes. "Giselle?"

I fake a deep breath. Eyes shut tight.

He exhales, and I feel him moving behind me, stealthily, as he doesn't crawl over me like I expect but goes over the back of the couch and lands with a thud on the hardwood. His footsteps pad into the kitchen, where I hear him opening the fridge and grabbing something, the fading echo of his feet as he walks down the hall to his room, then opens the door and shuts it quietly.

I jump up and dart for my bedroom. Eleven thirty. I have an hour to shower and get dressed, then drive to Daisy.

Half an hour later, I'm drying my hair when he knocks on the door of my bathroom.

"Hey," I say as I open the door a crack.

His eyes search mine, then take in the lacy blue robe that hits at my thighs—thank you, little boutique downtown. It matched my hair. Seemed like a perfectly viable reason to buy it.

"Uh, I made coffee for you and set out some muffins we had left over. I know you have to get going."

"Thanks."

"Thank you for last night, this morning." His gaze is hesitant.

"Anytime," I say as I ease the door open more with my foot. He's wearing pin-striped baby-blue tailored summer slacks with a matching jacket and a white shirt that contrasts with his tan. His belt is white-and-blue striped, his shoes brown loafers with no socks. Judging by the perfect fit of his suit, it must have cost more than my rent, and the way it hugs his shoulders makes me gulp. His dark hair is swept back, the royal-blue highlights glistening. He looks—have I died and gone to Devon heaven?—mouthwatering. Sophisticated. Sexy. An ovary explodes.

"Where are you going?" I ask, shutting out the disappointment that lingers, knowing I won't see him today.

He shrugs, straightening the little white square in his jacket pocket. "Got to see Lawrence."

I huff. In that?

"How did you get showered and ready and make coffee so fast?"

He pauses. "Head start. I was up before you. Didn't I wake up first?"

"Hmm," I say, my chest seizing as I resist the urge to give him the right answer. I reach over for my hair dryer and wave it at him. "My hair takes forever."

"Do you need any help before you meet Mike? A few last-minute tips?" His words are light, but his face is set in granite.

"Oh yeah, Mike. The old crush. Can't wait." I wave at my face in a "He's so hot" expression.

He flips around and heads inside the depths of my room. "What are you wearing? Let's start there."

He marches to my closet and starts pushing things aside. There's barely anything there—a few skirts, some dresses, two pairs of jeans, and some shirts.

He yanks out a long dress. "This one."

I sputter at the golden puppies frolicking on the velvet fabric as they chase a robin, the background a beautiful pastoral scene with tall trees and rolling hills. "*That* is a muumuu—for Myrtle. I forgot to give it to her. It's five sizes too big, and it will hang on me like a shower curtain."

"With your flip-flops," he continues, as if I haven't vetoed him. "Minimal makeup, no perfume."

"Your fashion sense clearly extends to males only. We'll blame this choice on your lack of sleep." I brush past him, pulling the dress out of his hand, my robe parting, my cleavage drawing his gaze. After hanging the muumuu back up, I snatch two new dresses and flash them in front of me. "Ready-to-ride red or no-back black?" I swish them back and forth. "I have lingerie to match either."

He lets out a breath.

The scarlet-colored dress hits several inches above my knee with a long slit up the back, the bodice a halter top with a plunging neckline and delicate see-through lace on the back. The black one is even shorter with a flirty skirt, skater-girl style. The torso is fitted with a scoop neck and a back that's open and laces up.

He juts his chin at Myrtle's. "Everyone adores puppies. He has a daughter, yes?"

I barely recall telling him that.

"Not trying to impress the kid; it's the man." I pull out the stilettos—three inches, black, and strappy. "Either dress goes with the shoes. Which one will make a man choke on his chicken leg?"

His jaw pops as he gives me a long look. "Black one."

I smile, but it doesn't reach my eyes. It's him I want to wear it for, him I want to be at my birthday lunch.

"Sold. Let's hope he likes it."

He moves to the bedroom door, his back to me as he mutters, "He'll love it."

"Are you jealous?" He can't expect me not to meet Mike, not when he's spelled out where we stand.

I follow him down the hall. He doesn't reply but keeps walking and gets all the way to the front of the penthouse and snatches his keys. He pauses, gathering himself, as he rolls his neck.

He turns to me, and we stare at each other.

Everything from last night—from the club, to Cindy, to him pounding on the wall—rises up and boils like a dark cauldron of emotion, simmering and churning, thoughts I put on hold, but after him touching me on the couch and his stupid dress idea, they can't be stopped.

"You are, and you can't stand it." My voice ripples with hard truth. *He wants me*—maybe more than just *want*, and the fierce girl inside me pounces. She's had enough. She demands.

He takes a deep breath, forest-green eyes on me as he grapples for the door behind him. "I fucking hate it," he snaps. "From Brandt to Greg to whoever the fuck that guy was last night, I'm—shit, Giselle, they don't deserve you, and I don't, either, but I want you, and I'm at a crossroads; it's go left or go right . . . to you. I'm scared you're gonna, I don't know . . . hurt me." He pulls in air. "I have to go." And then he's out the door.

All the air in the room disappears, and I fall back on the chair in the den. Just let me in, Devon. Please.

Chapter 19

GISELLE

The sun is blazing when I pull into Mama's driveway at one on the nose in the Maserati. It's only her Cadillac in the driveway, and I let out a deep sigh of relief. Maybe Aunt Clara was busy. Maybe Topher had something to do. Maybe it will just be me and her. With worry about the dynamic between Devon and me, I just want to sit at her house, eat, and go back home and wait for him. Just as I'm about to get out of the car, my phone rings with an unknown number. Thinking it might be one of the kids from class, I snatch it up. Final exams are next week, and they might need me.

"Hello?"

"Giselle Riley?"

"Yes." I don't recognize the voice, her tone brusque yet warm.

She laughs. "I apologize for calling on a Sunday. I do admin work on Sunday and thought you wouldn't mind, especially since you sent me the email with *urgent* as the header. I'm Dr. Susan Benson."

My hand clutches the phone. I'd sent an email to her after my disastrous meeting with Dr. Blanton. She graduated from MIT at nineteen, got her PhD at Harvard, spent time in Switzerland, then came back to the US and settled in Nashville. She was on a brief sabbatical when I entered the program, or I would have asked her to be my advisor. "Thank you for calling!" I say, trying to keep my excitement at a decent decibel. "Your research on the spin memory effect is groundbreaking. I've read it a hundred times. Being part of that study must have been incredible."

"Ah, yes, well, I read the LHC paper you sent me. Well done. I've seen you teaching your classes this summer."

"I prefer unconventional methods—"

"Not all learning is done in a classroom. I'm available Monday morning at ten. Can you come in?"

My stomach flutters, and I give her a resounding yes, already making a notation on my phone calendar. Well, at least she sounds promising. It is a good birthday!

After ending the call, I check my hair in the rearview mirror. I put in my contacts, twisted my hair up in a loose chignon, added smoky eye shadow to my lids with liberal amounts of mascara. Red lipstick coats my lips, and I quickly add extra gloss.

Mama meets me at the porch of her two-story colonial dressed in her finest, a pale-blue skirt and blazer, blonde strands artfully swirled in a style similar to mine.

"Giselle Riley, your hair—"

"Is gorgeous!" Aunt Clara says as she pops out the door and does a circle around me. "Can't even see the spots I missed."

I sheepishly admit I had it corrected as she plucks at some of the hair, a satisfied sound coming from her. I wonder where her car is.

"I can live with it," Mama says. "You need to show your wild side."

I start. "Have you been drinking champagne?"

She narrows her eyes at the car I drove. "Why are you driving Devon's car?"

My shoulders straighten. "Mine's in the shop."

"Still? It's just a busted window. Your dress is short, dear." She shrugs, *shrugs*, then smiles. Did my own mother manipulate me into wearing a sexy dress with just a phone conversation this week?

"Let's get this done. Where's Mike?" I say, pushing past them and into the house. Seeing no one in the den, I march into the dining room, where there are no place settings out, no food on the table. What . . .

Frowning, I head to the kitchen, looking around at the sparkling-clean counters.

"Mama? Didn't you cook?"

"Don't be mad, Giselle," she says gently, crooking her arm in mine.

"What have you done?" I breathe.

My eyes bounce around the room and snag on the window, a hiss coming as I see the large white tent set up in her spacious backyard. People mill around underneath, a band is setting up on a raised platform, and smartly dressed caterers are setting up a buffet table. There's even a champagne fountain. I blink.

My gaze skirts the yard, taking in the twinkle lights, the cloth-covered tables, the pink and more pink flower arrangements.

"Everyone parked across the street at Wilma's," she says brightly. "She has that long tree-lined private drive. It's a hundred or so people. You didn't get to have a wedding, so I did the next best thing."

"Surprise!" Aunt Clara jumps in.

"I told them to tell you," Topher says, coming in from down the hall dressed in khakis and a pressed shirt, lime-green Converse on his feet.

"You won't even see it coming when I kill you," I mutter, waving my hands at the three of them.

"Guess you'll have to put rat poison in my tea, too, then," comes a girlie squeal from behind me, and I turn to see Elena. I run to her, laughing; then I squeeze her in a hug. She's beautiful in a black pencil skirt, a white blouse, and heels, her auburn hair in deep waves down her back. Jack looms behind her, his broad shoulders against the doorjamb, an intense, utterly smitten look on his face as he stares at Elena.

I squeeze her arm. "Oh my God, you came back early? You didn't tell me!"

"We always planned on coming back today." She takes my hands. "Jack wouldn't get in the water anyway. The man can't swim."

Jack wraps his arms around her and pulls her into his chest. "Other things to do anyway."

Mama and Aunt Clara move to the window, talking about someone outside, so I take the opportunity to say what I want before this party gets started. I lean in toward the couple. "By the way, your husband here warned the whole team to not flirt with me. He told Devon I was a virgin."

She gapes, then glares at Jack. "That was a secret!"

"You told him," I accuse. "Apparently, no one keeps my secrets."

Jack winces and holds his hands out, not an ounce of remorse on his face as he gazes at his wife. "Sweetheart, I trust my best friend to keep her safe. You know the kind of men we hang out with." She sighs and tells him they'll discuss it later, then kisses him.

I tap my foot. "Well . . . I'm living with him." Take that.

Jack's eyes flare, and he starts to speak, but I cut him off. "I love you, Jack Hawke, but you keep your nose out of it. He's important to me. He was there the night my apartment burned and I came down the fire escape—"

"What?" Mama screeches. She's sneaked up on us. "I thought you walked out with Myrtle!" She clutches her chest. "You're living in *sin* with Devon?"

"Not enough sinning," I mutter, and Aunt Clara titters, the feather in her hair bobbing.

"I thought he would have nailed you by now," she says on a giggle.

"He hasn't?" Topher asks. "I was sure Greg would push him over the edge."

Mama slaps both their arms in one movement. "She's a virgin! Didn't you hear?"

"Bionic ears," Elena tells me with a wry grin. "Rookie mistake, sis." She pauses. "And when were you going to tell me you're writing a romance?"

I'm sputtering for a reply when the band taps out a drumbeat, and Mama gets on one side of me, Elena on the other, and Jack and Topher behind me as they drag me toward the back door.

"That's our cue," Mama grouses, her eyes taking me in. "Act surprised."

I dig my heels in. "I should fix my makeup first—"

"Stop that. Daisy Lady Gang is going to find your perfect match, dear," Aunt Clara winks at me. "Mama invited every eligible bachelor in a fifty-mile radius. If Mike doesn't work out, she's got backups. Uncle Farly's daughters are here, and they're on the prowl. Up front, they are marginally attractive but hussies. You've got to beat them out of the first picks. I told Cynthia not to invite them."

"They're family," Mama mutters. "Had no choice. And nobody is as pretty as my girl," Mama adds. "Oh, I see your preschool crush, Jude. Looked him up on the internet. He's not handsome—but single. Come on, dear." She opens the door, and I grudgingly head down the steps with her.

◆ ◆ ◆

They pull me under the tent to a mass of people amid pats on the shoulder and calls of "Happy birthday!" and "Good to see you!" Several are family, and the preacher and some of Mama's church friends are there, along with a few cast members from *Romeo and Juliet*, and so many men—most I don't know. One of them, an older man in his late forties, owns the Piggly Wiggly and keeps winking at me.

"Mama, why is Mr. Pig here?"

"Lance White, dear. Widower. Lost his wife in a car accident several years ago, bless her heart. Financially solid. Raised in Daisy, school board member, president of the Rotary Club, looking for his next girlfriend," is her hissed reply as she shakes hands with another distant cousin on Daddy's side.

"Likes to be tied up," Aunt Clara says in my ear. "Pass."

How do you know? my wide eyes ask.

She shakes her head. "Beauty shop talk."

Mama darts a look at me. "A submissive man might be the right one."

No, no, afraid not. It's alpha for me all the way.

A few minutes later, after meeting two single guys I went to high school with but who never paid me any attention, I've got it down. Nod, smile, inquire how they are; then say I'm thirsty and drift off to grab a glass of champagne or nibble on the bounty of food. I'm sucking down my second glass, feeling better but light headed, when Mama and Aunt Clara and Elena steer me to the back of the tent, where a group of people are clustered. The band has started and is playing Bryan Adams's "Summer Of '69."

Mama nudges her head at a tall broad man whose back is to me. She picks at my dress and fluffs my hair. "That's Mike. Go do your thing."

I inhale. "Mama, in case you don't know, I have no game."

Aunt Clara pulls on my arm, dragging me toward the group. Elena has the other arm. "I had a crush on him too," Elena says, her eyes going dreamy. "Pitcher for the baseball team, those brown eyes . . ."

"When did you turn into one of them?" I say to her. "My own sister. Betrayed."

She blushes. "They rub off on you. And I want you to be as happy as I am."

I eye Mike from behind, taking in the snug gray slacks, the french-blue shirt tucked into his pants, the loafers on his big feet. He's dressed nice. His hair is still that gorgeous chestnut color, messy with thick unruly waves that he keeps pushing off his face.

"Your cousin Cami is working him, and her boobs are big. You better go get him," Topher says.

A statuesque redhead, Cami is thirtysomething, single, and gorgeous. Her dress is a green sheath that clings to every voluptuous curve. Older than Elena and me, she lives an hour away from Daisy, but we spent our summers together out on the farm.

"Remember the toad?" Elena hisses, giving Cami side-eye.

Do I? Oh, heck, yeah. When I was ten, Cami dared me to put a toad in my panties. I did; then she teased me that I'd get warts on my "hoo-ha"—her word, not mine. "Toads and warts are a myth, but they do have toxic glands, which could have poisoned me," I say. "She's lucky I didn't give her a bloody nose and an anatomy lesson."

"She's meaner than a wet cat in a washing machine with a blowtorch," Aunt Clara adds. "When she was fifteen, she stole a bottle of my mama's whiskey, the twenty-three-year Pappy, no less, for a party with some kids and tried to blame me. It's worth two grand now, but she wasted it with a bunch of teenagers." She spits. "Blasphemy."

"Nobody takes Nana's whiskey but me and Elena! We inherited it!" I exclaim. Champagne has kicked in.

"Shush," Mama says. "Neither of you should be drinking. Your nana was just a collector."

We all look at her. Nana loved her whiskey. She nipped on it most evenings on her back porch with me and Elena at her feet while she told stories about the people in Daisy, every skeleton in this town.

I glance at Cami. She's laughing up at Mike, her eyes lasered in on him. "Someone needs to bring her down a notch."

"That's the fighting spirit!" Mama says and drags me the rest of the way to where Mike is, maneuvering her way between him and Cami, muttering "Excuse me, dear," then nudging Cami's hand off Mike's arm and replacing it with hers—like a claw.

A giggle erupts, and I stuff it down as I'm shoved in front of Cami. "Oops, sorry, new shoes," I say, apologizing for stepping on Cami's foot with my heel. I really didn't mean to. Honest.

Cami rears back and gives me the once-over, her eyes low as she rakes hazel eyes over me. I know her snark is coming in . . . three, two, one . . . "Any warts, Giselle?"

"Just the one on your nose," I say with a sweet smile.

She laughs, light and airy. "That's all right; do your best, little cousin. I've already given him my phone number." Obviously, she's aware of Mama's machinations.

"What cute hair. It looks *so* much better," she tells me, a fake smile matching mine on her lips. "You march to your own drummer, don't you? Nothing wrong with that, of course. I don't care what anyone says—you're attractive . . . in your own way." She waves her hand around at the crowd. "Have to say, your mama knows how to throw a good party. I guess Elena brings in all the football players and hotties. You never could. Wasn't your ex-fiancé one of her castoffs?"

Her comment has me glancing around. Aiden and Hollis are chatting at a table, heads bent as they devour chicken fingers and shrimp. Aiden looks up and blows me a kiss, and I grin. He points to the other side of the tent and mouths something, but I shrug, not catching on. He uses his fingers to send a message. Holding one index finger up straight, he curls his thumb and a finger from his other hand around it. *D*? Then he presses one hand together in a quack motion . . . like Pac-Man? Talk? What? I shake my head. He blows out a breath and rolls his eyes.

"Still a bit odd, aren't you?" Cami says as I turn back to her.

"Yes. I'm awesome."

"Weird. You're weird." Her gaze roams the people around us, snagging on someone behind me, a look of avarice growing on her face. *Holy hot guys, I'll take that one,* her eyes say.

"When you get a chance, send me and Elena the money for the Pappy you stole."

She laughs, the sound tinkling, eyeballs still on her target. "Keep dreaming, little cousin. Right now, there's a sexy man looking at me."

She flicks a strand of bright-red hair over her shoulder and pushes her breasts out.

A prickling sensation dances over my skin, and only one person makes me feel that way. Stiffening, I gaze over the crowd, searching—

"And she remembers you too," Mama's voice comes from next to me, and I stop and look at her. "You wouldn't believe how smart she is, a doctorate program at Vandy . . ."

"Giselle," Mama says firmly and manhandles (womanhandles?) me in front of Mike. "Meet Mike. I think it's been years since you've seen him."

The boyish boy is gone, replaced by a devastatingly handsome man, his face leaner, harder, and chiseled, his hair swept back, deep-brown eyes peering at me over a glass of champagne.

I'm aware of Mama steering an unwilling, muttering Cami to the buffet table, and Mike smiles, a flash of white, perfect teeth. "Giselle, all grown up. The last time I saw you, you had braces, glasses, and hideous bangs."

"You gave me those bangs after you tricked me and handcuffed me to the tree. Last time I saw you, there was a girl climbing out your bedroom window onto that tree." I point to the huge elm that sits between his house and Mama's. "She was pissed and yelling. You followed her out and kissed her, and then she went right back in your room."

He laughs.

I nod. "I'm sorry about your parents."

"Cynthia has been a godsend. Brings meals over and plays with my daughter. She talks about you constantly—and about having her own grandkids."

His shirtsleeves are rolled up, the sparse hair dark on muscled forearms. His shirt hugs the muscles of his chest, and he's at least six-one, his stance easy and relaxed, an aura of confidence exuding from him. I recall him in school, a slew of girls hanging off his letterman jacket, a charming smile as he fought them off, never giving too much attention to one or the other. Dammit. Mama can pick them. He *is* sexy.

"Don't encourage her. She'll have us married by Christmas. Unless Cami beats her to it." I smile.

He throws his head back and laughs, low and deep. "I'm not interested in getting married."

"Hard divorce?"

His smile vanishes. "Worst mistake I ever made. Right after our daughter was born, Leigh, my wife, ran out on us. Said she missed being single. That was three years ago." He tells me about the move from New Orleans after his parents passed, deciding on a fresh start. We chat about what I'm doing at Vandy, and he talks about his position as the principal and assistant baseball coach at the high school. He takes his phone out and shows me a few pictures of his dark-haired daughter and her new kitten. She's adorable with dimples and a big smile.

"She looks like you," I say wistfully.

"You want kids?"

I nod. "I want it all—career, kids, a big house in the country. You want more kids?"

"I love Caroline and can't imagine my life without her, but not really."

A waiter walks past with drinks, and I grab two—one for me and one for him—after setting our empties on the tray. He takes it with a smile, his gaze glancing over my shoulder before coming back to my face. "So who's the big guy giving me dirty looks?"

I freeze, and he puts his hand on my shoulder. "No, don't look. He's behind you, blue suit, dark hair with blue glints, diamond ear studs, built like he can bench-press a few hundred pounds."

"Devon Walsh," I say, butterflies going crazy, recalling those last words to me.

"I thought your ex was the lawyer . . . oh, wait, *that* Devon Walsh?"

"Yep." I suck down a sip of my drink, a hot feeling starting at my toes and rushing to my face.

"Something there?" He eyes me carefully, a hint of disappointment in his voice.

I exhale, thinking over the past week. "Yes. Maybe. I don't know. We're living together."

His eyes widen. "You're dating him? Holy shit. Is Cynthia trying to get me killed?"

"Not dating." I bring him up to speed on the fire and my new roommate status, and before I realize it, I'm telling him about seeing Devon on TV in college, then Elena and Jack introducing me to him, then Cindy the spider, and the "fuck and walk away" conversation. I stare at my drink. Too much alcohol. "I can't believe I just told you all that."

"Ah, we're old friends. Let it out." Mike takes a covert glance behind me. "You said he gave you his Maserati?"

"Borrowed. Why does everyone make a big deal about that? It's a *car*." Okay, a very expensive car.

He laughs, watching a scene behind me. "He just told Cami to get out of his face. I read lips well. All teachers do."

"You should call her, you know."

He blushes, and I find it endearing. "She only wants one thing."

"And it's not a Christmas wedding."

"Is that what you want?" he asks.

"I'm in no hurry. I just want . . ." To have the man I'm crazy about. And whatever comes after that.

"Devon?"

"Is it so obvious?" My shoulders slump.

He gives me that boyish grin that used to make me melt. "I said his name, and hearts popped out of your eyes."

I roll said eyes. "You're teasing me."

He pulls on my hair, making some of the strands fall by my face. "Keep looking at me," he says softly and takes my drink and places it on a nearby table with his. He grasps my hand and leads me to the area that's been designated as the dance floor. We walk past where I sense Devon is, based on the way my heart is hammering and the sweat dripping down my back. The tent has woven fans spinning every few feet, but they're not doing much to cool me off.

"What are you planning?" I whisper as Mike puts his arms around my waist and twirls me around as we dance to "I Want to Know What Love Is," by Foreigner.

He bends his head down, eyes gleaming. "I'm a huge football fan, and the chance to mess with *the* Devon Walsh cannot be passed up."

"That doesn't make any sense." My hands curl around his neck as we sway around other couples.

"I didn't say I was a Nashville Tigers fan. I've spent the last ten years in Louisiana. Last year, your guy demolished my Saints. We never had a chance. Devon is vicious. Nobody can tackle the guy. Consider this payback."

"Competitive men are fascinating."

"And you're a beautiful woman." His voice is husky as his arm tightens around me. "Now, smile up at me, because he's about to blow a gasket. Also, your mama is swooning—legit, her hand is on her heart as she watches us. Your sister is slyly taking pics of us on her phone and is already picturing the montage to show our children. Clara is mentally measuring me for a tux on our wedding day. In between 'Come hither' looks at me and Devon, Cami is seething and tossing back drinks." He laughs. "Definitely calling her."

I start giggling.

He grins down at me. "Your mama had me ready to meet you the moment she walked over with her chicken and dumplings and said she taught you how to make them. Leigh never cooked. She never got out of that sorority-girl phase." A brief look of sadness crosses his face, and I squeeze his arm.

"Don't fall for Mama's traps. I can barely make eggs."

"Honestly, this party and her schemes are the most fun I've had since I came back. Most of the time I'm trying to figure out who spray-painted graffiti in the boys' bathroom or where Caroline left her stuffed unicorn." His dimple flashes.

"I feel sorry for the women of Daisy. They're all going to be crawling in your window."

"Nah, I'm on the first floor now." His face grows serious as he stares down at me. "Devon's crazy if he lets you slip away, Giselle." He tugs more hair down, and it falls around my temple.

"You're messing up my style," I accuse with a grin.

Mike glances over my shoulder. "Update: he's pacing like a jungle cat."

"That's what I say!"

"Panther."

"Yes!"

He grins and does a dip with me in his arms, making me cling to him. "He doesn't like it when I touch your hair, and I bet I've only got a few minutes left." Glee colors his voice. "Just don't let him hit me. I'm an upstanding pillar of the community now and have a reputation to uphold, but I'm about to get all the tongues wagging. Me and Devon Walsh and you will be all the talk when school starts. I can't wait to call my buddies in Louisiana and tell them how I messed with him . . ." He trails off. "The song is almost over. I mean this sincerely: if you decide he isn't the one, call me. I'm not interested in picket fences, but I'd love to see you at my door."

A week ago, I would have been interested.

"I need a friend," I tell him frankly. His hand skates to my lower spine and presses me against him.

"I'm a good friend. Remember that." His other hand slides inside my hair.

"I . . . what are you doing?"

Mike lowers his head, his lips inches from mine. "Trust me. Close your eyes and think of England—or Devon."

Realization hits, and my startled gaze finds his. "No, Mike, no—"

"The lady said *no*," comes a deep voice behind Mike as a hand clamps on his shoulder. Devon wrenches him away from me and scowls, biting out his words. "Little handsy there, man. Not cool. Just walk away. While you can."

Caveman. Can't say I'm mad about it.

My throat dries as Devon puts me behind him and never takes his attention off Mike, who's currently digging around in his pocket and murmuring something about *the chance of a lifetime*.

Mike's brown eyes twinkle as he sweeps them over Devon. "She used to write my name in her diary with little hearts." He gives me an apologetic look. "Cynthia told me."

"Not shocked," I say.

"We're just friends," Mike says in a sly tone. "Like you and her. Only I've known her longer."

"Touch her again, and I'll punch you," Devon growls.

"You have no idea how exciting that drama sounds, but unfortunately I'm a teacher. Now, before I go"—Mike holds up his phone, and in a movement that reminds me of his athletic grace playing baseball, he takes a step toward us, putting his face next to Devon's—"I just need some proof." He tells me to smile, and I grimace as he takes a selfie of the three of us, then flips around and moves back, pocketing his phone. "A Maserati," he says while grinning, then waltzes off, making a beeline straight to Cami.

Devon turns back to me, eyes ablaze, all hard muscle and barely leashed temper. "Did you let him touch Red?"

It's too much—the champagne, Cami's sly barbs, Mike's antics, Devon's obvious jealousy—and I giggle. "He was messing with you."

"Did you want him all over you?"

I lift my chin, my gaze defiant. "I believe it's apparent *who* I want."

The moments tick by, the air thickening. "I need to go say hello to everyone," I say and turn, but he grasps my hand, pulling me back to him, pinning me with a mesmerizing look.

His lips part. "Giselle—" He pulls me into an embrace, his arms around my waist as he leans his head down to my ear. "There are things to say, that I need to tell you, but I can't say them here, not with everyone, *your mama*, watching." He runs his nose up my neck, his fingers brushing against the back of my dress, sliding under the lace as my stomach flutters. His hands drift and dig into my hips, his obvious arousal against me as he presses a deep kiss to my neck. Need flashes over me, curling inside as I melt into him. His scruff edges down my throat, and I gasp.

He groans. "Dammit, who cares where we are. I want you, Giselle. In my arms. In my bed. And I . . . I won't walk away."

My heart swells. "Oh."

He searches my face. "I'm close to dragging you out of here right now. Tell me not to."

"To fuck?" Heat flashes over me.

His lips twitch as he tucks a tendril of hair behind my ear. "Bet on it, baby. Do what you have to do with your guests, but later . . ."

I straighten my hair and dress, and my wobbly legs find the strength to turn and leave, past a gaping Mama and Aunt Clara and Elena. I catch Jack's eyes, and in spite of his obvious glower, I send him a smirk and keep going.

I bump into Mr. Pig—er, Lance—and smile brightly as I shake his hand and thank him for coming. "Mama adores you," I tell him. "You should call her. She can be a bit domineering, but some men like that."

His eyes light up, and he glances over at Mama and heads that way.

"One score settled," I say under my breath and wave as I see Myrtle and John arriving.

Chapter 20

Devon

"You should have called me," Jack says as we sit at a table under the tents.

"Didn't want to bother you on your honeymoon," I reply, my eyes on Giselle as she flits around the room, greeting people and chatting. At some point she went inside and put her hair back up, and she appears cool, as usual, but I know what's underneath: a hot-blooded female with a luscious mouth and long legs—

"Are you even listening to me?" Jack asks in a dry tone, pulling me back to the current conversation. "What's the plan for your dad?"

"Lawrence is checking with local bookies to see who he owes," I tell him.

Lawrence and I had a quick meeting before coming to the party—but part of me was still thinking about Giselle. I can't stop this, us, any longer. I've been pushing her away for days, turning off that internal voice in my head, the one that wants her. She's going to be mine. Having her with me at my dad's was a turning point—her acceptance, her kindness, her words that made my heart seize.

You are the best person in all my universes.

How often does a man find a woman like that?

My eyes find her near the food, chatting with Myrtle. She's a delectable vision in her sexy black dress, her pearls resting in the hollow of her throat, those "Fuck me" heels on her feet. I picture her in nothing but creamy skin, splayed out—

Jack makes a *tsk* noise, and I look back at him.

His eyes are hard. "Look, let's get this out of the way. I don't approve of you letting Giselle stay with you. You need to get her out of the penthouse."

She's not leaving.

"I don't have to say it, do I?" he adds.

"Say what?" I snap as Giselle sets down a piece of birthday cake and makes her way toward the house. Most of the crowd has left, and my leg bounces under the table. How much longer until we can leave . . .

"Dev. You and Giselle. You can't go there."

I swing my gaze to him. "I get why Giselle was angry when she found out what you told me. It's not cool when your friends try to manage your life." A grunt comes from me. "In a way, this is all your fault. After you told me, she was pretty much all I could think about."

"What did Jack tell you?" Aiden asks from across the table, a shrimp in his mouth.

"Nothing," Jack and I mutter at the same time.

"I just want to take care of my family. They mean everything to me, even the crazy mama." Jack looks over at Elena, his face softening—which changes when he focuses on me. "You and I both know you don't do permanent relationships. What was the name of that last girl you dated?"

Annoyed, I frown. "Mariah."

He nods and takes a bite of cake. "Right. How long did that last?"

I scratch my jaw. "A month. She went her way, and I went mine. She's dating Michael now. He's crazy about her."

"Only Devon Walsh can date jersey chasers, send them off happy, then set them up with another player," Aiden muses, admiration in his tone.

"Who was the girl before Mariah?" Jack asks as he sets his fork down, a hard glint in his eyes.

I take a sip of water, eyeing him. "I know what you're doing."

"You don't remember her name," Jack replies. "My point is, Giselle isn't going to be the next one. She's not that kind of girl. She's the one you get serious with."

"Her name was Kandi. The one before that was Lori. They walked away with smiles." I'm not an asshole. I remember names, just not warm, fuzzy feelings of the time we spent.

He waves me off. "But they disappear from your life and move on. Giselle isn't going anywhere. She's part of my life, a sister I never had, and you'll have to see her."

"You need to stay out of it," I reply as I stand. He isn't telling me anything that hasn't been running around in my head for the past few days, but *something* has irrevocably shifted, and I refuse to tame it any longer. My crossroads? I'm going right, straight to her.

Jack sits back and watches me, an enigmatic smile on his face. "She's driving your goddamn prized possession. You shoved Aiden around. You're ready to kick my ass. I'm the one who throws you the damn ball."

Aiden interjects, "I'm the one who'll throw you the ball next year, Dev."

"Dream on, rookie," Jack snaps at Aiden. "I'm the person you call *brother*," he continues, looking at me. "I don't know what is wrong with you."

"Check yourself," I growl. "You did your own playing around before Elena, so don't talk to me about my past love life." My hand taps my leg, my head scrambled, and I can't pinpoint what part of what he's saying is pissing me off more—the fact that I'm messing with the dynamics of our team or the fact that I go through women and he's lumping *her* in that category. Giselle is different.

"Settle down, you old farts," Aiden mutters. "This is a party."

Jack leans back and crosses a leg, watching me, a gleam in his eyes. "Giselle is getting over her ex. She is *vulnerable*. Remember those days after Hannah? How fucked up you were?"

A sharp inhale comes from me.

He nods. "So you do remember. You were lost. You didn't know what was left or right. You were devastated. Don't devastate *her*."

Never going to happen.

Something he sees on my face makes him drop his casual sitting position, and he stands and gets in my face. He's taller, but I'm leaner and meaner. We used to tussle in college—over girls, over games—and we laughed over those times minutes later, two alphas working out frustrations. It's been a while, but I know his weak points.

And it's been a hell of a week.

He gives me a quizzical look. "Dude. You won't hit me—"

"Don't be so sure," I say, hands tightening.

"Better tread light, Jack," Aiden chirps. "He moves fast."

Jack huffs. "Fine, there's no talking to you today. Let me say one thing. If you touch her, you better fucking *mean* it. And if you break her heart, I'll take you apart piece by piece."

Little did he know she'd be the one breaking my heart.

Chapter 21

GISELLE

It's six by the time everyone is gone, and I leave with Devon. My body tingles as he walks next to me, his hand in mine. I feel Mama's eyes on us as he opens the passenger door of the Maserati and helps me in, then goes around to get in and crank Red. She caught me earlier in the bathroom and asked me to swear I wouldn't have sex with him. I patted her on the shoulder and walked away.

Topher and Quinn offered to drive the Hummer back for us, and I can't wait to be alone with him.

We've barely spoken since the episode with Mike. Every time I turned around, he was watching me, eyes smoldering, a promise in those green depths. The emotion that rolled off him was palpable, cloaking me in anticipation.

I take the pins out of my hair and shake the strands out as his eyes linger on me.

"Eyes on the road," I say as I lean the seat back all the way and prop my feet up outside the passenger-side window, shaking my heels in the wind. "Black Velvet" by Alannah Myles plays from my phone.

His hands grip the steering wheel as he takes a turn on a familiar gravel road. I hear pings from the rocks hitting the car, but he doesn't seem to notice.

"The barn?" I ask. "Do you have any golf clubs in here?"

"I've got something else in mind." His voice rumbles, dark and thick, laced with heat, and shivers dance down my spine.

My heart flutters, and I swallow.

He handles the car with precise movements, shifting gears, his feet moving the transmission with athletic ease, and I close my eyes and sing loudly as Buddy Guy's "What Kind of Woman Is This?" comes on.

"Go faster," I murmur. My eyes drift over his shoulders, the peek of a butterfly on his wrist.

His hand shifts as he speeds up, and I squeal and let the ride and bluesy song sink in.

"I have to touch you," he says and slides a hand up my leg, a groan coming from him when I hitch my dress to my waist and flash my black lace underwear.

"Are you over Preston?" His hand tightens around my thigh.

"Yes," I rasp. "He wasn't even worthy of revenge."

"And Mike?"

"Hopefully banging Cami right now."

"Jealous?"

"Not even a little," I sing.

A purr of satisfaction comes from him. "You're with *me*, Giselle."

"Yes," I breathe.

We hit a straight stretch, with no cars anywhere, the lush trees on either side of the road thick and dense. Downshifting to a slower speed, he reaches over, cups my nape, and fuses his lips with mine, angling his head to go deep, his taste rich and heady, his scent teasing my senses as he takes and takes, marking me as his. Every stroke of his tongue sends bolts of pleasure to my body. "How much farther?"

"Five miles," I murmur as his teeth tug on my bottom lip. The car swerves to the right. He's using his knee to help him drive.

He straightens the wheel. "Scared?"

"No." I kiss his jaw, nibbling at the rough shadow. "But at twenty miles an hour, it's going to take us fifteen minutes, and I don't know if I can wait that long . . ."

"Any man who can drive safely while kissing a pretty girl is simply not giving the kiss the attention it deserves."

"You're quoting Einstein. Miniorgasm happening." I kiss him, twining our tongues as my hands dig into his scalp.

"Just trying to keep up with you. Lie across me in my lap, and maybe I can watch the road."

After maneuvering under his arms, I position my back on his door, parting my legs to give him room to shift. It's a tight fit and not easy—heck, the car itself can barely hold his powerful frame. His chest presses into my right side, and I start undoing his buttons, easing my hand inside to touch his hot skin. Looking down at me, he bites his lip, his free hand tracing my neck, the wing of my clavicle, down to my legs, where he toys with the waistband of my panties, teasing.

"How much traffic is on this road?"

"Barn," I mumble as I tug his shirt out of the front of his pants. "Speed up."

"Kiss me," he demands.

I take his jaw and mesh my mouth with his, liquid fire searing me as we get lost in each other. He's possessive and hard, then soft and slow and languid, licking at every secret place in my mouth, tasting the roof of my mouth, the bottom, his teeth nipping.

"Beautiful girl."

My insides quake, my legs scissoring as he lets me go to make the turn onto the road to the barn. He speeds to the side of the building, and I ease back to my seat. He parks, and before I can blink, the ignition is off, and he's out of the car and at my door. He sweeps me up in his arms, eyes burning with lust, and heads to the barn.

"On top of the car." I glance back at Red.

In two seconds he's set me down in front of the vehicle and is tearing off his jacket and spreading it out on the hood. Moving fast, he sets me on the car as he stands between my legs, takes my face, and kisses me, rough and hard and deep. Deft fingers find the hem of my dress, and it disappears somewhere behind me. His eyes burn as he takes me in, growly sounds coming from his throat. "Giselle, you are . . ." His fingers caress from my cheek down to the center of my black bra to my waist. "Perfect."

He removes my bra and throws it over his head, his mouth tugging at my nipple. He cups the weight and suckles one, then the other. My hands slide into his hair, running the mink strands through my fingers, arching my chest into his. I yank on his shirt, and he unbuttons it and shakes it off viciously, his lips attached to mine. His thumbs graze over my sensitized breasts, plucking the erect nipples. I gasp, need ratcheting over my body.

His mouth works down, brushing over my throat, his scruff mingling with the pleasure. His carnal, demanding lips cling to mine as he works my panties down with one hand. I don't know where they go. I don't know where anything is, just his lips and hands and tongue.

He bends to his haunches, eases me down, parts my thighs, and kisses me *there*, and my breath escapes in a whimper, spirals of lust curling.

"Devon . . ."

He consumes me like I'm a rich, dark chocolate and he's a connoisseur, his tongue skating over my clit.

"Everything about you, all your secrets . . . right here . . . on the tip of my tongue," he says gruffly, meeting my eyes, the effect of the intensity in his gaze enough to cause a quake inside me, a true miniorgasm rolling over me. But it's not enough, and I chase it, my heels digging into the bumper. His gaze goes molten as he slides a finger inside me, lazy and slow. "Has anyone ever gone down on you?"

"No."

"I'm the first," he purrs. "And I'm writing my name on you. Devon . . ." More tantalizing licks. "Kennedy . . . now that's a long name . . ." He sucks the center of me in his mouth and nibbles. "Walsh." He pauses to breathe me in, his fingers tugging on my curls as his palm presses on my mound. "I want you so slow, savor every little place, no rush, until you come hard and long." His fingers rub at the top of my entrance, teasing, in and out, never enough.

I lose my sense of perception, how much time is passing, the breeze in the trees, the hardness of the car, the silky feel of his jacket as pleasure buzzes and builds and sharpens until it rushes at me and pulls me under. I call out his name, a tsunami feathering down my spine to my core. My body clenches around him, my entire body undulating as I ride the wave.

"Do you want me as much as I want you?" He stares deep into my eyes, and my heart flip-flops. It feels like a deeper question, layered with more meaning, nuanced with significance.

My reply is smothered as I kiss him, my hands already working the buckle on his belt, the button on his slacks, the zipper. I can't believe he isn't naked yet. With trembling fingers I shove his pants and tight underwear down, his length jutting out at me, long, hard, and thick. The rose-gold crown has a bead of come, and I brush my finger over it, unsure if this is going to work. It's supposed to; that's how we were designed, but . . .

"Tell me." He stops my hand, his self-control vacillating when his lashes flutter.

"Yes, yes, yes, *I want you.* More than I've ever wanted anyone or anything. Please." My eyes lock with his. "Make me yours."

"Mine," he breathes, a shudder racking his body as he cups my face. "Giselle . . . fuck . . ." He groans as I grasp his hip and map out the topography of his cock. My eyes can't stop devouring all of him—the disheveled hair, the jerking muscles of his abdomen, the tip of him, mushroom shaped and veiny.

"I don't have a condom," he rasps out.

"I'm on the pill. I'm assuming you get tested regularly for physicals."

"I do. You are? Why?"

"I've had irregular periods for years, painful . . ." I stop, not wanting to explain my menstrual cycle now.

"I've never had sex without condoms, but it's you, baby, it's you, and I'll do whatever you want." A laugh comes from him. "You make me say crazy shit." His lips graze my neck, and I hold his head there.

"We can wait," he drags out. "We can drive back to the penthouse and do this in my bed."

My leg hooks around his hip, pulling him toward me. "Just put the tip in."

"Like we're in high school, huh?"

A slow smile curls my lips. "I've fantasized about the moment when the guy slides it in, the first bite of pain, then bliss—or I think. You're big."

"It will fit."

"I wouldn't be opposed to video."

"We are not making a sex tape."

"Yet." My hands curl around his shoulders. "I do want to watch it go in."

"You are insane."

"Mildly. Runs in the family."

"I don't know what this is," he says. "I don't know where it's gonna end up."

Regardless of his obvious hesitation, this is right, and I want it all, the ugly with the good. He said he wouldn't walk away, and I believe him. "We'll figure it out together." I flick my tongue over his nipple, making him shudder.

"Come here," he murmurs, adjusting my legs, bending my knees so that I'm halfway sitting up, my palms pressed to the hood of the car. He scoots the jacket closer to him. He steps back and stares, his chest heaving, his eyes dilated and low. I feel sexy and beautiful, bare and ready for him.

"Watch us, baby." Backing up, he lines himself up with my center and puts the crown in, then stops and slants his mouth over mine and kisses me. I dip my head to see through the space between us. His abdominal muscles shudder as he moves his hips back and forth slowly. My body has a primitive reaction, clenching around him. Trembling, I look up at him, seeing the glazed look on his face. He sets up a steady pace, rhythm sure and careful, never pushing hard. Sweat mists his skin, down his throat, through the trail of hair on his chest. In the distance, the sun is setting, the sky turning a vivid orange pink through the trees.

"More . . . ," I whisper.

"Not yet, beautiful."

His thumb caresses my clit, rotating in sync with his shallow thrusts. He looks at me, and our eyes cling. His green depths shimmer, and I read the nervousness in that gaze, underneath the desire, the hope that he's making this everything I've ever wanted. Oh, Devon. You beautiful man.

"Baby . . ."

The endearment sets me off. Tension builds and explodes. I can't breathe as lights burst, fireworks releasing in a kaleidoscope of color. I soar over the edge of bliss, shaken and torn, writhing as I cry out. He captures my words with his lips, his hips thrusting all the way home. A bite of pain hits as his chest rumbles with soft, comforting words. Not able to hold the position I'm in, I fall back on the car, my arms weights. He grasps my hips and adjusts, swiveling deeper as he pants.

"Giselle, fuck, so tight. Are you okay?"

"Yes, please, Dev, more."

His jacket works its way to the edge of the car and falls to the ground as he thrusts, the cool metal of the car under me as he owns me, his hands lacing with mine as he leans down and kisses me.

My body arches up to his, my legs around his hips, my pelvis dragging out every long, perfect stroke. Kicking up his tempo as he mumbles my name, he hitches my leg to his shoulder, grabs my hips, and finds a new angle. He shouts into the darkening night and releases inside me, the spill of him hot and sticky.

He leans his elbows on either side of my face and stares at me. My hands rub his back, tracing the line of taut muscles, the ridge of his spine. "Devon . . ." I don't know what I'm going to say. *Thank you for being you. Kind. Possessive. Unsure.* Even the part of him that's been holding back from me, I want to cherish. He's a little broken from the past, but if he wasn't, then we might never have happened. *Fate.* I swallow down those words. Too soon, too fast.

"Yeah?" His hands play with my hair.

I settle with . . . "Well, it fit."

"Was it good?" I feel the grin in his voice.

I pop him on the arm.

"Just the tip," he teases, his wicked lips curling.

I mock growl at him, which only makes him chuckle more, the softness of his breath against my lips as he kisses me. I sigh into him. This day, this place, this moment—I want to capture it forever.

Chapter 22

DEVON

My alarm goes off at six, and I turn over, reaching for Giselle, but she isn't there. Disappointment hits, but hearing the distant sound of water, I decide she's in her shower. Checking my phone, I see I don't have any calls, and I plop back on the pillows, my head wondering about Dad, hoping he's okay. Before long, my mind drifts to last night with Giselle, snippets of us replaying in my head. I've never been with a virgin before, and unbidden, a smile crosses my face, and I laugh into my pillow. God, I'm such a weirdo when it comes to her . . . I don't know, shit . . . but knowing that I was her first, that I'm the only man she's shared her body with—that feeling, it's fucking heady.

We drove home with her music blaring, my hand in hers the entire drive back to the penthouse. We made out in the elevator, kissed down the hall to the door, laughing as I tried to get the key in the lock. She wrapped herself around me, and I carried her to my shower and cleaned us up, then placed her on my bed and let her take the reins. Girl checked me out like I was the most fascinating science experiment she'd ever seen. I laugh up at the skylight. We didn't go to sleep until one in the morning.

Jack pops up in my head, and I kick him down. I'm not going to hurt her. Every bone in my body rebels at the idea.

So what are you doing?

I stare up at the ceiling, the peek of the sunrise shining. I have no clue. I'm operating on instinct and going with the flow. She hasn't made me promises, and neither did I. It's possible she's just exploring her sexuality with me; it's possible this won't last.

Later I come out of my shower with a towel around my waist and head to my closet, anxious to get dressed and talk to Giselle before I head out. My closet is huge, about the size of a bedroom, suits on one side, jeans and casual shirts on the other, clothes for the gym folded in cubbies in the back. Loafers, sneakers, and a myriad of other shoes are in boxes, neat and organized, but I can't see anything because the light doesn't come on when I flick it up and down. The bulb must be blown. A sound scrapes, like nails down a chalkboard, from the vicinity of the darkest part of the room, a spot near my tailored shirts. Maybe I'm hyperaware since the Cindy episode, but it makes me hesitate, picturing a giant spider with babies ready to pounce on my chest. I'm not scared of bugs, not really, but I don't want an infestation in my house. Better tell Quinn to call the pest guy.

A light crawling sensation dances over my foot, and I skitter back. A beam of light flashes in my face, making me blink; then the light bounces down to a pointy-headed monster with a wide mouth and bloody, sharp teeth. It growls, and I yell and jump two feet back.

Laughter spills from Giselle as she whips off the shark mask and rolls on the floor. A flashlight falls from her hands. "Dev, oh my God, your face . . . dying . . ."

"You took out the light bulb?" My voice sounds incredulous.

"While you showered." She giggles and throws the *Jaws* mask at me, and I catch it, holding it out with a disdainful finger. It's hideous, and I throw it behind me. Will burn it later.

"Where did that thing come from?"

She bites her lip. "Ordered it the first time we watched *Shark Week*. Amazon Prime delivery." Another fit of laughter. "I told you I'd get you." Her eyes narrow. "Why are you smiling?"

"Oh, I'm just picturing fake spiders in your bed, on your laptop, in your panties."

She rolls over to her back, her fingers playing over the edge of my shirt she's wearing as she looks up at me with innocent blue eyes. "Try it. Give me all you got."

I'm on her in a heartbeat, tickling her as she cries out and tries to scoot away from me, but there's no escaping. She twists and turns under me as I run my hands under her shirt and dance my fingers over her ribs. Squealing, she begs me to stop, promising she'll never scare me again, and I laugh, putting my face in her neck and inhaling the smell of her, soft and all Giselle. I've got her. *I've got her.* Here in my arms, with *me*. Fear spears me, snaking around, making my heart jump in my chest. I shove it away.

I've stilled, and she pulls my jaw up. "Whatever you're thinking, I don't like it."

My eyes shut briefly. "In one of your universes, in the future, what am I doing? Where are you?"

Time stands still as we look at each other.

She swallows thickly. "You just scored the winning touchdown, a sweet pass from Jack where you ran seventy yards. There's already a Super Bowl championship ring on your finger, and your heart is light. Your dad is clean and sober. Your girl is crazy about you. She travels with you when she can. She always knew you'd win. She's special, a little quirky, not like anyone you've ever met, and before each game you look up, see her, and send her a kiss with your fingers. That's your signal that she's the one."

My breath hitches. "What's she like?"

"Smart. She has a serious career, but nothing would exist if you weren't there."

I press my forehead to hers. "What if we're too different?"

"You aren't different—not underneath, where it counts. Life doesn't decide who you fall for. Love knows no rules at all, and your girl, she's never boring, and you're constantly wondering what she's going to do next. She brings out your soft side, and no one makes you laugh like her. One day, you take her hand and beg her to be yours. You make a home with her, a wild little family of boys who play football in the yard and girls who grow into intelligent women. You can't believe how lucky you are. You guard them with your life. The first time daughter number one has a date, you follow them to the movies until she confronts you, and you back down and hope she chooses a good man like you. Your wife kisses you when you get home, and you make another baby that night. Five kids total. Maybe more."

The world spins, and I gasp to keep up, the air in my chest frozen. "I always thought I'd never have kids."

"My universe."

"Where are you?"

Her lashes flutter as her fingers skate down my back. "You tell me."

I suck in a breath. "You're happy. You got your doctorate. You're famous for your research and your books. You travel the world, speaking at conferences to authors about incorporating science in their novels. You go to CERN and give them a few lessons about dark matter."

Her mouth curves up. "What a dream."

I brush a soft kiss over her lips. "My universe."

"Do I have a guy?"

I nod. "He's a handsome devil with a high-profile career. You crushed on him years ago, but he didn't know you then. He's never met anyone like you, and he has a past he's working on. He tries to go slow and keep his distance, but once he sees how smart and talented and beautiful you are, he can't let you go. He's afraid he'll never be enough, but he puts his heart in your hands and takes a chance."

"Kids?" she asks.

"Five. Maybe more. He builds you a dream house right next to your barn, a three-story craftsman with a big front porch and rocking chairs. Your mama cooks for your family on Sunday. Your man spends his free time playing with the little Giselles while you sit in your office and write. At night, he carries you to bed and worships you."

My chest twists as nerves swamp me.

Where are we going with this?

I dip my head and trail my lips down her neck. My voice has grown husky, my mouth trailing down to her shoulders. I push her shirt up and brush my fingers over her breasts. "Are you sore?"

Her response is a moan as I latch on to her, suckling the erect nipple, then trailing down to her stomach. "I've got to be at the stadium soon, but if you want to try that reverse cowgirl you mentioned . . ."

"Can I wear the shark mask?" she says, reaching out into the closet, snatching it, and taunting me with it.

I kick it back and pull her up, sweeping her into my arms, then stalking to my room and placing her on the bed. My breath stutters as I take her in—tousled hair, ruby lips, heated eyes. "Baby, if you want to be a shark, be my guest. I won't be looking at your face."

She throws a pillow at me, and I tackle her, caging her in under me as I kiss her. "How about a cowboy hat?"

"You have one?" Her eyes gleam, and I burst out laughing.

"Everyone in Nashville has one. I've never worn it. It's in the closet on the left top shelf. Let me get it—if I can see in the dark!" I call back as I rise up, drop my towel, and stalk off.

"Nice ass," she breathes.

"I know."

When I swagger back wearing the Stetson and a hard-on to rival last night's, she scrambles to her feet and jumps up and down on the bed, then snatches the hat off my head and slams it on hers.

Fuckkkkkkk.

I can't believe she's mine.

For now, a dark voice reminds me. *How long will she stay?*

"I've created a monster."

"Yeehaw. I'm ready for a ride. Get ready, little pony!" she yells, waving her arms in a lasso motion.

"Nothing little here," I grouse as I pull her into my arms.

"I'll bring dinner home at seven?" I ask her later as we walk out of the Breton together. She's heading to Vandy, me to the stadium. The valets pull up with the Hummer and Red, and I relish the slow blush that starts at Giselle's throat and moves up to her face as she stares at the car. She's wearing her hair in braids again, and I keep flicking at them, winding them around my fingers, itching to take them out and run my hands through her strands. In dressy slacks and a silk blouse, she looks classy and good enough to eat. I'm going to be worth shit at training camp. I take her hand, following her eyes to the hood of Red as I lean over and whisper, "I came down and cleaned the hood while you were on your laptop. There's a dent on the top, but don't feel bad. Quinn will take care of getting it to the shop soon."

"Your jacket. I can get it dry-cleaned."

I threw it in the trash this morning, but she pulled it out, hugged it to her chest, and swore she wanted to keep it. "You're funny, baby. I can get a new jacket."

"It's a memory. I'm going to put it in a shadow box with a miniature Maserati inside."

"Shadow box?"

"A display case for treasured keepsakes. Don't you have some with sports memorabilia in it?"

No. My dad didn't do those things. Whatever I have is kept packed away.

I grin. "I kept your underwear. Never did find your bra. Too dark, and I was afraid an owl might get me."

"Poor Bobby Ray. I meant to introduce you to him yesterday, but it didn't feel right."

"Hmm, don't want to meet the guy who almost got what I have." I kiss her lips, and she sighs into me, her arms wrapping around my shoulders. "I can't wait to see you later."

"Same," she murmurs.

"Mr. Walsh?" comes a scratchy male voice on my right, and I pivot, putting Giselle behind me.

"What?" I growl.

It's not the guy who was here last time, but he fits the description of the man from Walmart—and I know exactly what he wants. He shuffles his feet, and I narrow my eyes, body tense and ready to take him down if he so much as moves a muscle.

He holds his hands up, his gaze darting from me to Giselle. "No disrespect, sir. I'm just a guy doing a job."

"You're a bad guy!" Giselle snaps and steps around me to confront him. "And don't think I don't remember you, *Harold Pittman*. You used to work at the body shop on Main. It took me a while because you look different, but I figured it out."

The man exhales. "I lost that job, Ms. Riley. My cousin got me this one. It's not the best, but it puts food on the table."

"So you're, what, an enforcer? I played volleyball with your niece!" She crosses her arms.

What the hell . . . I frown. "You figured out who he is?"

She nods.

Harold holds his hands up. "I swear. I'm just a messenger."

"For bookies," Giselle mutters. "Harassing women and approaching an innocent man just because he's Garrett's son. Despicable."

He pales and looks at me beseechingly. "Please. I'm just looking for Garrett. He owes my boss fifty grand, and if he doesn't get it, then

I'm the one in trouble." His shoulders slump. "I honestly don't like approaching you, sir. Not what I'd like to be doing today."

The doorman has noticed us and comes over, but I hold my finger up to let him know to stay but not interfere yet.

"I assure you no harm will come to either of you," Harold continues, his throat bobbing. "It's just a large sum of money—"

"You used to change my oil and rotate my tires, Harold! There are plenty of places to work with your skills. Is this how you want to be remembered? As some kind of hit man?"

Harold looks mortified. "Not a hit man, Ms. Riley. Please understand."

As fascinating as this is, I pull Giselle back until she's behind me. "Stop looking for my dad. He's moved." I pull a card out of my wallet and thrust it in his hands. "That's my guy. Call him, and he'll settle the bill today. I won't pay any more after this; you got me?"

He flicks the card through his fingers, obvious relief on his face. "Thank you."

He turns to leave, and I call out, "I have friends in high places. Politicians and cops love me. I see your face again, and we've got problems."

He gives me a jerky nod, still eyeing Giselle. "I hope I never see y'all again. Please don't tell Cynthia about this."

"Call her, Harold! You don't have to be an assassin! She'll find you a real job!"

He pales and sends a final harried look over his shoulder, then dashes across the street to his vehicle and leaves, truck tires squealing.

"Giselle, that man is scared of you," I muse as relief rolls off me, a burden lifted. No matter how screwed up my relationship with Dad is, I want to take care of this debt for him. He's struggling every day with his addiction, and maybe somewhere out there, he's figuring himself out. I tap out a quick text to Lawrence to let him know they'll be calling.

Giselle laces her fingers in mine. "I can't believe Harold has sunk this low. He used to be the nicest man."

I pocket my phone and stare down at her. "You really are crazy."

"I prefer *southern*."

My lips twitch. "Beast."

"I'll show you fierce tonight. BDSM is a particular interest of mine—I think. No ball gags or Saint Andrew's Cross, but maybe some spanking—"

I groan and plant a kiss on her lips. "How the hell did any man ever let you get away?"

"Fate," she says simply and searches my face. "You okay?"

As long as I have you.

"It's a relief, actually, to have his debt paid. Go get your new advisor. I'll bring Milano's. Just text me what you want."

I open the door to Red, she gets in, and I shut the door. She rolls down the window and calls out as I'm walking to the Hummer. "Tonight is episode ten on *Shark Week* about an eighteen-footer in the Guadalupe waters—"

I jog back over and kiss her before she can finish. "No."

She laughs, and I walk backward and watch as she pulls away. I stand there until she disappears in the traffic.

"Your car, Mr. Walsh," interrupts the valet, who's been holding the door for me.

I start and look over at him. Right. I guess I've just been standing here.

My heart flutters in my chest. I miss her already.

Chapter 23

GISELLE

"Giselle? Are you still listening?" Dr. Benson says, and I snap to attention in the seat across from her desk. What was she talking about? Her studies at CERN. Right. "You seem a little distracted."

Oh, I am. Devon, *Devon*. His mouth, his hands, his laugh. My mind tangles in memories—me sleeping tucked in his arms under the stars, the slide of him inside me this morning . . . I feel giddy, like I'm flying over rainbows on a real-life unicorn. In other words, in love.

"I tend to ramble, but it's been a joy speaking with you. I'm glad to be your advisor," she continues, shuffling papers in front of her, copies of my grades and papers.

"Thank you so much for taking me on." My relief is obvious.

"You're welcome." She studies me, then nods, making notes on her laptop. She's an attractive woman with bobbed strawberry-blonde hair, stylish yellow glasses, and a svelte figure. Her clothes are well made, a jacket and slacks—the same taupe color as mine. According to her bio, she's thirty-five. Will I be her in ten years?

"No need to email Dr. Blanton now; I'll tell him today." The words come from her with a touch of malice, and I bite back a smile. She's had her own run-ins with him, I bet. "Women in science need to lift each other up," she adds solemnly.

"Fix each other's crowns," I murmur.

"Or our particle accelerators."

We laugh.

I stand when she does and shake her hand, my eyes snagging on a framed photo on her desk of her with two boys in her lap. They're little, maybe three, and look identical. My gaze traces their faces. "Twins. Yours?"

"Nephews. My brother's kids. Little rascals. One of them stole my phone last Christmas and hid it in his diaper. We didn't find it until he made a poo. 'Susu, I poo on you,' is what he told me, and I couldn't even be mad, even though I had to put on a hazmat suit to get my phone." A melancholy expression crosses her face. "I love kids, but raising them alone feels daunting."

"Oh." My interest rises. No rings on her fingers. Must be a story there, but I don't know her well enough to ask . . .

"You're single, I assume?"

She cocks her head.

I grimace. "Sorry, I blame my nosiness on my upbringing. My mama owns a beauty shop in Daisy, and it's the usual to grill every woman who walks in. 'Who are you dating? Is he employed? Does he own a home? When can I meet him?'" I laugh. "She threw me a surprise birthday party yesterday with over fifty eligible bachelors."

"Ah, it's fine to inquire. We're going to be friends."

"I'd like that." I sensed an instant camaraderie with her the moment I walked in.

"I've had relationships, just none that stuck," she continues, "mostly because I didn't have the time to devote to anything meaningful. My first love will always be physics."

We share a brief moment of rapport, two women who've worked diligently to get where they are, with goals and aspirations that sometimes don't leave room for relationships.

"People say women can do it all, a career and a family, and it's a pretty picture, but it's not for me," she adds. "There are plenty of women who make it work, and I salute them. My own mother worked a factory job my entire childhood, then came home and cooked dinner and read us bedtime stories. I don't know how she did it." Her breath hitches. "She passed away recently. I wish I'd asked her what kept her going all those years."

"I'm sorry for your loss."

"Thank you."

She picks the picture up and smiles down at it, but there's a lonely look on her face. "I get my dose of cuteness when I see my nephews."

We say goodbye, and I'm heading to the door when she calls my name, and I turn around.

"About Switzerland. I have some pull at CERN, close colleagues who are collaborating on various studies. I was half tempted to join them a while back, but I came to Nashville to take care of my mom, and time just got away from me."

"Ah."

"Dr. Blanton didn't approve your application, but I wonder if he puts enough importance on theoretical physics. He's, well, quite, um . . . old school." She clears her throat and straightens her jacket. "I don't want you to get your hopes up for a fellowship, because there's no availability at CERN at the moment; however, I called some friends last week after I read your paper and shared it with them. They were receptive—and impressed."

I gasp. "Oh."

She smiles. "We have a new school year ahead of us, and now that you have me, your chances are better for next year."

A frisson of excitement washes over me. Next year feels far away, but with my writing and classes and Devon, time will fly. "Thank you so much for recommending me. It would be a dream to go," I say, then pause and say on impulse, "Dr. Benson, you should come have Sunday dinner at my mama's. She'll try to set you up with any man with a job, but it's worth it to eat at her table."

She starts, then smiles. "I'd love to."

◆ ◆ ◆

My happy bubble expands. I stop by the library for a quick study session with my students, and they surprise me with a giant cupcake with pink icing that we huddle over in a closed room and split between us while discussing their questions for the final they'll take at the end of the week. Afterward, Quinn meets me at my apartment, and we finish boxing up my things. He says he'll take them to a storage unit that's close to Daisy. After grabbing some takeout, I dash over to Myrtle and John's complex, then take her to a follow-up appointment with her orthopedic doctor. With assurances from John and myself that we'll help her with her recovery, she agrees to schedule a knee replacement in the fall.

I'm bringing your present home is the text I get from Devon once I get back to the penthouse. He adds a heart emoji, and I squeal.

What is it? Give me a hint. Is it your body? After a moment, I delete the last line before I hit send. It's not his body that calls to me—well, I mean, yeah, he's the most gorgeous man I know, but that isn't why my heart is full. It's his hesitant care when he took my virginity, the way we laugh at the silliest things, the universe he described in the closet.

It's going to bring you full circle. I've had it planned since your first morning in my kitchen.

Cookware?

You can't cook.

Sex books?

You have me for that. Don't be wearing a mask when I come home. There will be consequences.

A delicious shiver races over my skin.

I like your "consequences".

Laughing, I dash around the penthouse, deciding to create my own surprise.s

It's not much, just a red bikini from Walmart—on sale!—that I've put on. The silky fabric barely covers my breasts, and the bottoms are a tad skimpy. Okay, it's a size too small, but who cares? I'll use what I have.

With Def Leppard crooning from speakers, the lights dimmed, I stand at the far side of the den, posing against the backdrop of his windows, and when I hear his key in the door, my heart races.

Shuffling sounds come from the foyer as he enters, and I picture him taking his shoes off, managing our takeout as he deposits his keys on the table in the hall. He calls my name and flicks on the lights to the den.

He's changed since this morning, the joggers and T-shirt replaced with jeans and a tight black shirt that emphasizes his broad chest. He freezes, and his heated eyes flare, a slow grin easing up his face. Low eyes drift over me, making my nipples stand to attention, my core with its own heartbeat. "Oh, baby, you look . . ." He rakes a hand over his mouth. "You're gonna want to put something on."

"Why?" I sashay toward him, as much as a lanky girl can.

"Because you've got company—*holy shit*, Giselle—" comes from Aiden as he emerges from behind Devon, a wide grin on his face.

A petite girl around my age with spiky pink hair and a leather jacket appears on the other side of Devon, her face reddening, eyes checking me out, then looking up at the ceiling.

My mouth opens and closes, and I tumble to my knees behind the couch.

I hear Devon's voice. "Erase those thoughts and images out of your head right now."

I look over the edge of the couch. Devon has gotten behind Aiden, with his hands over his eyes, and Aiden's wrestling to get away.

"I'm just going to get out of this, um, bikini I was trying on," I call and make a run for the hallway and Devon's room.

"That's barely a bikini!" Aiden says from behind me.

"Shut up, Alabama," Devon growls. "We were going swimming."

"You don't have a pool!"

"I'm going to build one!" Devon replies.

I slam the door and sprawl out on his bed, dying, when Devon cracks open the door and peeks in at me.

"Baby? You okay?"

I can't bear to look at him. "Is my present a foursome?"

"Nah, I don't share."

"Thank God. No judgment for those who do, but you're all mine."

He laughs as he slips in the door and walks over, his gaze running over me, then the room, seeing where I've unpacked some of his boxes and laid out some of his high school and college football mementos.

"Been busy?" He sits on the bed.

"I was looking for stuff to make you a shadow box. I found your senior football picture from high school and the program when you won the state championship," I mutter. "What are they doing here?"

"Danika is the girl who does my ink. She's here to finish your tattoo. Surprise." He chuckles. "Aiden popped up in the lobby and begged to come up. I'm really sorry."

"She's going to fix my tattoo?" Some of my embarrassment fades. She's probably seen a lot of skin. As for Aiden—I'm sure he's seen worse.

"I like your bikini," he murmurs and stretches out next to me as he brushes a knuckle over my collarbone.

I press my face to his chest. "Ugh. It's too small. I wanted to surprise you."

He laughs. "You run fast."

"So a tattoo?" I mumble.

He plays with my hair. "Yeah. I figured you'd never walk into a tattoo shop again, so I brought her to you. My girl needs a finished tramp stamp."

I rise up and give him side-eye. "*Tramp stamp* is not a term I like."

"Right," he teases and touches my cheek. "It's a lower-back tattoo, and I insist you wear low-rise shorts and crop tops every morning when I walk out and see you bent over your laptop."

I never said I wouldn't go in a tattoo shop again, but he knew. Unexpected emotion rises. "That's such a thoughtful gift."

"I got you something else." He moves around, reaches in his pocket, and pulls out a black velvet box. "Never got around to giving it to you yesterday. Meant to, but we did other things." He gives me a wicked grin.

I sit up against his pillow and open the box, my fingers trembling as I pull out two black bobby pins, a royal-blue glass butterfly on the end of each one. "Kick" is engraved on one wingspan, "Ass" on the other. I trace the scripted gold writing.

He watches my face. "I found them in a jewelry store downtown. A necklace didn't feel right—you always wear your pearls. Earrings, you don't wear them and . . ." He stops, dropping his gaze, a hesitant expression flitting over his face as he speaks. I get the impression Devon doesn't give gifts often. "Anyway, I saw the pins, and they reminded me of the night in the VIP room when you took yours out and left them on the table. I had them engrave the words so you'll always be reminded that you can do anything you want."

"How do you do it?" I ask as emotion overwhelms me and a tear escapes and slides down my face.

He wipes it away. "Aw, baby, do what?"

"Make me imagine every morning with you." Make me fall so deeply and irrevocably in love that my soul belongs to him, every beat of my heart in sync with his.

He sucks in a breath and kisses me long and deep. There's a hint of desperation in the way he clings to me, in the words he doesn't say.

We part, our breaths heavy. "Giselle . . ." He stops as a frightened look grows in his eyes, and I put my fingers to his lips.

I can wait for him. He's right there with me; he just doesn't know it.

Fifteen minutes later, I'm past the embarrassment and dressed in a green Buddy the Elf T-shirt—on sale—and shorts. I lie on my stomach on a fold-up apparatus Danika brought along with her tattoo machine.

With gloves and a mask on, she leans over me, her machine buzzing as pricks of needles tingle over my back. I showed her the pins, the azure and turquoise colors, and she's retouching the other side of my old tattoo to match them while creating the other wing.

Aiden munches on garlic bread from our dinner as he reclines on one of the loungers. Devon halfheartedly attempted to get him to leave, but I told him it was fine.

"What were you trying to tell me at my party?" I ask him after Devon gets up to grab a water and Danika takes a break.

I hold my hands up in the "sign language" he tried to convey at the party.

He smirks, moving his fingers in the motions. "This is *D*, genius, for Devon." He presses one hand together, the fingers tapping against his thumb. "This is *talk*. In other words, we need to talk about Devon."

My gaze catches Devon answering his phone and heading down the hall for privacy. "About what?"

"Dude. He pushed me around last week. Over you."

My eyes narrow. "Did you deserve it?"

He rolls his eyes. "I said some stuff, but I was sincere when I told him I wanted to ask you out, but whatever, that ship has sailed—you're his."

I grin. "Your master plan of pissing off Jack failed."

He blushes. "It wasn't like that. Anyway, I've never seen him like this. He's always had girls around him, but he doesn't get upset or jealous. So you and me, we're just friends, so forget all that flirty stuff I said. Just don't fall for me, 'kay?"

Danika snorts, and he shoots a glare at her. "Women adore me, tattoo girl. I'm every girl's dream."

I stuff my face into the table and try not to laugh. "Ah, Aiden. You're like a playful puppy I love to cuddle."

Danika picks up her tattoo machine. "All bark, no bite."

Aiden huffs and glares at both of us. "You two aren't taking me seriously. I can prove how addictive I am. Give me an hour, Danika. You busy after this?"

I look over my shoulder at her. She rakes her eyes over him, lingering on his shoulders. Shrugs. "Meh. If I throw a ball, will you fetch?"

He glowers at her. "You're gonna eat every word."

"Okay, I'll see what you got, quarterback," she chirps.

"Devon, your boy is hitting on your artist," I call out, giggling.

"Not a boy," Aiden says around a breadstick. "Danika's gonna get the full awesome Aiden treatment."

"In an hour?" I laugh.

He points his food at me. "You make a terrible wingman, and after all the things I did for you with Greg."

"That was you, huh? Putting the jersey chasers on him."

"True colors, Giselle. How a man reacts around other women is a big clue—even if it is a first date. Devon never looks at anyone but you," he says. "Been that way for a while; guess it just took me a while to realize it." He grins. "I saw you in your underwear. I'm never letting Devon forget it."

I make a moue with my lips. "Ah, little puppy, you need a pat on the head?"

He bares his teeth, and I smirk.

Devon comes back to the den and sits next to me, picking my hand up and threading our fingers together. He gives Aiden a look that says, *Mine.*

It makes me feel warm all over. If another woman gets near him— my brain explodes at the image, a scowl forming on my forehead. My hand tightens in his, and as if he reads me, he leans down and gives me a slow kiss. "Yours," he whispers in my ear.

A few minutes later, Devon and Aiden help Danika pack while I check out the artwork in the hall mirror, a gorgeous blue butterfly with black edging around the wings and swirls of curvy black ink fanning out on the sides. She dabs Vaseline over it and puts a bandage on, filling me in on the aftercare instructions to remove the bandage after twenty-four hours, then clean it with antimicrobial soap, pat dry, and apply ointment, but leave off the bandages.

Aiden and she leave, and Devon walks them to the door while I go through the food left in the kitchen.

"Hey, who called earlier?" I ask when he returns.

He leans against the counter. "My dad."

My eyes flare. "What did he say?"

He tucks his hands in his pockets. "Not much. Just that he's okay." He pauses. "He sounded sober." There's a hopeful look on his face that makes my heart snag.

"Did he say where he was?"

He shakes his head. "No, just that he's with friends and wanted to make sure I got his note and that he didn't want me to worry about him. I told him I paid off the debts."

"Do you want to call him back?" It might have been hard to talk with company here.

"Nah, he said he had to go. I told him I'm here if he . . . wants to go to rehab." He rakes a hand through his hair. "He said he'd think about it. He's never been, you know, and I feel like if he could get therapy and a quiet place to figure things out, it might make a real difference. It's his move now," he says, weary acceptance in his voice. "He'll always be my dad, but I can't keep giving him money."

"Whatever happens, I'm here for you."

He stares at me, searching my face. "I believe you."

"You hungry?" I indicate the food on the counter. "I can warm up the pasta? Aiden ate the bread."

His eyes drift over me. "Not hungry for food."

"Me neither," I murmur and step closer and toy with edges of his hair, running it through my fingers. "I couldn't sleep last night, hence the hiding in your closet, and I barely ate a thing today. Studies show that when we're feeling this . . ." Intense early stages of romantic love . . . "Euphoria, our bodies forget about basic needs and beg for more elevated dopamine, almost like cocaine—not that I know, but—"

He kisses me long and slow, until I'm breathless. "We can talk later." He pulls my shirt over my head and undoes the snap on my shorts, mindful of my back as he eases them down my legs. His eyes burn as he stands and takes in the lingerie. I do a little twirl, and he chuckles.

"You looked like a dream when I walked in; you know that? It was all I could do to keep my hands off you with them here."

I put my hand on his chest. "Give me one sec." I run to my room, grab the item, and rush back to him. He looks down and pops an eyebrow. "Pineapple lube?"

I work his shirt up his chest and over his head. "Hmm, you're a big guy, and my inner cowgirl worked hard this morning. Myrtle gave me the lube for my birthday."

"What if I don't like pineapple?" he murmurs as I unbutton his jeans and push them down his legs; then he kicks them across the room.

"Got strawberry and cherry. You don't eat it anyway."

"I'll eat you in every flavor. Does it come in bacon?"

"Gross!"

He laughs and hops around, taking his socks off. "I'm gonna show you what I can do with that lube. You had control this morning; it's my turn."

"Uh-huh," I say and ease down his black underwear. Magnificent warrior.

After stepping away, I make a dash for his bedroom, looking over my shoulder. "I've put the mirror from my room in yours. I want to see your face for what I have planned."

He chases after me, and I squeal when he catches me and sweeps me into his arms and places me at the foot of his bed. After jumping up, I switch around on him and push him down to sitting. "I get one more time in charge, and then you can do whatever you want."

"Let me grab my flogger."

"Hush." I angle the mirror I grabbed earlier, making sure it displays his incredible physique.

"You know what you're doing?" he asks slyly as I get on my knees in front of him.

"Books taught me everything I know, football player. Prepare to have your mind blown—and your dick."

His lashes flutter against his flushed cheeks as I take the tip of him, my tongue dabbing as I lick up his steel rod. "Like a very delicious, very long lollipop," I murmur against his skin.

"Dirty talker," he says in a rough voice as his hands go in my hair.

My gaze finds him in the mirror, tracing the flex and ripple of his chest as he inhales deep breaths. My mouth swallows his crown, and he hisses. Using my tongue until he's slippery, I take in several inches, flatten my tongue, and slide him against the roof of my mouth—little trick I read about—making it appear as if he's in my throat. I meet his eyes, and he groans. With an exhale, he eases me off him and stands up, tugging me up.

"I wasn't done," I say with a pout.

"When I come, it's inside you."

Desire makes me weak as he kisses me, his hands digging into my hips, smashing me against the full length of him as he turns me and walks me to the mirror. In a blink, he has my bra and panties off. Standing behind me, he bends and kisses my shoulders, the back of my thigh. "Mine." He sucks the bend of my knee. "Mine." His finger slips inside me. "All mine."

Languid, I lean against him.

His thumbs tease over my erect, aching nipples, his mouth on my neck. "Every part of you."

"Devon . . . ," I moan, shocks of pleasure curling around me, at the feel of us, the intimacy that we've created, so soon, so fast, but yet, here it is, and I love him . . .

"Look how beautiful you are," he says gruffly, pointing my face to the mirror. His eyes hold mine in the reflection as he clutches me, his tan forearm around my waist, holding me as if he'll never let me go. "Kickass girl. *With me.*"

Chapter 24

DEVON

"With you," she repeats, and I kiss her, angling her head to slant my mouth across hers. I won't ever get enough of how she tastes.

"Devon, am I crazy? With you . . . this . . . it's so good. Is it always . . ."

She whimpers as I sweep her up and move to the side of the bed, positioning her on her hands and knees so she can see herself in the mirror.

A long breath comes from my chest as I run my hand down the arch of her back, skating around her bandage and then kneading her ass. I don't reply, just stare at her, and she watches me, her cheeks flushing, her hair a mess, her two bobby pins haphazard and close to falling out. I ease them out and set them on the nightstand.

Her chest rises as she watches me put lube on my length, then spread her apart with care, tasting her, groaning as I make her slicker. I'm past any finesse at this point, all man, just want to get her off so good and hard and make her fall for me until she can't ever think about anyone but me.

"Dev . . . ," she cries, wriggling as my fingers dip inside her. So fucking wet. One hand on her hip, I guide myself all the way inside, letting her adjust to the angle and fullness.

"Nice and slow," I groan, knowing that's going to be a lie in the next few minutes. I can't get enough of her, I can't think, I can't . . .

"Please . . . ," she begs, her shoulders bent to the bed as she presents her ass.

I set up an easy pace, muscles vibrating with tension. She clenches the blanket as I take her in a measured pace, barely hanging on to my sanity.

"Giselle . . . ," I mumble as she clenches around me, and my control snaps. Speeding up, I fuck her hard, my pelvis grinding into her as my fingers find her clit. My heart pounds as the air around us intensifies, sharpens. I'm not aware of anything but her gasps of pleasure, the shape of her mouth as she gasps for air, the music in the den, the hard slap of our skin. "I couldn't stop thinking about you today, baby. Dropped five passes at practice. Coach chewed me out, and I didn't even care. I want you like this, want to make you beg me, make you cry when you can't get me. You want that?"

"Yes . . ."

My fingers caress her. "I'm going to be the first thing you think about, the last man you fuck." I can't stop the torrent of insane words. "I want you"—thrust—"all those theories you got"—thrust—"and I got one for you: you're in deep with me." Thrust.

"Yes," she moans.

I lick at the mist of sweat on her shoulder. "I'm gonna be needing this every time you walk in the room; every time you say my name, I'm gonna be right there, ready. I don't give a fuck how different we are—no matter what happens, I don't care as long as you're here. I want you all the fucking time on your knees for me, and I'll get on my knees for you, baby; just tell me, just tell me how to make it work . . ."

She screams out my name and tightens around me, spasming, her hips jerking as I come, the pull of her sizzling down my spine. Still thrusting, I ride out the wave, milking every tingle of pleasure that swallows me whole as she rocks against me. Sex with her feels different from anyone else, emotion in my chest clinging tight.

Shaking, I land on top of her, breathing hard, feeling uncertain and scared. I slip out, kiss her around her tattoo, and grab a towel and clean her up as she lies limp on the bed. Crooning to her softly, I scoot her to the head of the bed and hold her against my chest. My hands play with her hair as I try to get my own lungs back to normal. "You okay?"

She nods and looks at me, searching my face. She opens her mouth—then shuts it and licks her lips.

Yeah. That.

I kiss her, soft and slow, heart hammering, as I try to stay chill, when my head is a wreck. She's so trusting, open, giving. "That was . . ." Best I ever had. "Intense."

She lays her head on my chest, and we rest, my fingers idly tracing her shoulders. My head races, tumbling around with thoughts of how this relationship is supposed to work. She isn't like anyone else. She's not a girl I can let go. She's shoved me over that cliff, and I'm lying at the bottom on the rocks, waiting for her to finish me off.

Just . . .

Please.

Stay.

◆ ◆ ◆

The days fly by as the team prepares for our preseason game in Miami. Giselle and I stay up late at night talking or watching TV or playing video games. She begs for *Shark Week*, and I relent on Thursday and get grossed out while she giggles. I called her a bloodthirsty scientist, and she said I was a *wittle scaredy-cat jock*.

On Friday, she pulled out *The Complete Illustrated Kama Sutra* and showed me the Lotus position, where the man sits down with his legs crossed, and the woman straddles him, wrapping her legs around his waist . . . and she asked, *Could you do it?*

"Starting to think you just want me for my flexible body and stamina," I teased her. She laughed and kissed me, and I forgot about everything else.

At night, we crawl in bed and talk with the stars over us. Not even tired, we get up early and eat together; then she walks me out in workout clothes. She's getting back to her running before the semester starts.

She spends the rest of the day writing, and when I come home, tired and worn out from camp, I take one look at her, and exhilaration rushes over me. I'm barely paying attention to camp. I'm on a high. There's a nagging voice in the back of my head that screams that I'm rushing, that I'm going to fuck it up, that she's going to disappear, but I shove it down.

The team flies to Miami on Friday for a Saturday preseason game, and we win, 28–7, a tight game with our offense running the show. Jack is resting his arm, and Aiden gets a day in the spotlight, trash-talking Jack the entire flight home. When we land in Nashville late that night, Giselle's in the parking lot next to the Maserati. She and Elena stand chatting as Jack and I hoist our duffel bags to our shoulders and head their way.

"Giselle seems happy," he says, shooting me a glance. "And you. How are things?"

"Good."

"Look, we've been friends a long time . . ." His voice trails off, a torn expression on his face as he grabs my arm.

"What?"

He studies me. "I haven't seen you this happy in a long time."

"But?"

"But she's staying with you. It's going to make ending things hard, don't you think?"

"Who said I was planning on ending it?"

"Come on. It's you."

I'm really fucking sick of this.

"We aren't temporary," I snap.

We stop under a parking lot light, and he takes in my tight face and tense shoulders. "All right, all right. Maybe I'm wrong. I hope I am."

Before I can respond, Giselle runs up to me, and I drop my duffel and wrap her in a hug when she jumps at me. I twirl her around, my hands on her sweet ass. "Baby, fuck, I missed you. Barely slept." She's wearing low-rise jeans and one of my shirts. "You look good."

"I watched you on TV. Two touchdowns," she calls in glee, eyes shining.

We're in our own world, but I feel the heat of Jack's and Elena's gazes, sense the puzzlement radiating from them as they watch us from his Escalade. Who cares if they don't *get* us together? I do. She does.

"I finished my book," she whispers in my ear, and I laugh and give her another spin. "And I saw Cindy in the basement when I went to check on the hood of the car. Quinn had it fixed in a day. Cindy wants to know if you're available to babysit sometime. I told her you'd love to."

"Did you miss me?"

"Terribly. I invited Myrtle and John over, and we ordered sushi and watched a French film after the game."

"Hopefully not the one with the 'nice' cinematography?"

She grins. "No." Then her face grows serious. "I couldn't sleep without you."

She's still in my arms, her legs wrapped around my waist, and I don't want to let her go. "Come with me next time. I'll buy you a first-class ticket, and you can sit in the stands, and I'll blow you a kiss."

She nods rather distractedly. "Okay. I have some news."

"Oh?" I let her down as Jack and Elena finish stowing Jack's duffel, then walk over to us.

"You remember Robert, the guy who gave me his card at the diner?"

"Yeah. John's son. He wanted to have lunch. Did you meet him?" I frown.

She waves me off. "No, I told him I was dating you, but it turns out he wanted to talk about my book. He's a literary agent. Myrtle had given him a copy."

I arch a brow. "So he wasn't interested in you?"

She blushes. "Maybe a little, but he also wanted to talk business." Her eyes light up. "He's going to shop it around to a few publishers and see if they want my book. Can you believe it?"

Elena walks up, pride in her voice. "I told her I have contacts in publishing, but she wants to do this on her own."

"Good news," Jack says.

I take her in—the way she looks, the softness in her face, the happiness that radiates. "Going places, baby. You deserve it all."

"She does," Jack murmurs, his gaze on me.

Chapter 25

GISELLE

"Dear Heavenly Father, we come to you this Sunday with a meal before us, prepared by hands that work for you. Please bless this food, and use it to nourish our bodies. Thank you for bringing my family here. Encourage their hearts to visit more. A mother's love never ends; she knows the words her children cannot say, and she supports them through good and bad, even when she knows they might fail along the way. Mothers are the pillars of generations to come, which brings me to my daughter Elena and her husband, Jack. Please make her fertile and give them babies to populate the earth. Lord, I need grandchildren in my life to fill the empty places."

Elena and I both look up at the same time from across the table, and I make a pregnant motion over my belly. She rolls her eyes while Topher smothers a laugh with a cough. Aunt Clara snags a roll, takes a bite, sees us looking, then mimes rocking a baby.

Mama keeps her head bowed and continues. "Lord, give special attention to my sweet Giselle, who recently got a book agent when I spent thousands of dollars to send her to college to be a scientist. She's writing romance about aliens. Dear Lord, I'm sure there's no extramarital sex in it. She would never do that. Please, Father, let her finish her doctorate. I've invested enough money to retire in Boca, and I don't want it to go to waste."

Ugh. I'm going to finish school, and I have plenty of scholarships to help with my education. She's still salty. And she'd never live in Boca! It's too far away from us.

Elena mouths *sex* and makes a hole with one hand, then pokes her index finger inside with the other. Aunt Clara, who's since read my book and knows there's sex, chokes on a sip of tea, then dashes off to the kitchen.

Mama took my news of my writing with a straight, slightly disapproving face when I told her, but when my sister designs sexy lingerie, there's not a whole lot she can say—except for now—in her passive-aggressive mama-prayer kind of way. I was shocked yet thrilled to hear from Robert on Friday. I never would have dreamed of seeking out an agent at this point, but with Myrtle's encouragement over the past months, I discovered I want Vureck and Kate's story out in the world.

"Father, thank you for our guests today, Dr. Benson and Devon."

Devon's hand tightens on my knee. He was nervous this morning when we got ready to come to Mama's. His head is bowed, eyes shut, and I'm tempted to lean over and kiss him. Instead, I lean into his neck, inhaling his scent. He peeks at me with one eye and gives me a look that says, *Behave.* He admitted he's never gone to lunch with a girlfriend's family.

"We pray that Dr. Benson finds solace and comfort in the absence of her mother. Guide and help her navigate this world. Let us be a light for her. Let us find her a good husband."

I peek over at Susan—she insisted we all call her that—but Mama likes the doctor status. Eyes shut, Susan wears a slightly rueful expression. Sorry, Susan.

"For Devon, Lord, we ask that you bless his football season along with Jack. I've never seen a team that needs a Super Bowl more. They've come in second the last two years, and it's embarrassing for them. Help them be fast and quick and defeat their opponents with the vengeance of your mighty angels."

Eyes clamped shut, Jack's lips twitch, while Elena mimes throwing a football to me, and I pretend to catch it. Topher does the touchdown motion. Devon has one eye open and shakes his head at us. I sneak a kiss, just a peck, and he tries to push me off as quietly as possible. He darts a glance at Mama—*Behave or else,* his eyes say—so I stop, biting back my laughter. I can't help it. I'm crazy in love with him.

"Lord, be with Devon and Giselle. Forgive them for living together before marriage. She assures me they are not having sex. You know her heart and his. Help them as they date. Give him patience and gentleness. He will need it. Also give him the perseverance to not be tempted by her."

I glare at Mama. She's gone too far. Elena rocks in her chair and holds her stomach to keep from laughing. I flip her off, and she sticks her tongue out at me.

"Keep her chaste and sweet until the day she walks down the aisle."

Devon whips his hand off my knee—*Ah, so that one got to you, huh?*—and I snatch it back just as Elena throws a black-eyed pea at me and hits me on the cheek. I grab a roll and toss it at her head. It bounces off her and lands on the floor, just as Aunt Clara tiptoes back in and takes her seat.

"Finally, Father, bless my sister."

Aunt Clara throws her hands up in a "give it to me" motion.

"She's in love with a man years younger than her and is scared to tell us, when the whole town already knows he sneaks in her back door every night."

She means Aunt Clara's literal back door and not the other kind.

"I pray she sees the light and makes an honest man of Scotty—who isn't here because she won't invite him. Amen."

"Amen!" Elena says and smiles. "Wonderful prayer, Mama."

"Indeed," I mutter.

"I know," Mama says sweetly. "Now, pass the fried chicken around."

"This is a beautiful bouquet on the table," I murmur as I hand the basket of rolls over to Devon. "Red roses aren't your usual."

"Didn't see a reason to let them go to waste," she replies as she takes the bowl of green beans and spoons some on her plate. "I sent all the flowers from your party to the assisted-living facility, so they came in handy."

Aunt Clara titters. "Lance brought them by yesterday. Wanted to woo your mama." She drags out the word until it's *wooooooo*.

Looks like I might have created a monster with Mr. Pig. "How sweet of him," I say and picture Mama and him together—nope, can't do it.

"He asked her out," Aunt Clara tosses in. "She said no, and he said he'd be back with more flowers. I can't wait!"

"I told him I don't date and I didn't want to see him anymore at my door," she replies primly.

Elena smirks. "Hard to avoid him when he owns the Piggly Wiggly. Don't you go every other day? You still have those pink handcuffs in your room?" Elena asks me.

"Top dresser drawer," I say with a smug smile. "Might be some left-over twine in the garage from where we tied up those tomatoes. Lance likes bondage, Mama."

"Eat your chicken," she says, never batting an eye. "We have guests."

"Thank you for inviting me," Susan says, smiling carefully, and for a brief second I wonder if maybe I shouldn't have invited her, but it felt like she needed some cheering up. And if we're going to be friends, she might as well know my family is insane. "I haven't had a good home-cooked meal in a while," she continues.

"You need a man to cook for, dear. How old are you?" Mama asks.

"Thirty-five," she says hesitantly.

"Still young enough," Mama says with a wave. "They've got those IVF things now. Miracle babies. Tamara Wilkes had triplets using fertility drugs. Even if we can't find you a man . . . oh my . . . Mike would be perfect. Let me give him a call right—"

"No, Mama," I say firmly. "Let's eat together."

She sighs, settling back in her seat at the head of the table as she cocks her head at Susan, sizing her up. "There's also sperm banks if you don't like men. Topher is gay."

"I am?" He chuckles. "Yep."

Mama motions at all of us. "You'd have help. I'd love to watch your triplets."

Susan pales.

I hand her the plate of chicken. "We're having chocolate pie for dessert. I'll make sure you take some home."

Later, while Elena and I clean the kitchen, Mama sits with Devon and Susan, asking the newcomers a million questions. Devon manages to pull himself away, inch by inch, as he gradually gets up and shuffles his way out of the room and into the kitchen.

"You okay?" I ask, handing him a dried plate to put up in the cabinet.

He shakes his head, a harried look on his face. "The woman is terrifying. I told her about my dad before I knew what was happening. She just sucked it out of me. She wants to meet him."

I pat him. "She'll add him to her prayer list. It's very long."

He grimaces. "I don't mind the prayers . . . you told her we aren't having sex. But she knows, Giselle; the woman knows."

I grin. "She just doesn't want to think about it. Technically, she asked if I had my own room at your place, and I said yes. Then I ran before she asked me anything specific."

From behind, he wraps his arms around my waist and whispers in my ear, "She's got no clue how naughty you are."

I lean back against him. "Shh, no one does."

Susan pops her head in. "Hey, hate to interrupt, but I need to get going. Will you walk me out, Giselle? I'd like to chat a little."

Devon lets me go, and I grab her container with two slices of pie—the woman needs a reward—and head her way as she makes her good-byes to Mama. She and I stop in the foyer. "Congratulations on the book agent. You're a multitalented person. I had no idea you were a writer. I think it's incredible and exciting."

I blush. "Thank you. It's good to have your support."

"I hope it doesn't interfere with your studies." She searches my face.

"I had a rough last semester, and this summer hasn't been much better, but I'm ready for fall semester."

She breaks out in a smile. "Wonderful. I was hoping you'd say that. I spoke to a colleague Friday, and there's an opening at CERN."

I gasp. "Now?"

"Yes. I didn't tell you right away, but he just texted me during lunch, and I got excited! He wants to talk to me tonight. I'm sure he's going to say 'Send her over.'" The rest of her words jumble and get lost, my mind racing as we move out the door.

I find a seat on the porch and sit, my hands clasped tightly in my lap. Her words seem far away, and I strain to listen, but there's a roaring in my head.

"Sent him your records and a copy of the application you filled out for Dr. Blanton. He'd already read your paper and was suitably impressed, but I want to make sure it's what you want . . ."

"Of course." My chest feels tight. And wrong. I rub it.

I notice her taking the seat next to me. "It starts September sixth, so you'll need to expedite a passport if you don't have one—"

"Devon's first home game is September sixth," I say, interrupting her. "We play the Cowboys."

She gives me a quizzical look. "Is that a problem? The football player?"

He isn't *just* a football player. He's everything.

She continues. "We can use your research as credit for your classes. Usual internships range a year or longer if you get in a deep study. Some students are awarded doctorate degrees based on their work—just an incredible opportunity. Giselle? Are you okay?"

I nod, but my head bangs, a throb right in the front. I swallow thickly.

Twenty-one days, and I can be in Geneva, Switzerland. "Yes, I'm fine, just shocked. I . . . I didn't expect this."

She smiles and pats my hands. "Of course. I don't have the *okay* yet, but I feel confident I will tonight after I talk to him and tell him you're on board. I'll text you what he says; then we can meet at my office later and work out the finer details. Sound good?"

I picture Devon in his yellow-and-blue jersey, taking the field and looking up to the stands for me. And I won't be there. Dread washes over me.

"Giselle? Are you sure this is what you want? He's already had one cancellation, and I don't want to disappoint him."

Right, he's her friend and colleague, and she's gone out of her way to work this for me.

"Are things serious with you and Devon? I thought your mom said you'd only been dating a short time, but . . ." She trails off, waiting on me to reply.

Are we serious?

He hasn't said, but my gut feels what he can't say, and I know that leaving right now would not be good. Nausea bubbles in my stomach.

"I don't know" is what I settle for, and she nods.

"I was in a similar situation at Harvard." She half grimaces. "He left for Caltech, and I went to CERN. Leaving him was the hardest thing I ever did."

"You couldn't make it work long distance?"

She shakes her head. "We tried at first, but eventually work took over, and we drifted apart. He's married now with kids." A sad laugh comes from her. "She's a physicist as well, and I ran into them at a conference last year. Talk about awkward. I barely made it back to my room before I cried."

My heart dips. "That's terrible. Do you still have feelings for him?" It helps to talk to her; it gives me time to think through my muddled mind.

A sad smile graces her face. "Sometimes I think I made a mistake, you know, but then if it was meant to be, then . . . well, he wouldn't have married her, and we would have ended up together somehow. Silly, right? To believe in fate?"

"No, it isn't," I assure her and describe how Jack and Elena met, a mistaken blind date, then how he showed up to be Romeo to her Juliet. "There's an ancient Chinese myth that says if two people are destined to be together, then no matter how long it takes, their paths will continue to cross and intertwine. They believe there's an invisible red thread that ties destined couples. The thread may knot or tangle but will never break."

She sighs. "Ah, that sounds very romantic. I guess he wasn't my thread." She pauses. "Will your and Devon's thread break if you go to CERN?"

"I don't know," I whisper, a niggling sense of doom tugging at me.

She gives me an unsure look, then nods and tells me goodbye and leaves. I watch her drive away, my throat dry.

Devon comes out the door. "Hey, you were gone for a while. Everything okay?"

I start, a long breath coming out of me as Devon laces his fingers through mine. Trepidation sneaks over me, thick and vicious. I can't leave him. Right?

"Was she weird about your book?"

"No, not at all," I manage to say. "She's no Dr. Blanton."

"Good." He smiles. "So why do you look like someone just stepped on Cindy and her babies?"

Unease swirls in my gut. "Dev . . . I . . ."

"What is it, baby?"

I swallow down the words hanging in my throat. I can't say them. "I want to go home." It's the truth.

He stands and holds me, rubbing his hands down my back, and I cling to him. "Me too," he murmurs, his lips pressing a kiss to my neck. I arch closer, needing the reassurance of us.

My heart is already breaking. My body already misses him, picturing nights without him next to me, his leg thrown over mine, his arm curled around my waist as we lie under the stars.

We can do this together. We can.

I just have to tell him.

Chapter 26

GISELLE

I was going to tell him on the way home. I really was, saying the words in my head over and over: *Devon, my dream of going to CERN is here. Will you wait for me?*

Preston never minded the possibility of CERN, or perhaps he never believed I'd go, or more than likely he just planned on screwing around on me while I was gone.

I've made so many stupid mistakes over the past eighteen months—picking a terrible advisor, choosing Preston over my sister—and I can't make another wrong move, not when it involves my future. I have to be sensible and pick what matters the most without involving my feelings. I don't know where Devon and I are going. How can I? He doesn't tell me—and it's too soon to ask.

But you know the words he doesn't say, a voice reminds me.

I have to tell him.

But I don't, and desperation is a thorny vine around me as he drives the Maserati to the door of the Breton. My chest is cracking open as we walk into the lobby and get on the elevator, my insecurities bubbling to the surface, exposing themselves in capital letters in my head, doubts about our status as a long-term couple, misgivings about his abandonment issues, worries about a virile man who's faced with sexual advances from beautiful women every day. They chase Devon, give unwanted kisses and hotel keys. If I'm not here one day, one night, maybe he'd give in. And our red thread would be irreparable.

Stop it, Giselle. Stop.

I don't tell him while he looks for a movie. I don't tell him when he changes out of his slacks into plaid pajama pants and walks around shirtless and puts freezer cookies in the oven and sends me long questioning glances. An hour later, when my phone pings with a text, I dash to the hall bathroom and read it.

It's official. You're in.

My fingers cling to the counter, and I gasp for air. It's real; it's happening, right there in Susan's words. I splash cold water on my face, then hunker over the sink as emotions I can't name, terror and dread mixing in a toxic concoction, make me dizzy. Seeing a dream manifested shouldn't make me so unhappy; it shouldn't. *It's because you haven't told him; just do it, and he'll understand, and he'll hold you and tell you everything's going to be okay.* It's such a lie.

He's lying back on one of the leather loungers when I come out of the bathroom. His eyes darken, and his voice is thick. "You're naked."

"I know." On legs that don't feel stable, I walk over to him and bend down, stroking the tent in his pants. He arches up, a long groan rising from his chest. After shoving down his underwear, I take him in my mouth with desperate eagerness and ferocity, laving his tip with my tongue, licking down his skin, my hands stroking him with feverish devotion. He pumps into me with careful motions, his hands tangling in my hair, his fingers clasping on the ends, the sharp pain welcome, igniting my arousal, my core soaked and primed.

"Giselle, baby, you're off . . . something isn't right . . ." He jerks me up until I'm lying on him, and his eyes search mine, and I feel tears building, gaining momentum in my throat. I close my lids and kiss him with vengeance before he can ask, before he insists I tell him what's tearing me up inside. Our mouths collide over and over, finding new angles, darker than the other times we've kissed, my tongue searching out for his, sucking and pulling and taking, until I get the essence of him. Desire has me in her grip, from the top of my head to the soles of my feet, as he picks me up, and my legs wrap around his hips.

"Don't stop kissing me. Ever," I breathe against his mouth. "I want you so much. My body aches. My mind is consumed with you. I can't get enough, never enough," I say, and my voice is broken and ragged, my mouth peppering his cheeks, his nose, the corner of his lips. "Please, *please* make love to me . . ."

The air thickens around us, knotting and twisting, his fingers digging into my ass so hard I'll have bruises, his eyes mirroring mine, acknowledging what I crave. He pants and tries to speak, a question on the tip of his tongue, but instead he kisses me with electrifying clarity, sensing my need, feeding off the intensity of my emotions as he shoves me against the wall. His cock does not wait, slamming into my slick entrance with a full thrust, his fit tight and deep, all the way in and back out in a furious pace as I cling to his shoulders. He ravishes me, plunders me, crawling in and making me his. He drowns me with his rough possession. My cries are loud, my hands deep in his hair, latching my mouth to his, never letting go, begging him to take all of me, forever, no matter if I'm going away. When I come, my body clamps around him. Tears pour down my face, and he kisses them hungrily, lapping them with his tongue as we end up on the floor, and he drives inside me. He takes me with greed and lust, his eyes on mine, that questioning look gone, replaced with a frantic need to make whatever is wrong right. Driving, grinding, lunging, he uses me until I fall apart again and scream his name, only to want more. He flips me over and puts me on my knees, his tongue tasting me as he groans, his fingers kneading my ass. I gasp when he fills me back up, pushing hard and wild, no gentleness, just hard and dirty, undeniable need to crest. We spiral into grunts and groans, our skin slapping against each other's, wetness running down my legs. He roars his release, still pumping inside me, the spill of him coating my entrance, and still, I want more.

Take my heart, Devon. Take it, even if you aren't there with me yet; use it and hold it and nurture it, and always, always wait for me.

◆ ◆ ◆

Devon stirs next to me in the bed, tightening his arm around me, as if he senses my turmoil. I can't sleep. *I can't tell him.*

Moving as stealthily as possible, inching away, I ease his arm off of me, slip out of bed, grab my phone on the nightstand, and tiptoe out into the kitchen, my fingers dialing.

"Giselle?" comes my sister's sleepy voice. "Honey . . . it's midnight."

I walk farther, putting as much distance between me and the man I love as I can. "Elena . . ." Tears fall, and I swipe them away. "Something terrible is going to happen," I choke out.

Rustling sounds come over the phone, and I picture her sitting up and getting out of bed. "What's going to happen?"

I shake my head, as if she can see me, and cling to the phone. "Susan . . . Dr. Benson—I got the fellowship, and I can't tell Devon."

"Oh, sweetie."

I put my hand on the window in the den and gaze out at the city lights of Nashville. "I'm going to leave, and he's going to break up with me. Everyone leaves him, Elena. His dad just left. His mama abandoned him years ago. Hannah . . . I . . . she left him for someone else. What am I going to do?" A fresh wave of remorse washes over me, and I sink to the floor. "Am I doing the right thing? Do I go?"

There's a long silence on the phone as I hear her breathing and picture her thinking. "How long have you wanted to go to CERN?"

"Since I was ten years old . . ." My voice cracks.

"How long have you been dating Devon?"

My spine straightens. "That's not fair—it feels like more, like he's always been mine. I've known him for months."

"A few weeks versus years, sweetie; don't you think the answer is obvious?" She sounds confident, and I want to bang the phone on the floor to shake some sense into her.

"No, it isn't," I cry out. "I'm in love with him, Elena, so deep that I won't ever forget him, but he'll forget me—he will; he'll push me away like he used to. He'll go on with his life as if I never existed."

"Shh, it's okay, it's okay," she croons. "Preston hurt you just a few months ago, and maybe things are moving too fast with Devon for you to really consider what your true feelings are—"

"No, this is nothing like Preston," I grind out, falling into more regret for the sweet relationship with my sister. "Elena, God, forgive me for thinking I wanted him, please. I didn't know what I was doing then; I let myself get sucked into his vortex, and I didn't love him, not like this—"

"Shh, Giselle, please . . ." I hear her breath hitching. "I have forgiven you. You can't forgive *yourself*. He manipulated both of us, used you to get to me, and when it didn't go like he wanted, he took advantage of you, and none of it is your fault—"

"We lost part of what we have," I cry into the phone. "And I missed you so much those months; I couldn't focus, and it bled out into everything I touched: my grades, my life." My chest crumples, and I lie on the floor, staring up at the ceiling.

"And we got *us* back, baby sister; we got us back," she murmurs. "I can't be without you, okay, and you can't be without me, and he tried to rip it apart, but it didn't work. You're my friend, my mirror opposite, my confidante, my smart little sister who gives and gives. Sweetie, *I* should have talked to you and made things right with us from the beginning of that bastard. You're part of the fabric of my life, Giselle, and our quilt is stronger now. You have to see that. Forgive yourself, and things will be clearer, your heart open, major decisions easier."

My free hand balls at her words as I rub my eyes, surrendering to the thought, letting myself finally release those leftover feelings of regret that have hovered over me like a storm cloud. I made bad decisions that cost me, but I'm only human and fallible—and so is she. "I love you," I whisper. "Daisy Lady Gang forever."

"Ditto," she replies.

A half-garbled huff comes from my throat. "I called you for advice, and we ended up talking about us."

I can hear the smile in her voice. "We've been fine for months; you've just needed to find who you are and what you want. You have wonderful options: teaching, researching, writing novels . . . Devon."

"I just want to make the right choice this time." Panic washes over me. What if I choose him, and he breaks my heart? He said he wouldn't walk away, but what does that really mean?

"Talk to Devon. Lay out your cards."

"If we'd just had more time together." Turmoil swirls as a hollow feeling fills up my chest. "He suspects something . . ." I close my lids, picturing the probing looks when he carried me to bed, as if he were searching for my soul . . . "He's afraid to ask, because he knows I can't *not* tell him the truth."

We talk a little longer; then I get off the phone and sit in front of the window as I search the skyline for answers. Four thousand five hundred ninety-eight miles away, there's CERN.

When the first rays of light peek over the horizon, I pull myself together, tired and broken, my chest aching. I tiptoe back to Devon and run my eyes over his face, hypnotized by him, the high forehead, the stark cheekbones, the taut forearms with butterflies. I'm flying away from him, and no matter how many times I keep trying to convince myself our thread won't break, my heart knows the truth.

Lay your cards out.

I will, I will, just not today. I slip into his arms, my cheek to his chest, listening to the steady beats as I drift off to sleep in his arms.

Chapter 27

DEVON

"Numbers spiked this week. Ten percent profit, probably fall semester starting at local colleges," Selena tells me, shuffling papers around on her desk inside her office on Thursday.

"Hmm, right." I frown as I glance down at the spreadsheet she put in my hands. I pace around the small space. "You need a bigger office," I tell her, my tone distracted.

Giselle.

I rub my forehead, scraping down my face to my jaw. She's up and down, one minute reaching for me with greedy hands, the next hiding her face in her laptop, barely noticing when I say something. This morning I made us breakfast, and she didn't even complain when I ate most of the bacon.

"Did you get me tickets to the pregame Saturday?" Selena asks.

"Hmm, yeah."

"Did you get me the seats I wanted?"

"Fifty-yard line with Elena and Giselle."

"Postgame room entry, so I can see all your bumps and bruises?"

"Sure, whatever you want."

"Can I bring ten friends?"

"Yeah."

"What about Evan, the superasshole? The one I met online who stalked me. Can he come?"

"Fine."

"You don't say. Fascinating. How about comps for that brisket vendor who puts waffle fries on the top? Plus all the drink tickets?"

"Okay."

There's silence, and I'm vaguely aware of Selena tapping her pen as I pull out my phone to see if Giselle's texted me. I told her I'd be late for dinner, and she hasn't replied. She had a meeting with Robert about a publisher, but that was earlier. She said something about Hobby Lobby and shadow boxes, then taking Myrtle to the doctor, but she'd still have her phone—

"What's up with you?" she asks on a laugh, interrupting my thoughts, as she walks over to me. "I told you you're making bank this month, and you acted like it's chump change. If I asked for a company car to drive the one mile from my place to here, you'd probably give it to me right now. I'd like an old-school Trans Am, white with a blue stripe down the hood—I know, redneck, but there it is."

"Yeah, not redneck. Sounds good. Giselle . . . something's not right with us." I rake my hand through my hair, unease crawling over me as I plop down on a chair. On the surface, things look fine, she and I consuming each other in heady doses, neither of us able to get enough of touching and kissing and fucking. Maybe I'm crazy to worry; maybe it's just her mama's prayer messing with me, about Giselle being chaste on her wedding day, and knowing I've pretty much shot the hell out of that pipe dream. I'm *in* with Giselle, and I want her, and there's more, so much more eating at me, itching to make us permanent—wait, no, that's crazy; it's too fast. I'm just reaching, reeling in the off-the-charts sex and intensity of my heart wanting to cleave to hers, wanting to bind us, to kiss her every day, to make her need me like air. My thoughts shift direction, fear pricking as I replay Sunday. Was it Dr. Benson, something she said . . . ?

But why wouldn't Giselle tell me?

My fingers trace one of the butterflies on my arm. Is she tired of me already? My head recalls some of the revealing shit I've said during sex. Am I too intense? Too needy?

"Ah, dude, you're crazy about her," Selena murmurs as I look up to meet her soft gaze.

My shoulders heave out a long exhalation, and I bend over and just . . . breathe. "Yeah. I'm fucking terrified."

My phone pings, and I grapple to get it back out of my pocket, to get it back in my hands and see if it's her. Just Aiden. I sigh.

Yo. Saw you come in. Where you at? There's a chick out here asking for you.

On my way, I send and stand up, relief washing over me.

"Giselle's here; I need to go," I tell Selena, and she nods and follows me.

"Cool. I need to get to know her better. I get the feeling she's going to be around awhile."

I hope so.

"You think she likes Trans Ams?"

"Red is hers, so probably," I say, my steps lighter, the tension loosening the closer I get to Giselle as we weave through the hallway and head out to the club. My eyes search the bar for her blue hair, not finding her but seeing Aiden at the end. I stalk his way, shifting past patrons with eager steps. My baby, my girl, my sweet, sexy scientist. I'm going to kiss the fuck out of her.

"Where is she?" I ask Aiden, who turns to face me from his stool, a water in his hand.

He nudges his head at the girl next to him. "Right here." He waggles his eyebrows and leans in. "Says you guys talked about getting *married.* Came in to say *hi.* Didn't recognize her, but she said she went to Ohio State—"

"You're a moron, Alabama," Selena breathes from behind me. I'm aware of her popping Aiden on the arm and his exclamation and curse, muttering something along the lines of "What is her problem? I didn't know it was that big of a deal."

The girl turns on her stool, and my chest seizes, the same hazel eyes behind thick lashes, the round face, and the straight black hair.

"Hannah?" I say, not believing my eyes. "What are you doing here?"

She stands in a graceful motion, petite and as curvy as she used to be, dressed in a black dress, pumps on her dainty feet. Her hair is shorter now, around her shoulders instead of down her back.

A blush rushes up her face. "I would have called, but I don't have your number. I messaged your IG profile, but I'm not sure you even see those." A half grimace crosses her face. "I probably shouldn't have done that—a bit forward of me, I suppose, but . . ." She trails off. Her voice is small and lyrical, pulling me further down into the past, into when I hung on her every word. I see her in my dorm room, telling me she's breaking up with me. *I found someone else. You have football. I have medical school. He knows me better than you do. He's the one for me. I'm sorry, so sorry . . .*

She walked out and never looked back. I didn't breathe right for a year, always looking for her face in crowds, wondering if she was happy, if she thought about us, if she'd really loved me at all.

"Because you're married," Selena mutters, easing next to me and crossing her arms and glaring at Hannah. "You dumped my cousin, married some guy, messed with Devon's head, and I've never forgotten it."

I hear Aiden sucking in a breath. "My man getting the shaft from a girl? No fucking way." He scowls, darting his eyes from Hannah to me. "Nope, can't see it. You two don't go together. As Giselle says, no zing."

Hannah sighs, her eyes on me, looking for something. "Right. It's been a long time—seven years. I'm in town with some friends and read somewhere that you owned this place. Thought I'd just take a chance and pop in and see you. You look different." She looks at the floor, then back up to me, holding my gaze.

And by *different*, she means the hair and earrings.

"I'm living in Cleveland and started a dermatology clinic with some colleagues."

"Congrats," I say, not sure why she wants me to know the details of her life. After that first year, I placed her on the shelf of people who deserted me, and I've never once reached to find her pages and read more. The pain of what she did lingered—not denying that—but she's been written off, finished, closed, *over*. Once you hurt me like she did, once you leave me broken with scars that fester, I will rally and erase you.

Selena looms closer to her. "Well, Devon is famous and rich. Not that you ever cared about football, but he's the best wide receiver in the country." She pauses. "His girlfriend is younger, prettier, and a *physicist*." She lets out a derisive laugh. "She doesn't pop zits."

"Selena, ease up," I murmur. "She's just passing through, right?" I glance at Hannah.

"I was hoping you were free for dinner, actually?" she asks in a hopeful tone.

Aiden's eyes are wide, and I figure he's still trying to understand how a girl could have dumped me. Poor guy. His heart has never been broken.

Hannah takes my hand, her gaze soft and inviting as she takes me in, and I let her, curious and bemused about where this is going.

"I'm in town for the weekend," she says, an obvious meaning in her tone.

She wants to play on the wild side while hubby stays at home.

Have I thought about her showing up someday? Maybe.

Did I think I'd feel this disconnected from her, even with the rawness of her betrayal? No.

I feel nothing . . . except . . . regret that I've let my scars hold me back from Giselle.

She won't leave. She's the real deal.

"Sorry," I drawl, disentangling her grasp and putting some space between us. "Don't think it's right to have dinner with you when there's a beautiful girl waiting on me at home." I stick my hands in the pockets of my slacks. "It was interesting to see you. Enjoy your visit, and tell your husband . . ." I hold a finger up. "What's his name?"

"Edward."

"Yeah. Tell him hello." I turn, then pivot back. "Drinks are on the house, appetizers, whatever you'd like." I give a wave and walk away.

Glancing in the mirror behind the bar, I see Selena doing a fist pump. Aiden still looks confused, while Hannah frowns.

She isn't anything to me.

No zing.

Not even a little.

There's only one person in this world who holds my heart.

I walk into the penthouse and call out Giselle's name. With no reply, I check the place, but it's empty. In the den, I bend down to a glass box with pics of me from high school pinned to cutesy football paper, my name in gold stickers on a goal post next to it. Grinning, I find another box, mementoes from the national championship game, the one she watched when I didn't even know she existed. Old photos of me and

Jack and Lawrence dangle from little ribbons. In the kitchen, I find one in progress, her name and mine written in script on a pink heart, a photo of us at Elena's wedding, a plastic spider, a silver shark charm, a pic of Red, and blue butterflies laid out on the counter.

I grin like a lunatic. "Ah, baby, you make me so happy . . ."

After changing into joggers and a T-shirt, I text her again and hear her phone ping next to her laptop. Huh. I pick it up, my arm accidentally brushing the space bar on her computer, and her Gmail pops open. The first email has the subject line of Expedited Passports. I frown as a dark premonition crawls over me. Why would she need a fast passport?

Oh, what if . . . no way. Giselle wouldn't be going somewhere. Not without telling me first.

Still, doubt slips in, hanging on to the threads of just seeing Hannah, and my mind jumbles.

Giselle's been *strange*.

Fear wraps around my gut and sticks like cement. Heart hammering, I flinch back from her computer, shoving my hands in my hair. I hear a pounding in my ears, the echo of a drumbeat, blood rushing in my veins.

Oh, fuck . . . nah, nah . . .

With trepidation creeping in, I bend over and gasp in air, then touch the laptop again. Just to make sure, because it can't be true; it can't. Dread piles up brick by brick, building a goddamn skyscraper in my head, as I scroll down, find a message from Dr. Benson, and read the first few lines—

"What are you doing?" Giselle asks, walking in from the foyer. Her face is flushed from exertion, hair up in a ponytail. She's in running leggings and a blue sports halter top, her hand clutching envelopes. "I went for a quick run and grabbed the mail downstairs." Her breathing is erratic, her gaze wary as she watches me snap her computer closed.

"Did it come in?"

She shakes her head. "What?"

"Your passport," I grind out, nudging my head at the mail. "Saw the message on your laptop."

"No." She swallows hard, her lashes fluttering. "It hasn't arrived yet. Devon—"

"Stop." A harsh laugh comes from my chest as I put my hands up to ward her off when she takes steps and reaches for me. "Don't touch me. You applied for a passport on *Monday*. For days you've been acting weird. You're going to CERN. Yeah, I saw the email. When were you going to tell me?" My voice rises and reverberates around the place as she wraps her arms around herself.

"Goddamn!" I stalk out of the kitchen to get away from her. I end up in the den, pacing in circles, my hands tugging on my hair, spiking it up. I stop and look at her. "When do you go? For how long?"

"Sixteen days." She gulps in air, her words rushing out. "I'll be gone for a year—or longer." Her blue eyes water.

"So *years*?" I pinch the bridge of my nose.

Her chest rises, a slow nod coming from her, dread etching her face. "Possibly. I . . . I didn't know how to tell you." She places her hands to her eyes, then drops them. "I wanted to tell you a hundred times, but I just couldn't."

She just *couldn't* . . .

An important life decision that affects both of us?

A turning point in our relationship?

Days, weeks, months, *years* without her in my arms.

Our eyes lock, the windows to our souls clinging.

"I love you, Giselle. I fucking *love* you. And you . . ." My hands clench as I shake my head. Her eyes glisten, a tear slipping down her cheek.

"I love you too," she whispers.

She doesn't. *She doesn't.*

I'm nothing to her, a blip on her way to Switzerland, useless and *unwanted*.

Haven't I seen it enough now to know?

They come. They *leave*.

Same fucking shit.

"I'll be home for a few days at Christmas and two weeks in the summer," she says in a small voice.

I bark out a laugh. "I'll be in LA for a game. Merry Christmas."

She flinches. "We can make it work long distance, Dev. We can chat online and fly back and forth, and when I get back, it will be as if I never left . . ." Her breath hitches as her face scrunches, fear shining in her eyes. Even she knows those words are a lie.

Years. *Years.*

She's killing me slowly, piece by piece.

"Don't," I say, my voice low and tight. "You can't stop the clock on us and expect things to still be the same when you decide to come back." Still not able to believe it, I fall back on the couch, shoulders bent as I try to tackle my emotions and get them under control. Every time we kissed, every time I made love to her for the past five days, she lied to me. *She knew* we were going to end. I clench my teeth. I was worried about what was wrong with her and if her strange behavior was *my fault?*

What a joke.

What a fucking joke.

Would I have tried to change her mind if she'd told me? Grimly, I realize I would have. I would have cajoled and begged—hell yeah, because I'm greedy and hungry for her, my need fucking embarrassing. But . . .

CERN is her dream, a nagging voice tells me. *You knew it.*

She wants to go, and I can't . . . *do this.*

I stalk into the kitchen. "What do you want most in the world, Giselle?" I just need to hear her say it's CERN, and then, maybe then, I can handle the aftermath.

The air thickens, damn near suffocating. "I've messed up before, with decisions, and I want to make the right one . . ." Her voice trails off.

"What do you want?"

Her lashes flutter. "I don't know."

She does know. It's not me; she just can't say it.

She rubs her eyes. "You mean everything to me. I've never felt this way about anyone before. Since the moment I saw you on TV, I wanted to know you, to discover who you are. You're part of me, and somehow in this crazy world, fate brought us together. We're connected, and it's . . . killing . . . me . . ." I hear the desperation in her voice, the brokenness, the deep sadness.

My eyes shut, and I let out a long exhale, wrestling for control. My shoulders dip, and I sit down on a stool, just breathing, breathing, in and out, low and slow. I will my heart to slow its fast pace. Steadily, a desolate calm sinks into my bones, sticking and adhering to my body, giving me strength as I methodically take my raging emotions and pack them away. I need to say the right things. Treat her the way a good guy would. I'll take care of my bumps and bruises later. "Giselle," I say and wince at the wreck my voice is, need for her scratching to escape from my raw throat. "What we have is incredible. We had a . . ." *Baby, you're the best fucking thing in my life . . .* "Good time."

She whimpers, and I steel myself, hands tight on the edge of the counter, anchoring myself.

"And now you have an opportunity to go to CERN." My chest aches to crack again. Not yet. Wait until she's gone. "I wish you'd talked to me. I wish you'd trusted me. I wish you'd let me in." I suck in a shuddering breath. "I would have freaked out, yes, but it's your dream . . ." I can't finish.

"I'm sorry."

"I'll . . ." Be devastated, ruined, inconsolable. "Be okay. Don't worry about me. I want you to be happy."

She cries silent tears, her shoulders hunched over. "Devon. No. You're breaking up with me."

Agony spears me, and I gasp. "Yes. You should absolutely go to CERN without entanglements. I'll be honest; I can't take knowing if I might not see you for a week or a month, much less years. I didn't even want to spend one night without you on the road, Giselle. It's not fair to either one of us, and just dragging it out would kill me." I exhale. "This is why we never should have been together. I saw it coming, shit, from a mile away and still went right over the cliff."

"Devon . . ."

"Go and be well, and get the fresh start you've talked about. Go and be the awesome, smart, beautiful girl *I love*." The words are torn from me, and I rack my head for more, to be the positive she needs before leaving me for a whole new life, but I can't think of another goddamn thing to say without breaking down. There's nothing left anyway. I want to run. I want to go and hit something. I want to—shit, I don't know. Crawl away and hope I feel like getting up tomorrow.

She stands too far from me, her tears silent, but I feel each one like a nail in my heart.

She's really leaving me.

"I love you, Devon. I have for a long time. I knew for certain that night in the garage with Cindy. The words just slipped out, but they were true."

Yeah? Maybe love isn't enough.

The enormity of how far she'll be away from me claws at my chest. No more her. No more kisses. No more laughter.

Her weeping destroys me, and I shove away my anger, leaving only gnawing grief. Groaning, I scrub my face and look at her. "Baby, come here."

She eases in closer, and I stand and pull her against me, slow and easy, as I wrap my arms around her. I kiss the top of her head and inhale her vanilla scent, rubbing my cheek against the strands. I should have told her how I felt days ago, not that it would have mattered. This is what she wants regardless.

Shoving back my own pain and the primitive instinct that battles to try to change her mind—*it wouldn't be fair*—I say the things I should.

"I fell for you that first night at the barn. Best kiss I ever had," I say, my voice ragged. "Felt that zing every time I looked at you, and I couldn't stay away. You're everything I never knew I needed. You're perfect; you know that?"

And not *mine* anymore.

Someday she'll find someone better. Maybe a guy at CERN. That image hurts, cutting like a knife, and I push it away.

"It's gonna be all right. You'll be okay," I murmur, yearning to soothe her as my fingers drift up and down her back. "You're going to go over there and kick some serious ass. Wear those bobby pins."

She clutches my shirt, lips trembling, anguish on her face. "I have no right to ask you to wait for me—I don't—but there's no one else for me *but you*. Can't we try?"

I stare down at her, misery and heartache echoing around us.

Getting pieces of her when I want everything?

When every day without her would be razor blades to my heart?

No.

I cup her face and kiss her, my mouth tender. She tastes of salt and regret, and I end the touch, taking a deep breath as we pull away and gaze at each other, her blue eyes on my green ones.

Goodbye, baby.

Chapter 28

GISELLE

"Dear, it's eleven o'clock. Your phone is pinging. You need to get up." Myrtle's soft voice breaks into my reverie.

"I'm awake," I say and wince, my throat raw and sore from the tears over the past three days. I've been awake since five this morning. I barely slept. Swinging my legs to the floor, I sit up on her couch, my bed since I left Devon's on Friday. My fingers pluck at the sheets she laid out for me, trailing over the white material, thinking about Devon's bed, his fluffy down comforter; then I'm lost in images of him. I suck in a breath as fresh emotions hit me all over again, and I close my eyes and plop back down, putting my hands over my face.

A tidal wave of regret drowns me, and I don't want to move. I turn and face the back of the couch, pulling the quilt over my shoulders.

"Giselle. Do you have class?" Rustling sounds come as she walks in from the kitchen area and settles in a flowered armchair a few feet away.

"The fellowship takes care of my classes," I say dully.

"Your mama called again. I told her you were okay."

"Thank you."

"Should we go shopping?" she asks in a gentle tone.

"For what?"

"You're going to Switzerland. It'll be colder there, especially when fall gets here. You'll need warm sweaters, a raincoat, thermal underclothes, maybe some scarves and gloves. You still haven't picked up your things from the cleaners." She sighs.

"Yeah. Okay. If you think so." I draw circles on the flower pattern on her couch.

"Have you made flight arrangements?"

"I'll do it today." I blink away tears.

"You said that yesterday."

"Did I?" I don't remember. I can't recall much of the past seventy-two hours. Memories play back in my head: me leaving Devon's, grabbing my laptop and a few things while he told me to keep Red until I left, but I said I couldn't do that and caught an Uber to Myrtle's. I walked into her apartment, spilled my guts, then crawled onto her couch and tried to forget the world. I missed his pregame. I didn't reply to a text from Elena asking where I was. I didn't go to Mama's yesterday for lunch, too tired to put myself together and face them.

"You need a shower. Pookie is offended. Not me, of course."

I huff out a laugh, running a hand through my matted hair. "I'll get up." In a minute.

An hour goes by. And another. Myrtle comes and goes, offers me lunch—"No, thanks," I say, and I drift off, my body bereft, my heart split open, my muscles and my brain so very tired.

What do you want most in the world?

Why can't he wait for me? My hands clench, and I punch a pillow. He's right; it isn't fair to ask him to wait for me, to commit to a long-distance relationship when we've been together only a brief time—*but when you know, you know*—yet I'd barely see him. Sure, my parents made it work, but it was a different time, and my dad was gone only for months, not years.

Our phone calls would get fewer and fewer, him with football, me researching. I'd fly home at Christmas, and we'd have to scramble to see each other. The summer? Sure, we could meet, but what's that brief time compared to being with him for real? I longed for him when he was in Miami, watching him with bated breath on TV, just to see his face, and I think I can go a year or more? Please.

I flip over and stare up at the ceiling fan. He'd let me go and move on, and I guess I would too. Someday. Would our threads bring us back together in the years to come? Maybe. Fate is fickle. Threads may cling to a true love's heart, but with enough time and distance, they choose other people to love.

"Giselle! How could you let it get this bad?" Myrtle calls as she hobbles into the den from the bathroom.

"What's wrong?" I cry out, throwing the covers off and sitting up so fast I get dizzy. My stomach rolls, nausea bubbling. Might be a good idea to eat something. Myrtle has been pushing food at me three times a day, and I've picked through it. A throbbing pain shoots through my head, and I grimace as I cling to the edge of the couch. Okay, okay, three days is enough time to wallow. I *have* to be better.

She points to her roots. "Gray!"

I squint and walk over to her in one of Devon's shirts. I couldn't leave it behind and stuck it in my bag. The fact that it was clean when I took it killed me. I miss his smell. God. I miss his eyes. His wicked grin.

"You're pretty as ever." I push out a wan smile and fluff her brown hair.

She tsks. "You should have told me how old I look. With the fire and the renovations, I haven't had time to get it done. Lordy, John is already younger than me! I need all the tricks! He might get tired of the sex and take a good hard look at me. Can you drive me to your mama's? You think she'll fit me in?"

"I'm sure Mama or Aunt Clara will fit you in. Mondays are never busy." I sigh. "I know what you're doing, you know, trying to get me up and going."

She shrugs. "There's no shame in my game."

I swallow and nod. "All right. Let me grab a shower—and take some Tylenol. You call Mama, see what her schedule is. I'll get us an Uber, and we can pick up my car at the body shop, then head to the beauty shop."

"Good plan," she says in a voice that smacks of victory. "Glad you thought of it."

"Uh-huh." I trudge off to the bathroom.

◆ ◆ ◆

Two hours later, we pull up in my white Camry and park in front of the Cut 'N' Curl. The only bright spot in this day is that when I went in to pay for my repairs, Harold was working the cash register at the body shop. He gave me a wide-eyed look and begged me to not tell Mama about our recent meetings. Apparently, once he got Garrett's payment taken care of, he resigned his other job.

My head pounds, even after the Tylenol, and I dig around in my bag to see if I have some extras. Instead, my hand clenches around my birth control.

"What's wrong?" Myrtle asks, her hand on the door. "You just went white."

I jiggle the pill pack, showing it to her, seeing her eyes widen. Licking my lips, I say, "I took my last active pill last Sunday, which means I should have started my period three days later, which was Wednesday. I don't take the inactive ones usually . . . so . . ." My brain freezes, then unfreezes, as I count . . . "I'm five days late."

"Oh my," she says in an oddly serene voice. "Is that normal? I don't know anything about birth control these days."

"No, it's not normal. I'm always on time . . ." My voice trails off as I set down the pills and yank my phone off the console and search for articles about my prescription, my fingers tapping.

"Are you pregnant?"

I shoot her a look. "I never missed a dose."

"You've been having sex every day, a thousand times a day, right?"

My body clenches at those memories. I keep reading.

"His sperm is so mighty it defeated your pills."

My stomach swirls. I hold my phone up. "It says here that stress and changes in diet and exercise can cause me to miss my period. That qualifies. That's *me*. I'm under stress. I didn't run for days, then picked it back up with a vengeance. I haven't eaten a full meal since Sunday, and that was fried chicken and corn bread."

"Are you nauseated?"

"It's grief nausea."

We look at each other.

"You gonna go with that, huh? Just trust an article?"

Butterflies flip-flop in my stomach. "Let's go in," I say, dropping the topic as I grab Aunt Clara's Chick-fil-A and get out of the car. My head swims, tendrils of something I can't name pricking at me. What if . . .

We walk into the shop, and just as I thought, it's empty except for Mama and Aunt Clara and Elena.

"Bless your heart; you look awful!" Mama yells and gives me a hug, then holds my cheeks in her palms. "Poor baby." She searches my face like a hawk. "You need to eat. That'll make it better." Her shoulders slump. "That Devon, he broke your sweet heart, and now you're leaving me for Switzerland!"

I lean into her, tears roaring back. Seems to be a new normal. "I'm going to miss you so, so much." My head lies on her shoulder, and I breathe her in, peppermint and sweetness.

She pats my back. "There, there, it'll be okay. We've already planned a girls' trip to see you on Thanksgiving. We'll stay in a fancy hotel and eat out."

My eyes press shut. I want turkey and dressing at Mama's, her fall decorations and fancy plates and napkins with little squirrels eating acorns. I want Aunt Clara sneaking rolls during the passive-aggressive prayer. I want Elena and Jack kissing when they think no one is looking.

"Thank you for my lunch," Aunt Clara says, taking the bag but not opening it, just pouting at me, then huffing and giving me a hug. "I'm going to miss your face."

"Sorry it took me so long to come. Just needed some time to regroup." I haven't regrouped worth a shit.

Elena hugs me next. "Whiskey at my house after this, and we'll talk, okay?"

"She can't drink anymore," Myrtle says brightly, fluffing her hair in one of the mirrors. "Damn, I look good. I don't think I need a touch-up after all." She pauses as we all turn to look at her. "What? She might be pregnant."

Chaos ensues. Mama screeches, and Aunt Clara falls into a chair. Elena covers her mouth. I'm trying to explain that I'm *not*, amid the overlapping voices, but no one hears me.

"A virgin . . . ," comes from Mama as she stares at me with wide eyes. "Someone grab my smelling salts . . ."

"You don't use smelling salts," Elena says, then "Oh my God, you're gonna have the *first* grandchild. You little hussy . . ."

"Nausea and *late* . . . ," Myrtle says.

"Hope it's a girl with Devon's eyes . . . ," Aunt Clara says as she munches on a waffle fry.

"Stop," I shout, my hands fluttering. I glare at Myrtle. "I am not pregnant. Look what you did."

She shrugs, the shoulders of her muumuu shifting. "Maybe you are, maybe you aren't, but doesn't it make you think?"

"About what?" I say.

"The future," she says, her kind eyes on me.

"You're pregnant?" Topher gasps, and I realize he must have come in halfway through the mayhem. "Can she call me Uncle Tophie? Please?"

"Y'all need Jesus," I drawl, my voice a testament to my southern roots. "There's no pregnancy."

"Don't bring the Lord into this." Mama grabs her purse and heads to the door. "I'm going to the Piggly Wiggly and buying a test. Everybody just wait here. Elena, get that whiskey. I might need a nip."

"Say hi to Lance!" Aunt Clara calls to her back as she gets to the door.

"Get the early-detection one, Mama!" Elena yells, and Mama says she will, and the door shuts.

◆　◆　◆

"You are not coming in here with me," I say to Mama as she follows me into the small bathroom at the beauty shop twenty minutes later.

She hands off the grocery bag and shows me all five tests. "Yes, I am. Now pee on all of them."

I take the bag, ease her out, and shut the door in her face. Holding the first pink box, I read the marketing tagline: *Accurate up to six days before a missed period.*

That's fast in detecting hCG in my urine. Despite my random information gathering over the years, I realize I know zilch about pregnancy tests. I sit down on the toilet lid as I unwrap the box and take out the stick and read the instructions. Remove the cap and reveal the absorbent section, pee midstream—oh, that's nice—then place it on a flat surface and wait six minutes. If you're pregnant, a line will appear under the control line. Seems easy.

My hand trembles.

And hope, feathery and sweet, blooms and takes flight in my heart, the vision of me with Devon's baby making me tremble. Is it crazy that I want this? I can have a baby, finish school, be a sci-fi author by night, a teacher by day. More kids, I don't care—give them all to me, running around our big house and the barn where I'd put my office, renovated with white paint, rustic crossbeams, and industrial lighting.

What do you want most in the world?

Devon. You. Always you.

God, what a mistake I made.

I've been clinging to CERN because it's been part of me for so long, yet part of that desperation revolved around the mistakes I made with Elena and Preston, a lifeline to escape and start fresh, but now . . . dreams are meant to evolve. Goals readjust. I want family. I want love.

Einstein said many great things, and his favorite quote hung in his office at Princeton: "Not everything that counts can be counted, and not everything that can be counted counts."

Science is important to me—it's the core of my personality—but love and happiness, those intangible, beautiful, hard-to-hold things, are what *count* the most, and physics is just icing on the cake. I can't be me without him, knowing he's in the world and I'm thousands of miles away. What good would I be at CERN, not caring, missing him with every breath I took?

A knock makes me start. "You've been in there for half an hour!" Mama says. "Can't you pee? Let me get a Sun Drop."

She shuffles off, and I hear talking from the shop. They're probably out there planning a baby shower. I shake my head and stare at the magical pee thing. "Thank you, little stick," I whisper. "I would have figured it out before I left, but you helped. Let's hope Devon . . ." My voice cracks. What if he doesn't let me back into his heart? Worse, what if I'm pregnant and he . . .

Don't go there.

Might as well get this over with. I take care of business, using two sticks, one after the other, then setting them on the counter—and wait.

I can't breathe as I watch the minutes tick down on my phone. My fingers clutch the edge of the sink as I breathe, anticipation building and rising with each moment. I want this, I want this, I want this—and him.

Six minutes later, I clean up the mess, throwing the package and instructions in the trash. Leaning my head against the door for a minute, I attempt to get my emotions under control, grappling with the torrent of feelings as I swipe at my face.

Walking down the hall and out into the beauty shop, I watch my feet, my mind tumbling. I need another shower. One wasn't enough. I need to put some makeup on, some decent clothes besides his shirt—which I haven't taken off. I need to see him. Friday night rushes back at me: his anger, his disappointment, his *I love you.*

"Why are you crying?" Mama asks, rushing over to me.

From her perch in a stylist chair, Myrtle says, "Bun in the oven. Knew it."

The door opens, and he walks in.

My whole life. Right there.

His eyes are wide, and his face . . . "Baby, don't cry," he says in a deep husky voice.

My body reacts, spinning toward him as he rushes to me, broad shoulders swaying as he stops in front of me, and I jump in his arms.

"I called him," Elena offers with a grimace as she waves at the rest of them and shoos them out the front door. They file out, not willingly, but they do.

He's here. Really here.

My heart throbs, squeezing inside my rib cage. I press my face into his chest and exhale. His hands go to my scalp, massaging the skin, trailing his fingers through my hair. His lips brush my ear, and I tighten my arms around him. How did I fool myself for three days? I'd choose him every single time.

"I'm not pregnant," I say glumly.

"Hmm, I see." His voice is too calm, and I can't meet his eyes as I let him go and slide down his body. He sways with me in a gentle motion.

"I wanted to be," I choke out, admitting the truth, trying to push the disappointment away. "I was already making a nursery in my head, with a mobile to foster brain development, toys for optimal tactile touch, painting butterflies on the wall."

"Ah, that sounds nice." His voice is hoarse.

I look up at him then, seeing details I missed before. He's wearing his football pants and a white vented practice jersey, and his hair . . . I half smile. It's a mess, sticking up in a million directions. His gaze is heavy on me, low, speculative, and hesitant. He looks haunted, his face thinner. Is that possible in just three days? My fingers run over his face, outlining the details.

"How freaked out were you?"

A long exhale comes from his chest. "Let's just say there's a state trooper who now has season passes."

"Were you scared?"

His lashes flutter against his cheeks, emotion pulling at him, his throat working. "Not for me. I can handle a baby, but I don't want anything to hold you back from what you want."

I gaze up at him, and our eyes cling. Oh, Devon.

Tears clog my throat, and I push them away to say my words. "Dev, you *are* my dream. You are what I want most in the world. You and me and babies and a house in the country. CERN can't compare. Maybe it will be in the future—they let people teach classes periodically—but Switzerland will always be here. You are now. You are mine, and I'm yours. That morning in the closet, you described what I want with you. Every detail of that life." My eyes close as I replay his words. "Me and you and a life that's worthy and good and precious. I want to be in all your universes."

Gathering strength, I tell him my Einstein quote, and he watches me, listening carefully, his beautiful green eyes all over my face, drinking me in. "I'd be nothing but a shadow of who I am if I left you," I whisper.

His hands tighten as he bends his head to mine. He kisses me with all the longing we've been denied for the past three days. "Are you sure, Giselle? I . . ." His voice hitches. "These days without you have desolated me, but I'm willing to be yours and let you go, and we can try and see how it works out . . ."

I put my hand to his lips. "From the moment Susan mentioned CERN, I was sick. It just took a pregnancy test for me to figure it out. I love you so much, Devon."

A long heavy breath comes from him, and his eyes glimmer with hope, a soft shine there. He presses his forehead to mine. "I'm going to make you proud, baby; I'm going to make you happy, and you're going to get everything you want, I swear."

He kisses me soft and slow. "So are we going to go out there and tell them you aren't pregnant?"

"You tell them while I dash to your car."

He groans. "Your mama knows for sure we're having sex. I can't even look at her. You do it."

"Okay. You tell them I'm not going to CERN, and I'll tell them I'm not pregnant. They'll be disappointed about the baby," I say wistfully.

"There'll be other babies," he murmurs after another drugging kiss, his voice soft and wondering, as if he's amazed at the idea. "I love you, Giselle."

"I'm yours, Dev."

That rich red thread of fate wraps around us.

We hold hands and walk to the door, a whole new future waiting for us.

Epilogue

DEVON

A few years later

I wake up and look over, and she isn't there, causing a brief bite of disappointment, until I laugh up at the skylight above our bed. Knowing her, she's either hiding to jump out at me, or she's up and working.

I shower in the bathroom of our house, the one we built out on the farm after we were married. I dunk my head under the water, thinking about that day, her in a white dress, an amethyst ring surrounded by diamonds on her finger, her nana's pearls around her neck, her hand in mine as we said our vows in her mama's church. It was a perfect spring day in April when she was halfway through her doctorate, and I was giddy to finally make us official.

My dad was at my wedding, sober. A few months after he left Nashville, he came back, took one look at me and Giselle in my penthouse, and wept. I think . . . he saw my happiness, my contentedness, my deep love for a woman who adored me right back. He saw that I had something real, admiration mixed with devotion, respect, and commitment. He never had that. Eventually, a few months later, he let me pay for rehab, got straight, and moved back into his house. He's his own man and makes his own way. He might slip, yeah, but we'll deal with it together, me and Giselle and our family.

I walk into our spacious closet, and when I see there's no mask-wearing wife, I shake my head. "She's slipping," I murmur. After throwing on joggers and a hoodie, I pad down the hall and open the nursery door as quietly as I can, tiptoeing in on Gabriel Kennedy, our one-year-old son. His thumb is in his pouty mouth, and I tuck the covers around him, my heart swelling.

After slipping out, I pad into the bright kitchen, my eyes searching for her. Not in the den that overlooks the rolling hills of Daisy. Nerves hit as I grab the pics from a drawer in the desk. I can't wait to show her. After shoving my feet into sneakers, I head outside and jog the yards to her office, the barn we renovated as we built the house.

When I slide open the doors, her tattoo winks at me from her skinny jeans as she reaches up to a shelf, organizing her books. Three bestsellers for my baby. I grin. Always knew she'd do it. The baby monitor sits next to her laptop, the sound of Gabriel's soft snores reaching my ears. After easing up behind her, I kiss her neck, and she melts against me, sliding her arms up and tangling in my hair.

"You left me," I growl.

"I had to get work done before the baby wakes up." She laughs and turns around, her hair down and thick, the color silver and gold. It's been a few different colors, but her original is my favorite.

She kisses me, and I'm lost in her all over again, just like the first time.

"I have a gift for you," I say against her lips.

"And it's not even my birthday. Is it what's in your pants?"

"That's free anytime you want it." Anxiousness hits as I show her the pics in my hand, then spread them out on her desk.

She gasps. "Devon, is that . . . a villa . . ." She stops, her finger moving to the next house. "And that one . . . where is this?"

"That one's an apartment in the Saint Jean neighborhood, nice enough at three million. Four thousand square feet and a pool with a view of the lake. The real estate person says the sunsets are spectacular." I wrap my arms around her from behind. "The villa is my favorite, though, just under five mill, with a view of the Alps, six bedrooms, a renovated kitchen, and a garden—but you get to pick."

She blinks. "You want to buy a house in Geneva, Switzerland? For just under five million?" Her voice is incredulous. "I mean, you've joked about it, but . . ."

Just testing you, baby. And your eyes lit up when I brought it up.

"I have plenty of money, and so do you. I have the best life any man could ask for: a beautiful woman, a baby, and so much love that some days I wake up and have to look around and think . . . damn, is this really me?"

"A villa?"

"Come on, baby, this is a gift. I'm giving you a part-time home in Geneva. If you don't like these, we'll pick out more and fly over and make a decision." I pause. "I'm giving you all your favorite universes."

"Devon . . . you . . . God . . . I love you," she chokes out as she turns around.

I kiss her. "You have your doctorate, and Susan has already checked with CERN—"

"What! She hasn't said a word to me!" She and Susan have become close friends. Giselle isn't a full-time faculty member, preferring to teach one class a week until Gabriel is older. She goes to every home game, most of the away ones, a laptop bag over her arm so she can write, a baby in her arms. Elena is tagging right along with her, her two girls in tow.

"Don't blame her; this is on me, my idea. She and I have been talking about how to get you to CERN."

She gapes.

"She said they'd be thrilled to have you come in, meet the researchers, and check out the place behind closed doors, hug the LHC, make out with it, lick it—that might sting, but whatever gets you hot."

She shakes her head at me.

I pause, this part really making me nervous. I'm springing this on her, and she can always say no, and that will be cool, but I just want her to have fucking everything. "She mentioned there's open interim teaching positions there, from January to May, for their winter term. It's a temporary job, usually filled by students, and that's where you rock, baby—all those kids adore you. It's mostly the off-season for me, so Gabriel and I can come with you after the playoffs in January." I arch my brow and let the words hang for a moment as her mouth opens and shuts.

"What if I don't get the job? What will we do with a house in Europe?"

I shrug. "Vacation home for us—rent it out, make a ton of money. I can't play football forever, and as long as you're with me, any country works. We can settle there someday or fly back and forth between homes. It's a pretty place to write your next book." I tangle my hands in her hair. "Where you go, I go."

She blinks, tears shining in her eyes.

I kiss her softly. "Bring your mama and aunt. I'm sure the whole lot of them will want to come stay for a while. Jack and Elena and their girls, Topher and Quinn, Aiden, Myrtle and John, my dad—we'll fill it up. We can hang around, check out the city, and if you don't want the job—I know they'll hire you in a snap—then we'll do the regular tour, and I'll sneak you into the room with your particle accelerator."

"You are crazy," she breathes, and I smile at the stars in her eyes.

"Nah, just in love with the smartest, most beautiful girl in the world."

She laughs. "I'm deliriously happy. I don't need a villa"—her eyes linger on the pic—"or CERN."

"Baby, I'd give you the whole world if I could. What's a house in Europe?"

Several moments pass as we stare at each other, and I smile knowingly. "Level-five gaze. I know what that means," I say and ease her shirt up and off her head. "Somebody wants my body."

Five minutes later, she's undressed, I'm naked, and we're rolling around in the room off to the side, a place with a big plush bed she had put in here for stolen moments like this. I'm staring down at her under me, her hands pinned above her head as I slide inside her and kiss her. She whispers that she'll take the villa and that she'll think about the job. I laugh and promise her that I'll always be with her, no matter where she is, that she'll always have my love, my soul, my everything.

BIBLIOGRAPHY

Carroll, Sean. *The Big Picture: On the Origins of Life, Meaning, and the Universe Itself.* New York: Penguin Random House, 2017.

Greene, Brian. *The Elegant Universe: Superstrings, Hidden Dimensions, and the Quest for the Ultimate Theory.* New York: W. W. Norton & Company, 2003.

ABOUT THE AUTHOR

Wall Street Journal, *New York Times*, and *USA Today* bestselling author Ilsa Madden-Mills writes new adult and contemporary romances with humor and heart.

She loves unicorns, frothy coffee beverages, and any book featuring sword-wielding females.

Please join her Facebook readers group, Unicorn Girls, to get the latest scoop and talk about books, wine, and Netflix: www.facebook.com/groups/ilsasunicorngirls.

You can also learn more about Madden-Mills by visiting her website, www.ilsamaddenmills.com; signing up for her newsletter at www.ilsamaddenmills.com/contact; and visiting her page on Book + Main: www.bookandmainbites.com/ilsamaddenmills.